Past Forward

Volume Five

Chautona Havig

Copyright © 2012 by Chautona Havig

First Edition

ISBN-13: 978-1483952291
ISBN-10: 1483952290

All rights reserved. No part of this book may be reproduced without the permission of Chautona Havig.

The scanning, uploading, and/or distribution of this book via the Internet or by any other means without the permission of the author and publisher is illegal and punishable by law. Please purchase only authorized electronic editions and avoid electronic piracy of copyrighted materials.

Your respect and support for the author's rights is appreciated. In other words, don't make me write you into another book as a villain!

Edited by: Jill. Just Jill. Kathleen Kelly would not approve.
Fonts: Book Antiqua, Alex Brush, Trajan Pro, Bickham Script Pro.

Cover photos: AVGT/istockphoto.com
gradyreese/istockphoto.com

Cover art by: Chautona Havig

The events and people in this book are fictional, and any resemblance to actual people is purely coincidental and I'd love to meet them!

Visit me at **http://chautona.com** or follow me on Twitter **@chautona**

All Scripture references are from the NASB. NASB passages are taken from the NEW AMERICAN STANDARD BIBLE (registered), Copyright 1960, 1962, 1963, 1968, 1971, 1972, 1973, 1975, 1977, 1995 by The Lockman Foundation.

Chapter 141

Babies slept in each arm as Willow rested in the corner of the couch. *"Six days,"* she thought to herself as she watched her sons sleeping. Little milky mouths moved rhythmically in their sleep, while Willow catnapped between feedings. She had felt great when William and Lucas were first born—well, after the first thirty-six hours or so—but the past twenty-four hours had been rough. She was exhausted, achy, and Marianne insisted she get as much rest as possible to avoid mastitis.

"Want me to take one of them?" Marianne's voice near her ear nearly made her jump out of her skin.

"If you like. They're just sleeping, though."

"True, but you'd sleep better if you passed them to me and went upstairs to your bed."

"Is it really possible to get mastitis if they're draining me every time I feed them?" Willow looked at her chest curiously. She had been warned that when her milk came in and they were just a little larger, her chest would expand dramatically between feedings—nearly an entire cup size sometimes. She didn't believe it.

"It is, and you don't want it. I remember the worst heaves ever with mastitis."

Without further discussion, Willow stood, handed William to his doting grandmother, and carried Lucas to the stairs. Marianne's voice stopped her. "Willow, I'm really not trying to take over, interfere, or all of those other ugly mother-in-law things, but don't you think you'll sleep better if you just go up by yourself? I can keep them content for a while and then bring them to you when they get hungry."

"It just feels so—so—well, like I'm using you."

"That's what I'm here for, though. I won't always be able to do it, but I can now." As she spoke, Marianne laid William down in the little Moses basket she'd purchased and reached for Lucas. "I'll bring them the minute they demand their lunch."

Willow's yawn betrayed her. She gave Marianne a sheepish look, hugged her, kissed her son, and climbed the stairs slowly. If rest was essential to recovery, she'd rest. Never, not even those last weeks of pregnancy or the early weeks of her leg injury, had Willow ever tired as easily as she did now. A trip up the stairs to the bathroom made her hungry and sleepy both.

However, much to Marianne's amazement and Chad's amusement, she'd already managed to embroider initials on sleeper feet to help differentiate between her boys. She had an unreasonable fear of mixing up who was who, until she'd finally taken a permanent marker to each boy's right foot. Carol and Marianne both were certain that they'd be permanently tattooed if she continued to mark them that way, but Willow didn't care. She wanted to know which child was which. Chad, David, and Christopher all thought the initials were a great joke, but none of them sympathized with her. In their opinion, it didn't matter if the boys got switched a time or two. No one would be the wiser.

Upstairs, Willow grabbed her journal and started an entry before she fell asleep.

March-

The babies are already on a slight schedule thanks to Mom's excellent diversionary tactics. She managed to convince them to eat every two and a half hours and she staggered their sleep times by half an hour giving me a chance to feed one thoroughly before the second woke up and opened the floodgates with his little cries.

I already can tell Lucas's cry. He has more volume. If both are crying, I know who is who just by the cry alone. Chad says I'm crazy, but so far, I've been right every time. William is quieter but much more persistent. He'll fuss and cry until he gets what he wants, but Lucas just lets out a huge fuss and then goes back to sleep in disgust if we don't meet his needs quickly enough. Fortunately, (or is it unfortunately?) he wakes up again quickly and repeats the performance.

I've never eaten so much food in my life. It is unreal how much I eat and how often. I am eating almost as frequently as I was those last weeks of pregnancy, but instead of a quarter of a sandwich, I eat the whole thing. Chad mocks me, but Mom hits him with a pillow and tells him I need nourishment to feed the babies. I think she's afraid I'll feel bad about how much I'm eating or that I'll worry about gaining more weight. Maybe she's worried that Chad is worried about me gaining more weight. I don't know. I think it's all very funny. It seems the more I eat, the more the babies eat, and the thinner my face, ankles, and hands get. My stomach isn't anywhere near flat again... I think I still look like I'm several months pregnant, but I can tell that I'm already smaller than I was when I left the hospital. I should remember to get on the scale. I wonder how long it'll take me to get rid of those extra thirty pounds. I gained six pounds that last week alone!

After much prayer and a bit of last minute panic, we finally chose names for the boys two days after we brought them home. Chad drove us back to the hospital to fill out the birth certificate the next day. Christopher Lucas and David William were named after four very special people in our lives. However, since we have a Christopher and a Chris, and now Granddad David is in our lives, we decided to call them by their middle names. I never imagined it'd be so hard to name children. With all of the amazing and wonderful names out there, who would expect choosing two (I can't imagine how parents narrow it even further to just one!) names would be so difficult.

Chad loved the disposable diapers we had for the first few days. It was comical how he'd try to sell me on forgetting the washable ones I'd made and sticking to the little paper thingies they gave us at the hospital. I admit; I did like them those first few days when that tar-like mess was coming. I can't imagine trying to wash that sticky stuff out, but once it *was gone, I put the dozen or so paper ones we had left in the van for trips and pulled out my super soft flannel ones. Chad thought we were out and bought another package. He was sure I'd prefer them after using mine for a few changes, but I just didn't understand why I'd want those smelly things laying around for weeks until he had time to run them to the dump. We can't burn them, but I think he'd forgotten that. I finally just used up the paper ones—I think he thought I conceded his superior wisdom, but I made sure that I asked him to take them to the garbage. After four days, he didn't really like the smell in there. We ran out yesterday, and he's been to town twice. No new paper diaper packages came home with him, and he took out the last load of cloth to be washed just before he went to work. I think he's decided that washing isn't as bad as composting non-compostable diapers.*

I should be sleeping instead of writing. I do feel weak... very tired. I almost feel chilled. Maybe we're going to get that storm after all. I wonder if I should close the window.

Willow closed the journal, pulled the covers over her, curled onto her side, and was asleep almost instantaneously. Downstairs, Marianne rocked babies, changed diapers, and did everything in her power to keep the boys happy as long as possible before carrying Lucas upstairs for his noon snack.

"Chad. I think you should come home. I also think you should call Dr. Kline."

"What's wrong?" Chad pointed to a couple of teenagers loitering near the Farmer's Market and motioned for them to move away.

"Willow is burning up. I don't know if it's normal or not, but I can't help but worry about infection."

"She seemed fine this morning. Are you sure she's not just over tired?" Chad shifted his phone and took a bag of groceries from Mrs. Hayfield, carrying it the three blocks to her house as he listened to his mother's concerns. "Well Mom, if you think so, I can see if the chief'll let me come home but—"

"This is your wife Chad! We're talking about postpartum infection—or the probability of it."

"I'm calling the chief now, Mom. Take a deep breath. We'll bring her in to see Dr. Weisenberg. Actually, can you bring her in? I could meet you there—"

"I couldn't get her in the car. I know I couldn't. She needs help getting dressed…"

"Ok. I'm coming."

Chad snapped his phone shut with more force than necessary. "Sorry, Mrs. Hayfield. My mother is a little over concerned about my wife."

"Mastitis?" The elderly woman nodded knowingly. "That can wear a woman down faster than anything."

"Mom didn't say. She just said infection."

"Probably mastitis. Better get her into the doctor. I've seen it turn ugly and fast."

Chad nodded, put the groceries on her counter, and waved goodbye. "Have a good day Mrs. Hayfield."

"I'll light a candle for her at Mass tonight, Chad."

"Thank you." Chad didn't know what that meant, but it seemed like a thoughtful gesture.

A call to the Chief gave him permission to take his wife to the clinic. Chad drove home more than a little irritated at being interrupted on his first day back at work for something so nebulous. His mom knew what mastitis was. If that was the problem, why didn't she just say so? It seemed ridiculous.

One look at Willow changed his mind completely. Her forehead and hairline were damp with perspiration, her pajama top clung to her body, and she whimpered at his touch. "Oh, Mom! What's wrong with her?"

"I don't know! She says she's not tender and I looked—no read streaks or anything to indicate mastitis. That's how mine looked anyway. Angry red streaks."

He struggled to carry her downstairs and laid her on the back seat of the van. For a moment, he debated between bringing his mother and the babies and leaving them at home. "Those places are full of germs. I'll call you if she needs to feed them. If they get hungry before that, just warm up some of the goat's milk. The doctor seems to think it's fine, or I think maybe they sent home formula samples. Use that."

Either one. I don't care."

He drove as fast as he safely could to town, and then nearly climbed the van walls as he crawled through the streets to the clinic. Sarah Malia met him at the van with a wheelchair. "Your mother called. She said maybe mastitis? This is a bad fever for mastitis. Did you take her temp?"

"No. I don't think so. Well, I didn't. Mom might have—" Chad's voice rambled nonsensically as he followed alongside Willow watching her with concern.

Dr. Weisenberg, busy with a broken arm, stitches for a toddler's split lip, and a possible appendicitis case, ordered an antibiotic. He had the nurse check for signs of mastitis and an hour later, walked into the room to examine her himself. "Sarah doesn't think it's mastitis—no tenderness of the breasts, no streaks, but her temperature was over one hundred three so we're looking at something infectious. I've got a call into Dr. Kline."

For the next hour he examined, consulted, and finally wheeled her to the lab for an ultrasound where they found the culprit. "She's retained a blood clot that won't pass. It's too big."

"Is that dangerous?"

"Well, it's not good of course, but we'll get it out and she'll be just fine." At the look on Chad's face, Dr. Wiesenberg smiled reassuringly. "Son, this isn't uncommon with twins—can happen with any birth, but you have twice the chance of little complications when you have twice the babies. It's ok. We're going to take good care of her."

"Should I have Mom bring in the babies to eat?"

"That'd be about perfect. By the time we get everything ready for the D&C, they'd be about done and we don't want her missing any more feedings than absolutely necessary."

"Does she have to stay overnight?" Chad knew Willow wasn't going to like that.

"It'd probably be best, considering the infection."

He sighed. "Ok. I'll call Mom. Thanks."

The next afternoon, Chad brought his wife and children

home from the hospital. Again. Already, she looked a hundred percent better than she had the previous afternoon. To save her the stress of walking up the stairs, Chad arranged her porch swing exactly how she liked it, brought the Moses basket out there to keep the babies close, and tucked her in for another nap.

"I've got to get in and relieve Joe. He's been covering for me all day, and he's got the late shift. Mom's taking a nap on the couch so just yell if you need anything."

Exhausted, Willow murmured something unintelligible and drifted into semi-consciousness. Portia sat next to the swing as though awaiting orders. Chad pointed to his wife and children and then took the dog's face in his hands. Staring into the animal's eyes, he entreated her to be on guard. "Watch them, girl. Watch them for me. I'll be home as soon as I can."

He hurried down the steps and to his truck. One last glance at the porch showed Portia, head lying on her outstretched paws, body alert and watchful. The coloring was all wrong, the location as opposite as the farm offered, but something about her guard over his wife and children reminded Chad of how faithfully Othello had kept watch over Kari's grave. Nothing else could be more different and so similar simultaneously.

"Lord, I am blessed. Did you know that? Of course You do. How stupid of me," Chad muttered as he drove toward town.

Chapter 142

Willow stared at the twins as they slept in the crib, weeping. So small—so helpless. Her mother's panicked journal entries hung heavy over her heart. The moments of terror with a shotgun in her hand, ordering strangers from her land, praying that her baby wouldn't cry and give them reason to come back with police—they made sense now. The overwhelming desire to protect and provide she had never expected.

For the third time, she checked the window. Wide open, there should be no reason she couldn't hear them if they wailed. Lucas would ensure she heard them. That thought made her smile through the tears. It would be all right.

The stairs should have produced a broken neck. Willow made it down the first three steps without mishap, but blurred, watery vision made her miss half a dozen more steps, almost twisting her ankle twice. "Stupid, stupid. Going to get myself killed, and then what?"

Before going outside to work in the garden, she grabbed a mason jar and filled it with water. She didn't make it to the back door before half was gone. As if the most tragic thing she'd ever seen, she stared at the jar, uncomprehending, and returned to fill it.

The garden stretched out before her—likely ten times larger than the one her mother had tried to grow that year. Had she screamed every time Mother put her down? How had Mother managed? Dread overcame her as the memory of those journals rubbed her heart raw. She hadn't managed. If Mother couldn't manage with just one baby, how did she think she could with two and ten times the work? Why had she purchased the lambs—the chickens? The chopping stump mocked her. Firewood. They had nearly frozen that winter because Mother couldn't keep up with the wood.

Chad found her there when he came home for lunch, surrounded by half-split logs, covered in chips, her sobs nearly drowning out their son's wails—make it their sons' wails now. "Lass?"

"I can't do it."

"Ok, then don't."

"No, I can't do it. We're going to go hungry but be warm, or we're going to be fat and freeze. I can't do both."

He wrapped his arms around her, kneeling in the dirt and woodchips. "You don't have to do either. If I can't do it, we'll hire someone else to. You can do nothing but sit in that rocker and sing songs to those boys for all I care. We won't starve and we won't freeze."

Willow stared up at him, a sniffle adding to the pathetic expression on her face. "I'm ridiculous, aren't I?"

"I think you're an overwhelmed mommy."

She shook her head. "That I'm even a mommy astounds me. I distinctly remember telling you I wasn't going to risk that."

He chuckled, pulling her even closer. "And I distinctly remember you telling me you were glad that one 'try' probably didn't 'work.' Sounds like someone who changed her mind about children to me."

"Chad!"

"Do you deny it?"

The wails grew quieter. "Lucas is giving up. I need to go up there."

"You're avoiding the subject."

"I wouldn't give up the little guys for anything." She tried to glare at him, but the exhaustion in her features made her look as if she were pleading for him to help. "You know that, right?"

"I know, lass. C'mon. I'll take Liam."

"No, you take Lucas. Liam is always getting the bottle

because he's quieter."

"I could try to keep him quiet," Chad offered. "Just until you're done with our strong, silent son."

Willow laughed. "We misnamed them."

"Wha—" Understanding hit him. "You're right. We did. Liam should have been Lucas. We could switch... No one but us would ever know..."

"They're two and a half months old, Chad. We can't now!"

"Not that old—"

"March twenty-first to May twenty-eighth is almost ten weeks, my laddie. Sorry to say, two and a half months already."

"That might explain the weepiness," he murmured, pulling her to her feet.

"What?"

With an arm draped around her shoulder, he steered her toward the back door. "Remember when Dr. Kline suggested that we should watch for emotional swings?"

"Because 'if they become severe or debilitating they may indicate PPD.'"

"Right."

"So you think I have PPD?"

He shook his head. "Not really, but if you're going to get it, I bet it'll hit soon."

She sighed. Halfway up the stairs she asked, "So what is PPD again? It sounds like something that fills a diaper."

Chad snickered. "I think most women would agree with part of that."

"Part?"

"Yep," he added as he opened the boys' door, "I think they'd say PPD definitely stinks."

Chad found her asleep, her arms sprawled across the kitchen table. His back protested at the sight of it. He glanced at the papers around her. What had been neat stacks of animal orders, butchering schedules, and copies of their year's tax forms were now fanned into a semi-homogenous mixture and he suspected the ones beneath her cheek might be christened with drool. "Lass?"

"...mmmget him." She stirred, her arm sending a few pages dangerously close to the edge of the table.

He shook her shoulder. "Willow, c'mon. Wake up. Go to bed."

The whimper squeezed his heart. "M'kaay... don't hear them..."

Hands on his hips, Chad watched her. Could he lift her? Even as the thought came to him, he knew it was futile. He might be able to carry her if he could get her over his shoulder, but he'd never get her over his shoulder without her cooperation.

Before he could decide what to do, her hand swung dangerously close to her glass. Chad dove for it and moved it to the windowsill above the sink. If the papers hadn't covered that table, if she hadn't stayed up much too late to do work that she couldn't get done during the day, he might have been tempted to douse her in it. *Another time,* he mused as he stared at the scene before him.

A new thought crossed his mind. He opened the icebox, knowing what he'd find, and sighed. No sandwich—nothing. She wasn't tired; Willow was exhausted. She hadn't failed to make him a lunch since those awful days when she wasn't speaking to him. He had to get her to bed.

Chad knelt beside her, pulling her arm around his shoulder. He stood, still trying to wake her. "C'mon. Let's go. You can do it. Take a step."

"Oh... is it lunch time already?" The words were hardly intelligible, but he knew she was waking if she could attempt to speak in a complete sentence.

"Yep."

"Forgot to make you lunch." She turned at the door as if to go back, but he nudged her back toward the living room.

"I'll get it. You sleep."

Her eyes focusing now, she froze. "Oh, no! The papers!"

"I'll get 'em."

"I spent too much time on the envelopes. It was just so relaxing."

"It's not wrong to put them in a plain envelope and

decorate it later." The moment he spoke, he realized that the words were the wrong thing to say.

"Chad..." her shoulders slumped.

A sick feeling filled him. She was too exhausted to argue—to stick up for herself. "It's ok. I wasn't saying it was wrong—just hate to see you so tired."

It didn't take her more than half a minute to relax and fall asleep. Chad jogged to the kitchen, his mind whirling. He scrambled to assemble the papers in some kind of order. He stacked them on the dining room table with a plate on top to keep anything from blowing them away. He grabbed a sheet of paper and scrawled a note, leaving it at her place on the table.

The babies played on the floor. Well, complained about being forced to lay on the floor—but Willow preferred to keep a positive outlook. While they had what Marianne insisted on calling "tummy time," much to Willow's disgust, she dusted the library and washed windows.

Chad's truck barreled down the drive, hours late. He'd said he wouldn't be home until close to noon and the clock proved his estimate correct. She gathered her supplies, put them away, and met him at the door. The twins wailed their welcome. "Was getting worried."

"But not worried enough to call," he joked.

"Right. Close though. I put the phone in my pocket." Willow smiled.

He followed her through the kitchen, pausing only long enough to stare at the boys. "Tummy time?"

"Chad, do you have any idea how ridiculous that sounds? Can't they just play on a blanket without making it an event with an asinine name?"

"Aw, lass. You make coming home six hours late a joy." He sank into Mother's rocker and closed his eyes. "Any chance I can talk you into making me a cup of coffee?"

"Nope. You're eating your chicken salad sandwich, inhaling your bowl of soup, and going to bed."

"Ogre."

"That's Mrs. Ogre to you." She bent to kiss him, but he grabbed her, pulling her into his lap. "I can't make your dinner if you don't let me go."

"But I don't want to let you go." He winked. "What do you say to that?"

Willow pushed away from him. "Go get changed, lock up your gun so the babies don't shoot each other with it, and change—or take a shower." Once he was on his way upstairs, she pulled out the soup from the icebox and poured it from the jar into a small pot. As she started to add a log to the stove, she sighed. "It's probably too hot in here for this for him. Time for the barn."

By the time she carried in the pot of soup and plate of sandwiches into the kitchen, Chad lay on the floor by the boys, half asleep. She started to call him, but something on the kitchen table caught her attention. Setting the food aside, she stared at the package of large envelopes and single colored pencil. What could he possibly want with those?

"Chad?"

"Ready?" He pushed himself from the floor, his hand caressing Liam's head before he stood.

"Yep." She pointed to the envelopes and pencil. "What's this?"

"Think about it."

She did. All through his sandwich, eating two of his turnips, and three cookies when the meal didn't satisfy, she thought, but nothing made sense. Had he remembered their discussion about her decorating the envelopes and decided to change to white—even though she had told him she didn't like it? "You do know I said I wanted to stick with the old style, right? I love the idea of decorating on white, but the tops..." She sighed. "I want the tops to match."

"Yep." He grinned. "I love this. I'm the creative one this time. You're going to love it."

It still made no sense to her. None. What could it mean? Her fingers stroked the pencil as she stared at the envelopes. A new box perhaps? Maybe he wanted her to keep their records in different colored envelopes to differentiate between hers and Mother's? It seemed weird, but it would be easier to know at a glance if she was in the right decade—or half a decade even. From the glint of excitement in his eyes, she doubted it was anything quite that simple, and it still didn't explain the yellow colored pencil.

"I give up."

Chad took the envelopes and opened them. Her heart sank. What a waste. She knew she'd never be able to do it. She liked the tops matching—being able to move envelopes around as she wished without it looking silly. Then he pulled her pencil case from the corner of the table and removed the sharpener. If he took up coloring, she'd cry, and Willow wasn't sure why.

As he ran the side golden pencil tip across the top of the white envelope, giving it the exact shade as her manila envelopes, understanding dawned. He gave her something new, something fun, and still within her comfort level. So simple, but the meaning behind the gift was enormous. He supported her.

"Oh, Chad..."

"I'll take the boys to bed with me. You color."

"I love you."

He grinned, kissing her temple. "I know."

Chapter 143

In early July, Chad whistled low as he read Willow's take on her early weeks of motherhood. To watch her now, she'd always done her work with a baby in one hand, and one nearby. He had almost forgotten the long nights of round the clock nursing, weepiness, and panic at the thought of the future. He flipped the page.

April-

Tax day. I was excited about our little deductions, but Bill says we don't get to claim them until next April. I think it's a government plot to reinforce the erroneous idea that babies are not human until they are out of the womb. I have to feed them, pay for their medical care, purchase the things they'll need for when they arrive, and all in nine long months before they get here, but they don't exist and aren't deductible until they're born. I can, however, give birth, and if the baby dies before the end of the year, I still get to claim him. That just reinforces the appalling attitude our country has regarding the unborn and it angers me.

Bill was visibly touched when I introduced him to little David William. We've taken to calling him Liam because Will sounds so old, William is too stuffy, and we already have a Bill. Chad laughs because we didn't want matchy names like Dirk and Dick and we got Liam and Lucas anyway.

The look on Bill's face as he held his little namesake was priceless. I saw Chad swallow hard a few times. I think Bill has finally moved from frustrated suitor to a "friend closer than a brother." I can see his comfort level has changed, and now with the boys, I think we'll see more of him. That blesses me immensely. I hated that awkwardness after the engagement.

The little chaps are three weeks old and thriving. Apparently, I do not have Mother's milk supply issues. We finally, to give me relief and give Chad a way to get to feed his sons, purchased a breast pump. Yes, they make milking machines for humans. It amazes me what kinds of things are out there. I was determined to milk myself, but when I saw the difference between what I could express and what the machine managed to get, I decided to go with the machine. I'd used it for a week before Chad came downstairs laughing. He'd just lit the bathroom candle for me and then realized that I could always turn on the light since we have to leave the breaker on for the milking machine. Oh, and he really hates how I call it that. It's so fun to tease him

My Chad is adorable with his sons. He talks to them, sings to them, and already lectures them on how to treat their mother. When they fuss at feeding, he reminds them to eat what they're given with thanksgiving and without fussing. I can't help but think he's being a little ridiculous, but it is charming nonetheless. When they soil their diapers, he talks about how men don't make extra work for their wives, sisters, and mothers and as his little men, he expects them to become efficient at doing all of their business in one diaper so that I have less to wash. Hysterical. Absolutely hysterical.

Yesterday was my first day alone. Mom Tesdall stayed for almost two weeks and then Grandmom came for five days. Yesterday I woke up to a house that was empty. I now understand mother's slightly desperate tone in her early journals. It isn't easy doing all of this work when you have babies clamoring for food, dry diapers, and cuddles. I woke up, fed all of us, and was ready to go back to bed. However, Petra and Repetra both expected me to get out there and milk them. Chad didn't get off until eight so the job was mine. I felt strange leaving the babies in their crib while I ran out to do it, but they slept through it just fine.

We weeded the garden yesterday afternoon. I've

discovered that their little car seats are nice for them out there. They can sit comfortably and watch me and be shaded by the sun. Ok, I doubt they see much. From what I've read, their eyes are shortsighted still. It's a nice thought anyway.

I have become much more efficient in my work. We've always taken our time, done the job, moseyed along as we weeded, cleaned, or worked with the animals—well, if we chose—but now I have to get the job done, get it done right, and as quickly as possible in order to be available to the lads when they need me. It makes some jobs less enjoyable, but I've learned that it really helps with the ones I tend to drag out due to dislike. Laundry on the line is such a good prayer time for me that I don't want to rush through it. So, I chose to work very swiftly in putting the clothes up, but I take my time bringing them down and folding each one as I put it in the basket. The little diapers flapping on the line look so charming I've taken half a dozen pictures of them already. Mom thinks I'm nuts.

*She's been invaluable. She came for two days after Grandmom left. Her idea was to be here in case I really needed her but she didn't do anything. Occasionally she'd speak up, but she resisted the urge to jump in and help and just gave input. It was wonderful. I know it must have been terribly difficult not to pick up the babies and hold and cuddle them but she didn't. She was just **there** in case I needed her. It made the transition easier.*

Mom also asked me about my recovery. She was concerned that it'd take me longer to recuperate after the D&C (I need to look up what that means), but I think it actually helped. When I came home from the hospital, I was able to quit using those huge paper pads and go back to my nice comfortable flannel ones. Now, the only time I have any spotting is if I overdo something.

I'm still wearing my early maternity clothes. To be honest, I'm a little disgusted with them. How can I still look so pregnant! Isn't it a bit ridiculous? I'm already down five more pounds, but that still leaves me at twenty pounds overweight. I feel huge. Chad says I've discovered American female vanity, but honestly, I mostly object to the waste of perfectly good clothing in my closet and how difficult it is to wash dishes in my deep sink with all that blob around my gut.

I hear Lucas. Right on schedule. Time to eat and again, I didn't take my nap as I should have. Maybe if Chad gets home before he's done, I'll ask papa to feed Liam for me.

She'd written the entry over two months ago. The lads were already four months old. Her birthday was only a week away. He wanted to do something special for her twenty-fifth birthday but had no idea what to do. The little tykes were too small to be left overnight with his mother... or were they? Perhaps... He shook his head. Forget Willow, he wasn't ready to leave them.

Willow's voice called him to dinner. "Coming!" He stepped inside the boy's room, checked to see that they were still sleeping, and hurried downstairs. Willow would have a list a mile long for them to try to get through in the next two days.

Omelets and muffins sat on the table but the kitchen was still cool from the night's refreshing rain. "Cook in the summer kitchen?"

"The little tykes have a harder time cooling off than we do. I thought it'd be nice to keep the house cool for them today."

"I was thinking of your birthday..."

"Me too."

"Really?" Chad had never seen her show much of an interest in the day. From his reading of Kari's journals, he'd decided it had started at her death because Kari wrote of birthdays as delightful holidays and special surprises.

"I wondered if maybe your mom—"

"Not leave the lads!" He couldn't believe it. He'd been sure that she'd object even if he wanted to do it.

"Not really leave them. I thought maybe we could get a nice room in the city. Leave them with Grandmom and Granddad for a few hours, go get them, take them to your mother's, stay for a while, leave them while we go get dinner and then maybe she or Cheri could bring them to us when it got time for their last feeding." She shook her head. "No, that's too late to ask—"

"She'd love it. Mom's been dying to have them again."

"We can go?"

"I'll see if Caleb thinks Ben is ready to be responsible for all of the animals. If not, we'll have to see if Charlie might be willing to come out."

"Ryder can come on a weekend. He doesn't care much for the animals, but he'll do it in a pinch." She polished off her eggs and popped the last bite of muffin in her mouth. With eyes that reminded him of the Willow he'd discovered after those awful months of her deepest grief—a gleam of mischief glistening in one corner—she jumped up with a new spring in her step. "Oh this'll be so much fun! Where should we go? It's silly to take the boys with us, isn't it? I mean, what on earth would they get out of a trip to the zoo at their age? Or a museum... they wouldn't get anything out of that. Our dinner..." She stood at the sink thinking as she mused aloud.

"They'll just sleep through it. Let the grandmas have a turn with them and when they get two or three, we'll take them."

She spun in place, a huge grin on her face. "We're really going to the zoo! I can show you the pandas. They're so huge! And the penguins are so funny..."

Chad didn't have the heart to remind her that he'd seen them many times. He also made note that zoo was what she wanted the most. "What about dinner?"

"I want an excuse for a new dress—I'm sick of these tenty things—but I don't want something stuffy like The Oakes. Maybe we should stay and eat in Westbury. It'd be less hassle..."

"That'll work." He couldn't resist a chance to tease. "You know, Mom wouldn't care if we just stayed there..."

Before she realized he was joking, Willow shook her head. "But I thought it'd be nice—" A glance at his twisted smile sent her eyes rolling. "You're just terrible."

"And you like me that way."

"I do. Strange isn't it?" Willow snapped her dishtowel at him as she left the kitchen to answer the call of her sons. Lucas' hearty wail informed them that the boys were hungry and most likely quite soggy.

"A picnic?"

"I've worked hard all week fixing fences, weeding, picking, cleaning, laundering, and so forth so we could enjoy your day off. Don't you want a chance to prove your superiority as a fisherman, or are you just scared you'll be upstaged by a *girl?*"

"But you wanted to make a dress..."

Willow shook her head bemused. Even as he'd spoken, he'd hurried up the stairs to retrieve his tackle box. If she followed, which she couldn't with one milk-drunk baby tucked into her crossed leg and the other happily nursing, working hard to 'tie one on' himself, she'd find him critically examining every fly he owned for the best ones before he grabbed the lot and went to change clothes.

A drawer banged. There it was; he was changing. He'd come down in swim trunks, holey t-shirt, and Rockland Warriors baseball cap. He'd forget to put sunscreen on his ears and when the sun shifted, the tops would get red. She needed to make him a fishing hat. Her floppy sisal hat dropped onto her head.

"Thanks. I worry about the amount of sun I get in this room..."

Chad ignored her teasing. "Sandwiches? Should I make some?"

"They're in the ice box in the cellar. We need to clean the kitchen box. I didn't get ice in it quickly enough and there's mold in there."

"Oh ugh. I'll do it. You shouldn't be breathing that stuff."

"It's just mold. I'd have done it already, but I need bleach and I'm out."

Every time she ran out of something, Willow felt inadequate. How had her mother noticed how much of everything to order and keep ahead of everything? They'd been through so many bleach tablets since the boys were born. She'd asked Chad to bring home bleach once, and he'd arrived with a bottle of liquid bleach. It seemed horribly wasteful to her, and she hadn't asked again.

"I'll bring some home—"

Willow bit her lip. She had to say something. "Chad, I'd

rather you didn't."

"Why not? We need it. I don't mind." A look at her face enlightened him—or so he assumed. "It can't be that much more expensive. We'll order right away but you need it in the meantime."

"We don't have room for plastic bottles, and I can't burn them. We need to order tablets. I can let it dry out in the meantime."

"What about the boys' diapers?"

She groaned. The week she'd skipped bleach, the diapers had been dingy and a few of the stains hadn't washed out properly. "I guess. Thanks."

"I'll take the empty bottles to Adric. He's a survivalist type. He can fill them with water for his pantry."

Changing subjects, Willow pointed to Liam. "He's about done. Can you get the sandwiches and the cut fruit? Oh, and there's a jar of fruit tea down there. Can you get that too? I'll get the—"

"You'll sit there and hold my children. What else do you want?"

In twice the time she thought it should take, they finally set off for her favorite fishing place. Each of them carried a baby and a pole. Under Willow's other arm was a rolled up blanket and in her hand, she held a bucket with most of their lunch in it. Chad carried the tackle box in his "free hand," while trying to juggle the baby and avoid whacking Willow with his pole.

Willow commented on how different this walk was from most of their fishing treks. She started to complain that she missed walking hand in hand with him, feeling that closeness and camaraderie when Chad dropped his pole. "This is insane. We should have brought the cart."

"I could go get it if you'd like…" Her lack of enthusiasm was not lost on him.

"You wait here. I'll go get it." Chad dropped everything but Lucas and hurried back to the barn.

"Hey, Liam and I are going to keep walking."

All the way to the hole, Willow told Liam about her fishing dates with Bumpkin and how Othello was too noisy to bring. "Portia is a good dog, though. She doesn't make much noise." Liam's toothless grin was the baby's only reply.

At her favorite tree, Willow was forced to lay the baby in the grass in order to spread out the blanket. "Now I wonder if Mother did this all those years ago. Do you think so, little man? I think she must have at least once." The blanket snapped in the breeze as she spread it out over the ground. "There. Now, we'll just sit here and look cool and refreshed when your daddy arrives. Do you think I should pour him something to drink?"

In spite of its rocky beginning, Willow's picnic was exactly what they needed. While the babies slept, they fished, catching little in the midday sun, and they talked about everything from their expanded operation to further plans for her birthday. They would have stayed out there for hours, but Liam's diaper demanded a change, Lucas insisted that it was dinnertime, and the magic of the afternoon was lost in the shuffle to make the boys happy again.

Late that night after babies slept curled next to each other in one corner of the crib across the hall, Chad brushed an escaped lock of hair from her face and tucked it into her braid. "Thanks for the picnic, lass. Man I needed that."

"It was refreshing, wasn't it? Made all that extra work this week worth it."

"Don't do that too often. As much as I liked it, I don't want a worn-out wife."

"Yes m'lord."

"Watch it, or I'll start calling you Sarah."

Her laughter rang out before she clamped her hands over her mouth giggling. "It's like I don't *want* to sleep or something."

Seconds passed. Willow thought Chad had fallen asleep and rolled over to get more comfortable. His voice made her jump. "What were you talking about earlier? You said something about walking being different, but I dropped my pole. I kept meaning to ask what you meant."

"I just missed the way we used to be able to—" Suddenly, she felt silly. "Oh never mind."

"No, what did you miss?"

"We just used to walk together. I missed holding your hand and talking about things that didn't matter—just because they were interesting. This time it was just different. Not bad—different." She sighed. "Is it terrible that I'm really looking forward to our time alone in the city?"

"From where I'm sitting—"

"Lying," she corrected sleepily.

Conceding, he amended his statement. "Lying, it sounds just about right."

"Good. Night."

"Goodnight, lass." Seconds ticked by before he added, "Goodnight, John boy."

She didn't bother to ask.

Chapter 144

July-

    I think I had the best birthday of my life this year. Chad and I had a delightful time shopping, wandering around the zoo, and relaxing in the hotel room. We didn't even go out to dinner. We ordered room service, watched a bunch of ridiculous TV, and talked for hours. It was wonderful. I think I already said that, but it was.

    The boys didn't seem to mind spending the day with doting grandmothers, grandfathers, and aunts, well aunt, and I got to spend time with Chad. I told him that I thought it was ironic that a couple of years ago I thought he was ever-present and a bit clingy, and now I was abandoning our children for a few hours so I could be clingier—more clingy—no, I guess clingier. Surprisingly enough, he isn't complaining.

    One of the most wonderful parts of the trip was a walk around Granddad's neighborhood. He showed me where Mother's best friend's house was, told me he'd written her to tell her about me and what happened to Mother, and even pointed out where she got on the school bus every day. It was strange to see everything that Mother knew but probably wouldn't recognize anymore.

    We've gotten very close, Granddad and I. The boys' birth changed something in us and for that, all the pain was worth it. I'd wondered about how he'd take our naming Liam after him, but when he picked up his little namesake he said, "David William. I never imagined you'd use my name." It wasn't the words that affected me so deeply, it was the way he said them. My Granddad was honored in our choice.

Wow. I don't think I've ever said or written that before. "My Granddad." My little lads are going to know their granddads and have a lifetime of memories with them if the Lord will see fit to let them live long enough.

Liam is through nursing. I guess it is time for me to put down my pen and pick up a bucket. Tomatoes are calling.

Willow stared at her journal as she nursed a very fussy Liam. She'd missed journaling for nearly three weeks, and now her little guy was teething, making it hard to keep current. Chad had mentioned something twice about how she'd be sorry if she didn't take the time to write down the little things that kept her days so busy. *"Those entries of your mother's are so meaningful to you, Lass. Don't you think that our sons or their wives and children will want to read them as well?"*

A fresh feeling of shame washed over her as she remembered her snappish retort and the look in Chad's eyes. She now knew exactly what he'd look like if she ever slapped him. Her words already had.

August was already half-gone. In another week, Ryder would be off for his first year at Rockland U. They would miss the help just as things were entering the busiest season of all. The thought almost choked her.

"Hey, lass? You up there?"

Hoping not to kill the drowsiness dropping over little Liam's face, Willow tried for a cough. Chad's footsteps echoed in the stairway growing louder as he neared the top. He leaned against the bedroom doorjamb smiling at the picture of Willow in her chair nursing the baby, her feet propped on the foot of the bed. "Still fussy?"

Nodding, Willow whispered smiling, "He's almost out, though."

Her hands caressed his little head smoothing the hair into place. He had a three-inch piece of hair growing near the crown of his head forward like an elderly man who combed one long piece over a bald spot. Chad's voice brought her attention back to him. "I could watch this all day."

"Better get a picture then because I cannot sit here all day. My leg is growing numb, peaches are screaming to be processed, and now that you're home, I can pick some more while you rest. Lucas stopped fussing about half an hour ago and he's," she stood gingerly and shifted the baby and pulled her shirt down discreetly, "going to stay out this time. I rubbed his gums with a little brandy. Mother's journals said that seemed to soothe me and two of her medical books recommend it, so I tried it."

"Did you ask Dr. Wesley about it?"

"I didn't think about it. Two books and Mother were enough for me, but I'll call when I get a chance."

Willow settled Liam next to Lucas and patted his back until he wiggled his head into his brother's stomach and settled into sleep. The boys slept like that often—one head tucked into the curve of the other's fetal position like a human "T." She closed the door behind her and crept downstairs to make Chad a sandwich before she spent the next couple of hours picking peaches.

Chad carried his sandwich out the back door, dropping crusts for Portia as he crossed the yard, wandered around the barn, and back between the tree break to the orchard. As he neared, he could smell the comforting scent of alfalfa. It was time to harvest that too. The next day was his day off. He'd get started on it then.

The baby monitor crackled in his pocket and he paused to listen, but there was nothing. The garden cart had four buckets filled on it already and Willow was carrying a fifth to it. "Wow, you're working fast."

"My body seems to be screaming for some hard physical work, so I decided to reach as far as I could, work as fast as I can, and carry things a bit in order to give me some exercise. I think I'm even weaker since having the boys than I was while I was pregnant."

"Of course you are," Chad teased taking the bucket from

her and forgetting that she wanted the work. "When you were pregnant, you carried weights with you everywhere you went."

"Well, now I need to give my body some real work or its going to protest." She punched her still-paunchy stomach ruefully. "And if this doesn't start looking a little less pregnant, I'm going to protest. I don't mind looking pregnant when I am but the boys are five months old and I look at least that pregnant."

Chad wisely kept the mental adjustment to himself. *Sorry, lass,*" he thought amusedly, *that'd be six months for the average pregnant woman.* Aloud he reassured her with something his mother had mentioned the last time they spoke. "Mom says it takes your body nine months to get out of shape so it is only reasonable that it'd take that long to get it back where it belongs."

She nodded absently as she grabbed another empty bucket and walked away pointing toward the house. "Go to bed, Chaddie lad. I can see you've had a rough day."

"How?"

"You don't want to sleep, but you don't want to talk either. You just want me to talk to you."

She whipped her head around, and Chad sucked in his breath sharply at the sight of her smile half hidden by her wide hat. How did she do that? How did she go from being just "attractive" to amazingly gorgeous at the oddest times? Why had God chosen to bless him with this life, this wife, and the two most amazing little sons a man could ever hope to have?

Willow waited for him to protest and then nodded satisfied. "Tell it to Jesus, Chad. He's waiting for you to talk to Him about it anyway."

He waved and hefted the handles of the garden cart, forcing it down the path, around the barn, and carried the buckets into the summer kitchen. It wasn't much help, but Chad hated thinking of her pushing all that weight. She thrived on it, but to Chad, it was like expecting a woman to change her own tire. Sure, she *could* do it, but that didn't mean she should. Even as the thought entered his mind, Chad brushed it aside. If Willow knew he had thought she shouldn't do any work she wanted, she'd let him have it.

Cart returned, he dragged himself back to the house, up the stairs, and kicked off his shoes. A peek at the boys found them sleeping soundly. Hopefully, Willow would be back before they woke him with their demanding cries for sustenance. As he lay in bed waiting for sleep to erase the mental images of twisted metal and broken bodies, he remembered Willow's not-so-gentle reminder to take his pain to Jesus.

Lucas' piercing wail sent him flying from his bed almost the moment he fell asleep. Chad hurried to the crib to grab him before Liam woke again. Fortunately, the boys were deep sleepers or neither would have ever gotten any good sleep. Chad shoved the little pillow Willow had created to simulate their sibling's body against Liam's head and absently wondered just how helpful it was. By the time he reached his bed, Lucas snoozed again in Chad's arms as though he'd never awakened at all.

Willow found them there two hours later, Chad snoring softly laying on his back propped by pillows, while Lucas gave his own impressive snore for someone so tiny every now and again. "Like Father, like son I suppose," she muttered as she grabbed clothes for a quick shower.

"If there is one thing about motherhood I don't like," she said to Chad that evening, "It's the loss of a good, long, hot shower."

"What on earth are you doing, woman?"

Chad rounded the corner to the orchard to find Willow on the ladder, shirt flapping open in the breeze, breast pumps strapped to her body, pumping away as she picked peaches. "Where are the boys?"

"Lily and Tabitha picked them up an hour ago. This fruit is going bad, and they heard Jill say she'd buy all the preserves I could give her in the next three weeks. They volunteered to take the lads so I could get it done."

"And how is your pump running without electricity?"

"Lily went and got me a battery pack. I didn't know it

was an option! We can turn the electricity off again."

The excitement in her voice told him that she'd been more bothered by keeping the breaker on than he'd realized. He also realized he'd grown accustomed to flipping on lights that now had working bulbs, plugging in fans at random, and suggesting a movie much more often than they'd ever done before the boys were born.

"So, you're pumping while picking? Am I the only one seriously bothered by this?"

"No one is around, it only takes about twenty minutes every few hours, and this way I'm not stuck in a chair while these milking machines drain me." She pointed to her canteen. "Can you hand me that? I'm parched."

"Mom would have come…"

"I know, and it's not that I didn't want her, but Lily called and asked, and you're always saying that I never take help from the church so I thought I'd accept this time."

For the second time in just a few minutes, her words irritated him. First, the glee in finding a way around using electricity as if it was some great sin, and now casting his words back at him like he didn't know what he said and she didn't know what he'd meant. It was as though she deliberately tried to provoke an argument or something. Chad's irritation threatened to erupt in anger.

She grabbed the bucket and awkwardly carried it toward the cart. The sight of her arms, fighting to move around the pumps and hold the bucket with both hands, would have made him laugh if Chad was in a better mood. Irritably, he took the bucket from her and hoisted it onto the cart, waiting for her protest that she could do it herself.

"Thanks. It's not so easy with these things in the way."

Unaware of the storm brewing in Chad's heart, Willow unstrapped the pumps, poured the milk into a jar in the ice chest at the back of the cart, and set the pumps in a basket. "Why are you home? I thought you didn't get off until four?"

"Judith swapped beat with me, and then the Chief came in grumpy and said I could either sort the filing or go home. I opted for home."

"Joe and Judith'll kill you."

"Brad too, but hey."

Unaware that Chad needed to talk out some of his thoughts, Willow pointed to the cart. "Mind taking that up to the barn for me?"

He sighed and reached for the handles. Willow mistook his sigh for dismay at the weight and moved to the front of the cart to help pull. "I'll help. Sorry."

"I've got it, lass," he growled and jerked his thumb, ordering her out of the way.

She stood watching him wheel the cart through the trees until he vanished from sight, but he ignored her. Chad wheeled the cart back to the orchard, his temper smoldering hotter with every step. Any moment, the slightest spark would make it flash into a full-blown fire. The sight of Willow teetering at the top of the ladder as she stretched for a lone peach on a branch just out of reach struck the final blow.

"Are you trying to get yourself killed? Get down from there!"

She missed the seriousness of his tone and laughed. It was the wrong move. Before he could dive to save her, Willow and the ladder crashed to the ground, Willow laughing harder than ever. "Can you get that thing for me? I think I'm going to lose a limb if I try again!"

With an impatient jerk, Chad righted the ladder, gave his wife a helping hand, and climbed to get the peach. "Is a stupid peach really worth the risk? Would it have been so difficult to move the ladder? Twelve seconds and no injury or spend that twelve seconds leaning for it? Why do you have to be so selfish!"

"Chad, I just fell off a stepladder. I fell five feet for heaven's sake. Maximum!" She looked at his red face and stepped closer. "What's wrong? You seem out of sorts."

"You have done nothing but criticize me since I got home." He dropped the peach in her bucket. "I'm going back to work. At least files don't have sharp tongues."

"What!" Willow stared at his retreating back before exploding in her own fury. "I don't *think* so mister! Who do you think you are?" Her words grew closer and closer, but Chad didn't turn around until her hand grabbed his shoulder. "What are you talking about? When have I criticized?"

"First the electricity, then the jab at my mother, then the

implication that I'm not capable of doing any work, and now it's all about how I'm out of sorts. I think you're working too hard, overheated, and possibly dehydrated. I also think you need to realize that you don't have to do everything just because you used to do it."

All the way to the back porch, Chad ranted about everything from lack of sleep to the "insanity" of her insistence that she make the boy's clothing. "Did it ever occur to you that I might want to buy them little RU t-shirts once in a while?"

"Who said you couldn't?"

"You did! 'I don't want to buy their clothes until they need jeans. I enjoy making them.' Well what about what I enjoy?"

"You asked if I wanted to go shopping for clothes instead of stitching their little rompers myself. I said no. I didn't say you couldn't buy something. I said I didn't want to do it myself." He heard the tone in her voice. He knew it meant she thought he was ridiculous, but her next words toned him down—for a moment. "What about your mother? When did I make a jab about your mother?"

"Well, not really about mom I guess, but you did have to throw my own words back in my face when I asked why you didn't call mom. You know how much she wants to be with the boys and how she tries not to intrude too much."

"She's *family*, Chad! How can she intrude? I don't care if she moves into Mother's room indefinitely if it makes everyone happy. I love your mother, Chad!"

Had she managed to make the statement without a hint of laughter in her voice, Chad might have dropped the subject, but feeling ridiculed, he threw back the first thing that came to mind. "You didn't act like it when Mom was concerned about you and your pregnancy. You thought she was interfering."

"Chad, she was. Everyone was. I was pressured from all sides to reproduce, but that didn't mean I didn't want her, and she knows that." Her voice grew exceptionally quiet as she opened the back door. "For that matter, you know it. I don't know what has gotten into you, but I don't know who you are right now." Without another word, she disappeared into the house leaving Chad standing on the back porch, livid.

He threw open the door and at the sight of her chipping ice into a bowl threw up his hands in disgust. "Look at that. If you'd just keep ice in the freezer in the barn—or better yet, put a stupid freezer in this kitchen, you wouldn't spend so much time chopping ice."

"We don't need a freezer in here and in there. And fifteen seconds to move a ladder is something you want me to spend my time doing, but fifteen seconds for my personal comfort in getting some ice for my lemonade isn't? It's too much work to chip a bit of ice?"

"Why does everything have to be a contest with you, Willow? Why must everything be done *your* way? Would it kill us to have a fridge in here where we could keep a never ending supply of ice for water, lemonade, maybe a smoothie every now and then?"

"We don't have electricity in here most of the year to run it. It'd be a nuisance and a waste of space."

"We could have electricity if you weren't so determined to live in the past!"

Her amusement was completely gone. Her irritation had started to rise but now fizzled in a puddle of hurt. He saw it in her eyes, in the quiver of her lips, but he refused to yield. She took a deep breath and whispered, "I can't believe you just said that. After all the times—" Without another word, she left the kitchen, grabbed her purse, hurried down the front steps, jerked open the mini-van driver's door, and in a cloud of late summer dust, was gone.

The irony of her action wasn't lost on Chad. "Of all the absolutely modern and normal ways to duck out of an argument, that has to be the most hysterical," he muttered to himself. A new wash of fury prompted him to slam his glass on the edge of the porcelain sink, shattering it into a hundred pieces. "The only thing better would have been if she'd chewed me out by text."

Ten minutes later, Chad stared in shock as his phone rang and Willow's text message flashed on the screen. "The animals need food and tending. Let me know if you're not going to do it."

Chapter 145

The front porch creaked in rhythm to Chad's push. As each moment passed, he created quite a list of grievances in his mind until he jumped from the swing and strode into the house. He grabbed his keys from the kitchen table, and hobbled down the back steps. At the truck, he remembered the boys and returned upstairs for more diapers and out to the barn for a few more containers of Willow's milk. He'd see if Lily could keep the boys a bit longer. It was time for a talk with his father.

"I just don't know where she's gone or why she's being so impossible."

Christopher listened to his son, confusion growing. The argument didn't make sense from either standpoint. Neither Chad nor Willow was so unreasonable and vindictive. Such spiteful conversation didn't make sense. "Chad, none of this makes sense."

"You're telling me—"

Grabbing his phone, Christopher dialed Willow's number much to the chagrin of his son. "Willow, where are you?" He listened and then suggested she come to their home to talk. "Of course, Willow; bring David. I think that'd be a good idea."

An hour later, they sat in the Tesdall living room. Marianne tried to get everyone to eat and drink, smiling as though the very sight of her forced good humor would somehow erase the ugliness of the situation. Willow had entered the house and gone straight to hug Chad, but his aloofness sent her into a nearby chair nearly hugging herself. The others stared at one another in shock, and Christopher no longer assumed that they both shared equal responsibility for the argument. He had a sinking feeling that this time Chad was way out of line.

"I'd like to take Willow into the family room and hear what she has to say, Chad. Will you let David know what's bothering you while we're gone?" Somehow, he knew hearing it together would start an argument.

How two people could use the same words and make it sound exactly opposite the other story, Christopher didn't understand. Listening to Willow, he heard the same description of the "milking machine," the ladder, and the electricity, but from a much more logical viewpoint. Even as he listened, Christopher thought he knew the trouble—or part of it.

"Willow, I think there's something bothering Chad. My guess is work."

"There was a bad accident the other day."

"He's probably taking it out on you. City cops tend to have to decompress after hard days at work and sometimes they take it out on those closest to them. Not much happens like that in Fairbury, so I doubt you've seen it very often, but I'm imagining that there were children involved or something?"

"I don't know, he wouldn't talk about it."

"I could be wrong," Christopher admitted trying to avoid taking sides, "But I think Chad was picking a fight. I don't think he realizes it, and once he does, he's going to feel terrible." His hand covered hers in an attempt to reassure her. "It'll happen again, I imagine. Next time I hope you'll be able to recognize it and maybe that'll help."

"What do I do? He's upset about things that don't make any sense. I can't just ignore him; it's rude, not to mention he'd be livid."

"You guys are both going to have to recognize this. You can't laugh at his unreasonableness; he can't deny or bottle his reactions."

"Ok." Her voice sounded small and confused.

"Let's go then."

"I need to go upstairs for a few minutes." The way she crossed her arms over her chest told him it'd been too long since her last "milking."

"We'll be waiting."

When Chad didn't invite Willow to sit with him or even acknowledge her return to the discussion, Christopher realized it was going to get worse before it got better. "Well now, I'm very proud of both of you. Things went wrong and instead of lashing out repeatedly at each other, you both came for counsel. This is good."

Chad grunted. Willow's hands wrung miserably and uncharacteristically, she cringed almost looking like a whipped puppy. This was harder on her than any of them had realized. Marianne's arms went around her, and she whispered something in Willow's ear, making Chad glower even more. Had the situation not been so strained and uncomfortable, Christopher would have laughed. He looked exactly as he did when sat on a chair to "cool off" after getting mad at Cheri over something when he was still in elementary school.

"This all started when Chad found Willow working in the orchard, is that right?"

Both of them nodded. "Chad seemed annoyed by it," Willow added confused.

"Of course I was! My wife was walking around outside with her shirt unbuttoned and breast pumps attached to her. How *did* you rig those things to stay attached like that?"

"It wasn't hard, and I can't imagine why you'd be bothered. No one knew I was out there but you; no one could see me, and frankly, even if they could, I was pretty well covered by machinery."

"See what I mean!"

Marianne sat up sharply. "Knock it off, Chad. That was uncalled for. It makes perfect sense to me."

"Did you know she sent the boys home with Lily and Tabitha for the day? She knows how much you love to spend time with them, but when she wants to get work done, does she call you? No. She just sends them off like they're going to daycare or something."

The entire room erupted in a shocked and unified, "Chad!"

"What!"

Willow's voice was small and quiet. "Did you really think that's how it was? Did you really think I couldn't wait to get my little chaps out of the house so I could go do my own thing without them underfoot?"

"You did it quickly enough."

She bit her lip trying not to cry. "Chad, every week at some time or another, you tell me how much the church is supposed to bear each other's burdens. You tease me all the time about how I'm willing to help someone else, but I'm not willing to accept help. You tell me that relationships with the church aren't an option—that we need to invest time together and that this is what you want for your sons." A sob escaped, but she kept going. "So Lily overhears me talking with Jill, and she knows I've been slower with my work this summer so she insists on taking the boys for the day so I can get some things done."

Encouragingly, Marianne patted her hand. "It was thoughtful of Lily to do that."

"But of course that means she sent the boys to Lily instead of letting you have time with them when she knows how much you crave it." The defensiveness in Chad's tone was more belligerent although it had lost some of its angst.

"I don't know what I should have done! Should I have said, 'No thank you, Lily, it's a kind offer, but I'd rather the boys spend time with Marianne. I think I'll see if she wants to come take them while I pick peaches?' Do you think I wanted Lily to take them at all?"

"At least Mom—"

"I'm the mom here and I'll tell you, I don't know how she can please you in this. Have you told her she needs to deepen fellowship ties with your church?"

"Well yeah, but—"

"And have you told her she needs to let people serve her?"

"Don't you think Willow could—"

"Answer the question, Chad." Marianne's tone took on a familiar "don't mess with your mother" tone. Christopher relaxed a little. This was going to be good.

"Yes, but—"

"And am I right in assuming that you've mentioned it quite frequently?"

"It takes that to get it through Willow's head."

"Well it got through," Willow muttered, audibly exhausted. "I remembered what you said, thought I was being difficult about things, decided I could always go and get the boys early if necessary, and accepted their offer thinking you'd be so proud of me."

The last words were choked out with emotion that wrung the hearts of almost everyone there. Christopher watched a flicker of emotion across Chad's face and sighed as he saw his son harden again. "Proud of excluding my mom—"

"I didn't mean to exclude anyone. I tried to include!"

Marianne didn't let him respond. "Don't be an idiot, Chad. If you've told her these things in the past, it is not unreasonable that she assumed this was a good opportunity to follow your counsel and do as she knew you wished. If you were my husband, I'd have thrown a glass of ice water in your face by now."

Willow's head shot up quickly. "Can I?"

The room erupted in laughter. Chad's mouth twitched ever so slightly, but no one but Christopher saw it. Without a word, Christopher passed her his glass of water and crossed his arms, challenging Willow and his son to step up to the plate. To his disappointment, she didn't use it.

"What about the electricity?" David hadn't spoken much since he'd arrived, but this part of the story had greatly confused him.

"What about it?"

"Well, the last time we talked, you told me that one of the things that drew you to Willow in the first place was how different her life was. You said you loved how she and Kari kept the convenience of electricity but had removed themselves from it just enough to ensure that they didn't allow themselves to be controlled by modernity. You liked having to decide if a movie was worth setting up your laptop, turning on the electricity, and you said that the simple act of lighting a candle was a daily reminder that one Christian can bring a lot of Jesus' light into the world. What changed?"

"Nothing. I just saw her hacking away at the ice, and with all she had to do, I thought it'd be nice if we had a refrigerator in the house to save work."

Without a word, Marianne stood, went into her kitchen, and returned with the ice bin from her freezer. This, she unceremoniously sat on his lap, stood back, and said, "So when you have an ice machine, you can avoid having to chip apart ice cubes, right?"

Chad had the grace to flush. "It was just a thought, but she—"

"Chad, after you said that, I commented that we didn't use electricity most of the year and your response was, 'well we could if you weren't determined to live in the past.' Considering you've told me time and again that you love how Mother and I kept the best parts of the past while embracing the best parts of today, that was the biggest slap in the face of all. I felt like you had lied to me all this time."

Christopher stepped in before Chad could say something he'd eventually regret. "Not a week before those babies were born, you told me that you were the most blessed man alive to have a heritage like Willow's to pass onto your children. I have to admit," Christopher admitted, "I felt a little insulted. We may not have had the same kind of rich traditions and unique lifestyle, but we taught you to love the Lord and about community and family, but your heart was wrapped in the life that you wanted for your sons."

Those words knocked the first brick out of Chad's wall. "Oh Pop, I didn't mean—"

"I know you didn't, son. You didn't mean that then, and you didn't mean to reject it all when you spoke to Willow today, did you?"

"Of course, not. I just—I—"

"I have a feeling that's a little bit how Willow felt tonight; am I right Willow?"

A slight nod accompanied her faint, "I had no idea what to think."

Marianne couldn't take it anymore. "It sound to me like

you came home and tried to pick a fight."

"So it's all my fault. I see. I would have thought my family could see—"

"What a jerk you're being?" Marianne's expression dared her son to argue with her.

"Tell me about the accident this week."

The room went utterly silent and still at Christopher's question. Chad's face grew hard as though shutting off everyone around him. "It was ugly, ok? Is that what you want to hear? Do I now have a family of verbal sensation seekers?"

"Stuff it, Chad. I'm asking a legitimate question. Was a child hurt?"

"As a matter of fact, yes. A little girl not much older than the lads riding on the seat without a car seat. The babysitter wanted a soda and didn't have the car seat. She just put the poor thing on the front seat and tried to get there and back before anyone missed her." He crossed his arms again. "Are you satisfied? Is that what you wanted to hear?"

"Of course we don't want to hear about that kind of thing; no one does. But Chad, can't you see it's eating at you?"

At the words "not much older," Willow had stood, crossed the room, sat next to Chad, and wrapped her arms around him. "I'm so sorry. That must have been so awful."

"It's the job."

"Doesn't make it easy. Is the baby going to be ok?"

At the choked sound in Chad's voice, the room emptied quickly, leaving Chad and Willow alone. "She's better off than she's ever been—than any of us are. She's with Jesus."

With those words, Chad broke down and wept, speaking of holding the dear little girl's broken body and trying to find some kind of life left in it. He told of having to notify parents at their places of work that their little daughter was gone and of how he'd had to arrest a broken and shocked babysitter for several broken laws.

"Why didn't you tell me?"

"You don't need to hear about the ugly side of my job."

"But Chad, the ugly side of your job is usually a domestic dispute or a drunk driver. It isn't like you deal with child deaths every day. You can't just let that eat at you."

"You seemed to mock everything I said today."

"I wasn't trying to. Actually, I thought you were teasing me—at first at least." She glanced at his face seeing the change slowly wash over him. "I didn't mean to offend you with leaving the boys or not wanting the fridge. If you want to leave the electricity on in the house, just tell me. I'll learn to adjust."

Seeing the sacrifice she was willing to make for him crumbled the rest of the wall he'd erected between them. "Was I really as awful as it seems like I was?"

"Let's just say I didn't quite know who you were for a while. If I'd realized that the accident was probably affecting you, I might have been a little more understanding."

The sight of Christopher's glass on the coffee table caught Chad's attention. "Still want to throw that at me?"

"Not this time."

"I don't want there to be a next time, lass."

'There will be. I have no doubt that there will be." She smiled. "I'm warning you, though. Next time I'm going to call it like it is, and I'm not going to play along. You can pick all the fights you want, say all the ugly things you can think of, but I'm not engaging. I let this get under my skin this time, but I won't let it happen again."

"If you tell me I'm just decompressing, I'm liable to blow up at you."

"Now that I understand why, I can take it," she assured him with an air of confidence Chad prayed was genuine.

"Now what do we do?"

She glanced at her watch. "Pick up our sons before I explode?"

Chapter 146

"I don't know what to do! I can't keep up with processing and picking and—" Willow's wail cut off her words.

Jill wandered the huge garden plot, the greenhouse and checked the trees in the orchard. "Do you have all the food your family needs?"

"All the produce, but—"

"Well then you have two options. The first is that you could just hire a bunch of teenagers to pick the fruit and you could bring it to the store." She glanced around the farmhouse, observed the tidy yards and huge flowerbeds, and watched the sheep grazing. "But, if I was you, I'd have a 'Self-Serve' Sunday. Open your farm up to visitors for a few hours in the afternoon. Allow them to pick all the produce they want and charge by the pound. That way, you'd only have to hire one or two teens to man scales and cash box."

Relief quelled the rising panic in her heart. This could work. "I like it. As fast as things are getting mature, I think I'll do it on Wednesdays and Sundays. Once a week will allow too much waste."

"How about the pumpkin patch? How is it doing? I haven't been out there in a while but it looks good from the road."

Excitedly, Willow made Jill promise to look as she left. "The first pumpkins will be ready around mid-September I think. I'm so excited about it. When Chad showed me those city patches, I just cringed for those kids. He wants to do a corn maze next time, but I don't think we have the time for it."

"Well, get some scales, some more buckets, and paint a sign."

A wail from upstairs sent Jill home and Willow upstairs to rescue her "starving" sons from apparent imminent demise. Chad found her on the swing, Lucas rolling around trying his best to fall off while Liam nursed. "Well, this is a sight for weary eyes."

"Rough day?"

"No—good day, actually. Just long when you'd rather be home."

"Good day? How?" Willow sat Liam up and rubbed his back firmly until he managed to burp up the air he'd swallowed.

"That's m'boy." Chad winked at her. "Aiden Cox."

"What about him?"

"He came zipping down the street, on his scooter, wearing his helmet and elbow and knee pads. He even jumped off the sidewalk when he saw Alexa Hartfield walking toward him."

"Will wonders never cease?"

"I just wish he didn't have to learn the hard way like that."

"The hard way?" Willow passed Liam to her husband and grabbed her basket. It was past egg gathering time.

Chad scooped Lucas up in his other arm and carried them around the house talking to Willow as he went. "He was there the day of the accident. He saw me working on the baby. I didn't have time to stop and make him go away."

"Oh, Chad! How horrible!"

"I think the reaction of the sitter made the biggest impact on him." It was as though Chad couldn't stop talking about it. All through the egg gathering, he told about calling Mrs. Cox and suggesting she come and get her son, how he'd blocked Aiden's view of the child, and tried to comfort the sitter before her hysterics drove Aiden into the street just to get away from it all.

Abruptly, he changed the subject. "So what did you do today?"

"I know how we're going to save the produce."

"Really?"

Willow outlined the plan for the produce stand and by the time they went to bed that night, an extra-large sign was ready to attach to the fence out by the gate. Excited at the idea, Chad was certain it'd ensure success for the pumpkin patch as well. More than everything else, they were both happy that Willow's hard work wouldn't be wasted. If she had to choose farm work or time with her sons, her sons would win diapers and little hands down, but she preferred not to see the rot and waste that would come from her inability to finish her projects.

No one could have predicted the success of the produce stand, but it exceeded anyone's expectations. On Wednesday and Sunday afternoon and evenings, she walked through the gardens, pointing at ripe, mature foods, and shaking her head if someone reached for something not quite ready. Customers did the work of picking, and she managed to keep them from stripping the plants.

Everyone loved the boys, and the sling Willow fashioned out of athletic jersey kept her and the boys as cool as possible. She strapped one to each hip, and strolled up and down the rows, explaining what each plant was as if they could understand. Marianne showed up on opening day and spent ten minutes on the back step clutching her stomach, laughing at the sight of Willow's "humongous hips." However, it proved an effective way to keep abreast of what was happening with her garden and keep the boys occupied with something other than wrestling in the playpen.

With less to do in processing the extra food, Willow found time to butcher her meat chickens on schedule and kept her egg layers happy with their new extra-large run. She and Chad still ate the laying hens as new layers came up in the ranks, but she used meat chickens to serve her customers, who were looking for free-ranging and hormone-free chickens. For some inexplicable reason, the boys would sit for hours in a playpen in the new barn and watch their mother pluck, skin, and wrap chickens. They rattled their toys, took an occasional wrestling tumble, but seconds later, their eyes roamed back to watch each fascinating movement. Chad was disgusted.

In a vintage overnight case that Marianne found in an antique store, Willow stored the cut out clothes she planned to sew for the ever-growing boys. It sat beneath the coffee table and Willow had great plans to cover it with fabric or paint it to match the room, but for now it was just a plain brown case looking like it was put there as part of the décor. Inside were flannel-lined overalls, Jon-Jons, rompers, and of course, more rompers. She knitted "longies" out of the white wool that Chad still hated, and no evening went by that Chad didn't find a new pile of something or another on the coffee table when he got home from work, waiting for her to put away the next day.

One evening late in September, he arrived home at two in the morning to find her journal lying on the coffee table next to three piles of new diapers, several longies, and to his amusement, four hand-knitted and sewn footed pajamas. She'd just spent twice the cost or more making something that could be purchased at Wal-Mart for five dollars each. Even as he thought it, her words from those early days came back to him, "I can't afford to buy cheap things. I need to invest in quality so that I don't have to replace them as often." She always assumed that cheap equaled inferior.

He picked up one of the sleepers and felt the softness of the fabric, the carefully knitted wool feet, and attached hoods. "She's right," he murmured to himself. "This will last through another ten children and look almost as good then as they do now." Something Dr. Kline had mentioned caused him to add even more softly, "Even if maybe they aren't *our* children."

In the kitchen, on the back of the woodstove, he found a bowl of stew on the still-hot stovetop. Using potholders, he sat it on a plate and grabbed a spoon, some cornbread, and a glass of milk, carrying them back to the living room. As he ate, he read the latest entry into Willow's journal.

September-

The strain on our friendship is all but gone now. Chad

seems to have taken his father's words to heart, and when things get stressful, he simply talks about it—even when he doesn't want to. I think he's amazingly brave. It's hard enough stopping drunks, breaking up fights between families, or dealing with an accident. It's even harder to come home and have to make yourself vulnerable to the very people you want to shield from those things.

The little chaps are growing and growing! Mother marked my growth inside the door of my closet, so I've been using each side of their closet for their growth. It's easier to mark them now than at first. I used to have to lay them down and use my measuring tape and transfer, but now they'll stand up against the door just like Mother used to do with me.

Liam is crawling. He can't seem to go forward, however. He sees something across the room, gets up on all fours, crawls with all his might, and ends up farther away from it than ever. It is hysterical watching him and the look of utter confusion on his face. One of these days, he'll put his knee forward instead of backward to go and actually get there.

Lucas, on the other hand, gets to anywhere he wants to go by crawling on his forearms and elbows. Chad calls it the "army crawl." It is slow, and it looks horribly uncomfortable, but he can get anywhere he wants to go. Liam seems to understand this and it annoys him. Lucas also has all four front teeth whereas Liam only has three.

Mom says that the boys are growing amazingly fast. The clothing she buys them are all designed for children of twelve months instead of six, so in her opinion, that means they're exceptionally healthy. However, Dr. Wesley concurs that they are larger for early babies (although for more medically substantiated reasons), so I guess that's good.

Lucas knows Chad's voice and has a very keen sense of hearing. When he comes home, if Chad even says one word to me, Lucas hears it and wakes up, unless he's in a very deep sleep. If he's playing on the floor, he starts crawling and has even climbed up on Chad's leg to get closer. Liam is definitely attached to Chad, but it's not the same as watching Lucas. I don't know if it is a personality difference or if maybe he's a little less advanced. I just don't know, but I think it's interesting. We're going to have a lot of trouble keeping the boys from the stoves this winter. They're too little to really understand or obey and too old to leave them alone.

The garden is under control again. Most of the produce is either ready for me to process, all picked and processed, or just growing in the greenhouse. We started new tomatoes outside just to try it. We have the water walls all around them and can't wait to see how well they work. We always used to start them that way when it was getting warmer but not when it was getting colder. I don't think it'll work, but we can't know unless we try.

All the fruit has been picked, and the alfalfa is in the barn. We had so many acres of alfalfa this year that Chad rented a baler. It made storing the hay easier. We've got enough to keep the animals fed for most of winter without calling the feed store. I'm excited about that. Fortunately, we didn't have to remove very many trees to plant those crops either. The property we bought from Adric was old cropland that just needed a good tilling and a couple of young trees removed. Those trees are now in our front pasture for shade for the sheep.

Ryder revamped the greenhouse to be twice as productive. He's built "loft beds" for shallow growing vegetables and herbs. He almost doubled our produce with that one move. Alexa Hartfield found out I could grow corn year round and has offered me obscene prices to keep her supplied. How could I say no? We'll get some too, so it'll be good for all of us. Meanwhile, the work Ryder does in the greenhouse has given him lots of material for his first term paper. I don't understand it all, or why they even have to do it, but Chad says it's normal.

I met Ryder's girlfriend the other day. She seems like an intelligent girl—very pretty—and showed an intelligent interest in what he's doing here. She took a tour of the house and asked questions about why we do much of what we do. I guess a cellphone next to an oil lamp is a bit of an odd sight. Chelsea, his girlfriend, is a senior in high school and plans to attend Rockland University next fall. She says she is interested in nursing. Ryder seems very taken with her. I hope he's not too young. I'd hate to see him or her hurt.

Granddad still comes once a week, without fail, on

Thursday afternoons. He sits with a boy on his lap, talks to them about Mother, tells him about Uncle Kyle and about my cousins, and plays with him. Then he passes the little lad to me and picks up the next. Those boys adore their G-G-Dad. I had no idea that children so young could become so attached to someone other than possibly their mother or father, but they are. When Grandmom comes, they both fall asleep to her lullabies and curl up with her as though she's the greatest thing in their little worlds. I love it.

I think we need to make an effort to become part of Uncle Kyle's life or at least to try to include him in ours. I don't know my cousins. I should know my cousins.

We see Mom and Dad Tesdall around every ten days or so. It's never quite two weeks, but usually more than one. Why that matters, I don't know, but there you have it. We take turns making dinner for each other, and when they come, they insist that Chad and I go into town for ice cream or a movie. At first, I was annoyed by the idea that we needed to get away from the children. Now I think I understand that it's not about getting us away from the babies, but rather about giving us time alone together. It's about giving us something rather than getting us away from something. Fine nuance, but a big one. I can see that it means a lot to Chad, and the more we go, the more I look forward to those couple of free hours to focus on him alone.

I've been invited to speak at a Christian Women's Retreat in New Cheltenham next spring. Chad recommended that I accept, but I still haven't decided. They are asking for women around the greater Rockland area in hopes that people will make friends of both the attendees and the speakers. They requested that I speak on infusing beauty into life and journaling. How did they find out that I journal? Chad wants me to try to get mother's journals "edited" so that I can offer them for sale at the retreat. He thinks they'd be a huge encouragement to other women, but I'm not sure. I don't know if I have time for that project. Chad, the lads, and the farm must come first.

Chad found the changes in pen color and the fine differences in writing or penmanship style between paragraphs amusing. She'd taken to starting one journal entry for each month and just adding to it as she had a moment. A paragraph or two at a time, the information that meant most to her ended up on paper. Sometimes she wrote about what was on her heart, the wrestling she had to overcome her own sins and weaknesses, and other times specific details about how to do something with the children or the work to make it smoother or more efficient.

He hadn't realized how pressured he'd made her feel to do things he thought were important. Reading about the retreat and Kari's journals through her eyes, he could see the pressure she felt, and if he was honest with himself, the pain it would cause her to do something so intense with her mother's journals. He'd have to tell her not to worry about it.

He crawled upstairs ready to climb in bed only to find it empty. With a sigh that only Willow understood how to translate, he made an about face and went back downstairs, onto the front porch, and found her curled up on the porch swing with several blankets. A closer look showed tearstains on her cheeks.

Were they evidence of more grief at the loss of her mother? A result of the pressure she was under? Were they something between her and the Lord? Why the tears? Could they have been prevented? And finally, why did he always feel so helpless when he saw evidence of tears, but a little irritated when he actually saw her crying?

Chapter 147

Willow hummed her favorite song from Chad's "Argosy Junction" CD. Occasionally, she'd sing a line or part of a line, before returning to her absentminded hum. *"...my mother, she's my sweetheart..."*

"Lass, you were sleeping on the swing when I got home last night."

"Mmm hmm. I heard the babies around four and came inside."

"When you weren't in bed, I went looking for you."

She turned, an egg clinging to the spatula as she stared at him curiously. "Does that bother you? My sleeping outside I mean. I thought you didn't care..."

He hastened to assure her that wasn't his concern. "Of course, not. I wouldn't have made the extender if it bothered me; I just wondered..."

The egg slid back into the pan just before the yolk broke. "Wondered what?"

"It looked like you'd been crying."

As she buttered the pancakes coming off the griddle, Willow told Chad about her evening. "The boys went down early. I think they're getting more teeth or coming down with something, because they've both been so sleepy the past couple of days. Anyway," she shook her head as though trying to clear the fuzz from her thoughts. "I went out onto the swing for a while and was having a nice chat with the Lord."

From his chair, as he ate the stack of pancakes and his

fried eggs, Chad listened as Willow talked about her tryst with the Lord. She spoke of her prayers for him and his safety, for the town and for their appreciation for all the police and firefighters did to protect them, and for wisdom for the town council regarding several issues facing the community. "I just felt..." she struggled for the word. "Well, *burdened* about it."

"I know what you mean. I've been praying for the town a lot in past weeks."

"Well, from there it went to your family and Mother's..."

Chad only half-listened, his mind mulling the tendency for her to consider the Finley's her mother's family rather than her own. He noticed she'd stopped speaking and was looking at him expectantly. "I'm sorry, you said something that distracted me. What did I miss?"

"I asked if Cheri was taking the trip with the missionaries in Guatemala or not."

"Yes, she is."

"Good. I prayed about it and then suddenly felt ridiculous for praying for something I didn't know for sure was happening." She stabbed her pancake stack with her fork. "Anyway, that led me into praying for the boys, and their health and growth and their relationship with us and the Lord. Before I knew it, I was praying about our home, our lives, and suddenly I was overwhelmed with just how blessed we are. Gratitude like I've never felt before almost smothered me. I don't know how else to explain it. I was sobbing, but it was a good and thankful sob. Weird, I know."

"A good sob?" Chad thought he understood, as much as a man who hates feminine tears can. His mother and sister had drilled the concept of "happy tears" into his head at a very young age. However, happy sobs—grateful sobs—he could not comprehend. To his mind, only Willow was capable of taking a basic fundamental feminine accomplishment and turning it into a full-scale production.

"It was like that Christmas list I made. Remember? It was good—cleansing—but I'm still wiped out from it."

As though the words were their cue, both boys sent up wails of sogginess and hunger. Willow wearily started to rise, but Chad jumped to his feet and gently pushed her shoulders back into the chair. "I'll get them. You finish your breakfast before they start demanding theirs."

"Too late for that."

"Well, it's about time they learned some manners. Clean diapers before breakfast and ladies first." Chad's wink warmed her heart as he turned to collect his sons.

September dissolved into October. The leaves that changed to the warm colors of autumn contrasted with the now crisp and sharply cool weather. The produce stand sold little more than pumpkins these days, but the idea had been a reasonably profitable one. With every passing day, the leaves fell, the grasses died, and the barren bleakness of the upcoming winter crept slowly over Walden Farm.

Ryder, however, kept the plants in the greenhouse growing succulent tomatoes, fresh lettuce, celery, and of course, carrots for Lacey. Spinach filled their salads, and he was attempting to try watermelon. The tomatoes in water walls in the garden were spindly little things. Willow had little hope for them, but Ryder refused to give up yet. He also had great plans to plant five acres of Christmas trees in the spring and five more acres each year afterward. He'd convinced Chad that by the time the first crop was mature, the boys would be old enough to take over most of the responsibility of care for, and later sell, the trees.

Willow's days slowed into a new familiar rhythm that allowed her to relax and enjoy the dozens of firsts her boys seemed to achieve every week. Some, like first crawls and belly laughs, were balanced by first illnesses and unexplained screaming fits. More often than she or her mother ever could have imagined, Willow poured over her mother's journals, reading about how to handle a tooth that nearly erupted and then moved back up into the gums, how to make lotion for chapped lips and cheeks that didn't irritate sensitive skin, and how to double rinse diapers when rashes appeared.

Chad remarked more than once that the journals were nearly priceless. He'd grown concerned that they'd be damaged and worn with so much use. So, the scanned copies became reference copies. He put the originals away for times when Willow just needed to feel close to her mother. However, no matter how strongly he argued for a fireproof lockbox, Willow refused to put them out of sight.

This had created a new project for Willow. Kari's journals were written with little regard to organization—much like Willow's journals. When she'd needed gardening information from one or more, she'd copied the information into a specific gardening journal that she later organized by dates, crops, and similar ideas. However, she only added information as she needed it, resulting in much being lost in the original journals until someone read it later and commented or copied into another journal.

Armed with sticky-note "flags" that Chad provided, as she nursed the boys, she read through her mother's journals again but this time with an eye to organization. She marked gardening topics with green flags, childcare, much to Chad's disgust, with pink, and housework yellow. She had flags for recipes, maintenance, and clothing plans. There were addresses, family history, and enough subgroups that some flag colors had asterisks, boxes, and circles to differentiate between others of the same color.

As the month drew to a close, she'd managed to do all of the fall canning and winter preparation, flag most of the journals, and nothing else. Chad didn't understand her frustration and despair, but Willow became nearly distraught at the lack of accomplishment in her days.

"I haven't made their next sets of clothing, I barely got the house wiped down much less scrubbed, and if Ryder wasn't taking care of the greenhouse, we'd be hurting for next spring."

"Did you hear yourself? You cleaned the house—"

"Wiped. I really didn't get to do any serious scrubbing. I'm going to have more work next spring because of it, and by then, the boys could be walking, which means it'll be harder than ever to get things done."

Patiently, Chad tried again. "Willow, wiping is all it needed. You keep a clean house. It didn't need seriously hard scrubbing. My mother doesn't scrub our house half as much as you scrub this one."

"She doesn't live in the dirt! My house has twice the dirt in it since bringing in the sheep, having vehicles coming up and down the driveway every day, and that horse stirring up dirt in the yard."

Unaware of how her words sounded, Willow picked up her sleeping son and carried him upstairs to his crib. Chad sat, stunned in his seat. Their changes caused more work, he knew. He'd calculated the time expense of shearing, of more work in the gardens and processing. He'd ensured that what work they added was doable with growing boys that would need more and more of their time the older they grew. He had even calculated the cost of another pregnancy or two and how to downsize quickly if the demands of family became more than they could handle. The idea of additional housework caused by the animals and vehicles arriving and departing simply had never occurred to him.

He knew that cleanliness was very important to her. The Finley women didn't spend all of their time working hard and working fast at their work. They took their time, enjoyed the process, and left enough time at the end of the day to relax and do something they enjoyed. Whether reading a book, playing a game, or creating something beautiful just because they could, they kept a part of their life available to refresh themselves in that way. With a sinking heart, Chad realized he hadn't seen Willow do anything "for fun" in weeks— months even. In fact, the last time he remembered her doing anything creative had prompted a trip to town for a yellow pencil and some white envelopes.

He needed to talk to someone before he talked to Willow. He only managed to hold his immediate desire to sit her down and go over the situation in check by the lessons he'd learned in how differently Willow thought than most people. At last, he hurried upstairs and asked if she'd like to take a drive into the city.

"Oh, I've got much too much to do today. If you see your mom, tell her the boys are trying to pull up on things, and she needs to hurry out here before she misses it."

"I do think I'll go by and see them. They have a DVD from Cheri with her trip to Guatemala on it. I'll burn us a copy so you can see it too."

The relief Willow felt as Chad drove down the driveway bothered her. The boys were sleeping, the day was unusually warm—nearly sixty degrees—and if she worked quickly, she could cut out several sets of diapers and a couple pairs of Jon-Jons each. Eventually, her tasks drove the discomfort out of her mind as she worked as quickly as possible to get everything accomplished before Liam and Lucas awoke from their morning naps.

Chad drove past the Westbury off-ramp and drove toward the Chesterhill area of Rockland. He passed small bungalows that reminded him of Fairbury, around a park that sent a lump into his throat, and down the Finley's street to the colonial style home where Willow's mother had spent her childhood. As a last minute idea, Chad prayed that talking to David was the right answer.

"Chad? Is everything ok?" The voice made Chad spin, hand automatically going to his hip. David Finley grinned at the sight of his "grandson" in "cop mode."

"Oh hey, Granddad. I've got something to discuss with you."

David's eyes narrowed. "About what?"

"Well, I was talking to Willow this morning, and—"

"Does she know you're here?"

Frowning, Chad shook his head. "I started to go talk to my parents, but then—"

"I'm not discussing anything with you about Willow without her knowledge."

Without skipping a beat, Chad whipped out his phone and dialed home. He told Willow about his visit and passed the phone to David. Within minutes, both men zipped along the highway back to Fairbury. When they arrived, they found Willow elbow deep in flannel, corduroy, and denim. "Just walk around the mess. I decided I *have* to get this done before the boys wake up."

Stacks of cut diapers, threatened to topple as the men threaded their way through the room, but Willow kept cutting. David watched her with concern growing in his eyes. Chad cleared his throat and nodded as Willow's grandfather raised an inquiring eye. "This is why I went looking for help. I wanted to make sure I wasn't expecting too much of us with all the changes."

"What's going on around here? I've never seen Willow look frazzled before."

Willow's head rose wearily and shrugged her shoulders. "There's work to do and no time to get it all done. I do what I can, Chad does what he can, and we're both pretty thankful for Ryder these days."

"Are you expecting too much of yourself, Willow?" The gentleness in David's voice soothed away any hint of condemnation.

"What do you mean?"

"You have a lot on your plate, girl. Are you sure you can handle it all?"

She didn't miss a beat. "I'm doing no more than mother did."

"You have twice the children she had—" Chad took his cue from David and spoke cautiously.

"And I have a husband when she didn't."

"You have more animals and more land cultivated..." David knew, even as he spoke, they were taking the wrong direction.

"And I have Ryder and Chad to help with those." She looked up at the men confused. "Are you here to tell me that we need to change how we live?"

"No!" The men's voices echoed through the room in unison.

Chad shook his head vehemently. "I brought David here to help us see how to accomplish everything we want to and if I've added too much of a burden on you. I feel like I've let my ideas and dreams for this place override your personal workload and comfort, but I *knew if I said that, you'd object.*" His voice grew more intense as he prevented her interjectory objections.

"What do you see as adding too much to her plate?"

"Well, until today, I didn't realize how much just adding traffic to the driveway added to her workload. Before we got married, I don't think she noticed the extra dust that my truck stirred up around here. But add extra animals, Ryder coming and going, Jill coming and going, and then family and friends visiting, not to mention the produce traffic when the stand is open, and her workload is increased exponentially just keeping abreast of the dirt."

The defeated look on Willow's face bothered David. "What is it, Willow?"

"I didn't realize the dirt bothered him too. I thought it was just me."

"I didn't even notice it, lass. I just know how much cleanliness is important to you, and I've made it hard for you to keep ahead of the dirt."

Confused, David shook his head. "Ok, what do you see that is bothering you, Chad?"

"I see Willow working harder than ever, faster than ever, and never having any time to relax. She's always glowed with life and loved what she does. I don't think she resents her life now or anything, but I can see she doesn't love it like she did, and I think I've contributed to that. I want to know how to fix it."

"Oh, I don't think so, Chad. It's just adjusting to a new way of living with the boys. Once I'm—"

"I see it too, Willow. You look weary. I saw you cutting out clothing for the boys before they were born and while it was work, it seemed almost leisurely. Here, you're frantic. There are dark circles under your eyes, and I suspect you're on the verge of tears at the idea the boys might wake up before you finish."

As if given permission, the tears flowed freely as David spoke. "I don't want anything to change, but..."

Chad tried to take the scissors from her, but Willow jerked away from him. "Sit down and stay out of my way. I have to finish—"

"See what I mean? What you loved to do has now become a burden. You know that all I have to do is speak the word, and my mother will show up at the door with bags of clothing. You don't have to do this and part of you still wants to do it, but there is also a part that feels burdened by it."

Her vision blurred as tears obscured the fabric pieces she tried to cut. Dropping the scissors, she pulled her knees up to her chest, wrapped her skirt around her legs, and dropped her head to her knees. As if it was a perfectly logical time to comment, she added one last desperate whisper, "I can't get rid of the leftover baby weight either."

The men stared at each other in horror. A discussion of work, expectations, and plans was reasonable in their minds. Adding in a woman's weight and tears made both of them miserably uncomfortable. Instinctively, they knew they were in for a difficult discussion.

"Lass, what does—"

David interrupted quickly. "Ok, well, I have a question." Frowning at Chad and giving him a quick shake of the head, David Finley drew upon years of dealing with women and stopped Chad from escalating the focus on her appearance. "What is most important to you? Is it doing everything yourself because that *is* the life you want to live, or is it having the benefits of the life regardless of who does the work?" He watched the gears start and put his hand up. "Don't think, answer with your gut. You can change your mind later. I want to know your gut answer."

"Live my life regardless of the division of labor."

At the corner of the couch, Chad relaxed visibly. David nodded understandingly. "That's a very good way to put it. I have another question."

"Shoot."

"What is keeping you from working at a reasonable pace and doing the things you love to do?"

"The interruptions. The boys need me right when I'm in the middle of something so I have to leave it. Then, when I return, I often have more work than ever because I have to undo what dried out, or caked on, or whatever while I was with the boys."

"Are you mothering your sons or are you making yourself a slave to them?"

Protest died on Willow's lips as Chad sucked in air and his eyes grew wide. "That is a very insightful question. I think you may have a point."

"You think I—"

"I don't think anything, lass. I just heard the question at the same time you did, but immediately, I thought of the way you drop everything when the boys want you, and I could see why Granddad asked the question."

"I do that, don't I?" A frown wrinkled her forehead as she

thought about the question. "I didn't—not at first. I'm sure of it."

"You don't with the phone. If you're doing anything when it rings, you wait until you're at a reasonable stopping point before you answer. If it stops ringing, you finish all together and then go listen to voice mail. But the minute either of them stir, you're there."

"But I didn't do it at first, right? I remember deliberately making them wait sometimes."

"I think," Chad answered as he tried to recall how it could have happened, "It started when the boys got louder."

"Ok, so we know," David interjected before they got too far off topic, "That you do need to consider how to teach them to entertain themselves while you finish things that shouldn't be left standing or are almost done. That alone will help with the frustration level."

"What about the work I've added with the expansion?"

"Is it profitable?" David's mind was already into a business solution.

"What?"

"The changes you've made. Are you making a profit yet?"

"As in have we repaid everything we've spent and now are earning money or are we bringing in more than we're putting out now?" Willow stood even as she asked, and went for the hand written ledgers that she kept. Her meticulous lines of expenses vs. income on old-fashioned ledgers drove Chad crazy. He'd tried to show her how easy it'd be to run a bookkeeping software program on his laptop, but Willow wanted nothing to do with it.

"Well, I want to know if right now, your income is greater than your outgo."

Chad and Willow nodded simultaneously. "Definitely," Chad said. "It's lower now that the produce stand is over, but we still have the chickens for meat and eggs, the produce we sell Jill, and of course, we don't have much in the way of expenses to begin with."

David looked at the numbers. "When Carol is feeling overwhelmed at home, she always says, "I wish the chef fairies wouldn't have gone on strike this week. I could use them.""

Willow giggled. "Mother used to say that about the dishes."

"If you could have fairies to come and do part of the work while you were sleeping, what would they do?"

To Chad, the question was brilliant. He'd never have thought to ask the question in a way that he instinctively knew she'd answer truthfully. Willow's answer surprised him. "I think right now, the laundry, everything in the greenhouse, and maybe watching the boys for a while every now and then so I could do some of the other things I want to get done. Maybe a little cleaning too."

Before Chad could voice the surprise on his face and ruin a moment of open honesty, David leaned forward, his forearms resting on his knees and his hands clasped together. "My advice, Willow-my-wisp, is hire a fairy. You two can obviously afford it, you aren't trying to prove anything to anyone here, and you don't have to do it forever. Just do it until you feel confident that you can and want to do the work again yourself. I have a feeling you just need a little time to adjust. Farms, for centuries, have had hired help to do some of the work both indoors and out. Why does this one have to be any different?"

Chad and Willow stared at one another with questions in their eyes and answers in their hearts. Willow glanced back at her grandfather. "Hire someone, huh? For how long? Indefinitely?"

"As I said, however long you need. Just until you adjust or if you discover you like it, keep them on as long as you can afford it. Talk to Bill Franklin about it and see what he thinks of the long-term effect on your finances. If you want to take over some of the jobs again, take them on one at a time until you are confident again."

Willow jumped from her place on the floor, leapt over the stacks of cut clothing and diapers toppling one in the process, and wrapped her arms around her grandfather. "I think you're the most brilliant and wonderful granddad ever."

"Gee, thanks. Glad he thought to come out here and offer help..." Chad's tone held a deliberate aggrieved air.

With a grin at David, Willow jumped to the other couch and into Chad's lap. "—but I think you're the world's best and most considerately thoughtful husband in the universe." She tossed a wink back at David again. "The handsomest too!"

"I think you're both nuts," David said as he rose to answer the wailing duet from upstairs.

Chapter 148

"So then I was thinking that there was no reason to assume we had to pay anyone for anything. I mean, we have produce, chickens, eggs, wool, I spin so that's yarn, and there is all that food I canned and such, so why not try to barter first? If I gave a better price on each item to whomever worked for us, then it'd be a savings for them and wouldn't cost us cash. It's a win-win if we find someone willing to work for goods instead of dollars."

Chad smiled at the eagerness in Willow's voice. Ever since the discussion with David, her old bounce and energy had returned, although slowly. He wondered at the change in her when there was no change in their situation. "Lass, what happened to you? You seem a bit of your old self already."

"I don't know. I think maybe I needed to see that I don't have to do it all by myself. Just knowing I don't need to freed me somehow."

"I was thinking we could put an ad in the Fairbury Gazette. You write it, and I'll drop it off on my way to work this afternoon."

Willow dropped the dishcloth into the sink, dried her hands, grabbed a pen and paper, and began writing. He nearly went crazy as she meticulously wrote each word in her perfect and artistic penmanship. "There. What do you think?"

Chad read the paper aloud. "We are a family of four and are looking for part-time house help. It is our preference to barter food and fiber items in exchange for the work, but will also consider monetary compensation. Please inquire at Walden Farm or call 555-3525."

He took the pen and made a few scribbles and adjustments before passing the sheet back to her. "This is how most people write an ad."

Willow read the note under her breath. "~~We are a family of four and are~~ Looking for part-time house help. ~~It is our~~ prefer~~ence~~ Willing to barter for food and fiber items. ~~in exchange for the work, but will also consider monetary compensation.~~ ~~Please~~ Inquire at Walden Farm or call 555-3525."

Her nose wrinkled as she looked at Chad. "But it's a grammatical nightmare. You also removed the possibility of payment."

"See if anyone will barter first. If we get no calls this week, then we'll add that to next week's. Why tell them it's a possibility until we know if we need that possibility or not?"

Willow's arms slid around her husband's waist. "And that is why I married you. I needed someone to tell me how to live in this crazy world of yours."

Chad finished his coffee in one gulp and then reached for his coat. It was time to take Lacey for her ride. He kissed her temple on his way to the door and then paused as he stepped outside. "Well, that and you were awfully curious about smooching. I heard the end of *North and South* so many—" He slammed the door quickly before her soggy dishcloth could smack him in the face.

The ad came out in Wednesday's paper. To Chad and Willow's great surprise, they had four calls within an hour of likely delivery. The next day, two more calls came and then they received a call from Aggie. After speaking to her for a few minutes, Willow disconnected the call and raced to the barn where Chad fed Lacey and the goats. "Chad! Aggie just called about the ad—"

"Aggie wants to work here? Is she nuts?"

Playfully, Willow shoved him and reached up to pat

Lacey. Absently, and much to Chad's stunned amusement, she stroked the horse's neck as she continued with her news. "If you'd let me finish... She said that she has a friend who lives in Ferndale. Iris..." Willow glanced at the pad of paper in her other hand. "Landry. I guess they helped Aggie a lot when she first got the children and moved out to their place. She said Iris was a wealth of wisdom and a hard worker. When she saw the ad she called Iris and told her about it, and Iris said she'd love to work in exchange for fresh food and yarn!" Willow hesitated. "Her only stipulation is that she'd have to bring her son with her. He's almost thirteen, though, so he shouldn't be too loud and rough, should he?"

"What's wrong with loud and rough?"

Nearly sending Chad into a seizure in trying to keep from reacting, Willow laid her head against the horse's neck and sighed. "I am not bringing someone out here to make more work. Loud and rough means babies that don't sleep. What's the point of hiring help if they undo all you gain by hiring them?"

She stepped away from the horse, brushed her hands off on her jeans, and started toward the door talking all the while. "So what do you think? Should I call her or not? I like that she has such a good reference, but that boy..."

"Would you have Aggie out here if Laird or Tavish came with her?"

"Definitely."

"There's your answer then."

"Thank you! I'll call her right now before the boys wake up again."

At the barn door, she turned wide-eyed and stared at Chad and his equine friend. "Did I just touch that animal?"

"You not only touched her, you stroked her neck and snuggled up against her."

Willow shuddered visibly. "This is proof that I need some help." She shuddered again blinking very slowly as if trying to gain self-control. Her eyes narrowed slightly and she glared at Chad. "You enjoyed that."

"Just a little, yes." He met her icy eyes and sighed. "Ok, so I barely contained my helpless laughter. It *was* pretty funny."

To his surprise, she retraced her steps until she stood nearly at his shoulder with Chad between her and the horse. "Do not *ever* stand by and watch me put myself in a situation like that again. If I want to cuddle up to that beast, I'll do it, but it's very unjust of you to let me do it unknowingly."

As he watched her leave again, he shook his head and fed Lacey another carrot. "They talk about no fury like a woman scorned? Forget it Lace... the real fury comes when they're scared out of their wits."

In the house, Willow leaned against the back door, shaking. She had all sorts of theories as to why horses terrified her as they did, but none of them made sense. All she knew was that they did, and she hated how she lost all sense of logic and reason the moment she was around them. Weakly she pushed herself away from the door and grabbed her journal. According to her calculations, she was two weeks behind on her Christmas gifts. She could get an early start on butchering chickens, or work on gifts. A glance at the clock told her she had an hour at most.

The sound of Chad's boots on the back step made her decision for her. She just couldn't go back outside in the cold right now. She sighed. "More like you can't stand to go near that animal right now," she muttered under her breath.

While Chad loaded the wood boxes for the stoves, Willow went upstairs to the craft room and pulled out a box. She'd work on the boys' main gift while she and Chad talked. He might even be able to keep them occupied so she could make some serious progress on it.

"Did you get a hold of the woman—Iris?"

"Oh! No, I need to call. Thank you."

Several minutes later, she danced into the room and pulled out her box of felt squares. "She says she can start Monday and thanked me for the opportunity."

"Did you work out payment?"

"I'm 'paying' her twelve dollars an hour. From her earnings, she's buying anything we produce that she wants at a ten percent discount. On the first of every month, we'll settle up. Either she'll take more food home to make us even, or I'll give her cash."

"Sounds fair." He pulled out a fence picket from his pile,

spread it on top of a tack cloth, and grabbed his sandpaper.

"What are you doing?"

"Making a fence for the stove. I thought it might as well be attractive. I knew you'd never go for a plywood box."

"I think Mother has something like that up in the attic. I know there are pictures somewhere of a fence-like thing around this stove and the one in the kitchen. I don't think she made one for the upstairs."

Before she finished talking, Chad raced up the stairs. She reached for a cutout of a sun and the letter S and chose a light blue square. With orange embroidery floss, she carefully stitched the sun to the block. By the time she finished, she heard the faint cry of, "Eureka!" from the upstairs.

Minutes later, Chad came downstairs with something wrapped in a huge blanket. "It's covered in dust. I thought I'd take it outside and sweep it off there."

"Is that all of it?"

"No, this is just one side. It looks like it attaches directly to the wall I saw several more pieces so I think the kitchen one is up there too."

While Willow sewed trains, umbrellas, violets, and wagons to block squares, Chad carried down huge sections of fencing to the front porch. He took a broom out, swept them carefully, and then brought them into the kitchen to wipe them down well. "I thought about hosing them off, but I was afraid they'd just freeze and then melt all over the floor."

"They would. I tried that with the hearth tools when I was six. Mother was very irritated."

"Honest mistake..."

"Yes, but then I was told not to mess with them in the first place. I thought I knew more than she did."

"You *were* a little stubborn..."

She laughed at his studied air of diplomacy. "I still am, and you know it."

As Chad assembled the fences around the stoves, he and Willow made their Thanksgiving plans. The Tesdalls and Finley parents both had plans with other family members. They'd also both invited Chad and Willow to join them, but the couple had declined. They wanted their first Thanksgiving with the boys to be at their own home.

"We could invite Ryder. I heard him talking to someone on his phone the other day that his parents were going to be gone all weekend. Apparently they're going skiing in Aspen for Thanksgiving."

"They didn't invite their own son to join them?" The idea seemed impossible to her.

"Apparently they need 'us' time."

"Translating into, 'You aren't becoming a high powered professional in a highly successful field, therefore we'll punish you in the hopes that you'll feel guilty enough to switch majors before it's too late."

Chad dropped his screwdriver. "I can't believe you said that."

"I know it's awful, but it's true. That poor boy works so hard out there and is doing amazing things. He's cultivating all new plants—well, old ones really. He's trying to turn the entire greenhouse into heirloom plants. It's amazing what he can do, and his parents refuse to recognize it."

"And if Lucas or Liam chooses a life like Bill's in Rockland, will you accept it as equally valid and important as the life you've chosen?"

Shock filled Willow. "I can't believe you'd assume otherwise! He's my son! He lives his own life just as I chose mine. I didn't have to stay here. Mother made it plain, the whole time I was growing up, that the day would come that I'd have to choose whether I wanted to keep my life as it was or change it. I changed it drastically."

"You stayed here—"

With deliberate patience, eyes welling with tears, Willow set down her sewing. "Chad, you forget that I am not living my mother's life." She swallowed hard. "I invited you into my home. I invited the Varneys, the Allens, and Bill into my life. I took an isolated farm and welcomed people who would have been met with a shotgun in my mother's lifetime. I added cellphones, laptops, and DVDs to my life. I increased production of food and expanded our property to accommodate it. I did that to serve people my mother would never have spoken to. I got married. I did the one thing that my mother feared most. I let a man into our home, willingly. I let him hold me, love me, and together we became parents—the thing my mother feared only slightly less than men in general."

Chad started to interrupt, but Willow plowed through his words continuing her own at a slightly higher pitch. "I confronted my grandfather, learned to pity and then fear my grandmother, and in general, turned my life upside down." After another deep breath she stood. "I very nearly moved to the city and took a job as a children's clothing designer and store manager, and you can sit there and tell me my life is no different than it was when I was, say, ten years old. I don't know whether to laugh, feel hurt, or if I am just insulted."

Stunned into silence, Chad watched slack-jawed as his wife opened the front door and closed it firmly behind her. He jumped to follow, but cries of consciousness from the boy's room stopped him. If he knew Willow, she was far enough away from the house already to be unable to hear them. Shoulders slumped, he hurried upstairs to greet his sons.

Liam clapped happily in the crib at the sight of Chad, but Lucas slept through the noise his brother made without stirring. Even when Liam fell over, his head landing on Lucas' feet, the baby didn't move. Alarmed, Chad placed his hand on the boy's back and sighed with relief as he felt the rise and fall of the little boy's chest. He moved his hand to the lad's forehead, but Lucas was as comfortably warm as any baby should be and not a smidge more.

As he grabbed the "diaper basket" and hurried to their bedroom to change a soggy Liam, Chad realized his own life was vastly different than he'd intended as well. By now, he'd planned to be expecting a move to the Rockland police force if not on it already. Instead, he was in an old farmhouse, sans electricity, diapering a child with what Willow insisted on calling "washable" diapers, and milking six goats every morning. Just as he dumped the soggy diaper into the pail in the bathroom, another thought hit him. He was also living his dream of being a police officer. His dream had expanded and changed to suit new dreams—much like Willow.

Liam sucked contentedly on his bottle as Chad dialed the Allen's home. Even as he did it, he realized the irony of choosing to bring in the Allens for help instead of calling his mother or the Finleys. What had seemed like such an affront at one time was now his first reaction. Would he ever learn the kind of wisdom and discernment that his father seemed to exude naturally?

Lucas awoke the moment Chad saw the Allen's car coming up the drive. He opened the front door, despite the frigid temperatures, and hurried upstairs to grab his other son. Liam tried to escape their bedroom as Chad changed another soggy diaper until he finally shut the door in the adventuresome tyke's face. "You stay in here. The last thing I need is you falling down the stairs. That wouldn't go over very well."

The sound of Lily calling him sent Chad into a rushed frenzy of snaps, soakers, and a fresh pair of sweat pants that did not match the carefully tailored striped shirt Lucas had been wearing with the funny overalls that Willow always made. With a boy in each arm, giggling and laughing as they played their private games with each other, he hurried to greet Lily and Tabitha. "Thanks for coming out. I really blew it this time and we need to talk."

"Everyone has those moments in their marriage, Chad. That is something you both have to learn and deal with."

Passing the boys to his rescuers, Chad grabbed his jacket. "Thanks. I'll be back in a while."

"Chad?"

He popped his head back in the door, "Yeah?"

"I don't know what the problem is, but I just thought of something on my way over."

"What was that?"

Lily snuggled with Liam for a second and then pointed to the huge barn behind the house and the vehicles out front. "In less than three years, her life has turned upside down. For twenty-two years, she lived one way and now she's living another. On top of mothering responsibilities, it's probably all hitting her at once."

Chad nodded and shut the door behind him. "Looks like everyone has realized that but me," he murmured under his breath as he pulled his collar up around his neck and started looking for footsteps.

Chapter 149

The Monday before Thanksgiving, Liam and Lucas awoke with gunky noses, slight fevers, and coughs. Willow held one son on each hip and glanced from boy to boy, flummoxed. Her list of things to do in preparation for Thanksgiving had already grown to mountainous proportions. "Listen, chaps, if you won't cooperate, I can't get anything done. So, here's how it's going to be. You're going to have your breakfast—"

Liam wailed.

"—and then you're going to play on the floor while I clean the kitchen."

Lucas rubbed a snotty nose into her shoulder.

"Ugh." Willow went to retrieve a stack of handkerchiefs, but when Liam splattered his own nasal contents onto her neck and shirt, she dropped them back in the drawer and went to retrieve a box—no two—of Chad's beloved Kleenex.

She couldn't hold the boxes and the boys, despite her best efforts. Hating the betrayed looks on the lads' faces, she plopped them back in the crib and went to change her shirt, wash her face and neck, and carry the boxes downstairs. Their tortured screams of abandonment followed her down and back up again.

"You are two very spoiled little—darlings."

Once more, she hoisted a tot on each hip and carried them downstairs. Even snuggled against Mama, the lads wailed and sniffled, swiping her shirt with a fresh coat of mucous. "Ugh." She gave Liam a mock-glare. "You know, bud, I'm starting to understand Mother. Fluids and semi-fluids are revolting to see, touch, smell, and you'd better not give me a taste!"

Liam wailed louder.

Once downstairs, she settled them into the couch with her. Lucas fussed and whined as she tried to nurse Liam into some kind of contentedness. However, with his stuffy nose, the poor baby couldn't manage a gulp without coming up for air, creating a mess for both of them. Frustrated, Willow tried feeding Lucas, but he too struggled to breathe and nurse at the same time.

As both boys wrestled beside her on the couch, she stared at her soaked shirt and at their milk-splattered clothes. Time for another change—another one. It seemed futile, but she gathered her sons once more and carried them back upstairs to change them—again.

They tumbled over her bed as she pulled out a sweater—twice nearly falling off—and then mauled each other as she changed their clothes. She glanced at the clock, trying to remember what time Chad went into work. It had been almost an hour since the lads awoke. An hour—wasted. Willow sighed. Then she sneezed.

Downstairs, she set the boys on the floor with toys she knew they wouldn't touch, and opened the stove door. Bending over the fencing Chad made for them hurt her back, her chest, and her arms. She struggled to settle a log in place. "I hate these fences," she muttered.

The temptation to remove it long enough to fill the stove grew. She glanced at the boys as each one tumbled over the other in what seemed an attempt to smother each other's wails. It was worth the risk. She'd be right there anyway. Decided, Willow unlatched the gate and pulled it apart. It took less than two minutes to scoop out the ash, refill the stove, and close the gate again. Willow glanced over her shoulder. The boys hadn't moved.

"Kitchen stove while they're occupied in being mutually miserable," she muttered.

Before she pulled away the fence, Willow peered into the living room again, but the boys were still engrossed in their wailing wrestling match. The fire had almost died in the stove, but she shoveled ashes, laid new logs, and stuffed a bit of kindling in it to get up a decent blaze, hoping to take the chill off the freezing kitchen.

As Willow shut the door to the stove, she sneezed. Ashes flew from the ash can and into her face. Half-blinded, she rushed for the sink, washing her face and blowing her nose until she could see and breathe again. She turned back to finish her job and nearly froze at the sight of Lucas crawling past the fence to the stove.

"No!"

Willow's head connected with the floor and then skidded into the brick hearth as she dove for her son. She managed to keep him from reaching for the skirt of the stove—one she had burned her hand on often—but barely. With one foot, she kept both boys at bay as she replaced the fence and carried them from the room. "Ok, that wasn't fun. Not—aaaachoo— fun at all," she finished with a sigh and a dash for Kleenex.

Her mind tried to race, struggled to whirl, but instead slogged through the mire of her thoughts until she found one that made sense. She sat her sons back on the floor, ignored their protests once more, and dashed for her phone. Her fingers tapped the doorjamb to the dining room as she watched her sons and waited. "Iris? What are you doing today?"

Jonathan Landry burst in through the back door and raced through the kitchen, uncharacteristically ignoring his mother's rebuke. "Mrs. Tesdall, I found something when I was cleaning the kitchen!"

"You found something?" Willow blinked, trying to comprehend the boy's words. Her head felt thicker by the second.

"I didn't want to touch it, but—c'mon. You really should come see this. Or maybe Mr. Tesdall should come home."

Iris stepped into the room, hands on hips. "Jonathan Landry! What are you talking about?"

"The barn kitchen—"

"Summer kitchen," Iris corrected automatically. "What about it?"

"Maybe you should come, Mom."

A sickening feeling filled Willow's gut. "Where in the kitchen?"

"The cabinet above the fridge. I was putting the extra candles up there like you said, and the wall fell out!"

"The wha—"

Willow stood and passed a sleeping Liam to Iris. "I'll be back in a bit. Would you rather he stay in here?"

"Is there a reason it shouldn't be ok?"

Willow shrugged. "I don't know."

"Just call if you need him then." As Willow opened the back door, Iris added, "Do you want me to call Chad?"

She shook her head. "If I need him, I'll call."

"She's gonna need him," Jonathan insisted.

Portia greeted her as she stepped from the back porch. "I've avoided this for two years, girl." She sneezed again.

The summer kitchen looked as if a bomb had exploded pots, pans, and other cookery and survival items all over the counters. At first, Willow couldn't imagine what the boy had been doing, but a bucket and an old rag on top of the fridge told her. That Iris was a smart woman. The boy would keep occupied, out of the way, and get some of the infrequently done chores while not making noise in the house. She'd have to remember that—for what reason, she didn't know.

Procrastination. Disgusted with herself, she growled, "Snap out of it. You know what's up there; just get them, and get them out." Why Chad would be needed, she couldn't imagine.

As she climbed the stepladder, Willow's hand reached automatically toward the back where she knew the journals would be hidden in the wall. Mother hadn't really talked about them, but Willow knew they were there. However, before she could jerk her hand back again, it connected with the cold barrel of a rifle. "Why—"

She started to grab it—pull it out from the hole in the wall—and stopped. Her hands patted her pockets, but even as she did, Willow remembered that she had left it lying on the coffee table. Her feet strode across the yard with long, purposeful steps. She didn't say a word to Iris or Jonathan as she passed through the house and snatched the phone. Iris started to ask something, but she was back out the door before the poor woman could finish her sentence.

"Chad?"

"Hey, lass. I was just going to call."

"What time do you get off today?"

His chuckle rumbled through the phone. "You sound adorable with your stuffy nose."

"Not funny. I'm serious. What time are you going to be home?"

Chad told her he got off at two o'clock. "Why?"

She glanced at her phone. "Half an hour. The day sure flew past. Anyway…" She hesitated. "I have a hypothetical question."

"Okaaay…"

"If a policeman's wife found a weapon on their property that, as far as she knew, they didn't own, would that policeman likely prefer to be told while on duty or wait to see it off duty?"

"Lass?"

"I don't know why, Chad, but I'm scared."

"Be there in five."

Willow took a deep breath. "Chad?"

"Yeah?"

"Maybe you should bring Joe too."

Pieces of a .357 Winchester lay spread out on the counter Willow cleared while waiting for Chad to arrive. Joe Freidan poked at it with his pen. "Do we have any record of Kari Finley's fingerprints?"

Chad shook his head, one eye on his wife. Willow sat in the corner reading her mother's journals. With each turn of the page, he saw the tension rise, the pain increase, her heart break just a little more. "Lass, do you know if Mother was ever fingerprinted?"

"No, but…" Her eyes slid to the stack of journals. "Maybe?"

Joe nodded. "Well, it wouldn't confirm anything except that the same person owned or used the gun and the journals, but it would be a reasonable conclusion."

Chad hesitated. "Call Judith?"

Without hesitation, Joe nodded. "She's the best." As Chad made the call, Joe glanced at Willow. "You okay?"

"No."

"Can I do something? It's going to be okay, Willow."

"Why did she keep a disassembled gun in the wall, Joe? Why would that be 'okay?'"

"Maybe she figured out it was stolen. Maybe it didn't fire correctly and she didn't want someone to get hurt. As alone as she was out here, she wouldn't risk just throwing it away, and she wouldn't take it into the police if she was trying to stay under the radar. She could have found it and been worried about it, so she took it apart and saved it. If that's the case, she probably used gloves or cloth or something to hold it. It'll be worthless print wise if she did."

"I thought gloves were better."

Joe shook his head. "On porous things, sure. Non-porous needs not to be handled—laser." He nodded at the journals. "Anything interesting in there?"

"A whole lot of stuff I never wanted to see or read."

"See?"

"I thought I'd seen all the photos of mother after her attack. I didn't."

He stepped closer and reached for the book. "Let me take it, Willow. We'll go through it for you."

She pulled back. "I'd rather you didn't—not before I know what you're going to be reading."

"We may have to take them—especially if those prints don't match."

"If they *don't?*"

Chad stepped in the door. "If what don't?"

"He says they might have to take the journals before I can read them if the prints don't match."

"We might, but I think they'll match. Mother probably ruined any other prints if she found it."

Joe and Willow exchanged amused glances. Willow nodded. "So he says."

"What have you found?"

"Chad?"

"Hmm?"

Her eyes barely met his. "Not now."

Concern flooded him. If she wasn't willing to talk, it had to be bad. Joe stepped back, offering to leave, but Willow shook her head. "I'd say the same thing with you gone, Joe."

As punctuation to her assertion, Willow sneezed.

Chapter 150

Dark circles rimmed Willow's eyes the next morning. She stumbled from bed, stepped into the boys' room, and stared at the empty crib. A rattle downstairs told her Chad must still be home. Strange—he was supposed to work at six again.

The boys slept in the playpen in the corner of the dining room. From the woodstove, Chad smiled and refilled the water pan before crossing the room. "You're up early, lass."

"It's got to be after eight. I am not."

"You went to bed after four. You're up early."

"Is that why you're still here?" Willow paused on the bottom step and turned. "Be right back."

"I'll get you water."

"Thanks."

They met at the couch at nearly the same time. Chad passed the glass to her. "Drink up. I can see from your skin that you need more."

"It gets so dry..."

"Yep." He stared at her. "You're sick. Go back to bed."

"You're supposed to be at work."

Chad sighed. "I'm supposed to take care of my sick wife—the one who stays up until all hours when she's already sick."

Liam whimpered in the playpen. Chad's eyes slid sideways and then back to Willow. She sank into the couch, holding her head. "I'm so tired. My head hurts."

She reached for a journal, but Chad pulled it away. "Not

now, lass."

"I have—"

"No. No, you don't have to read anything. You're sick." Chad jerked his head toward the kitchen. "Do you want breakfast? I made oatmeal and boiled eggs. Oh, and I ran and got some orange juice."

"Juice."

Chad tried not to snicker at the word. She made it sound like, "deuce." As tempted as he was, he forced himself not to grab the journals and take them with him. Ten minutes later, he found her half-reclined on the couch and struggling through another page of the journals. "Lass, please."

"I just want to get through it so I can be done. Don't you get that?"

"I get that you're worn out. I get that you're sick—"

"And I get that I'm way behind on stuff for Thursday. Can you please call Iris back?"

"She said she'd be here at—" Chad pointed at the front window. "Nine o'clock."

"Are you going to work now?"

At Iris' knock, Chad stood and shook his head. "I thought I'd help Jonathan finish up in the barn."

He hurried to open the door before another knock woke the boys. The action—futile. Iris and Jonathan weren't two steps in the door when Willow cried out. He didn't even have a chance to ask.

Willow began wailing about things he couldn't even understand. The boys screamed, Jonathan glanced back and forth between the noisemakers asking, "Mom? Wha—"

Chad pleaded silently with Iris for help while he rushed to grab his sons. The cacophony of sounds built as he struggled to soothe the boys and his wife. He heard cries of "What does it mean?" mixed with cries of misery and surprise. Jonathan took Lucas and carried the little guy out of the room.

Iris took Liam and followed asking, "Bottles? Rice cereal? Both? Neither?"

"Bottles, thanks." Chad turned to Willow, pulling the journal from her hands. "What is it?"

"I don't know."

"Ooookaaay..."

As she wept, he wrapped his arms around her, confused by her words. Nonetheless, he did recognize something in her—fear, confusion, and incomprehension. Something in those journals bothered her, and as much as he wanted to understand it, he knew that calming her would be the most direct way to start. "Shh... just relax. It's all ok. Whatever is in there—it's over."

"I don't think it is."

He stuffed a wad of Kleenex in her hands and winced as she blew her nose. He'd be sick in twenty-four hours. Another sneeze. Or less. "Okay, can you show me where?"

She fumbled with the journal, flipping too far forward, too far back, and finally stopping on the journal page. "There. I don't know what it means, but it's—I'm so confused, scared—everything."

He began reading, trying to make sense of the journal.

Think I've just blown it. This life I've crafted for myself is probably gone. They'll take her away from me. I hated him so much. Feared his father even more. I saw myself as better than they are, but am I? Not hardly. I hate going outside. I hate hearing cars out by the road. Every motor sounds like the death march of our life. I hate what I've done, and it's all my fault.

And my work has exploded exponentially. I must work faster than ever. I'll never get everything done for winter now, but I have to. I don't want to make it too easy on me just to order wood delivered or to turn on the electric—especially after I tore out all the baseboard heaters. I'd have to buy a room heater for every room and that's insane. I'd have to cook in the barn and then come back in—it's all too crazy. I need to start carrying more food back on my trips to and from town.

None of this makes sense. I don't even know why I'm writing it. I guess because I'm scared again. I don't want to lose my child. I don't want her in foster care. Should I leave a note somewhere—a note that tells people where to find my family? But then, wouldn't that make the news? Foster care would be better than death or worse, kidnapping. Would they want her? I doubt it. But if for some reason they did, they could just kill me and take her. No one would know about it until much too late to do anything about it.

The weight of all I've done crushes me. I've put my parents through what is probably their worst nightmare. I've let them believe a lie. I've accepted money from a criminal. I am living off the money of a man who I believe would and has murdered for his own convenience. And, now I'm guilty of more—so much more. I don't even know what else to do. So many innocent people hurt because I was flattered that THE Steven Solari asked me out. How stupid can I be?

The rest rambled even more, showing Kari's fragile mental state as she talked about things that only made sense because she knew what she wrote and why. From his perspective, none of it made sense, and from the look on Willow's face and the confusion she'd shown, she didn't understand either. He reread a few sections, shaking his head and trying to decipher something from it all.

"Lass, I don't know what she's talking about. I think she's probably under some pretty heavy PPD right about here, and she's seeing everything she's done in the worst light, ignoring the fact that she made her decisions out of protection for you. Right there—" he tapped the page again, "it shows that she's worried about her parents and is irrational."

"I don't know, Chad. I don't know how to explain it, but this means something—something horrible."

"Even if it does, it doesn't affect us now. That time is gone. What we need now is for you and the lads to get well so that we don't have to cancel on our guests. That's what we need."

He couldn't believe it worked. She stared at him as if he'd said the most brilliant thing she'd ever heard, stacked the journals, and stood. "I'm going to go take a hot shower. Can you get Iris to make me some ginger tea? I'll drink and go to sleep. I have too much to do tomorrow and I can't ask her to come again Thanksgiving week."

A bang awoke Willow sometime late that night. She

glanced at the clock, but her eyes refused to focus enough to read the numbers. Engine—she glanced toward the window—lights. Chad was off to work. Must be nearly two. She'd have until six to work. Once awake, she knew she'd never go back to sleep. The only times she'd been awake all day were whenever Chad brought one of the lads up for a feeding. Tentative pressure on her chest told her it hadn't been long since the last. How did she not remember that?

As she stepped from the room, she hesitated. Wasteful to take another shower—oh how she wanted one, though. Two seconds after she shut the bathroom door behind her, she jerked it open again and retrieved a towel. She'd skip an optional shower someday to make up for it. It sounded too relaxing to forego.

The longer she stood under the hot water, the better she felt. The achiness had almost completely disappeared, and though her nose had been full, the steamy air seemed to help clear it. She dressed quickly, brushed her hair, stuffed her feet into warm slippers, and hurried downstairs. The living room and kitchen woodstoves had been banked recently.

Pies—she could make her pies now. Willow built up a good fire in the woodstove, letting it blaze for a few minutes, and then began pulling ingredients from her hoosier. As always, her heart swelled at the amazing piece of practical furniture. She'd never been more surprised than when Aggie admitted she never had put flour in the hopper.

"Crazy girl. She could save herself so much time," Willow muttered as she began measuring flour, salt, and lard. Her hands worked automatically, cutting the lard into the flour, mashing the teaspoons of water into it, rolling, dusting, rolling, and filling several pie pans. Cherry, apple, and of course, pumpkin. She carried the pumpkin to the summer kitchen. The mess that greeted her nearly made her dump the pan and all into the incinerator. Still, it wouldn't be Thanksgiving without pumpkin pie.

With one eye on the clock, and shivering from the cold, she began putting everything back where it came from—everything but the journals and the gun that now sat in police custody. Judith had assured them that a cursory glance showed one basic style of print over the whole gun. "Of course, the laser might show something else, but I doubt it," she'd assured Willow.

That had been a relief.

The boy had done a good job. She'd have to tell him. Only the gaping hole in the drywall hinted that anything had gone amiss. Willow stared at it for a few long seconds before she shoved the boxes of candles into the cupboard and ignored it. Chad could decide what to do about that later.

By the time she had the room looking well, she had only twenty minutes before the pies should be done. After checking on the kitchen pies, she hurried back into the summer kitchen and dragged the turkey from the fridge. She rubbed it with butter and herbs, but there was no time to mix stuffing. Frustrated, she dashed for the house, irritating Portia with her sudden appearances and disappearances, and pulled out the fruit pies just in time.

Satisfied, she rushed back to the barn and closed the door behind her, shivering again. The minute the pumpkin pie was done, she pulled it from the oven, set it on the top of the stove, and carried the turkey to the house. It took a couple of trips to gather ingredients, but with sage, cornbread crumbs, celery, onion, and crushed pecans, she mixed stuffing and filled the bird with it.

Thanksgiving smells slowly filled the house. Chad arrived for his lunch break to find the hoosier covered in flour, some on the floor, dirty dishes in the sink, and Willow asleep in her mother's rocker. Smiling.

She didn't sneeze, even when he woke her and insisted she go back to bed. Just as he started to close their bedroom door behind him, she called out, "Chad?"

"Hmm?"

"Can you baste the turkey and stick another log far away from it?"

Chapter 151

Chelsea Vernon sat in the Tesdall kitchen and watched as Willow basted a turkey in a wood-burning oven. The room, so warm and smelling so delicious she thought she could taste each scent. Her mouth salivated as turkey, bread, pies, and mashed cranberries melded together into one scent that sang of Thanksgiving. The babies crawled around Willow's feet, but the odd fencing gave them protection from the hot stove.

Willow's voice startled her out of her reverie. "Ryder says you want to go to nursing school. So what about nursing interests you?"

"I like a lot of things. I want to go into geriatric nursing. I'm really close to my grandmother, and since she's been in the assisted living home, I've gotten to see what is involved. It's so cool to listen to them talk about living stuff that I read about in school because they were there!"

"Will you work at the place here in Fairbury when you're done?" Willow sounded genuinely interested—unlike most people of Chelsea's acquaintance.

"I don't know. There are a lot of places to work in Rockland, but it's more expensive to live there. I could commute from home, but I'll probably want my own place by the time I graduate. They're adding an assisted living part to that eco-community in Ferndale. That sounds really cool. I'm totally into going green with everything possible. They even do green burials there."

"What is green?"

Chelsea looked at her hostess in shock. "You know—eco-friendly."

Reaching down to pick up Liam, Willow moved to sit in the rocker and tried again. "Okay, what is eco-friendly?"

"You know, like you have here—living off the grid, organic farming, small carbon footprint…"

"I don't know what you're talking about, but okay. It sounds interesting anyway."

Passionate about the planet, Chelsea grew animated as she tried to explain. "Oh, you know, working to keep our planet sustainable. People are destroying it with excessive waste, fossil fuels, and the abuse of chemicals and stuff. The impact on our environment is catastrophic. First they were worried about a greenhouse effect, but it's actually worse. Scientists are seeing that the real problem is climate change. We're shifting from over warm to over cool."

"But the earth has done that for centuries—millennia. I remember reading about ice ages and then warming trends that later reverted back to ice ages over hundreds or thousands of years. Why is it any different now?"

"Because man is just trashing the place."

"But if the result is the same thing that has always been happening, how can you claim that the trashing of the planet is the cause of the climate change?"

"I thought you'd be environmentally conscious. I so didn't expect you to be an anti-environmentalist."

Willow stared at her guest, stunned. "Why must I be against the environment simply because I don't understand the logic behind a climate change theory?"

Before Chelsea could answer, Ryder and Chad came stomping into the kitchen, laughing about some football play they'd heard on the radio while working in the barn. Unknown to her guest, Willow watched, concerned, as all of the girl's attention focused on her boyfriend the moment he entered the room. In Willow's opinion, the relationship seemed awfully intense on Chelsea's part.

"Hey, dinner is almost done, why don't you guys set the table, and we'll be ready to eat?"

The table conversation revolved around environmental activism, conservation, and the effects of politics on science.

Though she carried her end of the conversation when her lifestyle seemed to conflict with her political views, Willow spent most of the next hour watching the interaction between Ryder and Chelsea. A nagging concern hovered in her heart, until Willow thought of a way to test her theory.

All through the meal, she fed bits of meat, cranberry sauce, and mashed potatoes to the boys and waited. She argued against legislation, dipped her potato covered fork in gravy before feeding Lucas the bite, and served pie to overstuffed guests, all while biding her time. Being too obvious would ruin everything, and she knew it.

She cleared the table, filled containers of food for Ryder to take home to eat over the weekend, did the dishes, mopped the floor even, and then went to join everyone in the living room. Chelsea, trying to be a thoughtful guest, brought a wrapped Apples to Apples game as a hostess gift and explained the rules as Willow took the boys upstairs for their naps. Though tempted to put her plan into action, she sat down and tried to throw her whole heart into choosing Charles Manson as a perfect definition for "gentle."

An hour later, she made hot chocolate and put homemade candy canes in each mug. From the fridge, she pulled a sprig of mistletoe and smiled. It was time. Chelsea looked restless, and if she read the girl well, their guests wouldn't stay much longer. She wanted to test her theory before they left. Putting the tray on the coffee table, she pulled the sprig from it and dangled it tauntingly over Chad's head. "I think we need to change our tradition just a smidge."

"What—"

Before he could ask questions that made it look like there was no tradition, Willow took the sprig and hung it on the little hook over the front door. "Thanksgiving should be the first day we put up the mistletoe, not the day we put up the tree, don't you think?"

Swiftly, she changed the subject to Black Friday sales, shopping trips, Christmas traditions, and anything she could think of to keep Ryder and Chelsea relaxed and comfortable. When everyone had emptied their mugs, she refilled the tray and carried it to the kitchen, calling for Chad's help once she disappeared around the corner. "I think the stove is getting low in here, and I have more bread ready to go in."

"We're going to have to be going soon. Her parents expect us at seven for their dinner," Ryder called from the living room. Chelsea's affirmative murmur and the shuffling sounds she heard told Willow it was time. She grabbed the containers from the icebox, counted to ten, and then strolled nonchalantly into the living room.

As she expected, Ryder and Chelsea were plastered against each other under the mistletoe. "Excuse me. Sorry. Don't forget to take these home."

Embarrassment flooded Ryder and Chelsea's faces, but Willow forced herself to act as if nothing unusual happened. She'd have words with Ryder the next afternoon. Now wasn't the time to embarrass him any further. "Thanks, Willow. I appreciate it. No one cooks like you— especially my mom!"

"Lass?"

"Hmm?" Willow glanced at her pattern, eyebrows furrowed as she worked a large circle of yarn into what looked to him like a doily with arms.

"What was up with the mistletoe this afternoon?" His wife's constant industry was wearing off on Chad, and he'd spent his evenings for the past few weeks sanding, gluing, staining, and oiling an unusually shaped guitar that he called a renaissance guitar. Just as Willow consulted her pattern, Chad followed the instructions for adding a string to the tuning pins.

"Well, other than the obvious excuse to break it in early..." She sent him a flirtatious glance that might have distracted a less determined man.

"Yes, other than that..."

"I saw something in their relationship, Chad. It scared me. I think Ryder is looking for respect and approval anywhere he can get it, and if he gets it from an adoring girl, there could be trouble."

"So, because you're concerned that they might get too physical, you put up an invitation to do it in our living room?" That train of thought was illogical even for Willow's unusual thought processes.

"I'd rather that than the alternative?"

"Which is?"

"Get physical where there is no chance of getting caught and therefore the freedom to go too far."

He had to admit, it made some sense. "Are you going to talk to him?"

"Yes. Tomorrow while you're at work. Iris is coming to clean and watch the boys so I can do some work in the greenhouse with him. I'm hoping maybe it'll come up naturally."

"Willow, he's not a Christian."

"I know that. What does that have to do with anything?" From his vantage point, it seemed that Willow had figured out her pattern and the needles flew again.

"You can't expect the unsaved to act saved."

"Hogwash."

Stunned, Chad's reply was less than eloquent. "Come again?"

"Hogwash. God expects it, why shouldn't we?"

"God doesn't expect sinners to do anything but sin."

"Then what's the point of hell and damnation if He expects nothing of humanity?"

Leave it to Willow to see things from a different angle that redefined what he said. "What I meant was, it is futile to expect those who are not saved, to see the value in following the Lord's commands for us. Those who are not washed free of sin cannot help but wallow in it."

"I'll concede that point."

"If you need a non-religious reason to be careful, ask if she's underage."

"She is, surely! Ryder's under age and she's a year behind him in school."

Chad shook his head. "No, Willow, under the age of legal consent. It's eighteen here. If he's over and she's under, he could end up on a sex offender registry for the rest of his life if her parents pressed charges."

"Registry?" The confusion in her eyes was only slightly less overwhelming than the stunned expression on her face.

"If she's not eighteen, then any sexual activity can land

him before a judge."

"Wait. The schools can push their birth control and their 'safe sex,' but the kids who take that as a license to use it are only allowed to be stupid with other underage kids? If they're intimate with their seventeen-year-old boyfriend all year, the minute he turns eighteen, they're supposed to dump him for someone younger if they want to keep up their extracurricular activities? That's insane!"

Amused, Chad listened as she tossed aside her knitting and ranted at the illogical programs that trained young people to behave in ways that would later make them criminals at the turn of a birthday. She had valid points. As an officer, he'd seen the life of a young man shattered by the very scenario she proposed. Vindictive parents didn't try to put a kibosh on their daughter's relationship when her boyfriend was under eighteen. They simply waited for his birthday and then had him arrested for statutory rape. On the other hand, he'd gone to school with guys who took great delight in stripping as many girls of their virginity as possible and was thankful that at least something put a stop to it.

"It's a flawed system, lass. I'll give you that. However, the flaw is in the presupposition that teenagers cannot control their sexual impulses. A married man is expected to be faithful to his spouse, even if separated by months, but a teenager cannot possibly be expected to save himself for his bride. We reduce young people to animals anymore. It's wrong."

"You're absolutely right it's wrong. Furthermore, I cannot believe that the law—"

"The law is not at fault, lass. We have to have a way to protect girls from men who would prey on them. I know that it seems unjust, but there has to be a cut-off. In some states, consent is over eighteen, others it's under. I agree that if a parent is legally responsible for their child's actions, then the child shouldn't be allowed to give that consent."

"Chad?" Willow's voice had adjusted to a tone he knew all too well.

"I know, lass. Our boys won't be taught that way. I wasn't, and I went to the same schools that some of the worst offenders went to. Rich boys who thought that it was a game to rack up notches on their belts like gunmen in the old west."

"You won't make me send our boys to be taught like that?"

He laughed. "I wouldn't let you send our boys into that school. My reputation was nearly destroyed because a girl was taught, in our classrooms, how to accuse a guy of misusing her." He thought for a moment. "Then again, I doubt it'll be the same by the time the boys are old enough for those classes. Surely, by then there'll be a new theory. Monasticism or something will be in vogue or something."

They talked for some time, Willow questioning everything and Chad explaining the reasoning behind decisions he didn't even agree with at times. Their lives were changing, sometimes at breakneck speed, and nothing they did could stop it. Just watching the changes in people around them affected every aspect of their own lives.

As he crawled into bed the next morning, Chad saw Willow's journal open and the day's thoughts on it.

Thanksgiving—

Each time I learn more about the world around me, the more I see the wisdom in Mother's choices. She sheltered me from the ugliness, the foolishness, and the sinfulness of this world. I'm always sorry to see a little of that person I was disappear with more knowledge of how things truly are.

Then again, if I had known where it would lead, would I have made a different decision the day that Mother died? I could have buried her myself. I wonder that it never occurred to me. I could have kept everything exactly the same as it'd always been, and I'd be ignorant of the things that trouble me like Ryder's relationship and the propensity for people to politicize everything.

I would not have met Chad that day. Granddad wouldn't have become a part of my life, and we wouldn't have the boys. Yes, much of the things that make me so uncomfortable wouldn't affect me, but isn't every good thing worth the sacrifices you have to make to have it? I wouldn't be bombarded with immorality in the lives of people I love, but I would also have no one to love. The Lord and I would have been fine here, but would I have truly lived Mother's dream if I was not living "deliberately?" How can it be a deliberate life if it's one spent hiding from life around me. Would I not have found myself, at the end of my life, discovering that I had not lived?

Chad smiled at the words and replaced the journal. He loved those glimpses into Willow's heart—to see the side of her that she so seldom voiced. Each word of her journal reminded him of the choices she'd made, many to please him, and how with all the good, she'd accepted things that while not necessarily bad, weren't always the good that made her comfortable.

Lord, help me do my part to ensure that this different life of ours does make all the difference so that at the end of her life, she may know she lived, deliberately, every moment of it.

Chapter 152

One advantage to greenhouse growth in winter was the absence of pests. Cutworms, aphids, spiders, and all the other usual pests were dead for the winter. In their place, however was the constant battle with adequate light and the unpredictability of heirloom seeds. All of Ryder's hard work had produced very healthy looking tomato plants with fruit that refused to ripen. He'd suggested removing the tomatoes to ripen off the vine, but the one Willow tried was pale and anemic—not to mention without flavor.

As she and Ryder debated fertilizer, location in the greenhouse, and other variables, Willow prayed fervently for words for wisdom in counseling him with his relationship. Just as she opened her mouth to ask how serious he considered his relationship, she looked at the full spectrum lighting system and flipped the switch. "The bulbs are dead."

Ryder nodded as he opened the greenhouse door. "I guess that's the disadvantage to the automatic timer. We didn't see that they didn't come on. I'll go get more."

When he returned, Willow was ready. "We enjoyed having you and Chelsea yesterday. She's a very passionate girl, isn't she?"

"She's really into the environment, if that's what you mean. She doesn't get how arrogant it sounds to say, "We have to save the planet."

"Save the planet? From what?"

"Us. The stupid things mankind does that is destructive

to it. I mean, I'm all for responsibility, but mankind can't singlehandedly reverse the second law of thermodynamics."

Willow nodded thoughtfully. "As in all matter tends toward decay? That's the amazing thing about birth. It is a constant proof that the 'law' is a generality rather than an absolute."

"I just don't see how throwing away all the plastic in your cupboards is going to solve anything."

His thought process made no sense to Willow, but she decided to work with it. "So, is she planning to attend Rockland University?"

"Yeah, unless she gets that scholarship to Northwestern. I don't think she'll turn it down to stay here."

"What are the chances of that?"

As he screwed in each bulb into the lamps, Ryder opened up with uncharacteristic candor. "Thankfully, high. She's great, but she's a bit needy. I don't have time to focus on my classes, do my work out here, and give her all the time she wants." Ryder had the decency to look embarrassed. "I'm not saying I'm trying to dump her or anything, but that scholarship would put us on a 'summers only' kind of playing field. Easier to manage if you know what I mean."

"I think it's probably wise. If she's the right girl today, she'll still be the right one in a few years when you have your education finished and a start in whatever field you choose."

Jonathan Landry found them working a while later and asked if he could help. While he worked compost and manure into one of the raised beds, he asked intelligent questions about how they managed to grow vegetables when it was so cold outside. Willow harvested carrots as she listened to Ryder patiently answer each of the boy's questions. He had a gift, her helper, for teaching while working. He made an art of doing it without dumbing down the subject matter, and she knew then that he'd become a teacher rather than a research scientist. Somehow, she also knew his parents wouldn't approve. There was no money in teaching from what Chad had told her.

As Chad turned into the drive, he smiled. How had she done it all by herself? Evergreen swags, twisted with twinkle lights and sporting bows at each fence post, lined the long winding drive to the house. Candles glowed in the window and lanterns hung from the porch, showing off the greenery there. No Christmas tree on the porch, though. The incongruity of it struck him as funny. She'd hooked up the driveway to the barn to have twinkle lights but hadn't attached them to the house. It was so like her.

As he opened his door, he grabbed the container of ice cream and hot fudge sauce. Maybe a treat after such a long day. She'd called him twice, wailing that there was no hope for her. She was a failure as a mother. Liam had a knot on his head from a tumble down three stairs after she'd forgotten to put the gate up, and she had managed to step on Lucas' little hand at one point. The chief had gotten a kick out of it. Truth told, Chad found it amusing as well, but he was determined not to let her know it—yet.

The front porch was missing its tree. Good, she'd left something for him to do with her. How had he gone from a bachelor who didn't own a single decoration to a man happy to spend a few hours decorating with his wife and sons? The question dissolved as he opened the front door and found his wife blubbering on the floor, surrounded by half-boxed Christmas décor.

"Um, lass?"

"We can't do almost anything!"

The decision hovered before him—ice cream now or console the wife? On the off-chance that the ice cream at least soothed whatever woe that had overwhelmed her, Chad held up the plastic bag—one she'd despise for its uselessness—and smiled. "Will ice cream make it any better? I brought peppermint and fudge sauce."

The look in her eyes sent waves of panic over him. Would she cry? Tears seemed too much to manage after the day he'd endured. There it was—a smile. "Yeah. That sounds just about perfect."

She followed him to the kitchen, grabbing the bottle and setting it in the pan of boiling water on the stove. She would think of making the fudge sauce hot. Should he ask what had upset her or wait? Waiting never hurt anyone.

Chad carried heaping bowls of ice cream to the table and smiled as she jumped up to grab the hot fudge. He took it from her, set it on the table, and pulled her into a hug. "Missed you today."

"As opposed to yesterday when you were glad to be rid of me?"

"Nah," he murmured, kissing her and holding her just a little closer. "Maybe I'll do that tomorrow."

"Tease."

Something in her—maybe it was just the crazy lamplight that always made her eyes sparkle and her hair almost glow—choked him. "God... man, He is good to me."

"Huh?"

Rolling his eyes, he nudged her toward the chair and paused for one more kiss. It had been a really long day. "That was my ineloquent way of saying I love you."

"You might not when I start complaining. Eat your ice cream first."

There it was again—that something. How had he ever thought he wanted to stay away? *Because you knew you'd fall and hard. You knew it'd keep you here and you stupidly thought that'd be the end of the world.* "Idiot."

"What?"

"Just reminding myself that I'm not too bright at times. So, what is up with the Christmas explosion and the tears. I assume they're related?"

Tears filled her eyes, making Chad regret asking. "We can't have a tree. We can't have the tree blocks on the tables or any of the little candles in their usual places. We can't have anything."

"Why?"

"I tried. I had the tree assembled and in place, and they pulled it over—twice." She sighed and added, "Each."

"So we teach them not to touch it."

"I can't spend all day redirecting them from that tree. I don't have time." She took another bite and groaned. "Man, this is exactly what I needed." To his astonishment, she poured more hot fudge over the top and took another bite. "Perfect."

"Ok, so we put the tree where they can't reach it this year."

"Such as?"

Possibilities clicked through his mind like one of her View Master reels. "Well, if it'll fit, we could put it in the library on top of the bookshelves in the center."

"There's nowhere for presents there, though."

"Ok, then what about the dining room table. We don't need to eat in there. This is big enough." Why it was such a huge deal, Chad wasn't sure, but he'd find a way to calm her if it killed him. And it might.

"That might work." She sighed. "It's always been by that window."

"And some people hang them upside down from the ceiling."

Willow laughed. "You're not going to fool me with that."

"I'm not kidding. They were crazy popular a couple of years back. Mom and Aunt Libby flipped over them."

"They liked trees that hang upside down from the ceiling."

Chuckling at the flat tone of her voice, Chad shook her head. "No, they flipped as in became indignant, flipped out, got ticked."

"Smart women those Tesdall-Sullivans."

He leaned over and kissed her—much too briefly for his taste. "Sure are."

"If I was, I wouldn't be sitting in an undecorated house."

"Make you a deal," Chad began.

"Okaay..."

"We table the décor problem until morning. I have three days off and I plan to enjoy them with my family. We'll figure this out. There has to be a way to enjoy it all—just differently for a year or two."

She didn't respond. Instead, she finished her ice cream, put away the fudge, and carried their dishes to the sink. "Okay."

He crossed the room and wrapped his arms around her, pulling her back against his chest as she rinsed their bowls. "C'mon upstairs, lass. This'll look less awful in the morning," Chad murmured, tugging her away from the sink.

They stared at one another over the wails of their boys. Chad shrugged. "If we can't make them happy, one of us might as well have some sanity. Go for a walk or something."

"What if they're sick?"

"There's no fever, they have no stuffy or runny noses—"

"They're both running like rainwater."

"Because they're crying. I think they're both overtired." Even as he spoke, Chad had a new idea. "We could drive to Mom's. They'd probably fall asleep on the way. We could go see a movie or maybe a game at RU."

"We're going tomorrow anyway though, remember?"

"So we go a night early. I'll call and see if Caleb—"

"He has school."

"Then Ben—or even Charlie Janovick."

"Charlie might like the money. I know he said something at church last week about it being slow right now."

"Charlie it is." Chad nudged her. "Can I call?"

"I'll go pack."

Chad met her in their room minutes later, one wailing boy in each arm, both struggling to get down and clinging to him at the same time. "Charlie said just to drop off the keys and he'll handle it. He promised to call if he needs help."

"Can you fill a backpack with diapers and longies? I'm almost done here."

"That was fast."

Willow grinned. "I need them to stop screaming before I join them."

Chad pulled up to his parents' house just after nine o'clock. "Looks like Chuck is here."

"I haven't seen him in a couple of months!" Willow climbed from the van and met Chad at the front. "Thank you."

"What for?"

"For getting me away before I went insane. I needed that

movie—ridiculous as it was—and I needed it badly."

"It was kind of crazy," Chad mused as he led her to the door. "But, Christmas movies usually are."

"I think I remember Mother saying that was the best thing about Christmas movies—that they were either so tender they wrung your heart or so silly that they forced you to be joyful in spite of yourself."

"Sounds about right." He pushed open the door and followed Willow inside.

She stood in the entryway, her eyes riveted on the sight of Chuck holding Liam. "Chad, look," she whispered.

Before Chad could respond, Chuck's voice boomed out, "Hey, they're back!"

Liam awoke, protesting against the jarring noise so close to his little head. Stunned himself, Chuck stood and began trying to soothe the little guy. Willow started toward them to rescue Chuck and then stepped back again. Chad, thinking she'd decided to let him handle it, also stepped forward, but Willow stopped him. "No, look."

Despite Chuck's best efforts, Liam refused to calm himself. Willow eventually reached for the boy, but Chuck turned. "I'll get him. We're good pals, me and Liam, aren't we Cheri?"

"He's been holding that kid since you left."

"Probably needs a diaper," Chad suggested.

"I can do that. Where's the stuff?"

That offer struck the three Tesdalls dumb. Cheri found her voice first. "They're cloth, Chuck."

"So? You still take a gross one off and put a clean one on. How hard can it be?"

Cheri stood and passed Lucas to Chad. "This I gotta see."

Lucas fussed and almost dropped back to sleep, but one eye fluttered open long enough to see Willow. He reached for her. The moment her arms wrapped around her son, Lucas practically demanded a before bed snack. She sighed. "I'll be back down in a bit."

"Just sit in Dad's chair."

"I can't, Chad!"

"Chuck is changing Liam. Trust me, you'll have time." When she didn't fumble with her sweater, he added, "I'll get a towel and throw it over you if they come in before I can stop them."

The hesitation lasted only long enough for Lucas to jerk at her sweater again. "Okay, but you'd better."

"Lucas is a speed nurser. He'll be done before you can finish trying to hide what you're doing from me."

"I do not!"

"Well," he conceded, "maybe not, but you sure try to hide you from me."

"It's not decent to sit around with your clothes half off!"

"And it's not indecent for your husband to happen to see a bit of skin whenever you feed his child," Chad teased.

She rolled her eyes before gazing down at their son. "And this from the man who flipped out because I walked around with my shirt unbuttoned and two milking machines strapped to my chest. Those things covered almost every inch of me."

"I've got news for you, lass."

With her hair half drooped over one eye, it looked as if she raised one eyebrow. "Yeah?"

"That was the real complaint—covering every inch..."

"Liar."

He shrugged. "Had to try."

Lucas popped off and gave her a milk-faced grin. Willow tugged her sweater into place as she murmured low. "Your daddy is trying to be ornery." As she shifted him, the boy responded with a deep belch.

"That's m'boy."

"Thankfully, he's almost out or I'd shoot you for encouraging such bad—ahem—table manners."

Liam's wails grew louder as Chuck and Cheri returned with the boy. Willow tried to cover Lucas' ears, but it didn't seem to make a difference. The little tyke was gone. "Does he need a diaper?"

Cheri shook her head. "Just changed him less than half an hour ago."

As they talked, as Willow carried her boy to her room and laid him in the playpen, and as Chad fought to keep from demanding his child, Chuck worked to quiet Liam. Twice Cheri offered to take him. Twice Chuck said no. Willow offered when she returned to the room. He still insisted that he was fine.

Several minutes later, Liam belched and sighed. "Good one, kid." Chuck almost beamed with pride. Chad and Willow refused to look at one another.

Liam giggled. "We've been good buddies, haven't you little Chuck."

"His name is Liam, you moron."

Appalled, Willow cried, "Cheri!"

"What? The kid's name is Liam."

"Right. After me. Love that name."

"Um, Chuck?" Chad couldn't follow the mental gymnastics that turned Liam into "little Chuck" and named him after the last man he would ever want to name a son for. "His name is Liam. How is that even close to Chuck or Charles, I suppose."

"Charles William Majors."

He opened his mouth to correct Chuck, but Willow coughed. "But we call him Liam, Chuck. We didn't want to use names that other people we loved used—too confusing. It's better to stick to Liam."

Nodding, Chuck sank into the couch again, blowing raspberries on Liam's cheek. At the gesture, Willow made a choking sound. Chad stepped closer and squeezed her arm. He started to thank Chuck for helping to watch his sons when the man sighed. "See, I knew he'd be fine. He's such a cute little thing." Chuck tickled the boy's neck. "Just like your Uncle Chuck—gonna be a lady killer."

"In your dreams," Cheri muttered.

Chapter 153

Two days before New Year's Day, Chad awoke at twelve-thirty in the afternoon, reached for his watch, and grabbed Willow's journal instead. Pulling the blankets up around his chin, he read her last entry with a smile on his lips.

December 26-

Grandmom and Granddad spent Christmas here this year. Uncle Kyle and Aunt Sheryl were here too as were their children. It's hard to think of people my age as someone's children, but then, I am Mother's child, so it makes sense in an awkward sort of way. Bethel Ann doesn't like me. I've tried to brush it off as shyness, not trusting the daughter of the woman who broke the family's heart and deliberately at that. However, after a full day of snide remarks about the boys, telling me about all the things our grandparents did with her and for her, and with the general unease every time she opened her mouth, I am forced to conclude that she's threatened by my existence. She was always the "only granddaughter" and treated like the family princess. I guess she thinks she's been de-throned.

So, aside from that little petite bundle of negativity, the day was really quite nice. I had fun making gifts for everyone, and everyone but Bethel Ann seemed to like their gifts. Apparently, personalized journals are "so 2002" whatever that means. That snide remark did get her a sharp reproof from

Uncle Kyle. I felt badly, but how was I to know that the only thing appropriate to give teenagers was a gift card? I am still recuperating from Cheri's silly gift card spree last year—the year before—whenever it was.

Chad loved his saddle blanket. I wasted a lot of wool and knitting on that thing until I got it right, but after a long time of boiling and then cutting to the right shape, I did it. Lacey should be one very happy equine. I hope he doesn't tell her I made it. She'll probably try to thank me with those fat hairy lips of hers. Eew.

At the risk of being ungrateful, I must say now that I don't understand children's toys. I made the boys felt blocks and busy books. Chad made them each a few interlocking train pieces out of a wood kit he found on the Internet. I really need to learn more about that. It's amazing how often he tells me something or comes home with something I needed and says, "Oh, I found it on the Internet." That's off topic though. His parents, my grandparents, Aggie and Luke, and even Uncle Kyle all bought the children brightly colored (cute!) plastic toys. I liked them. I thought they'd be easy to wash when they got dirty, but then out came the batteries. Every one of those things requires batteries. Furthermore, they're the noisiest piles of obnoxiousness I've ever had the misfortune to encounter. All I want for Christmas is a battery thief. I tried to take the silly batteries out after everyone left, but Chad thought I'd put them in to charge again and replaced them. If he's reading this, he should know that I hate those things with a passion he's never seen before. He doesn't want to see it. Trust me.

Ryder has been distant this past week. He's missed work twice and been late almost every other day. To say that things are out of sync around here is an understatement. I've been grateful for Iris Landry's help—even more than usual lately for obvious reasons. Without it, I would have had to let the plants in the greenhouse go. If I have to choose between the farm expansion and my children, there is no choice. Period. However, if Ryder finds himself unable to work, I can try to find another college student that is interested in our life here, or maybe that British guy, Nigel. He's been working on Judith's house, but that can't last forever. Meanwhile, I find it odd. Ryder has been off school for two weeks and has another four before he goes back again. You'd think he'd have more time than usual for us and yet he's been here less than during classes. I'm afraid I need to sit him down and talk to him.

Chad just came in to tell me that Ryder asked if he and Chelsea could come out to talk with us. I have a sinking feeling that she's the reason for his absence and that I'm going to hear they've gotten engaged or something. I thought he made sense after Thanksgiving, and he's acted like his old self again, but now this. I can't think what else it could be.

I hear my little lads. I guess I need to quit writing about a whole lot of nothing and enjoy even more somethings with my guys. I think Liam is going to walk any day. He zips around furniture faster than I can catch him before he crashes to the floor. Thankfully, he doesn't seem to care. I asked Chad about the potential for permanent brain damage from all the knocks on the furniture and floors, but Chad says that it just knocks sense into them, and without it, they'd be idiots. I'm going with his interpretation for my sanity, but I confess, it doesn't make sense to me.

So many of her entries these days were filled with productivity lists, the boys' milestones, and plans for the future. The little tidbits that read more like her mother's average journal entries were his favorites. Oh, Kari had written her share of laundry lists of factoids to reference at a later date, but the sheer size of their enterprise now demanded much more of her journaling time.

The entry about Ryder concerned him as well. They'd been so relieved to hear about the potential scholarship and Ryder's eagerness to avoid a serious relationship so early in his educational career. When Willow shared her opinion of his teaching skills, the young man had seemed eager to talk to his college counselors about it. Ryder wasn't the kind of guy who called to make an appointment for a discussion. Something was up, and Chad was sure he'd be announcing his intention to move to Chicago to be with Chelsea at the very least. An engagement seemed equally likely.

Willow peeked her head around the door. "I've got coffee, chili, cornbread, and ice cream sundaes downstairs. They'll be here in an hour, so if you want a shower…"

"Hey, c'mere."

The thick braid whacked his face as she bent to kiss him. "That's what you get for lounging around in bed reading rather than controlling your children."

"They're in bed."

"They are now! I just put them there." She swung her braid at him again.

"See, I know when to get up and when to stay in bed."

Grabbing the blankets, Willow jerked the covers from him and carried them out the door. "If you want to stay warm, come get them."

Twenty minutes later, freshly shaven and starving, Chad arrived in the kitchen to find his lunch sitting on the table and Willow pounding bread with a vengeance. "Does that make you feel better?"

"No, but it'll make the bread taste better."

"He's a man, Willow."

She sent a withering look in Chad's direction. "He's acting like a child."

"We don't even know what he wants."

"He's bringing her with him. To talk. It must be serious, Chad. You don't bring a girlfriend with you to tell your boss that you're quitting or you made the deacon's list."

"Dean's"

"Whatever."

"How modern you're getting." Chad's teasing didn't make her smile as it usually did. "You're covered in flour, lass."

"Good thing I've got on an apron then, isn't it?"

"Your nose doesn't have one."

"Well then, you know what to get me for Valentine's Day."

Laughing, he carried his empty bowl to the sink, wondering as he went, how he'd finished so quickly. "I must have been hungry, and don't tempt me. I wonder if Mom knows someone who sews."

"She does. Me. So there you have it."

A knock on the door sent Willow's eyes flying to the clock. "They're half an hour early!" She stared down at the dough on her hands. "Well, they'll just have to talk in here.

112

I'm not going to waste good dough just because they can't come on time."

Chad led the couple into the kitchen and pulled out chairs. "Willow is in the middle of bread ,and you don't come between a Finley woman and her work."

"We're early. We sat around Chelsea's house until we couldn't take it anymore. Sorry."

"Get them sundaes, Chad."

Chelsea shook her head. "No thanks. I—no thanks."

One of the most awkward silences of Chad's life nearly smothered them in the room until Willow's fist slammed into the pile of dough and she said, "You said you had something to talk to us about?"

"Lass…" his low warning tone wasn't lost on her, but she ignored it and he knew it.

"We have a problem. Possibly a big one."

"Possibly? You're kidding me, right? Possibly?" Chelsea's voice was pitched high enough to earn her a spot as a soprano in opera.

"Chels…"

"Are you quitting Ryder?" Willow's voice held an edge that Chad recognized. It was her 'You'd better not say what I don't want to hear, or I'm going to blast you' tone.

"No! I—No!"

"Just tell her, Ryder. My parents will be home in two hours!"

With a face as miserable as any Chad had ever seen, Ryder looked up at him, ignoring Willow's questioning gaze, and said, "Chelsea is pregnant."

"Oh, Ryder." Without another word, Willow dusted her palms off onto the dough and went to put her arms around Chelsea. "Are you ok?"

"I am not ok! Why the h—"

"Chels!"

"Why on earth would you think I'm ok? I'm pregnant! I'm seventeen, pregnant, and my life is ruined."

"That's a lie." Chad winced at the words as Willow spoke them. Leave it to Willow not to let someone exaggerate the truth at a time like that.

"What!"

"Your life isn't ruined. Put on hold, adjusted, made more difficult, yes. Ruined no. Lying to yourself like that just perpetuates the negativity."

"What do you know about it? You're infertile!" Chelsea's tears flowed freely now.

"C'mon, Chelsea. Being cruel isn't going to solve anything." Ryder sounded disgusted.

Before things went downhill any further, Chad decided to find out why the not-so-happy couple was telling them this news. "What did your parents say to it?"

"We haven't told them yet. They get in town this afternoon."

"So why are you here?" Willow beat him to the question. "I would think telling them first—"

"We—" Ryder choked. "That is—"

Chelsea threw Ryder a disgusted look. "My mom is really into all the pro-life stuff. She's not going to sign for an abortion, and I'm not sure I'm ready to deal with that anyway. So we're going to give the baby up for adoption, and Ryder wants you to consider it."

"Adoption?" Willow's voice sounded strangled.

With an arm around his wife's shoulder, Chad squeezed it to tell her to let him handle the discussion. Fortunately, she picked up on his cue before she blasted the girl for even considering an abortion. "Chelsea, how do you feel about asking us to consider adoption?"

The girl began weeping. "I don't know. I just want it over with. Ryder thought that if we had a plan in place before we talked to my parents, they wouldn't freak out as badly."

"I don't think you should be asking us to do this unless you're sure. What if your parents are more understanding than you anticipate? What if they want you to keep the baby?"

"No!" She looked embarrassed, but the resolute expression on her face couldn't be ignored. "Sorry, but no. I'm not ready to be a mom. I don't want a baby. I don't think I want an abortion either, and a pregnancy is going to be gross and disgusting, but the baby has to go."

"We'll do it."

Willow's voice was quiet, but firm. Chad stared at her, stunned, and then beckoned her. "Will you excuse us? We need to talk about this privately for a minute."

They grabbed their coats and walked silently to the barn. Just inside the door, Chad slammed his fist against the wall. "Will you tell me exactly what you're doing?"

"I'm agreeing to adopt that child."

"Without us discussing it." He used the tone he hoped would warn her that she'd crossed one of those lines she never understood, but it didn't.

"What is there to discuss? She doesn't want the baby; Ryder would get to see his child if it came to live with us, and she's mentioned abortion twice. If she keeps talking, she's going to desensitize herself to the idea, and that baby is going to die."

"Not without her mother's consent."

Closing her eyes, Willow took a deep breath and then nearly leveled him with a disgusted glare. "You really think I'm stupid, don't you? Weren't you the one telling me just a week ago about how the school nurse took a girl off campus to get an abortion in the city? Weren't you the one telling me that the girl's parents filed a complaint, but there was nothing you could do about it because the law states that while under the school's care the school can do as they see best regarding their students' medical care? Didn't you show me the form parents sign when they enroll the students that gives those same school officials the right to make that choice?"

"That baby would be born sixteen—"

"Seventeen I think."

He nodded, "Seventeen months after the boys. That's cutting it close age wise."

"Are you saying you are unwilling to adopt this child?" The shock in her face was almost his undoing.

"No, lass. I'm saying you can't just agree to adopt a child without us discussing it. It's a bit sudden for me just to agree willy-nilly."

She chewed her lip for a moment and then nodded. "You're right. How about this. We tell them it's something we'll consider. That way, they can tell Chelsea's parents that they have a couple considering adoption, which is the truth, but doesn't leave us committed."

"Deal."

As the barn swung open, Chad's voice murmured low in her ear, "Have you thought about names yet?"

Willow gazed up at him. "How about we do that after they leave."

Chapter 154

As her living room erupted in arguments, Willow pinched the bridge of her nose, folded her hands, clenched her fists, and eventually stood and screamed, "I cannot stand this!"

From the corner, Chad smirked. Marianne glanced at him and then at Willow. Jostling Liam on her knee, her eyes moved to Carol and then back to Chad again. "What, Chad?"

"I just can't believe, after all this time, that you guys don't know Willow well enough to know that animated arguments against something she obviously wants to do is an effective way of getting her to do that very thing."

"Stuff it, Chad."

"Furthermore," he added, ignoring his wife's admonition, "I can't believe the people who taught me that the reason the abortion industry is so successful is because Christians aren't willing to step up and make self-sacrificial decisions are now sitting in my living room telling me how it's too much for us to attempt."

"You don't have to be the single-handed savior of all mankind, Chad!" Marianne snuggled the baby closer. "These boys need their mother's and father's full attention."

Chad shook his head. "So if Willow brought you two pink lines tomorrow, you'd be upset."

"Of course, I wouldn't! That's a terrible thing to say." Marianne stared at her husband as Christopher choked on his coffee. "What!"

"Don't ever tell me again how hypocritical the Wheelers are about favoring their biological grandchildren over the two that Jayne and Mitch adopted."

Chad's mother had the decency to blush. "That's not what I meant, it's just that—" She fought to explain herself. "I mean, if Chad and Willow were talking about this in two years, I'd be all for it. If she got pregnant today, it'd obviously be something the Lord blessed them with—"

"But our God, in His infinite grace and mercy, couldn't possibly be blessing us with a baby right now, unless it is biological. I'm really glad He doesn't feel that way about us when we come to Him for adoption." Willow's eyes flashed. "I can see it now, 'Sorry my child-to-be, I'm a bit overburdened with children at the moment, but if you can wait a year or two, oh and pray you don't die in the meantime, then I'll be happy to make you one of my own children.'" She stood and grabbed her empty cup. "I expected opposition, but I expected it from an entirely different angle. I never thought I'd see Christians willing to risk abortion or that an unsaved girl would give the child to unsaved parents. Frankly, I'm disgusted."

Before anyone could reply, Willow carried her cup to the kitchen, added a log to the stove, grabbed her coat, and let herself out the back door, not caring that it slammed shut behind her. Chad surveyed the room curiously. "I haven't heard anything from Granddad. What aren't you saying?"

"I've been thinking. That's all."

"About what?" Carol's initial voiced disapproval hadn't been repeated, but it was clear from her features that she hadn't changed her mind.

"Well, a lot of the objections expressed are concerning Willow and her work here."

"She's up at sunrise, in bed late, and even has to hire help to get it all done. Where will she put in another baby?" Marianne nodded her support of Carol's words.

"All of that is optional." David looked at Chad. "What would happen if Willow discovered she couldn't keep up with the farm or the expansions you've made on it?"

"She'd either hire it out or put a stop to it. The boys come first."

"But she hired—"

"Someone to do the housework—"

"—instead of doing it herself," Carol finished without acknowledging Chad's interruption. She shook her head, visibly frustrated. "Her solution, when she couldn't keep up, was to hire out the work closest to home and family. What will keep her from hiring out child care from eight to five every day when the boys get more active?"

"That was *my* solution to her overworking herself." David's quiet correction seemed to reverberate around the room.

Seeing the shift in discussion, Marianne kicked Christopher gently. "Help me explain."

"I can't."

Stunned, she blurted, "Why not!"

"Because I don't happen to agree with you. Libby has children that close together. They never seemed to suffer for it. Aggie—"

"And what if Willow gets pregnant half-way through this girl's pregnancy? Can you imagine the turmoil for that poor girl when she has to find another couple to adopt her child when she thought she had the perfect family?"

Chad's quiet voice answered before Christopher could formulate a coherent response. "We wouldn't renege, Mom."

"Glad to hear it, son." The pride in Christopher's voice was matched in David's eyes.

"What!" Carol and Marianne stared at each other, stunned.

"If we agree to do this, we're not backing out when it becomes inconvenient." He took a deep breath. "Besides, the specialist in Rockland says that he doesn't think Willow can conceive without intervention."

"So, she does the drug thing again—"

Christopher nearly exploded at his wife. "I never thought that you could be such a hypocrite, Marianne. After the grief you gave Willow about doing it in the first place..."

"I was just upset that she left Chad out of the equation!"

"Um, Mom?" Chad's voice indicated a dissenting opinion. "No, you terrified her with stories of multiples. Willow won't risk Clomid again. Not that I blame her," he hastened to add.

David preempted a new round of questioning with his own. "So, tell us. Why did you ask us here? What did you want to hear?"

Before Chad could answer, Carol pointed to the back door. "Shouldn't someone go out there? Isn't she going to feel ignored?"

"Willow didn't leave to get attention. She's out there talking with the Lord, and we'd just be intruding."

David nodded at Chad's answer and gestured for him to continue. "Which gives you time to tell us what you think."

"We wanted to know if there were concerns we should have considered and didn't, and we wanted to know if you thought having the child's father around all the time would make things difficult."

"I take it you already decided that the closeness of age isn't a problem for you?" Christopher waited for his son's answer.

"Yes."

"So you are mostly concerned with this boy being in your home with his child that you are raising?" David rephrased as a way to stall his response, and the others knew it.

"Yes."

Seeing David's hesitation, Christopher broke in. "I think it could be hard—very hard. The boy may decide he regrets his decision. If he's around in a few years, if you have to discipline that child, he may find it hard to take. He may also think that because he is the biological father, he has a right to input on how the child is reared. All of that can make a hard situation harder." Before Chad could respond, Christopher continued. "But, I think it might also be a very nice thing for him. Even with the downsides, Ryder will see daily that his actions have consequences, even if they're good ones for someone else, and it might make him a more careful person in the end."

David nodded. "I was thinking that since this boy isn't saved, it'd be a perfect, in his face daily, example of how God adopts us as His own. It might open doors of discussion that he otherwise wouldn't have entered." Sending Carol a look of apology, he added. "I think giving this baby a home to avoid abortion is reason enough to accept. However, even without that, this is an excellent opportunity for Ryder to see Christ's love in action. He'd be unlikely to see that even from another Christian family, because he wouldn't see his child again. If you want a yes you should or no you shouldn't from me, I'm saying yes."

"I second the motion," Christopher added.

"But—"

Christopher turned to his wife. "Did you hear what Chad said? He said that Willow wasn't willing to use the Clomid again. He said the doctor thinks they won't conceive without intervention. We can't know that another opportunity like this will come."

"They can seek it out later, Christopher. They can go to an agency, go to China, go to Ethiopia…"

"How many people do we know who have said the same thing but never did it—including ourselves?"

"But—"

"You don't have to agree, Marianne. I'm not expecting you to hold my opinion, but Chad asked for it, and I gave it. I think they should do this."

Carol, wrestling in prayer while the discussion continued around her, opened her eyes and said, "My objections are personal and selfish. I answered based upon what I would have done. If Willow thinks she's up to the task, if you support her, I'm one hundred percent behind you. I do not want her to ever think that my concerns over this idea were out of a lack of interest in the child."

Grateful, Chad stood and hugged Willow's grandmother. "Thank you."

"Oh, Chad! You don't think we'd reject the child!"

"Honestly, no. I didn't. I don't even think Willow assumes that, but I can't be sure. You know how she is. She doesn't think like we expect her to sometimes."

"Ain't that the truth."

As Chad left to go get his wife and tell her they had the family's blessing, he overheard Marianne ask Carol, "Oh, I wonder what the baby's name will be!"

January—

It's been two weeks since we told Ryder and Chelsea that we'd adopt the baby. We made three requests of them. First, that she use Dr. Kline. After all, we're paying for it; we want a doctor we trust. She was fine with that. We'll take her to whatever appointments her mother can't take time off to go with her. She said she could drive herself, but if she got bad news at an appointment, I think she should have someone there with her. She agreed. Second, we asked for an ultrasound or two if necessary to find out what the baby is. That made her happy. I guess Ryder convinced her that I wouldn't want her to submit herself to unnecessary intervention. I just want to know if I can start sewing pink or not! Finally, we asked them both to go to counseling with us. We're all going to talk with Tom Allen. Since Ryder is such a part of our lives, and since Chelsea and her parents live so close and will see us with the baby, we wanted to be sure that we know how to relate to one another as things change.

When Chad first suggested it, I thought he was crazy. I'm not accustomed to thinking like that, but Granddad, Dad, Mom, and Grandmom all agreed that it was a brilliant idea. Renee the lawyer did some research for us and said that she thinks it's a good idea. I hope they all know what they're talking about. To be honest, I only agreed because I think any time at all with those two and an open Bible is a good idea.

Someone left the greenhouse door open and we lost everything. Ryder is out there now, clearing out the old, adding it to the compost pile, and replanting new. The celery was a huge disappointment for both of us. It takes so long to grow, needs such cooler temperatures, and my customers are disappointed. Apparently, it tastes better than store stuff. We'll see soon. Chad is bringing some home for soup.

Lately, I spend my days playing with the boys, working with wool and then spinning it, and planning the fall Boho line. I am so glad I got spring's done ahead of time. Chad found a place that will print my own fabric designs, so I had him order what I designed and it arrived today. This is going to be so much fun! Is it wrong to hope this baby is a girl so I can design for her too?

Lee and I talked about the designing thing. I wasn't sure if I'd be able to keep up and do the samples as well as the designs. I told her that I thought I should resign now, because it'd be hard for them to find someone to do it in time if I got too busy. Apparently, that isn't an issue for her. She assures me that if I draw them, they'll get someone to make them if I can't. She even offered to send a seamstress to the house to work with me so that any changes I want to make during construction can be done. I guess the line is that successful. I'm still amazed when I see a child walking down the streets of Fairbury wearing something that I imagined, drew, and then sewed into a sample for a store! Mother would be proud. Even though she would never have done it herself, she always liked what I came up with for us.

The boys are ten months old. Time seems to zoom by so quickly these days. They wander all over the furniture, but neither one is willing to let go. They'll walk all over the house holding onto our fingers, but I'm going to be stooped permanently if I let them do it much more. The pediatrician says they're almost dead center of growth charts even though they're twins. They say twins are usually a little below average for the first couple of years or something. I get confused with it all sometimes. You'd think with the numbers, I'd get it, but I just can't quite understand it all. Oh well. I suspect that it's really because I just don't care. They'll grow when they grow.

Chad says they'll be walking by their first birthday if not before. We already have to put the gate at the top and bottom of the stairs to keep them off the silly things. They like to bang things together and make noise, but I think my favorite thing is to watch them "talk" to each other. They do it. Chad thinks I'm crazy, but I can tell that they understand each other. They'll sit and play, one will grunt and babble something, and the other will respond. It's amazing. I thought they should try to talk more, but everyone tells me that they'll talk when they're ready. Liam says no, but he says no for everything, so I don't think he knows what he's saying.

I have some amazing pictures of them and Chad with them. I don't have Wes's talent, but I have managed to copy his style on several shots. It's obviously a copy—uninspired so to speak, but I love it and that's all that matters. There's one of the boys sleeping in the crib, Liam's hand is lying on Lucas's cheek. So sweet. I have it hanging in the hallway. Chad turned it into black and white before we printed it. I need to learn how to do that stuff, but I hate staring at that stupid screen.

Marianne cracks me up. She brought me this body brush, some kind of mineral salts, and some kind of body oil. I'm supposed to use them to help get rid of the excess skin and stretch marks. I don't know if it'll work, but since she obviously did it as a result of my whining, I kind of feel obligated to try. I'll be careful about complaining about anything too personal—who knows what she'd send then! Eek!

The boys are up from their naps. I hear them shaking the crib together. They do that. It's amazing. They stand there, and shake the upper rail until it sounds like an earthquake in there. Honestly, there are times I'm afraid they'll rock it over! I think we'll all take a nice walk to town and see Daddy on beat. He likes it when we do that. I need to remember to thank Grandmom for that stroller again. It is the best thing ever.

Chad set the journal back on her bedside table and tiptoed from the room. His shift started in thirty minutes. As he stepped from their bedroom, he glanced across the hall at the closed door to Kari's old room. The new baby would likely sleep in there. He opened the door carefully and glanced around trying to imagine it in daylight. It'd need a few changes, but he hoped Willow wouldn't change too much. If they moved the big dresser out of the room, there'd be room for a crib in the corner. That'd be good.

He drove away from home, ready for a new day at work and his heart swelling with gratitude. He'd had a thought for a while, and now it was time to talk to the Chief. "Lord, if Chief Varney would agree to it..." Sighing, he gripped the steering wheel harder, "I'd be so grateful."

Chapter 155

"I know it's unusual, but you've been saying you need another guy but can't afford one. Maybe if I was just part time—" Chad saw Chief Varney's expression turn south, and he decided to throw in the one thing he knew might help the most. "Besides, I don't care what days I do work, as long as I get a couple of days off in a row. Working weekends is good with me."

"Being a cop was everything to you when I hired you. What happened, Tesdall?"

"I got married, had kids, expanded the farm... I want more time with them. I could quit, I probably should, but I don't want to give up something that means so much to me. I'm not ready to go that far yet."

"I'll think about it, Chad. I'll talk to the mayor and see what he thinks about the budget. He's been talking about a quarter percent tax increase to pay for another officer and another fireman, but maybe if I presented him a budget with another guy but only a partial increase—" Varney gave Chad an apologetic look. "It'd mean a delay in your promotion. I couldn't give you one so soon after you cut your hours."

"I'm good with that. As long as I keep the insurance, income isn't what matters to me."

"Well, get that paperwork done and then get home. You've got a family that needs you." The chief waited until Chad sat at the community desk the officers shared. "Chad?"

"Yessir?"

"I'm proud of you, son. Adopting that baby like that..." Varney nodded approvingly. "It's a good thing you're doing— the right one."

"Thank you, sir. We think so, but not everyone agrees," Chad admitted.

"Well, they would if they were that baby." All the way home, Chad remembered those words. Willow would understand it more than anyone he knew. Chief Varney was right. Only their baby would truly understand what a right thing it was that his parents did.

Chad already thought of the baby as a him. His mother, Willow's grandmother, and even Willow all prayed like crazy for a baby girl, but he refused to think about it. It was better to expect a boy and get him than hope for a girl that might not come. Another son would be an amazing blessing. With all the work they were creating with their expansions, those boys, in just a few years, would be a huge help. He needed to focus on that aspect and ignore the occasional flights of fancy that included pigtails and pink gingham dresses. It troubled him that he knew what gingham was or that it was appropriate for little girls' dresses.

He sighed as he pulled into his normal parking spot in the driveway and stared at the empty space left by the van. They weren't back from the doctor's appointment yet. Chelsea was only ten weeks—hardly far enough along to hear the heartbeat, but Chad hoped Willow would hear it loud and clear. Her journal entries for the past few days had centered on a safe pregnancy for the baby and for Chelsea and requests that the baby would cooperate during check-ups and ultrasounds.

As was customary on the occasions when he arrived home to an empty house, a note on the table told him where to find his meal, where she was, what needed to be done, and interjected some tidbit of her day.

Chad,

Chelsea and I will probably be gone longer than we initially expected. She spoke to the nurse yesterday when they confirmed the appointment, and apparently, they're going to do an initial ultrasound—something about measuring her pelvis and stuff like that. I don't know why they can't do it when she does the one later to see what the baby is. Maybe the baby hides the bones or something. Anyway, poor girl, we'll be enduring one of those awful internal things together.

When I found that out, I decided to drop the boys at Lily's. You were in court, so I didn't call. I figured a note would suffice.

Your sandwich is in the icebox and there's chili in the crockpot in the summer kitchen. I'll move it to the stove when I get home unless you have the time to keep watch on it. Then you can move it if you like.

Clyde is bringing out a truck for 103 and 108 to butcher. He says they're ready, so I called the next people on the list and got their orders. We'll have some leftover for us too. He thinks 112 and 104 will finally be ready in another couple of months. He's never steered us wrong, so I'm going for it. If they're gone, he's already been there. If not, maybe you could move them into the barn to make it easier.

Liam said, "Daa—yeee" when you drove away today. It was so cute. I'm going to try to record him doing it with the camera next time.

Have I mentioned lately that you've made my life everything I could have ever wanted and more than I could have dreamed? Thank you.

I love you,
Willow

"Lord, how many wives write their husbands a 'quick note' that takes up two and a half pages?"

As he went to get his chili, Chad glanced out in the pasture to see if he could find the right cows, but either they were gone, or hiding well. He poured the bowl, grabbed a spoon, and stirred all the way into the house. By the time he sat down with a glass of "plastic milk," his sandwich, his chili, and with Argosy Junction playing in the background, the chili had cooled perfectly.

Idly, he reread the note, pondering what else might encourage his wife. "Come on, Lord. I need suggestions here. When you get a note like that, you want to show it was appreciated. What does she need done?"

They'd never done anything to the kitchen—despite discussing it dozens of times. Outdated beyond anything he'd ever seen, even Willow knew it looked shabby. Those TV shows with their love of miles of granite countertops and stainless steel would cringe at the cheap laminate left over from a bad remodel and stained cast iron sink. On the brighter side, it was functional. He knew she loved her pantry. His eyes stared at the walls, wondering where they could add more counters and cabinets. Next to the stove. He frowned. That was odd, why hadn't he—

Chad walked to the kitchen doorway and started counting paces. He guesstimated around the couches and coffee table, and then frowned again. Opening the door to the library, he didn't bother to count. It wasn't possible. He'd seen cleaned out that closet—twice. It wasn't deep enough to make up the difference. How had he not noticed it?

Mentally comparing upstairs to down, he shook his head as if he couldn't believe it. There was at least four to six unaccounted for feet between the kitchen and the library. Possibly more. The living room and dining room both had the same wall space—even if the stairs did take up some of it. The kitchen, although deeper, ran smooth along the side of the house even though the library and kitchen both should have jutted out a bit. Before he could go stare at the outside of the house, he heard the van drive into the yard and park.

Eager to hear about the appointment, Chad jogged down the front steps, nearly slipping on a small patch of ice, and hurried to help Willow with the boys. "I'll get him," he insisted, taking Liam from her arms. "I hear you said Daddy today!"

"Daa-yee"

"And you doubted me," Willow interjected smugly.

"What about Lucas?"

"Dumb as a post."

"I can't believe you said that!" Chad stared at his wife, a bit stunned at the nonchalant dig at their son's intelligence.

"What? He doesn't speak, therefore he's 'dumb' as the proverbial 'post,' which obviously doesn't speak. You act like I just said the worst thing ever."

"Well, people usually use that phrase to say someone is stupid."

Shaking her head, Willow grabbed the diaper bag and punched the appropriate button to shut the van doors. Carrying Lucas in the house, she muttered, "I don't think I'll ever get used to how different things are than I always knew them."

"Speaking of which," Chad began.

"Can you speak of it after we get them in bed? Lily kept them up for me, but I think Lucas conked out for a bit until we hit the drive."

As she spoke, Willow carried her half-snoozing son upstairs, pulling off his shoes as she climbed. Settling the tyke in the crib the boys still shared, she reached for Liam, curled him beside his brother, and put on a blanket that might or might not stay depending on their level of sleepiness. They stepped out of the door, put the gate up in the bedroom, and escaped downstairs.

"Ok, sleeping tots, check!" She winked at Chad. "Ok, so what is going to be different now?"

"Well not going to be, I just was looking at the house today, and there's a huge section of space there that doesn't make sense. It's like there is room missing."

"Where?"

Chad showed her what he meant, but Willow shook her head. "That's staircase space. Mother showed me once. There's that closet in the library, the under the stairs storage, and then—"

"It doesn't add up. Look." Chad walked her through the depth, width, and practical circumference of the room. "There has to be a minimum of six feet missing—maybe eight."

"Weird. I wonder if Mother knew."

A week later, Luke walked the perimeter of the house, the kitchen, the library, and knocked on every wall he could find. He explored the upstairs, downstairs, attic, and tried to estimate the amount of missing space. At last, he came into the kitchen, shaking off his jacket, and settled his hands on his hips. Willow, seeing he wasn't ready to give his verdict, poured a glass of milk and handed him a pile of cookies. "Warm up, Luke."

"Thanks." After his first bite, Luke asked for a piece of paper. Using a sheet of notebook paper, he sketched, using each line as if it were a foot. "Right here, it looks like there is plumbing in the cellar that doesn't go into the kitchen. It's close to the upstairs bathroom, but then there is plumbing here," he pointed, "and here that would be unaccounted for. I think there's a bathroom behind there."

Chad burst into the kitchen, grinning. "Did you tell her?"

"Barely."

"It would take you twenty minutes to tell that many words. A bathroom, lass!"

Luke nodded. "Either that, or a laundry room."

Willow folded her hands and nodded. "What's your best guess?"

"Bathroom. It's so unusual for houses around here to have a bathroom on the upper floor and not the lower. Maybe the other way around, but..."

"I think so too." Chad seemed beside himself.

"You want me to have to clean more toilets?"

"Toilet, Willow. Just one more. Think about potty training kids! No rushing them upstairs to do their business when they had to go five minutes ago. No more waddling up there when you're the size—" He swallowed hard. That wasn't likely to happen at all. "Sorry..."

"No, I get your point. If it's there, it's being wasted, so we should do it, I guess. If it's not, I don't want to invest in it for nothing."

"It's there. We just don't know what 'it' is for sure. Washing in the house would be nice for you though, wouldn't it?" Luke sounded almost apologetic for finding missing space.

"Do you think there's room for a shower?"

"Willow, are you ok?"

Distress filled her eyes and masked her face, making her look utterly distraught. "Mother had to know. She gutted this place. Why—"

"Maybe it was more than she could handle. Maybe she just walled it up so she didn't have to deal with it." Chad's suggestions didn't help.

"Maybe," Luke added, a warning tone in his voice, "this is a bit overwhelming for your wife, so I should go."

Later that night, Chad came to bed late after hours of playing with layout ideas for a new bathroom. Willow's journal lay on the floor near the side of her bed, the pen nowhere in sight. She'd fallen asleep while writing and eventually pushed the book off the bed.

February—

It's only two days until Valentine's Day. I heard our new baby's heartbeat, and if old wives' tales are to be believed, it's that of a girl. We'll see about that. I don't put much stock in them, but Dr. Kline says some of his patients insist that it was true for them. I think the next ten weeks are going to crawl past until I'm ready to go crazy.

I think we're going to put the child in Mother's room. I thought about trying to move the craft things into her room and revamp it for another nursery, but that's just ridiculous. If this is a girl, it'll be extra special that she has Mother's room, or perhaps we should move into there and let her have our room.

Speaking of rooms, Chad and Luke have determined that there was a room with plumbing next to the kitchen once. Based upon Luke's drawings, I can't argue with his conclusions, but I'm confused and to be honest, a little hurt. Mother had to know about it. Even if she didn't want to deal with it, she could have at least told me when I asked. Was it too much work? Was she too exhausted from everything else to finish it so she just walled it up? Is there something horrible inside that we don't want to find? I don't know the answer to any of my questions and truthfully, I am beginning not to want to. It feels like the day we found those horrible journals and the gun all over again. I just wish Chad had never noticed the discrepancy in size.

I did the math on the beef cows. We made a profit. I am stunned, to tell the truth. With all we spent getting them, feeding them, the two vet visits divided by their portion, I was sure we'd barely break even. I'm not sure it's enough of a profit to be worth it for just a few animals, but keeping a dozen rotating, I think it'll work. Chad says we'll raise the price per pound another quarter, and it'll yield another hundred to hundred and fifty dollars per animal of pure profit without burdening the average purchaser. If they buy half the cow, they don't pay the extra. I guess that makes sense because then we don't have to pay to freeze any of it. He also wants us to cook one steak out of each animal we butcher so we can ensure the meat is good for each animal. I've got that on a list in my butchering journal. I just think he wants an excuse to eat more steak. Why he'd need one, I don't know, but there you have it. Usually we won't be butchering in winter—mostly fall. A few just weren't quite plump enough for good marbling, or so Clyde told us.

I have a sinking feeling that my kitchen is going to get a big overhaul when Chad starts messing with the bathroom idea. I should be happy, I know, but it means the electricity is on, the noise is atrocious, and I'll have to keep the boys out of the way just in time for a new baby. I really don't want to think about it, but Chad has always hated that there's only one bathroom. He gives up so much for me, I can suffer through the mess of one for him, right?

Then again, the idea of a new kitchen—what an amazing thing. We could put cabinets all the way to the ceiling and have shelves on the wall next to the stove. I could have pretty colors. I've always hated how ugly the kitchen is. Maybe Chad could put butcher block counters in there and maybe two sinks!

Oh, Adric's Jael is working on arranging Mother's journals for publishing. She found a way to do it so that we don't have to order a bunch at a time and so we can keep them in color. She has someone she knows in the publishing business that she wants to try to get to publish a series of them, but she says we should try to see how many sell first to demonstrate interest. There's a women's day thing coming up where several ladies from area churches are sharing how they do what they do best, and Lily asked me to consider showing Mother's and my journals to the ladies and talk about what they mean to us. Jael says we could probably sell copies there.

I don't know if I want to make a habit out of teaching

journaling classes. I think that sounds kind of silly. However, there's something about this idea that won't go away. Every time I pray about how to turn it down, I find myself asking the Lord for wisdom in the best way to explain just how amazing it is to continue a life Mother started for me because she laid it out there.

The boys are quiet now. Chad is downstairs with his Bible, praying for our family and the best decisions he has to make for it. I am blessed to have such a man. He'll be down there until he feels confident of an answer—even if that answer is "Later." That's just who he is. Meanwhile, those boys will be awake before I've got the biscuits going so I should sleep. Maybe I'll reread this. How will it sound to my children twenty years from now? Will they be as blessed by the unimportant things I write about now as I am about Mother's little insights into our life, or will they think it's silly? I wonder.

Chad's heart squeezed as he read her words about him praying. First, he'd spent the last half hour or more of that time playing around with layouts when she thought he was praying. It felt deceptive. However, he had spent the first hour or so after Willow went to bed praying for wisdom. He hadn't realized it, but that's exactly what he'd seen from his father so many times. He'd come downstairs for a drink of water and find his father asleep in a chair, the Bible over his chest, and the most serene look on the man's sleeping face. It was one of the most comforting things he'd ever seen as a child. He'd have to thank his father for the example. Christopher Tesdall's faithful prayers and attention to God's Word had paved the path for his children to follow. It was a heritage, much like Willow's mother's journals. He needed to make sure it was preserved for his children.

Chapter 156

After much deliberation, Luke and Chad decided that the dining room wall, behind the chaise, was the most logical place for a doorway to what they assumed was a small bathroom. Measurement wise, Luke was sure it was a full sized bathroom, but Willow disagreed. Compared to the upstairs room, it wasn't possible to fit everything in what looked like too small of a space.

While Luke measured, tapped on walls, and made an educated guess as to the original doorframe, Willow ran her hands over the wall and pointed out to her son the hand painted stripes and flowers that she and her mother had painted so many years earlier. "See, Liam? Those flowers were the first things I painted in this house. Mother painted the stripes, and I painted the vines. Then, when she had all those little dots painted, I came back and did the flowers."

"We'll be careful, lass. We will. Luke won't tear up anything he doesn't have to."

"Chad's right. Your mother walled this up correctly, but I can still find where the studs are off. Listen." Luke tapped the wall from the smaller end of the staircase over to where he thought the door was, making note of each solid thud where he thought a stud would be. "The studs are exactly sixteen inches apart until here. Then there are these four in a row and they're much closer together. I think that's the door frame and two studs to fill in the hole—a bit of overkill, but it's my guess."

"I know," Willow assured them. "I just can't watch. Liam and I are going to go see if Ryder has picked out the heirloom house." She glanced back. "Just don't let Lucas get whacked in the head."

Luke gave Chad an amused smile and started to cut a hole in the wall. "She is so matter-of-fact about everything, isn't she?"

"That's Willow. I always think I'll get used to her quirks, but I never do."

"That's probably half of her charm, eh?" Luke pulled an eight by eight chunk of drywall out of the wall. Reaching in, he began cutting on the other side of the wall. "What is the heirloom house?"

"Ryder has done such a good job propagating heirloom seeds that Willow is letting him built a new greenhouse so that they aren't mixing pollination or whatever it is that plants do."

"Aaah. That makes sense. Are you going to have separate gardens too?" Luke popped another section out from the other side of the wall and withdrew his hand. After peeking through the holes, he looked at Chad with a grin. "This is it. I see a sink and where a window used to be. It's just sided right over without moving the window or anything."

"Well, cut out the rest of that section. Can we get through there?"

Luke shook his head. "There's only maybe ten inches. It'd be a rough squeeze. Let's see what we find at the top."

While Chad blew raspberries on his son's belly, Luke sawed the entire section from the wall. "Hey, grab me that Phillip's screwdriver, will ya?"

Chad grabbed it from his cousin's tool belt on the floor. "If you had that thing on—"

"Then I'd certainly be unable to squeeze through. It looks like Kari Finley added these boards with L-brackets."

"Makes sense."

"That woman," Luke began as he removed the screws that held the board in place, "was obviously a very sensible woman. Aggie has helped with all kinds of renovations, but I doubt she'd think of L-brackets." He started to push on the board, but then realized there were screws in the stud holding the drywall to it. Taking his knife, he cut the drywall across the stud and then used his saw to go back down the other side of it. "Here goes nothing." Luke kicked and the stud jerked out of place.

"Yay! Look, Lucas! Uncle Luke did it!"

"Do you think we're going to confuse our kids by using uncle when we're not brothers?"

"That is exactly what Willow asked," Chad said, shaking his head. "But what else do we do? First names seem a bit too casual, 'Cousin Luke' seems too formal, and what else is there?"

"That's what Mom says, but it still seems weird." With a final jerk, Luke pulled the board from the opening and carried it out to the front porch. While he was gone, Luke peeked in the hole, unsure what kind of critters he'd find. Willow would happily pulverize him if he took her son in a vermin or critter infested room.

"Looks like you were right. Willow owes you cherry almond bars. I see a tub, sink, toilet, and even a small cupboard."

"Aren't you going in?" Luke stopped next to Chad expectantly.

Chad passed his son over to Luke and stepped inside the room. A layer of dirt covered everything. Mold grew around the window, and the musty stench revolted him. The toilet had no water, the sink faucet, when he turned the handle, didn't work. He pushed the shower curtain aside, coughing at the dust it stirred, and frowned. "Hey, Luke. Can you put Lucas in the playpen and come look at this?"

As he stepped through the door, Luke frowned. "Why is there concrete in the tub?"

"That's what I wondered. I didn't know if it really was or not."

He ran his hand lightly over the rough surface of unsmoothed concrete. "I don't understand. It isn't even smoothed."

Confused, Chad glanced around the room again, trying to find some reason that Kari would have a tub filled with concrete. He lifted the lid of the toilet tank, opened the cupboards, and pried open the medicine cabinet. An envelope sat on the middle shelf. Dread filled his heart as he lifted the flap. The glue, deteriorated by age, gave no resistance. After reading the first few words, Chad looked up at Luke.

"Oh, no. Oh, oh, no."

Chapter 157

Ryder glanced up from his work as she entered. "Hey. I think I know which one we should get—want to see?"

"Yep. Exactly why I came out here." Honesty forced her to add, "And to get away from the deconstruction zone in there."

"You're not excited to see what's back there, are you?"

The words hovered between them. "Actually, I don't think that's it as much as I'm not excited for more change in my home."

"Change like another baby?"

The unease in Ryder's tone shook her out of her funk. "No, change like a wall not looking the same as it always has. So much has changed in there—fences around the stove, another couch, Mother's concordances gone, and baby toys everywhere. It's not a bad difference; it's just a difference."

"That's funny. My mom changes our house with the seasons it seems. We get new furniture, new paint, new everything so often that I could probably walk into someone else's house and not realize it wasn't ours until I went up to my room."

"I don't understand that. Where is the tradition—the memories? How can you point to something and say, 'This is from when we'... whatever it is that we did?"

"Mom just doesn't care about those things. She cares about looking good," Ryder added glumly. "It's why when Chelsea came and said she was pregnant, my first thought was, 'They just have to adopt the baby. They'll care more about the kid than how the kid makes them look.'"

"Oh, I don't think—"

"Maybe not," he interrupted, "but I know. I live it." Ryder slid the catalog across the counter. "This one. Look how it allows for growth. I think we want this one."

"I'll order it tomorrow."

She stepped outside the door but Ryder's voice stopped her. "Willow?"

"Yeah?"

"Maybe instead of seeing the wall as changed, maybe it would help if you saw it as restored."

"Thanks, Ryder. Make a list of what I need to order."

She stepped out of the greenhouse and went to sit on the porch. Maybe she would feel less unsettled if she listened to progress. Ryder's words tried to soothe an agitated spirit, but failed. Change hurt—Willow had no doubt that the hunt for the hidden room would bring more. Wallpaper ruined, a door where there had always been smooth wall—more of her home less like she'd known it for the majority of her life. Yes, change hurt.

Three seconds after she sat in the porch swing, the sound of a saw sent her from the porch and out into the yard. Her eyes roamed toward her mother's grave. Would it be overly sentimental to spend the time out there? She glanced back over her shoulder at the front door. It would hurt Chad. That wasn't worth it.

Instead, she strolled around the back of the barn to the swing tree. Seated there with Liam growing heavy in her arms, she prayed for strength and peace. It would be good. Her life had resettled into a new routine. She liked it. Yes, there would be a door in a wall. Did that really matter in the great scheme of things? There were two barns now and she didn't ache over the missing dirt. Why should it matter?

As she pushed the swing with one foot, allowing it to sway and twist as it chose, Willow gave herself a good scolding for being a little ridiculous about things that really didn't matter. Chad had always hated that there was only one bathroom. If there was another one back there, it would make cleanup so much easier—and much cheaper than Marianne's suggestion of a mudroom added to the back of the house. As lovely as it sounded on rainy days, the changes had made her want to weep. Even Chad had protested.

The sounds of saws and drills ceased. Only the sounds of Liam's jacket brushing against hers and Portia's whimpering at her feet interrupted the cold March morning. Was that a shout? Did it mean that they did find something or that something went wrong? Lucas—

What an absurd idea. Chad wouldn't let anything hurt the boy. He was probably jumping up and down at the sight of porcelain sinks and another toilet for her to clean. She'd present him with a toilet bowl brush tied with a ribbon for St. Patrick's Day. That would teach him.

The screen door slammed shut. Willow sighed. She didn't want him to come quite yet. She pulled off her glove and touched Liam's cheek. It was cool but he seemed warm enough. *A little longer, Lord,* she pleaded. *I'm not ready.*

Chad and Luke appeared much sooner than her idea of "longer." Luke's face, rather than Chad's, told her something had gone horribly wrong. "Lucas—" She stared at the boy in Luke's arms, but nothing seemed off.

"Is fine," the quiet man assured her.

Hesitantly, Chad passed her something. "You need to read this, lass. I'm so sorry. I wish I didn't have to—"

Willow unfolded the paper and read the note, penned in her mother's familiar handwriting, and dated the summer she'd turned two.

August 4th

To Whom It May Concern,

I, Kari Anne Finley, confess to the murder of Jason Rosser, a man with physical characteristics that are remarkably similar to Steven Solari Jr.

Mr. Rosser appeared at my door two days ago, on August 2nd, and tried to get me to talk to him. When I first saw him, I assumed he was Steven Solari Jr. and reacted on instinct out of fear for my life and the life of my daughter. I grabbed my shotgun and killed him. When I went to move the dead man, I realized that I had shot the wrong person. For this, I am deeply sorry.

I would have confessed my actions to the police, but I believe that my daughter's safety depends on no one knowing she's alive. This would certainly have made the news. I cannot risk that. The man's driver's license, credit cards, and vehicle registration are all in the envelope with this confession to help you notify Mr. Rosser's family. Please extend my apologies for what I've done. I know I cannot be forgiven, but I am so deeply sorry.

If it is not clearly evident, you'll find Mr. Rosser's body in my bathtub of this bathroom. I foolishly thought I could cover him with the concrete to prevent the stench of decay and then transport him out of the house with a dolly, but I wasn't strong enough to move it. I will wall up the room, and I assume (and pray) I'll be dead before this is found.

Mr. Rosser's vehicle is buried at the back corner of the east pasture just inside the tree line. There were no trees there when I rented the backhoe and dug it out, but I planted a row of birch diagonally across that section to make it easy to find.

Kari Anne Finley

Tears poured down Willow's face as she read the letter. Things that had seemed extreme in the light of her life of the past few years made a little more sense to her now. She now understood, in a way she never could have before, why her mother met strangers in the yard with a shotgun before they could even come close to the house. Even Mother's refusal to allow the animals in that east corner of the pasture, and a few ambiguous journal entries were no longer ambiguous. The discovery they'd made the week before Thanksgiving now made sense. The journal entries regarding her destroying their life and being just as guilty—heartbreakingly clear.

"Now I know why she didn't write about the hassles of climbing the stairs while pregnant with me. She didn't."

If the stunned looks on Chad and Luke's faces meant what she suspected it did, that was the last thing they'd expected her to say. Chad knelt beside her, saying in that ultra-gentle tone he used when he thought she felt especially fragile, "I have to call the chief, lass. He'll probably have to call the sheriff."

"Why? Can't you take this letter and the papers and use your Internet thing and find the family that way?"

"Willow," he tried again as gently as he could, "our bathroom is technically a crime scene."

"No, that would be our porch. The journal said that Mother shot him on the porch."

"She put the body in the bathroom. It is also part of the crime scene as is the east pasture. They're going to have to dig up that car."

"Why? It won't run anymore, it can't tell them anything Mother didn't... why ruin our pasture—"

"It's the law."

"It's a stupid law that infringes on my rights as a property owner. It benefits no one and damages my property. I understand the bathtub. They should get to take that and bury it properly, but to tear up a field for something worthless is ridiculous." A new thought came to her. "What if I offer to purchase the car from the family? I could pay whatever is reasonable; they could sign over the deed—"

"Title," he corrected automatically.

"Yes, title, and then my field won't be destroyed by machinery and a gaping hole."

He shook his head even as she spoke. "It can't be done, Willow. We'll do what we can, but we have to follow the law. This isn't your fault, but the family deserves that closure."

"Can we keep the newspapers and television people out of here?"

"You can keep them off the property, but not away from the road."

Willow's head snapped up. "They're going to say terrible things about Mother, aren't they?"

Luke's pained eyes answered her before Chad ever raised his head again. "Yes."

"And me too, I suppose." She took a deep breath. "I want you to arrest anyone who sets foot on this property, touches our fences—anything. It's trespassing and I won't have it."

Shoulders slumped, Chad turned and walked toward the house, pulling out his phone. Luke stared down at Willow still seated on the swing with a sleeping Liam in her arms. "Willow?"

"Yes?" She hardly glanced at him, still fighting the overwhelming desire to sob.

"Think of Chad a little as you deal with this. I know it's hard on you, but politically speaking, this might just be the death of his dream of becoming sheriff around here."

"Why? He did nothing wrong. I did nothing wrong. Why should this hurt him?" The idea seemed preposterous.

"Because people don't think in terms of a person's actions. They think in terms of what that person is associated with. They're going to hear Chad's name, remember that a body was found in his house, and they will recoil. It's what people do."

"I think people should start thinking in terms of wise decisions instead of irrational emotions. I would think they would want a man who found a body and did all the proper legal things to take care of it, even at the expense and inconvenience of his own family and property."

She stood, shifted Liam over one shoulder, and gave Luke a one-armed hug. "Thank you for telling me, Luke. I would never have imagined that this could be that kind of a problem. It's ridiculous. We'll find a way to fight it when that time comes. Chad always says that public opinion follows whatever those in power spin it to be. We'll have to find a way to be the spinners that time." Willow shook her head. "I can't believe how fickle people are sometimes.

Chapter 158

The nightmare began before she could put the children down for their naps. Chief Varney, sirens blaring, barreled up the drive as fast as he could in the slushy mud. Willow stood at the window, arms crossed over her chest, as Chad and Luke met him in the yard, pointing to the house. They'd be coming in soon. Her eyes roamed the room—filthy. Was she allowed to clean it or not? As long as she stayed out of the bathroom, it should be safe, shouldn't it?

Her eyes slid toward the opening in the wall—a perfectly smooth place with a nice doorjamb—her heart sank. She knew where the door was for it. She'd used it as a play table as a child. As Chad stepped in the room, her eyes jerked away from the offending opening. She still hadn't managed to allow herself to look inside.

"Can I clean up in here?"

"I'll do it, lass."

"No, my question is, 'Am I allowed to clean up this mess or is it somehow part of the investigation?'"

"Let Martinez get pictures first, and then you can have at it, Miss-rs. Tesdall. Still not used to you being married to this lug."

Feeling dismissed, she crooked her finger at Chad and strolled into the kitchen. Once he stepped in the room, she kissed him. "I love you. I'm sorry about this. I just wanted you to know that I love you."

"Aw, lass..."

"And the minute they'll let you, I would appreciate it if you'd get the door out of the attic and put it up. I'm not ready to look in there yet."

He held her. Whether he tried to draw strength from her or infuse her with his, Willow didn't know. She gave him a weak smile and added, "Should I get Chief Varney the new journals—the ones that mention this?"

"I'll get them."

"Good, then I think I'm going to work on something else—like starting a roast for dinner. That'd be a good idea."

He turned to leave the room as she reached for her coat. She had almost shut the door behind her when his voice called out to her. "Lass?"

"Yes?"

"I'm sorry."

"I know. So am I. We'll get through it, though. I trust you."

Outside, she strolled to the barn, trying to feel as nonchalant as she looked, but Ryder stepped into the summer kitchen behind her. "Is everything okay? Why is—"

Fresh tears fell down her face. "I'm sorry. I didn't think to tell you. It's—" She stifled a sniffle, reaching into her pocket for a handkerchief. "Proof that these are better," she muttered, waving the fabric square. "Chad's boxes are never handy like these."

Ryder patted her shoulder awkwardly. "Do I need to go home?"

"No, that body was cemented long before you were born. You can't possibly know anything about it."

"Body? Cement? It sounds like something out of one of those old mobster movies. What are you talking about?"

"In the bathtub," she said. "Mother buried someone in the bathtub in the house."

"Um, I've seen—oh in the closed off room."

"Yep."

"It probably wasn't your mother, Willow. I mean, come on. She's not—wasn't—"

"She wrote out a confession and left it in the medicine cabinet." Willow snickered, almost half-crazed with new and uncomfortable thoughts. "It sounds like one of Miss

Hartfield's novels." She stared at him. "Why does everyone call her Miss Hartfield?"

"Because it's her name."

"But she's—" Willow decided perhaps the question was better saved for Chad. How she'd never thought to ask before, she didn't know. "Anyway, I'm going to make a roast."

"Proof that you are part Solari."

"What is that supposed to mean?" Willow glared at the boy and then sighed. "Oh, because I have a body in my house and my grandparents were both murderers."

"Because," Ryder clarified, "your answer to a horrible problem is to cook food. Sounds awfully Italian to me."

Observed, heckled, and bombarded by the press as he did it, Chad screwed a large "No Trespassing" sign to the end of the drive. Microphones were thrust into his face, but he ignored them, shaking the sign for strength from the wind before he strode back up the driveway. Once out of sight, he allowed his shoulders to slump and kicked himself as he made his way back to the house.

Had he not gotten carried away with the idea of improving the house, Chad would have realized that Kari would not have walled up a room without reason. The idea simply did not fit her character. Although occasionally irrational when motivated by fear, Kari had always made very deliberate decisions, hadn't she? Some now made sense in ways they never had before finding that note.

"Lord, she feared being caught for an accidental murder more than the Solaris. Somehow, she transferred that fear to their name—understandably so—but I see why the isolation now. It wasn't just to hide from them. She was hiding from her own actions. How terrifying."

A new thought hit him. *The family. What if they sued Kari's estate? Could they?* Wrongful death suits could be expensive. Then again... no, there was no then again. Bill would know.

Chad pulled out his phone and scrolled through contacts until he found their friend/financial advisor. "Bill—Chad here. Look, have you seen the news?"

Bill's negative answer preceded a wary, "Do I want to?"

"No, but you'd better. What do you know about Kari and a man she shot?"

"Kari shot a man?"

Chad nodded illogically as he added, "Yeah. We found the body today."

"That's disgusting. Where was it?"

"Downstairs bathroom." Chad waited for the protest. It came quickly.

"There is no down—oh wait. Oh. Hmm…"

"What?"

"I just remembered a visit—one of the first."

"Yeah?"

"I came in and had to go to the bathroom, but Willow was in there. Kari didn't say, but I got the idea there was something about bad cramps or whatever."

What that had to do with anything, Chad couldn't imagine. "Okaaay…"

"Well, anyway, I told her that she should build a bathroom downstairs behind the stairs. It looked like enough room for one to me. She nearly bit my head off for suggesting it."

"Extreme," Chad muttered.

"I just took it as Kari going overboard. She often did." Bill murmured something to someone on the other end of the line and then said, "Look, Chad. I've kept my thoughts to myself for quite a while, but since you asked…"

"Just spit it out."

"There's been quite a bit of—oh, I don't know the word I mean. Willow has kept her mother on a pedestal. To some degree it's warranted, but I've always felt like Kari kept one step ahead of encroaching instability."

"Some of the early journals show that," Chad admitted, "but I don't see it in the later ones."

"Like I said. It's just something I noticed. The older she got, the more reclusive they were and that seemed to fuel a growing paranoia about the world outside them."

"Well, that leads to my next question." The words stuck in Chad's throat before he found his voice again. "What concerns should we have about lawsuits?"

Seconds passed slowly as Chad waited for an answer. He watched the trees swaying in the breeze, felt the touch of it on his nose and ears, and wondered what changes would blow their way in the next weeks. Would their world fall apart with a lawsuit that devastated them financially? Would they end up living in town in a little bungalow and he work fulltime again?

"I think we should take this to Renee. I know there are insurance policies, but I'm not a legal representative. I can't advise you—not legally or morally. I can only tell you what is in place, but I do know one thing."

"What's that?"

Bill cleared his throat. "Kari was thorough—about everything. If she *could* prepare for this, she did. I just don't know if she could."

"Do I call Renee or should you?"

"Let me do it," Bill insisted. "It won't be on your phone records or anything then. You won't look like you were scrambling if anyone decides to look at stuff like that—can they even do that?"

Chad sighed. "I can't think. I think so—well, the police could. Can a court? I don't know. Thanks."

"It'll be okay, Chad. In as much as she could, Kari provided for so much. I suspect that if she killed a man, she found a way to protect them from financial ruin because of it. The corporation will help some, but I don't know about laws to override that. Bill sighed, the sound almost ominous in Chad's ear. "One more thing."

"Yeah?"

"I haven't brought it up, but there is quite a bit of legal stuff with Solari. She's in the will. If it ever gets to the point where they actually disperse the accounts, she'll have more coming from him."

Bile rose in Chad's throat as he disconnected the call. "Could it get any worse?"

Willow stared out the window, watching as the big

machinery drove up the lane, through the fields, and out of sight behind the barn. Digging. Destroying her land— Mother's land. For what? Proof of what they already knew? How could that car prove anything except that Mother didn't confess to a crime she hadn't committed. Ridiculous.

Her eyes slid toward the door-shaped hole in the wall. Almost seventy-two hours and she had yet to look in there. Willow's eyes traveled upwards as if she could see into the boys' room and hear them sleeping or stirring. Twice she stepped toward the doorway, her eyes riveted to the floor. Twice she stepped back.

Oh, God help me get past this! Her soul wailed in anguish over something that made no sense. Why was it such a terrifying thing for her? The body was no longer there—no longer encased in concrete. The bathtub was gone if she understood Chad correctly. The room held something over her, gripping her in a terror she didn't quite understand.

A wave of nausea washed over her. Willow hurried outside, allowing the cool air to take away the sick feeling in her gut. *It's just a room. The man didn't even die in there.* She stared down at the porch—out in to the yard. Where exactly had the poor man been standing? Had he pleaded for mercy? Run? Did he think she was bluffing and tried to step closer? Had that move been the one that made the decision for Mother?

Her feelings about the porch and yard didn't change. She had no discomfort at all in exploring any of them except that she knew people could see her out there. Is this how Aggie had felt with news vans camped at the end of her little driveway? Prisoner in her own home. That's what it was.

Willow turned with a determination she usually reserved for someone trying to change her life. The thought made her smile. This time she'd direct that determination inward. *She* was the culprit this time. *She* was changing her life simply by allowing fear to dictate how she felt in her own home. Well, not anymore.

Her hands gripped the doorjambs and illogically, she wondered how she'd have the lovely carved trim for around it that every other room in the house had. She couldn't do it— and yet, how fitting if she did. That was a thought for another time.

Willow's nose wrinkled in distaste as the musty scent of mold and mildew assaulted her with the first step inside. Where a bathtub had once sat remained nothing but part of a tub surround in the ugliest green imaginable. That would have to go. Thankfully, the toilet was white—sink too. The medicine cabinet door hung partially open. *That must be where the envelope was.*

"Be sure your sin will find you out," she whispered. "How many times did you say that to me, Mother? Did you think of this when you said it? Were you ever tempted to tell me? Would you ever have told me?" That question wrung her heart and sent a lone tear coursing down her cheek. Mother would not have told her. She would have taken the information to the police—unaware of the intrusions that would come. Mother knew. Mother protected.

Mother hurt all alone with secrets she didn't know how to carry. That thought brought another tear. Covering sin rarely worked—never in the long run. Eternally speaking, each thought, action, word—all unveiled and lain open before the Lamb of God. The thought wrenched her heart. She wouldn't like to see what hers looked like through the lens of God's purity.

The call came as the third tear slid down her face. She smiled and then her heart squeezed as she realized it wasn't likely one of their casual weekly chats. "Hello Grandmom."

"Are you all right?"

Strange—no one had asked that question. "No. I'm not." She swallowed hard, blinking back any other tears that might try to escape. "But I will be once the Lord does His work." Her lips trembled and she added before Carol could respond. "It's the right thing to say. Somewhere in me I believe it. I just don't feel it. I feel like it's a lie."

"I know. It's so hard. I thought to come, but David didn't know if it would be better or worse for you. He's so worried about you."

"Chad won't let anything happen to us."

Carol's smile—heartbroken as it was—managed to make itself heard through the phone. "I meant that he—well both of us really—are worried about your heart. This can't be the mother you knew. It's not the daughter *we* knew."

"It's not. Mother wouldn't—well, I guess that isn't true, is it? She did." A new thought struck her sending her from the room to the couch. Willow curled in the corner and whispered, "But it was."

"What was?"

"It was the mother I knew. I just never really thought about it. If you had driven up our drive, Mother would have met you in the yard with the shotgun. I never doubted that she'd shoot to protect us. I never thought she'd need to, but I always knew she'd do it if she thought it necessary. That's what she did. It's horrible and tragic, but she shot a man she thought was there to hurt me. She defended me. As awful as it turned out, she meant only to protect."

Carol's voice choked and the line seemed to go dead. Willow stared at the phone, occasionally saying, "Hello?" until she was ready to disconnect the call. Just as her thumb slid to the button, she heard her grandfather's voice.

"Willow?"

"Granddad? Is everything all right?"

"No, but it will be—somehow."

"I was talking with Grandmom and then she was gone."

David's voice, deep and husky with repressed emotion both soothed and cut her as he said, "It's hard on her. It's hard on all of us, I imagine."

"I'm sorry."

"Willow," her grandfather's voice took on a stern tone she rarely heard but nearly always heeded. "This isn't your sin. My daughter answers for her own mistakes. They're not grandfathered into your life for you to bear."

"That article—just one article—gave you so much trouble when it came out. I can't imagine what this is going to do to you. Uncle Kyle and his children—"

"Let us worry about that."

Long after the call disconnected, Willow sat with her knees pulled up to her chest, her head resting on them. What would it mean? Would more people hurt? Of course, they would. That was the nature of sin. It snowballed, picking up momentum and size until it crashed and exploded all over... something.

When the first wail from the boys sounded upstairs, Willow practically bolted to the stairs. Taking them two at a time, she counted—the words sticking in her throat on ten. She pulled them from their crib, changed and redressed them, and stood at their bedroom window, her eyes straining to see the progress outside.

How long she stood there, Willow couldn't remember, but by the time she turned away, a light, fresh dusting of snow covered the ground and her boys screamed for their dinner.

Chapter 159

At two o'clock, Chad dragged himself up the steps and into the kitchen. Chili and cornbread waited for him on the warming shelf of the kitchen stove. Such a long and exhausting week. Between normal farm work, his job, and the excavation of the vehicle from their field, he'd barely had a moment to relax. Each day he had stumbled home from work, collapsed in bed, and then got up and did it all over without any time to unwind.

The sheriff's department had finished their excavation and investigation, but the Tesdall's nightmare had just begun. Once the media grabbed the story, their name, life, and history had been dragged through more muck than even he'd imagined. Thankfully, after the first day, Willow hadn't asked about what was happening anymore and had been too busy to go into town. He planned to do everything possible to avoid her going for the next month. Hopefully, by then a new sensation would grab the inhabitants of the Rockland area.

He felt jittery—too mentally keyed up to sleep and too physically exhausted to do anything but sleep. As he passed through the living room, Chad noticed Willow's journal half-covered by a stack of fabrics—obviously a new shipment from Boho. At least the news hadn't delayed shipment. A few minutes lost in his wife's latest thoughts and activities seemed like the perfect end to a horrible week.

March—

It's been one of the worst weeks of my life. Mother's death was obviously one of those, and then there was the time when I kept Chad away from me. Those were horrible weeks, but this is just a whole new level of awfulness. My mother murdered a man to protect me. A man's family suffered for over two decades, wondering where he went, why he didn't come home, if he'd abandoned them, or if he had some horrible thing happen.

I've decided fear is a terrible thing. Mother used fear to protect us. I understand how and why, but I don't want to use fear with my boys and with the new child that I pray we still get to have. I can't help but wonder if Chelsea and her family will refuse to let their child enter such a tainted home. It's strange how people think. I never can understand it. Somehow, I have to learn a new way to teach my children caution and yet ensure they learn to trust the Lord rather than listen to their fear. It's strange; I always saw Mother as a very strong and courageous woman. She seemed the epitome of reliant faith and trust, but I see now that along with all of that was the kind of mind-numbing fear that can destroy faith. In many ways, Mother trusted herself more than her Lord. Do I do that? I'd like to ask Chad, but I don't think I'm ready for the answer.

Chad is weary. I see him flexing his hand, which is usually an indicator of physical overwork, but he won't rest. He seems eager to be away from us right now. I can't decide if it's to protect us, or if the sting of what this all could mean just hurts more when he's near me. I refuse to believe that there is not a way to use this to help him in his career rather than allow it to damage it. Perhaps there is more of my grandfather in me than I like to admit.

Granddad and Grandmom Finley have been devastated by this. Some of their friends have shunned them, and Granddad has stepped down as an elder in their church. I understand why, but I hate it. It kills me that Mother's mistake is damaging so many lives and so long after it happened. She used to say, "Willow, every action you take has far-reaching consequences—both good and bad. Make sure when you choose actions that you can live with the resulting consequences." I now know a little bit of what she meant.

On a brighter note, Lucas walked today. He saw me in the kitchen doorway, stood in the middle of the floor, and toddled right up to me as if he'd been doing it for years. Oh, his little feet were unsteady and he stumbled twice, but he just got up and walked as if it was normal. Liam seems quite disgusted. He has tried to follow in his brother's footsteps, but every time he lifts that foot without his hand steadying him on furniture, down he goes. The wails are of absolute fury and frustration, not because he injures himself on the twelve inches from bum to floor.

We put the second greenhouse plans on hold during the excavation, but now that there are no more sheriff cars coming and going

Chad smiled at the abrupt stop. Had Liam fallen in another attempt and hurt himself that time? Did she get a phone call, have to change a diaper, or realize how late it was and stopped mid-sentence?

He hadn't realized how personally she'd take the potential damage to his career. He also hadn't realized that he'd been aloof. His attempts to protect her from media garbage had done little more than make her feel alienated. He'd have to remedy that.

"Lord, I had no idea when I wanted to open that bathroom that we'd be dealing with this kind of thing. Now what do I do with it?"

April Fools' Day hit and Chad found himself awake in a quiet house, and with nothing to do. He glanced at the clock. The darkness of the room made it impossible to see. His hand reached to push the shades out of the way and his eyes strained to adjust to light. *After ten o'clock. She's off with Chelsea to the doctor.*

A glance in the boys' room told him she'd taken them with her. That left him relieved. At least she hadn't told him to keep an ear out for them. As exhausted as he was, he might have slept through their cries—at first anyway.

Downstairs he found a note—one of her "short" ones lasting only just over a page. In it, she told of her plans, asked him to check "his animal," and suggested that he bring home oak molding for new door trim. "'I'm going to try my hand at carving something,' he read aloud, '"something like a simple vine with leaves maybe. What do you think?"'

Chad grabbed a muffin and poured a mug of coffee. The bathroom still stood open—cleaner now that Willow had scrubbed it down, but even Luke's careful cuts and sanded edges looked rough compared to the rest of the room. He ran his hand over where the hinges still hung as if waiting for the other half—the pin. That was what was in the medicine cabinet!

As much as he really wanted a full breakfast, Chad's eagerness to get one thing done that he knew would relax her overrode the call of a man for his meal. He grabbed gloves and a jacket before climbing his way into the attic. Experience had taught him that the entire top floor of the house had little insulation between it and the roof above, but Kari had obviously insulated well between the attic and second floors. His nose immediately felt the cold.

The door remained elusive at first. The place he remembered seeing it held a few shelving boards and nothing else—just as he'd remembered aside from the door being "something else." It wasn't on the wall, used as a table as he'd once seen, or in the rafters above him. However, as he started back downstairs, he saw it—right beside the stairs. "Willow. She was going to do it herself. Probably got sidetracked by the lads."

It needed a good scrubbing which normally would have prompted him to go out for a garden hose, but he hadn't pulled them from the barn yet, and well, Chad didn't really care to do it. So, he carried it into the kitchen and began wiping it down. After the fourth kitchen rag, he considered the laziness he had displayed proof of why laziness would never be virtuous. "She's gonna kill me," he muttered as he stared at the growing pile of rags.

Once hung, Chad stood back to admire his work. They'd have to paint it. The colors were so far off that it looked bad even to him. Willow's color aesthetic would likely send her straight to town. That thought brought a smile. "Bet a piece of cheesecake she goes."

Still, despite the deficiencies of hue and—whatever you call the colors and their nuances—the room looked better even without trim and paint. "Food. Now let's get some food—and maybe put something in for dinner."

Willow found him in the barn, cleaning a scrape from Lacey's leg. She waddled up to the stall, one boy strapped to each hip with her slings, and watched him. "I saw that and got worried. Seems like I read something about horses having to be put down for bad infections in the leg."

"Well, I doubt it would have gotten that bad," Chad said kissing her and ruffling the boys' heads, "but I think it's best to get it taken care of."

"So," Willow had had enough of horses for a day—or year. "Want to hear what the doctor said about gender?"

"I thought you had another month before that ultrasound."

She beamed. "I did, but the doctor heard the heartbeat nice and clearly. Said it's in the 'girl' range and laughed. Chelsea says that this means it's either a boy or a girl." She snickered at the confused look on Chad's face.

"Didn't we kind of know that?"

"What she means is that her mom will say that because it's a 'girl' heartbeat, it must be a boy. Apparently, all her babies were opposite the old wives' tale. However, Ryder's mom said he was spot on for the heartbeat thing, so she'll say it's a girl." She wrapped arms around her squirming boys and squeezed them. "So, I've decided to buy pink and blue, make something for both, and appease all the heartbeat gods."

"Funny."

Willow turned to go calling back, "Hey, do you want lunch? I was going to make some taco soup. That recipe your mother gave me is amazing."

"Yeah, that'd be great. Thanks."

Inside, she pulled out the chair harnesses and strapped the boys into chairs. While they babbled and gnawed on the tough biscuits she made for them each week, she made oatmeal and stirred in a bit of yogurt. It revolted Chad every time he saw her do it, but Willow fed the boys from one spoon and one bowl, alternating bites so that neither boy had to wait for their next bite. It kept their meals from dragging indefinitely and kept them from wailing as they waited—in theory. It didn't always work exactly as planned but better than when she didn't.

Once fed she hurried upstairs to clean them up and change them for their afternoon naps. As she went, something felt wrong, but she didn't take time to see what it was. Unease crept over her, settling in her heart with each passing minute. By the time she closed the door behind her, Willow leaned against the wall, panic gripping her. It felt similar to the days of terror when papers were moved or baby Jesus disappeared from the manger. Something was different down there.

Her hand slid toward her pocket. Should she call Chad? Would her grandmother have the ability to start another strange thing from prison? It didn't seem possible. A new thought kicked her in the gut, sending bile to her throat. The discovery in the bathroom—surely someone wasn't going to torment them over that! Did people do things like that?

Taking a deep breath, she forced herself back downstairs. Ignoring the resurging feeling of dread as she crossed through the dining room, Willow stepped into the kitchen. Her hand gripped the top of Mother's rocking chair. She wanted nothing more than to step out the back door, fly to the barn, and beg Chad to figure out the problem for her.

A semi-hysterical giggle escaped as she stepped into the dining room. The door. Chad had replaced the door for her. All that panic and worry—for nothing. Willow stared at it for a moment, opened it, closed it again, and hurried out to the barn.

Chad glanced up at her, visibly confused as she stood there giggling. "Wha—"

"The door. Thank you." Willow snickered. "Oh, and I'm going to go buy some paint. I'll bring home sandwiches from The Deli instead of soup. We'll do soup tomorrow."

Chapter 160

Trees budded all over Walden Farm. Although a few patches of snow remained under the larger trees in the wooded areas at the back of the property, spring had arrived in Fairbury. Willow spent her late April mornings walking with her boys around the property, showing them the trees, the flowers peeking through the thawing earth, and the animals that seemed happy to be out of the large barns.

One Thursday morning, she stood at the back porch and stared out over the landscape. It looked so different from the place she and her mother had built over the years. Kari would hardly recognize the view before her could she see it. Two barns, two greenhouses, a kitchen garden and a produce garden, the chicken pens and houses quadrupled in size, and cows, goats, and sheep scattered through the pastures. It was beautiful. Kari would have both loved and hated it.

The work had become overwhelming, though. As each separate function of the farm expanded, the work grew exponentially. And with that additional work came less time to do the things she loved. "Lord, how do I cultivate that balance between what *I* need to do and what needs to be done? We need fulltime help—maybe even another house for them so they can be here for animal birthing and such. How do I plan for that? Is it too much?"

Lucas' little eyes stared up at her solemnly as if he understood the words and his mother's latest dilemma. His little pudgy hand sought her cheek and rested there for a moment before he giggled. Then, as if embarrassed, he ducked his head into the familiar hollow of her neck on her shoulder and popped his thumb in his mouth.

"I agree, little one. The whole thing is ridiculous, isn't it?"

Before Willow could ask another question or her son make any sign of agreement, the back screen door creaked. *Oil that when you go inside*, her mind noted. Just as she turned to smile at Chad, the familiar feeling of his arm about her waist and Liam's hands in her braid stopped her. "Liam, let go."

Lucas' head popped up from her shoulder and the boy whacked the little fists that filled his mother's hair. Chad laughed and stopped the brawl before it could continue. "Married for two years and you still have men fighting over you."

"I am a catch, didn't you hear? You'd better feel mighty lucky to have tricked me into marrying you."

"I thought women did the tricking?"

Willow's eyes clouded with confusion. Her brow wrinkled in concentration and then understanding dawned. "Can't trick a guy into marriage who hasn't tried to get the privileges of it beforehand, can you?"

"I'd have likely been arrested for assault on any man that tried."

His grin gave Willow that same silly flutter to her heart that she'd grown to love in the weeks leading to and following her wedding. "I'd have paid your bail."

"What are you looking at now, lass?"

"I just noticed how different everything looks than it did. I think it's time for more change too."

"More? Since when are you the one who suggests change?"

"I think," Willow continued, ignoring Chad's teasing, "it is time to hire someone fulltime. I don't see how we can avoid it."

"Is the work getting to be too much?"

"Not yet." Her silence made him nervous, and she knew it, but Willow waited a minute before she added, "I just know that with the new baby..."

"I could quit—come home and focus on the farm."

"You've always wanted to be an officer. I don't think you should give that up—not yet." She pointed to the tree line. "I thought on the other side of those trees, we could put up one of those prebuilt homes."

"Who would live there?"

Willow shrugged. "Not sure about that. We need someone who likes animals and farming both."

"Maybe we should leave the boys with Mom and Dad and have a planning weekend."

"Planning weekend?"

Chad took Lucas from her arms and stepped around her. "I'll take them with me to do the milking. You get the oats on and we'll talk about it over breakfast."

Papers littered the dining room table. While Chad made notes about different options, Willow tried to sort calving, lambing, and kidding schedules from planting, rotation, and harvesting schedules. By the time she laid neat piles of papers front of him, Chad didn't know where to begin.

"Ok, so what things do you know you want to do yourself?"

"The family garden, our sewing, Boho..." Willow hesitated as she considered her options. "Well, most of what I did before Mother died really. I don't care who cleans the house or beats the rugs. I personally don't need to do the wood splitting—not usually. I like hanging clothes, but washing them isn't important to me; I just don't know how to separate that."

Chad's list split into two sides. On one side, he listed every task that he or Willow preferred to do and on the other he wrote everything they could hire someone to do. When finished, he scrutinized it carefully. "You know, it looks to me like we need a husband and wife team. How can we find someone who doesn't have more children to add to this mix?"

"Why no children? Maybe they'd want to make it a family thing like we do."

"True. It just seemed like it would be hard for a woman to take care of her family and ours too." He knew it sounded weak, but he wanted to ensure the idea would work if they hired someone. "Do you think we'll make enough to cover our expenses with two? Maybe we should just keep Iris for as long as she wants to stay and replace her separately—if she wants to be replaced."

Willow seemed lost in thought. At last, she reached across the table and covered his hand with hers. "Is there a way—" she stopped, her forehead furrowed in concentration. "I just mean—you know that man, that new one who works for Adric? What if there are other men out there trying to start a new life?"

"Criminals you mean? You want to invite criminals into our home?"

Laughing, Willow stood and grabbed cookies from the cookie jar. "Not into our home—onto our property. We did it with Ryder—"

"You did it with Ryder."

"Fine, I did it with Ryder and look how well it worked."

Chad didn't like the look in her eye. He knew that look; it meant their life was about to change more than he had ever imagined possible. "I so wish I could pull the husband card on this."

"But you can't?"

"Not yet, but if the opportunity arises…"

Five minutes passed—fifteen. The time seemed to roll by much as it had in the first days of their friendship. The pressing busyness of farm life had been different in past months. As he watched Willow hurry upstairs and heard the bathroom door shut, he added something else to his list. *Fix the downstairs bathroom.* It had to be done.

The skip of her feet down the stairs brought a smile to his face. That was his Willow—the one he rarely saw anymore, and the thought wrung his heart. Was it all too much? He'd spent so much money to expand the farm and the success couldn't be denied, but was it too much? Something in his heart told him it was.

Seconds turned into minutes as he tried to decide how to broach the subject. At last, he leaned forward, his forearms resting on the table, hands clasped together. "Willow, do you remember why you started selling your produce?"

"I had too much." The answer came swiftly.

"Why did you have too much?"

Her eyes glanced up at him, concerned. "Because we planted enough for two people to eat all summer, winter, and spring. Well, we always did Mother loved big gardens so much of it became compost. Mother was gone, so…"

Even now, her voice constricted at the thought of Kari being gone from her life. Chad felt ridiculous for thinking it. Of course, it would still hurt. Would she be the Willow he loved if she could so easily forget her sole companion for the bulk of her life?

"And the greenhouse. Why did you build it?"

"Fresh vegetables for us in the winter." Her pen scribbled out cost projections and expected revenue as she spoke.

"Why did you keep planting more and more then?"

"We had a good business. People liked our produce and wanted it."

"But did you want to become a produce stand? Did you want all this?"

Chad watched as her mouth opened to say, "Of course," and then sighed inwardly as the real answer dawned. An inward struggle showed itself plainly on her features. Willow couldn't say yes and didn't want to say no.

"I don't know, Chad. I assumed that I did. I mean, we're doing it, and you and I both know there isn't much that I do that I don't want to do."

His chuckle brought a smile to her otherwise troubled face. "This is true—very true."

"You're right, though. If people hadn't expected more, I don't know if I would have expanded as I did—we did."

"I talked you into more animals."

"You wanted them. There was no reason not to do it if you wanted it."

The words stung. Chad listened as she verbally worked through almost every part of her life until he could no longer stand to hear it. "Stop."

"What?" Confusion clouded her eyes.

"Let's try this another way. Does it bother you that these things happen here? Remove yourself from the equation. Does it bother you that people buy meat and produce grown on this land?"

"Not at all. I'm glad they do!"

"Ok, then. Forget everything and everyone else—including me." He saw her protest form, but shook his head. "Now, what would your days look like if you only did the things you really want to do and the things you're sure God wants of you?"

The answer was a long time coming. By the time Willow was ready to speak, Chad had grown nervous. She looked around her, smiled into his eyes, and sank back against the back of her chair.

"I'd get up in the morning and feed my family. Mornings when you were home, I wouldn't bother with milking. Other mornings I would. The boys would watch me clean up after breakfast and as I start lunch. Then we'd go outside and do the laundry together. We'd sing, play, chase each other through the sheets. While they napped I'd spin, work in my flowerbeds, sew, and keep house. On your days off, I'd do things like make soap or candles—things that are very difficult with little boys who could get hurt touching things. In the afternoons, we'd change the animals' pastures, play some more, and maybe go fishing. After dinner, we'd read books, put puzzles together, and listen to music."

She picked at her fingernails. "Is it silly?"

"Not at all. What around here would you want to change?"

"I don't think I want to change much. I just want to be able to call someone and say, 'The boys and I feel like fishing today. Will you come and butcher a dozen hens?'"

"But you want to butcher them on other days?"

"Why not? I can do a dozen while the boys nap if I'm on the ball." She scooted her chair closer and wrapped her hands around his forearm. "What is it, Chad?"

"I just don't want this farm to do things simply because I mentioned them."

"We need an employee—one who lives on the farm."

"And we need a downstairs bathroom," Chad added as he

stood to hurry upstairs himself.

"I'll call a contractor."

"Don't. Luke wants to do it. He, Laird, and I will be able to get it done in a weekend if we put our minds to it."

Willow carried their napkins to the sink, shook them out, and dropped them in the laundry basket under the counter. "Just let me know when that'll be."

Something in her tone caught his attention. "Why?"

"I fully intend to take our boys to your mother's house for that weekend."

Chad felt as if he'd leveled another blow at her. "I'm sorry, lass. It'll be hard at first, but don't you think—"

"Sure, I think and I agree with those thoughts. I also know that there will be music playing, power tools blaring, soda cans all over the place, and I'll feel like I should help but can't. It'll be nicer if I come home and you have it all done for me."

The room at the doctor's office slowly filled with more people than Willow had imagined it could hold. Dr. Kline and his nurse stood next to the monitor watching the screen. Cecily the nurse typed on a keyboard as the doctor measured and pointed out arms, legs, and other body parts as they went. Willow and Chelsea's mother stood on the opposite side. Ryder even stood near the end of the examining table, looking miserable and a little excited at the same time.

Dr. Kline glanced up at the group. "Ok, so we do want gender confirmation, is that right?"

Chelsea nodded. "Yes."

"Well if anyone in here doesn't want to know, you'd better step out. I've never been so certain in my life."

No one moved. Willow glanced at the doctor and said, "Would you mind showing us first and then telling us? I want to see if I can guess."

"Sure."

The wand moved away from the baby's head until he stopped it. "Right there. Talk about a frog-legged baby."

Chelsea's mother choked out, "Frog-legged?"

"It's ok, Mrs. Vernon. It's just what I call a baby who likes to pull the heels up to the bum and flap the knees outward—like a frog."

"Well it does give you a perfect view," the woman agreed, "but I can't tell if it's a boy or a girl at all!"

"I can." Chelsea smiled at Willow. "Do you see it? Or, rather, do you not?"

Willow nodded. "Yes."

"You never said it, but I could tell that you hoped for a girl."

Nothing seemed an appropriate answer. If she admitted the truth of Chelsea's words, she sounded unexcited at the possibility of another son. If she denied it, she lied. Neither option seemed to express the full veracity of her thoughts. "I did. I just can't imagine not being thrilled to know my boys had another playmate. Can you imagine three little dudes traipsing over the farm?"

"Dudes. Listen to her, Ryder. Willow is getting so modern."

Mrs. Vernon kissed her daughter's cheek and stepped out of the room. The doctor and nurse took the cue and followed. Willow glanced from Chelsea to Ryder and back to Chelsea. "If you have changed your mind, I will understand."

Ryder didn't speak, but Chelsea nearly shouted, "No." She swallowed and tried again. "I'm sorry, but no. I am happy for you. I'm glad this baby will be so loved and wanted. I didn't get why it was so important to Ryder before, but I get it now."

"Ryder?"

Her young friend stared at his feet for a moment and then raised his eyes to meet hers. "I haven't changed my mind. I'm glad that things worked this way. I really am. I'll get to see her sometimes too. That's pretty cool."

"Ryder..."

Willow interrupted Chelsea's warning. "I like that too. It's good that he'll be close. You know you're welcome out at our place too—even if you change your mind and want to come every week. It's ok. We'll make it work somehow."

The girl didn't speak, didn't respond at all for several long seconds, but she eventually closed her eyes, sighed, and said, "Look, call me callous or insensitive, or—or—non-maternal. Maybe it's true. But I just have no interest at all. Maybe I'm in denial—"

Willow stepped out the door and left Chelsea and Ryder to themselves. Sharon Vernon stood leaning against the office wall, a stunned expression on her face. "You ok?"

"I didn't need to see that. What was I thinking?"

"If you want to visit too—"

The woman pushed away from the wall. "We'll be moving." Three steps from Willow Sharon turned and stared at Willow. "When the thing came out about the...*thing* in your bathroom, I tried to get Chelsea to find someone else. I just thought—well, you know what I thought."

"If it makes you uncomfortable, I'll understand," Willow managed to choke out, "but honestly, I need to know soon before I become any more attached."

"No. That's just it. Seeing you with Chelsea—you're giving her what I need to be and can't. Thanks." A weak smile punctuated the confession. She took a little breath and added, "Tell Chelsea I'll be in the car."

"Would you like me to take her home?"

"No. I don't want to alienate her any further."

Willow waited until she was ensconced in the van, windows up, air conditioner blasting—freezing really—and squealed. She whipped out her phone and punched Chad's number. "So... I guess we should change our ideas for a baby's name."

"Boy? Okay, what were you thinking?"

"Instead of Karianne Olivia, I want Kari Olivianne."

"What!" Chad laughed. "You got me."

"Guess where I'm going?"

"Fabric store on Westwood?" Chad hollered for Aiden Cox to slow down. "Kid is determined to risk his neck with speed now that he wears that helmet."

"Nope. I'm going to the fabric store in Rockland. I want to tell Josh. Won't he be excited! When they came by last month, he said they had the most amazing pink wool flannel he'd ever felt. I want to make... something out of it."

Chapter 161

April—

 We're making changes around here. Doing it has dropped a weight off my shoulders that I didn't know I carried. Strange, when Chad first encouraged me to take part in the Women's Retreat thing, I resisted. Now I look forward to it and I know why. I'll be talking about my life again—my real one. This won't be a talk about how to journal a busy life filled with everything that can be done. This will be about journaling the life that you believe the Lord wants you to live.

 There lies the difference. I allowed good things to become more important to me than the things that God has chosen for me. I allowed myself to become caught up in the busyness of life rather than being busy with my life.

 The boys do not walk. I thought they would. I mean, Lucas took those first steps, and it gave me an idea of what darling little baby legs looked like as they toddled around the house. Liam was frustrated and fought for the same talent. Then, out of the blue, the boy stood and ran. He ran for my legs, threw his arms around them, and so help me, I swear the boy crowed. Lucas was clearly jealous. So, he ran to me too. They haven't walked since. Furthermore, their competitiveness is epic. I had no idea such tiny little people could be so much like James and John—fighting for preeminence.

 Oh! And it's a girl! We're having a girl! Walden Farm

will have a Kari again. Lucas, Liam, and Kari. They sound well together. Pigtails. Gingham. Chad keeps talking about gingham. I didn't know he knew what it was, but I bought some when I told Josh at the store. I wanted to have a nice visit, but he'd just gotten back from break, so I couldn't linger. We need to have them out again. I've missed them.

Chad and I are better. I didn't know we weren't "right" anymore, but we are now. There's a difference. Things seem back the way they were back whenever they were that way. Oh my, that makes no sense and is utterly accurate at the same time.

Tomorrow, the first person comes to interview. We've decided to put a travel trailer on the property. After six months, if all goes well, we'll bring in a modular home. It seems silly to buy a house for someone that might not work out. If we don't find a good fit for us, we'll scale back the farm. As Granddad said, "It's better to have an empty barn and full lives than full barns and no life."

God is so good to us.

Oh, and hydrogen peroxide is a very inexpensive stain remover for little boys who are learning to eat good food. Chad says we can buy industrial sized bottles in Rockland. I have it on my list for when I go stay with Mom the weekend they do the bathroom. I hope that is sooner rather than later. I am becoming worn out just thinking about it.

That's odd. Chad is coming up the drive. Two hours early. I hope he's ok.

Willow abandoned her journal and rushed out the door. "What's going on?"

"Let's talk inside."

She started to turn but Chad stopped her. "No, here is fine. Sorry, I'm rattled."

"So, what—"

"It's Leo. I don't know what's going on, but the chief is being really..." Chad shrugged. "I don't know how to say it but he's being weird and something happened in town—Varney's not even letting us say what."

"So you came home to tell me that something happened but you can't tell me what it is? Couldn't you call if you felt the need to share that non-information?" When he didn't laugh, Willow's heart sank. "It's serious then, isn't it?"

"Serious enough that I want to cancel the interview with that Rockland probation officer."

"You don't think Leo—"

He shook his head. "No, I don't. But this just drove home the point that criminals' pasts can catch up to them. Not at my house, Willow. I won't invite that kind of potential danger around my wife and kids."

"Fork it over then."

Chad stared at her. "What?"

"Your card."

"Huh?"

Laughing, Willow nudged him. "You can't play the husband card if you don't fork it over."

He blinked. Twice. After several seconds, Chad shook his head and leaned against the hood of the truck. "I can never predict you."

"What?"

"You're not arguing about how we can't blame one guy for another guy's problems or whatever."

Willow stepped into his arms and wrapped hers around his waist. She rested her head on his chest, listening to the steady, if a bit rapid, thud of his heartbeat. "Chad, would I have ever been okay with risking anyone's safety?"

"No, but—"

"And didn't you say you'd never do this unless you felt you had no choice?" She lifted her eyes to his. "Right? Something about never leading me where I'm not ready to go? I figured that applied to never letting me go where your conscience prohibited too."

"Well yeah, but—"

"So I suspect it was really hard for you to come out here and tell me this—probably why you did it in person—"

"Wouldn't I be more likely to avoid—"

Willow laughed, shaking her head as she said, "No way. Not you. The harder it is for you, the more likely you are to face it head on. It's one of the things I respect most about you."

"Really?" Despite his surprise, Chad looked pleased.

"I've noticed that a lot of men avoid confrontation with their wives. They'll call out a friend or someone they don't like, but with wives, they just work around the problem until it's solved or circumstance forces it. You don't do that."

His arms tightened around her and suspicious huskiness filled his voice as he murmured into her hair, "You don't know how much it means to me that you said that. I—man, Willow. I really needed that right now."

Even after two years of marriage, Willow still felt awkward initiating a kiss. She'd hold his hand, snuggle up to him anywhere and at any time, but other than a quick peck on the cheek as she left or he did, kissing just didn't come naturally. The times she did, she also knew he noticed and appreciated it. That afternoon was no different.

The boys' wails drifted from the upstairs windows. Willow sighed and stepped back. "Guess I have to go rescue them from the horrors of life in a crib."

Chad caught her hand and pulled her close again. He gazed down at her, smiling and then tugged the hair tie from the end of her braid. She didn't even protest; time had taught her it was futile. With familiar slowness, he separated the braid and ran his fingers through the sections to let them fall naturally.

"I love you, lass."

A lump swelled in her throat, but she managed a grin and choked out, "I know. I'm—" She kissed him once more, lingering only for a second before rushing off to the house and to her demanding sons.

Chad crossed his arms over his chest, listening, waiting for that moment—there it was. Instant cease of screaming. She'd entered their room. With him, they always gave one last wail of protest as if to assert themselves in some way, but with her—never. The moment they heard her voice as that door opened, the cries stopped and semi-toothy grins appeared.

Two days later, Cheri's car stood parked behind the van when Chad arrived home from work. He had expected Willow in the garden, but instead, the boys half-destroyed the living room while his wife and sister sat on the couch in deep conversation. "Hey, squirt."

"Shut up, dork."

"Well, she's in a lovely mood, isn't she?" Chad bent to kiss Willow's head before adding, "What brings you out here?"

"Because I can't want to see my nephews without another reason. Fine, I'll go."

"Knock it off, Cheri. He's not the enemy. That's exactly the kind of response you usually expect from him." The edge in Willow's voice told Chad more than his sister could ever imagine.

"What happened?"

The women answered in one unified name. "Chuck." However, Willow added, "Although, from what I can tell, Cheri—"

"So now it's my fault? The guy is a jerk. Everyone knows it. I try to help him—"

"Whoa..." Chad sat on the coffee table and tried to read his sister's face. "What's going on here?"

Cheri refused to answer, but Willow seemed to have no scruples. "They had a fight. Apparently Chuck's apology was... how did that movie we watched put it—about the cottage?"

"Insufficiently grand?"

She nodded. "Right. Chuck's apology was 'insufficiently grand' for her. Good way of putting it."

"He said, 'Well since it always has to be my fault, I'm sorry.'"

"He's got a point," Chad admitted.

"What! You know who he is. Of course it's his fault!"

"What is?" Before she could go off again, he clarified. "I mean, exactly what happened?"

His little sister pouted on the couch much as she had most of his childhood. Her arms crossed over her chest and her lip barely protruding—she looked six instead of twenty-two. When her little charade didn't produce the result she'd expected, Cheri threw up her hands and said, "Fine!"

"Oh, yeah," Chad said, winking at Willow. "This is gonna be good—and your son is about to destroy that book." While Willow jumped to save her prized copy of *Life with Father*, Chad settled himself beside his sister and draped an arm over her shoulder. "So, what's up?"

"We were just at this party—you know for Drake Thomas' graduation?"

"No, but okay."

"Anyway, one of the guys asked where the bathroom was. I tried to tell him but he came back twice asking which way again."

"The Thomas' do have a big house, but that powder room is right under the stairs."

"It was occupied. Mr. Evans."

"Say no more," Chad, insisted, wincing at the idea of anyone having to go in there after the infamous Mr. Evans.

"So I took him to the one by the mudroom, but it was occupied too. So then I took him upstairs. When he got done, he found me and started talking. I think he's family—seemed not to know anyone but Drake and Mr. and Mrs. Thomas."

"Okaaay..."

"Well, Chuck got all mad. At first, he did great—didn't say anything offensive, but when the guy—"

"Does this guy have a name?"

"I don't know. He didn't say—didn't get a chance to." Cheri rolled her eyes. "He just asked me if I wanted something to drink and Chuck said he'd get it if I did."

"What's wrong with that?"

"Well, nothing if he stopped there, but the next thing I knew, Chuck was going all alpha-dog on the guy. I swear I could smell the testosterone!"

Something sounded off to Chad. "What else did he say to unleash the dog within?"

"Huh?"

"What else did the guy say after Chuck said he'd get the drinks?"

She thought for a moment and then shrugged. "I don't know. Sheila Dayton stopped me and asked if I'd seen Brad, but I don't think the guy said anything. This is Chuck, Chad. It doesn't have make sense. He's ridiculous."

"Then why do you care?"

Tears spilled onto her cheeks. "I don't know..."

"That's a lie."

Chad and Cheri stared up at Willow. She stood a few feet away holding Liam and shaking her head. Chad spoke first. "What?"

"She knows why she cares; she just doesn't want to admit it."

"I do—"

"Willow's right," Chad agreed. "We all know why. So just admit it."

"I don't want to."

Willow stepped closer, kneeling to let Liam down again. "Why?"

"It just makes everything worse."

Chad pulled out his phone. "Dial Chuck's number. I don't think I have it anymore."

"Cha—"

"I'm pulling rank if you don't."

Cheri sighed. "If I wanted Dad's opinion, I would have gone to the store."

"You didn't, because you know you're wrong," Willow muttered.

"I am not! He totally freaked out and was rude to the poor guy, like he always is!"

He couldn't help himself. Chad laughed. "C'mon, Cheri. Do you hear yourself? Why do you think he made an apology that says, 'It's always my fault so I'm sorry?'"

"Well it is!"

"The number?" Chad stared pointedly at his phone.

Cheri punched numbers into it and passed it to him. While he waited for Chuck to pick up, Chad stepped out onto the porch and ignored the indignant tirade she began once the door shut behind him. "Hey, Chuck. It's Chad."

"That's what caller ID says."

"Cheri's here."

"Great. Look," Chuck sounded defeated as he continued, "just get it over with. I'm done."

"Get what over with?"

"Chewing me out for something—whatever it is this

time. I'll leave her alone. I'll leave everyone alone. It's not worth it."

Chad had never heard Chuck sound so wounded. The bluster and bravado that characterized the man didn't surface at all. "What happened?"

"Seriously? Why do you care? If you're not going to blast me, call back when you're ready—"

"Chuck, I'm serious. Something doesn't add up, and I want to know what it is. What happened after you said you'd get her drink. Oh, and why did you say that?"

"Look, the guy was totally coming onto her. I didn't care that she missed it—was kind of glad. I said I'd get the drinks because it seemed like what she's always telling me to do—hint. Well, I hinted."

"Okay. Sounds reasonable to me. How sure are you that he was flirting?"

"No doubt at all."

The words were pure Chuck. Their boldness, conciseness—everything screamed Chuck Majors has spoken. However, they lacked his usual confidence. Instead, hurt and a bit of fear hovered in the man's tone. "Ok, so what happened when she was talking to Sheila?"

"Who's that?"

"What happened," Chad said again, with more patience than he felt, "when she talked to the blonde gal with the green glasses?"

"Oh, her—funny looking gal. Weird glasses."

"Yes, and…"

"Oh, right. The dude." Chuck didn't respond for a minute. "Remember how Willow got all ticked off at me for saying something about Cheri's—"

"Um, yeah. Don't make me hear it again. Just go on."

"Well, this guy made a crack about her—"

"Okay. Got it." Chad rolled his eyes and prayed for another baby boy. *Lord, I don't think I can take listening to guys talk about another family member's assets like this. Boys are best.*

"Oh, and by the way, Chad?"

"Yeah."

"I get it now. I mean, I really never did before. It seemed

like a compliment. Now I get it."

"It's because you love her, Chuck. It helps you filter things in a totally different way."

"Yeah, well, it's not going to do me any good now."

"Don't give up on her. I know my sister—better than you do still, but you're gaining on me. She will want you to fight for her. Can you come out here?"

"Chad, she doesn't want me out there. I can usually push, fight for it, ignore protests. I can't right now."

"She wants you. You have to trust me on this. She does want you."

Several seconds passed as he waited for Chuck to answer. At last, the man sighed. "I'll come, but if she attacks me, *you* can arrest her."

That settled, Chad went inside to do the hard task. That thought prompted a snicker. Who would have ever thought he'd consider Cheri a harder task than Chuck?

"Ok. I got the story out of him."

"So what happened? The guy existed?"

Willow growled a warning but chased after Lucas instead of saying what was on her mind. Chad snickered again. "You're not naïve. You're not dumb. You had to know the guy was flirting with you."

"Well, duh."

"But Chuck is supposed to ignore that."

"No, but he's not supposed to freak out either. We're not even 'official' or anything."

"Official? Seriously?" Chad rolled his eyes. "What makes someone official?"

"These days? Facebook. If the relationship isn't 'Facebook official,' it's not a relationship or it's doomed to failure. Obviously, we know which it is for me."

Willow interrupted. "What's Facebook?"

"Seriously, Chad? You haven't even shown her Facebook?"

"And how would I do that? We don't have Internet out here."

"But honest, social media—"

"Wait," Willow interjected, "can we discuss my lack of cultural literacy at some other point? I want to know what happened with Chuck."

Before Cheri could say any more, Chad nodded. "The other guy made a crack about your... assets."

"Top or bottom?" Willow's eyes narrowed.

"Bottom."

"Good choice of word then," she muttered.

"So a guy complimented me and Chuck lost it over that."

"I remember a certain girl giving Chuck a serious dressing down for the same thing at your house a couple of years ago—or did you forget that too?" Willow shook her head and took the boys' hands. "I'm getting out of here before I smack some sense into you."

Cheri stared at the empty doorway as Willow disappeared into the kitchen and out the back door. "What is her *problem*?"

"Well, she's just saying what we both know I won't. Instead, I'm going to tell you this. You're wrong."

"About..."

"This thing with Chuck for starters. This time, he made the right call and you blew it."

"Oh, come on, Chad." Cheri glared at him. "Do you really think that—"

"Stop. Just listen to me. Chuck has pretty much walked through the fire for you—fire you laid down for him to walk over. You're the one who got through to him when he made the remarks about your chest. Man, Cheri. He defended those remarks until you set him straight. And," Chad added with a smile he couldn't hide, "you'll be happy to know that he gets it now—really gets it. When some guy said it to the girl he loves, suddenly it sounded to him like it sounded to us."

"Loves. Chuck only loves himself."

"So then tell him to go away. Tell him you don't want to be his friend. Tell him he has no chance with you at all. Tell him you've been leading him on all these months—"

"Come on, Chad. That's a little dramatic, even for you." Cheri shook her head and glared at his shoes.

"He's trying, Cheri. Don't you see that? Chuck Majors, the guy who—until he met you anyway—thinks he is perfect, is trying to please someone other than himself. He loves you. He's going to make a million and one flubs every day of his life, most likely. But—"

"Yeah, yeah. I hear you." Despite her efforts to hide it, the corner of her mouth twitched. "I was talking to one of the gals from the mission team. She's got a degree in Special Ed. or something like that. She says he either sounds like he has Asperger's or some social development disorder."

"Makes sense. I don't think Asperger's, but he's got some screw loose." Chad hunkered on his heels and smiled into his little sister's face. "He does love you and not how I always thought he would."

"Huh?"

"I always thought he'd love you 'as much as someone like him can love.' He's going to drive everyone crazy until the day that he dies, but if you care about him, you've got the chance to be probably the most cherished woman alive. You noticed him. You chose him rather than the other way around. You love him—not just tolerate him. That's going to be pretty incredible."

"Yeah…"

Chad shook his head. "I can't believe I'm doing this."

"What?"

"Trying to convince my sister to give Chuck Majors a real chance. I've lost my mind."

Willow and Chad stood at the front window, watching the scene with great interest. "See how stiff she is. He's gonna run," Chad said with a hint of disappointment in his voice.

"Give him time. He's hurt and everything, but he loves her. Chuck is nothing if not tenacious."

Cheri's arms, crossed tight over her chest, didn't budge when Chuck's hand reached out to touch her. Willow winced. "I did that to you a few times, didn't I?"

"What?"

"See how she's holding him aloof—almost punishing him for being him—I know I did that to you."

Chad shook his head. "I don't think it's the same."

"No, Chad, it is." Willow stepped closer, lacing her fingers in his hand as she looked up at him. "I remember once in the craft room—about education I think. It was when Ellie and Tavish were here anyway. I did it then. I wanted you to get upset and leave because then it wasn't my fault and things could stay the way they were."

"Lass, I—"

"I also wanted you to make me see reason. I wanted you to fight for me." Her breath became shallow as she realized what she said. Making herself that vulnerable—even to Chad—terrified her.

"I wasn't going to give up that easily. By that point, keeping you from running was a point of survival for me."

She couldn't respond. Across the yard and under the tree by the pasture, Chuck's hand brushed Cheri's cheek. "Oh, Chad."

"I didn't know he knew how to be tender."

"I did."

"What!"

Willow felt his eyes on her, but she shook her head. "Not with me, Chad. I just saw it in him. He ached to have someone who accepted him—someone other than his mother. Even Nathan doesn't—not really."

"I didn't know you knew Nathan. I've never met him."

"I haven't either, but if you listen to Chuck—"

Chad laid his cheek on her head, pulling her into a hug. "You would have been good for him—Cheri's better, but you would have been. You guys both took the time to listen and see what was behind all the stupidity."

"Gee, that's a very flattering comment about your future brother-in-law."

He stepped back, eyes wide. "I—" Those wide eyes grew wider and he turned Willow's head toward the tree where Chuck and Cheri stood—kissing. "I'm doomed."

Chapter 162

Willow sat in the middle of the garden, sobbing. The boys played nearby in their little exer-saucers, flinging their cereal snacks all over the ground. Had she any doubts of the wisdom of changing their farm plans, they disappeared one late May afternoon.

As she wept, the enormity of the work pressed closer in on her until she thought she'd crush under the weight of it. Despite a healthy crop of weeds growing alongside her first plants, Willow stood and brushed the dirt from her hands. "That's it, lads. We're going. Don't ask me where. I don't know, but we're going."

It took an hour—or most of one—to get ready to leave. She started a roast in the crockpot, and wrote a note for Chad to add potatoes and carrots when he got home from work. The boys needed new diapers and new clothes after drooling and smearing partially masticated Cheerios all over themselves and their jon-jons. She shoved a clean shirt into the diaper bag, changed her own clothes, and managed to stumble down the stairs and out the door. Halfway down the drive, she realized she hadn't locked anything. Her foot hit the brake and then released. It would have to stay unlocked.

Not until she pulled onto the Rockland loop did Willow decide where to go. She took the off-ramp that led to her grandparents' house and pulled up to their door a little over an hour after she left the farm. "Note to self," she muttered as she climbed from the van. "Make sure you always drive this way between two and four o'clock."

Her grandfather hurried down the steps and to the drive before she could pull the boys from their seats. "Is everything all right?"

His panicked tones caught Willow off guard. "Why? What? Yes, everything is fine and horrible both, why?"

"You just showed up without a word in the middle of the day. You don't do that."

Tears sprang to her eyes again. "I know and I'm sorry. I just—I needed a hug from my granddad. I needed out of there. I hate that I needed to get away from the place—" The rest of the words she uttered were unintelligible even to her.

"Carol!"

The call brought Willow's grandmother to the door and grinning. "Oh, Willow! David didn't tell—why is she crying?"

"I don't know yet. Can you take Liam?" David passed the boy to his wife and reached for Lucas. "Let's go inside."

"They need naps. They chattered all the way here instead of sleeping."

Several minutes later, with the boys wailing upstairs and demanding out of their playpens, David hurried downstairs and wrapped his arms around Willow. "Wha—"

"You said you came because you need a hug."

"It's too much. I can't do it."

"Do what?"

"Live my life. I can't."

"So you want out?" David asked. "You want away from home and Chad and the boys?"

"No, I want away from gardens the size of pastures and chickens enough to feed all of Fairbury—"

"I hardly think—"

"Let me be miserable!" Willow wailed. A giggle escaped. "Ok, so maybe half of Fairbury."

"I worried about this, remember?"

"We've been talking about it—trying to find someone to come to help fulltime, but—"

David led her to the couch and pulled her down beside him. "What's wrong? Why can't you find someone?"

"A lot of people who answered the ad we put out hung up when they found out where we are. They knew about Mother and—"

"As sad as it is," David murmured, "that doesn't surprise me."

"It didn't surprise me either—not after I saw how people were after the discovery. But the people who came to gawk..."

"What?"

Swallowing hard, Willow fidgeted, her fingers picking at everything in reach. "The first time, I just thought it was an odd personality—like a Chuck sort of person. But it became obvious after several others that some people just wanted to see the bathroom where it happened. They'd ask, Granddad! They'd ask to use our bathroom and get upset when we sent them upstairs."

"Oh, girlie..."

"Chad started meeting them at the porch and saying that if they asked to use the bathroom, the interview was over. A dozen walked away right there." Willow giggled. "One guy was clever. He waited until he'd been interviewing for half an hour—he seemed so perfect—and then began shuffling awkwardly now and then. Chad almost offered, but I kicked him. Sure enough, the guy said he had to go early. He never returned our call for a second interview."

"So what are you going to do?"

The question couldn't have been a worse one. She looked up into David's concerned eyes, her own filling with tears again, and choked, "I don't know."

Chad's phone rang as he walked the last ten minutes of his beat. David Finley's name flashed across the screen. "Granddad?"

"Willow's here."

"She wha—" He frowned. "What happened?"

"It all became very overwhelming for some reason. She says she just fell apart, got in the van, and found herself getting off at our exit. When I asked why she came she said, 'I needed a hug.'"

The words cut. She could have come to town for a hug from him. "I—"

"You should know that I think she's so overwhelmed she can't think properly. Her first words after her crying jag were, 'I need Chad.'"

"So what do you think I should do—besides show up after work, of course?"

"Keep her away from the farm for a few days. She needs a break."

"Ok, so bring more diapers—"

"Forget the diapers. She's in town where we can throw them away. It'll be good for her to have less work here too." David didn't speak for a moment and then added, "Bring her journal too. I think she de-stresses by writing."

"Writing..." He glanced at his watch and then strolled back toward the station. Each step sent his mind in new directions and brought resolve. "Ok, I have a plan. I'll see you guys in a couple of hours."

Once disconnected, Chad punched Luke's number. "So, what do you have planned for the next few days?"

Chad arrived by dinnertime with a crockpot full of beef and suitcases to last a week—just in case. Willow met him at the truck, and for the second time in a month, gave him a voluntary kiss to knock his socks off. "I'm sorry."

"What for?"

"For just leaving without even saying anything. I just wanted to go for a drive. I didn't really mean to go anywhere but then I was here."

A chuckle followed. "That's hilarious."

"What?"

"Willow Finley, miss 'I'm not driving it if I don't have to' herself decided to go 'out for a drive.'"

She snickered at herself. "I guess it is pretty funny." Her eyes traveled to the suitcases. "What are those for?"

"You're staying until the bathroom is done. We'll start when I get back tonight and work until it's done. Your job is to stay here, rest, and work on your talk for the women's conference."

"But—" She bit her lip. "But I was going to stay with

Mom for that. She's been counting on a few days with the boys."

A slow smile spread over his face. "Then we'll just have to pack them up and drive over to Mom's after dinner. I promised Grandmom that I'd bring that roast."

"She's got potatoes and carrots in the oven—and she made some kind of lime cheesecake."

Just as she reached for the doorknob, Chad stopped her. "Lass?"

"Hmm?"

"I'm probably going to stick my foot in my mouth for this, but I have to say it."

"What?"

"Thanks for remembering about Mom. I wasn't going to say anything—not this time—but she would have been disappointed."

Willow stared at him, stunned at his words. "Well, I would too. I've been looking forward to it."

Her notebook slowly filled with the words Willow wanted to share with the women at the conference. Never having written something like it, she found herself destroying page after page until Marianne suggested she just strike out the words she didn't want and rewrite later. "I'll even type it up if you like."

"That'd probably be good for Mrs. Lanzo. I should learn how, but I don't have time." She glanced up at Marianne. "Where are the boys?"

"Cheri and Chuck decided to take them to swing at the park."

A smile hovered in Willow's heart and spread slowly to her lips. "That's good."

"She's going to marry him."

Willow noted the lack of emotion in Marianne's voice. "Are you sorry?"

"No... not sorry. Surprised and yet, I'm not. I overheard her tell Chris that she'll probably have to propose to him or it'll never happen."

She wrote a few more words before glancing up where Marianne dusted the mantel. "People always underestimate him. I think that's part of why he is the way he is."

"Can you imagine him as a father?"

Willow nodded, grinning. "He sure loves the boys. I've never seen anything like it. Most men seem to push away a fussy child, but it's almost as if Chuck sees it as some kind of challenge. He's going to be a great father."

"Who crushes his kids without knowing it until it's too late."

Those words swirled in her heart as she painstakingly wrote the next few lines. "I don't think so."

"Come on, Willow. He does it now. Stomps all over people's feelings—even when he doesn't want to or tries not to."

"But the child will grow up knowing that. Children are resilient. Don't you tell me that all the time? 'They have to be to survive our mistakes.' Those were your words. If he shows half the love and acceptance as I think he will, it'll help them see the truth. And he is learning to apologize—sincerely."

"Why are you so set on it?" Marianne swiped her duster over the door trim and turned to await Willow's answer.

"Because I can see how much Cheri loves him. Her only hesitation is how he'll be accepted."

Marianne didn't respond to that. She finished dusting the living and dining rooms before putting away her cleaning paraphernalia and moving into the kitchen. "She does love him, doesn't she? I wonder why?"

"Chuck is a little like Chad. I think Cheri knows how to—"

"What! Chad is nothing like Chuck! Chad would never treat people the way Chuck does! He's—"

"Mom!" Willow laughed. "Claws in. I'm not saying he would. Well, that's not quite true. I think Chad raised in the Majors home might have been more like Chuck than he is, but the root of it all is the same. They're both sensitive men. Chad built walls of protection from others around himself. He had good training to show him how to die to self and serve others and it worked."

"And Chuck learned to protect himself."

"Pretty much." She waited until Marianne had poured herself a glass of iced tea and sat down at the table before she added, "Can you imagine how much fun Cheri's wedding will be?"

"He'd better ask soon."

Before Willow could answer, her phone rang. "It's Chad. I'm going to go for a walk while we talk. Be back in a bit."

"Can I read what you have so far?"

"Sure!"

Willow hurried from the house, listening as Chad told of the slow progress on the bathroom. "You were smart to leave. It's a nightmare here. Luke has brought Vannie and Aunt Libby—tomorrow Tavish and Ellie too—to help with weeding, the animals, and things like that. So, we're not getting far behind on everything else. He's even taken Lacey for a few rides for me."

"That's good. I miss you."

"I've got to come out to Westbury and see you. My boys will be half grown by the time I get in there."

"Well, that's probably excessive, but you might enjoy watching Cheri and Chuck."

"Really?"

"Mom has figured out that they're going to get married and she's going crazy."

Chad sighed. "Think you can convince her to give him a chance?"

"I already did. That's why she's going crazy. She wants to do the wedding thing."

"Very nice. So have you been sewing anything? Did you get the peroxide? What about your presentation?" Chad's questions fired at her, one after the other, until she screamed in protest.

"Whoa! Let me see. I haven't bought fabric yet, so I haven't sewn anything. I did get the peroxide and my presentation is about half done I think. Mom's reading it now so it might be less if she says it's awful."

"How can it be awful? It's just you telling who you are and what you do."

Willow sighed. "Because if I write my life exactly as it is today, I'm not writing about what I'm supposed to. If I write it how it's going to be when we find our helper, I'm lying about today."

"So write about how it was, how it is, and how it's going to be. If we have someone by the time you speak, change the last bit to how it is then."

She stopped mid-stride. Glancing around her, she wondered where she was and how far it was to get back home. "You just finished the thing for me. I know what to do now."

"You're welcome."

"Thank you, Mr. 'I won't give her a chance to thank me.'"

Chad laughed. "Now don't forget pink. I know how you're dying to sew more pink."

"And purple, and yellow, and peach, and white—lots of white." She glanced up at the street sign. "Chad?"

"Hmm?"

"How do I get home from the corner of Lake and Sunset?"

Chapter 163

Willow stepped into the fabric store, reveling in the same amazing feeling as the variety of fabrics, trims, and notions filled her eyes again. Why had she not felt awed and invigorated over the volume of clothing at stores in those first days off the farm? Had she already been numbed to variety by the time she entered, or did the promise of creativity override what would have been overwhelming?

Josh saw her first, calling out as he wove through round tables of fabrics. "How are you!" He frowned. "And where are those adorable boys!"

"I'm great and the boys are being properly spoiled by their grandmother. Came for that pink flannel you told me about."

"It's a girl!" Josh's enthusism spread to a few others who sent them curious looks. "I just knew it would be. I told Becca last week that I was going to cut some and bring it out to you, but I got sidetracked."

"I was hoping you and she might want to go out to dinner with me."

"Let me call her right now. Hold on." As he dialed and waited for Becca to answer, he led Willow to an heirloom-sewing corner of the store and pointed to the Swiss wool challis. "This stuff is just fabulous. You have to feel that."

While she chose the colors she wanted, choking at the price per yard, Josh arranged with Becca to meet after work. She added more diaper flannel to the pile, preparing for the boys' next sizes, and added a bolt of embroidered voile. "It's crazy to buy it now," she admitted as he disconnected his call, "but it's so pretty and maybe I'll have time to make something by the time it's warm enough to wear it."

"I was going to show you that. I saw it and thought, 'That just fits Willow. It's perfect.'"

He dragged her to a shelving unit full of books. "I saw this book come in the other day and I almost bought it for you then, but I wasn't sure. It seemed very you, but some of the little notes are so New Age or Neo Pagan that I hesitated."

She flipped open the book and smiled at the little patterns for dolls, clothes—everything in classic Waldorf style. "Oh, this is adorable. I do want this. The ideas are exciting."

"Becca said you would say, 'I don't know if I have room on my shelf for it. I'll have to look first.'"

Laughing, Willow tucked it under her arm and carried it and her fabric to the registers. "She knows me well. We have several craft books of Mother's that I will never use. This will replace those." She nodded at the phone he stuffed in his pocket. "Can she come?"

"Her exact words were, 'I'll get Mae to come over so that I can meet you at the store at five o'clock sharp.'"

"Good." She hesitated, unsure if she should pry, and then couldn't resist asking, "Any reason you guys aren't married yet?"

"Only one?"

"That sounds like a question."

With a sigh that spoke before he did, Josh shrugged. "I'm not ready to hear no or not yet, so I keep putting it off."

"I cannot imagine what would make her say either."

"I cannot imagine why she wouldn't say anything but, 'no way.'" Josh waved and went to put away the bolts she had used. Just as it was her turn to pay, he beckoned to her, hissing, "Willow!"

Excusing herself from the line, Willow hurried to where he stood by the yarns. "What is it?"

"I forgot about this stuff. Come feel it." He led her to a rustic display case. "It's so misleading. You'd expect jute and other rough fibers, but these are the softest yarns and threads

I've ever felt. Wool, bamboo, silk, silk and bamboo combined—heavenly stuff. I just pictured little booties and baby caps and well…"

Before he said the word "softest," Willow's hands ran lightly over the skeins and balls. She fished out a pink, two whites, and a yellow in different weights. "This is lovely and it's less expensive than the yarn store."

"That's what I was thinking. It's just been so long since you've been in, I keep remembering things." His eyes widened. "I just realized something!"

"What?"

"You're going to have fresh inspiration for the Boho line!"

As the server left with their orders, Becca cleared her throat. "I have to ask now or I'll never get the courage."

"What?"

"How are you holding up after the… discovery?" Becca flushed and reached for Josh's hand. "Sorry."

"No, it's fine—well, asking is fine," she clarified. "Let's just say that the ordeal was."

"Was what?" Josh's eyes bounced back and forth between the women, trying to follow the silent conversation they carried.

Becca spoke first. "Was an ordeal. The ordeal was…an ordeal. See?"

"Right." His other hand stretched across the table and covered Willow's arm. "I'm sorry."

"I keep thinking it's over—done. There is no more ugliness, and then bam. Something else happens to prove it's still a problem. At least the reporters stopped bugging us. That RAT strike helped there."

"What kinds of things happen?" Becca scooted her chair closer to Josh's and laid her head on his shoulder. "Man, I'm tired. The kids were crazy today. I swear we're going to have a storm tonight."

"Any excuse to get my arm around her…"

Willow grinned. "I needed this. You two always make me smile."

"You didn't answer the question." Becca's eyes bored into Willow's. "Name one thing—just so I can get a feel for how it's affecting your life in a real way. I live vicariously through you as it is. Why not 'weep' vicariously with you too?"

"I told you about wanting to hire help, right?"

"Yeah... some guy to come out and do all the—what is it you want him to do?"

"Just everything I don't have time to do. Gardens, animal rotation, crops—stuff. We'll have to increase production a bit to be able to afford him and a place for him to live if it works out, but not much. All we care about is breaking even."

"So, with today's job market, why would it be hard to find someone to do that? I mean, even without experience, those aren't hard things to learn, are they?" Becca fidgeted with her silverware as she spoke.

"It's easy enough to learn with training. We're giving that. People just don't want to work where a murder happened *or* they *really* want to see where it happened but that's about all."

"Why a man?"

Josh and Willow stared at Becca. Willow spoke first. "What?"

"Why are you looking for a man? I mean, it's all work you're doing now, right?"

"Yeeesss..."

"So why specifically do you want a man?"

"I don't particularly want a man." She blinked, trying to follow Becca's thoughts. "I don't understand."

"Well, you said you were looking for a man, so I wondered why if a woman has been doing this stuff all these years."

"Well, it was less work," Willow clarified, "and two women. I don't think the ad specified a man, but maybe I'm wrong."

"So man was just generic for person."

"What's with you, Becca? Why hound her about the choice of words? I've never seen you like that."

"Because I want the job."

Becca's answer hung over the table as if waiting to crash

into their dishes. The server arrived with their food as if to maximize the potential invisible destruction. As seconds passed while the server set their plates before them, Josh and Willow stared at one another and then at Becca who fumbled with the napkin in her lap.

"What do you mean," Willow asked cautiously after the server left.

"I mean I want the job. I want to work there. I don't care where there I live as long as I won't freeze. I want to dig in the gardens and make the soap, and butcher the chickens—"

Josh's forkful of chicken lowered to his plate, and Willow could have sworn his skin took on a green hue. "You want to do what?"

Willow shook her head. "Don't say it. I get it."

"What's the problem, with—"

Once more, Willow preempted her. "I think it's a man thing or something. Chad turns green at the idea of it too—particularly chickens. Not sure what the deal is, but there you have it." Her eyes slid to Josh before focusing on Becca again. "What about Ida?"

"Gram would come too I think—maybe not at first. But if it got to the point where we really did consider putting up a real house, she would."

"You'd be so far away," Josh whispered.

"But Chad and Willow have a couch. They'd let you sleep on it now and then." Her eyes begged Willow to confirm her statement. "Wouldn't you?"

"Every night if you wanted, but—"

"But my job—"

"That you hate."

Josh shook his head. "I don't hate my job... just the lack of advancement opportunity. The lack of a chance to be truly creative because I spend all day helping other people find what they need to create."

Tears slowly filled Becca's eyes. "I don't want to see you less. I'm not saying that at all, okay?"

"Yeah..."

"I just don't want to spend the rest of my life watching other people's children grow up. I don't want to spend my life changing other people's children's diapers and teaching other people's children how to count or do fractions. I want to do something that I love if I can't spend my days teaching my own kids to do those things."

"And you love the farm."

"She came alive on the farm, Josh. You should have seen the difference in just a short while. Part of that was meeting you," Willow admitted, "but she really took to all of the work."

"Could she do it?"

"Do what?" Willow blinked slowly, trying to think fast.

"The work—whatever you need someone to do. Could Becca do it all by herself?"

"Sure."

"I want to apply." The first tear spilled. Becca blinked others back and turned an apologetic face to Josh. "I—I don't want to go, but I do want to do this." She stood. "Excuse me."

Willow watched her weave through the tables to the back of the restaurant. Josh stared at his plate. "Should you go with her?"

She shook her head. "I think she needs a moment alone." Willow leaned forward. "Are you all right?"

"No." Josh swallowed. "I can't even try to fix it or it will seem like I just feel manipulated into it—and I don't!" His eyes widened. "I really don't."

"I can't imagine thinking you did."

"The gas will kill me. The hours in the car—so much wasted time. I mean, she's worth it, but—" He sighed. "Here she comes. Do me a favor?"

"Sure."

"If she ever asks if I am sincere, will you try to assure her I am?"

"Going to let her go?"

"Can I stop her?" Josh sighed before smiling up at Becca. "You ok?"

"No, but I will be."

"Becca, you don't have to commit—"

"If you don't want me, then I understand. I don't have a lot of experience and I know I'm going to need a lot of training. If you think I don't really want it, though…" she sniffled before adding, "Willow, I want this almost more than anything else I could think of."

A hairline crack streaked across a corner of Willow's heart. How would someone like Becca stand to choose between a lifestyle she loved and a man she loved? Surely, Josh wouldn't put her in that position, but did she know that? Really know that? "Excuse me. I want to call Chad and make sure he has no objections—what they would be I can't imagine—before I tell you the job is yours."

She hurried outside, fighting back emotions that squeezed another crack into her heart. Her fingers fumbled for the phone keys. "Chad?"

"Hey, what's up? I just put up the first sheet of drywall!"

"Two things—"

He must have heard the pain in her voice because he interrupted her. "Lass, what is it?"

"First," Willow continued as if he hadn't spoken, "thank you for not putting me in the position of choosing you or my lifestyle. At the time you would have done it, I would have chosen my life over you. I would have been wrong, but I couldn't know that then."

"Aw, lass really... what's wrong?"

"Becca wants the job."

"What job?"

She swallowed hard and tried again. "She wants the job on the farm, Chad. She wants to move out there and do it. You saw how much she loved it that week she spent so much time with us. Every time she comes back, what's the first thing she asks?"

"'What do we get to do today?' Get to do. She says that every time. It's so—I don't know, charming."

"And she means it. She wants this job so bad I think it'll crush her if I say no."

Chad grew quiet, the sounds of the drill ceasing. "Wait. Why would you say no?"

"Josh."

"He doesn't—why doesn't he just marry her then!"

"He's afraid of rejection."

Willow snickered as Chad began ranting—at first incomprehensibly. "—think every man has to do? It's part of being a man. You have to risk rejection. I think God set it up that way to keep us humble or something. But so help me if

Chuck Majors can gather the—the—courage to ask Pop if he can propose—"

"He did what? Why didn't you tell me? Does Mom know?"

"I don't know. I assumed you both did."

"Wow." Willow smiled. "Well, that cheered me up a little."

"So Becca and Josh…"

"Can she have the job? I want to give her an answer before I leave so that she isn't left torn any more than she is already."

Chad's answer came swifter than expected. "Of course. Tell her we'll have the fifth wheel delivered the day she wants it. I've already got the septic guy coming out on Monday."

"You do?"

Chad grinned. "I figured we'd be needing it someday, so why not get it ready for that day?"

"I told Josh he could sleep in our house any time he wanted."

"Sure." Chad sighed. "We have to be prepared to lose her. The day Josh gathers the grit to ask, she'll give her notice."

"I know, but at least she'll have a few months or so and maybe that'll give us time to find someone else." Willow laughed. "Maybe absence will make the heart grow fonder."

"I always thought that was a stupid line, but this week I'd say it's true."

"I miss you too." She sighed. "So it's okay?"

"Yeah. And if you get a chance, tell Josh to call me. I have a feeling there's more to this than we think."

Willow hurried into the restaurant and stopped their server on her way to the table. "Can you bring something festive to the table? Dessert, cool drinks—non-alcoholic preferably. Please?"

"Celebrating…"

"New job for my friend."

The young man nodded. "I've got you covered."

Once seated, Willow furrowed her forehead, gave the most apologetic expression she could manufacture and said, "I'm really sorry… Josh. Chad said yes."

Becca squealed, flung her arms around Josh, and kissed him before pulling back again, blushing. "Sorry I—"

"Well, I'm not... I mean I am but—" Josh groaned. "You know what I mean."

The air at the table changed. Trusting her instincts, Willow picked up her purse and pulled it over her shoulder. "You guys finish up. I've got a surprise coming for you. I'll see you later. Call me when you're ready to talk move in dates and things, okay?"

Becca nodded as Josh protested. "Don't go now..."

"You guys need time to process. It's a big change for both of you. I'll see you at the Mission on Sunday if I'm still here." At the front desk, she waited for the check, sliding her card across it. "Can you ask the server to give the third dessert or drink, or whatever he was going to bring, to someone in the kitchen?"

"Oh, we can cancel—"

"He's already put the order in. I'm happy to pay for it. I just hate to see it go to waste."

The server stopped by the front desk just as she pushed the door open. The hostess must have shown her tip and told about the dessert because as the door shut behind her, she heard a single word. "Wow."

Chapter 164

Chad led her onto the porch and through the door, covering her eyes with his hands. She protested with each step, insisting that she wouldn't see a thing until she got to the bathroom door anyway. "I don't care. I want to make sure you see it all at once," he insisted.

Once in position, he ordered her eyes closed tightly and then hurried to stand beside the bathroom door. Gesturing like a game showgirl, he said, "And behind bathroom door number one..."

Willow stood there, unmoving, unblinking, eyes tightly shut.

"I said, and behind—"

"I heard you."

"Then open your eyes!"

"You didn't tell—" She swallowed hard. "—me to open them." Her eyes turned to Chad. "Oh..."

"Don't you dare cry."

"It's perfect."

"Isn't it? I don't know how Luke managed, but—"

She stepped forward, running her fingers over the hand-carved trim. The door looked as though it had always been there—blended into the wall as a natural fixture of the room. Willow turned to thank Chad and found herself alone. The boys.

The doorknob—how had they found one to match the rest of the house? She turned it and pushed the door open.

Nothing about the room felt familiar and yet it did. They had moved the tub and sink to different walls. She'd never open the medicine cabinet and picture that letter standing there. The cast iron claw-foot tub looked very different from the old tub and tile surround that had been in there. In fact, the bathroom was now identical to the one above.

Liam's babbles behind her made Willow turn. "I can use this." The words seemed inane—almost rude, but she knew Chad would understand.

Chad sagged in relief. "I hoped. I tried. Luke thought I was crazy. He kept saying, "Make it her dream bathroom. Give it all the features you know she's love if she knew they existed or had a chance to try them." He shook his head. "I just knew that you'd feel best with something that felt like it had always been part of your life."

"That's why I married you. You know me—even when you don't get me, you know me."

"You married me to find out what was so great about that *North and South* kiss and you know it."

A slow smile crept over her lips. "That too."

Her fingers toyed with her napkin as Chad read her notes. She had written every word of her speech—jokes and all—and now she awaited his opinion. He hadn't gone far when he paused. "What are the asterisks for?"

"I wondered if maybe I couldn't have large prints made of photos of things to switch out at those intervals. Like this!"

Willow jumped from her seat and rushed to find a few scrapbooks, talking all the while. "I thought maybe later when I talk about the changes to the farm and then scaling back again—showing before and after pictures." She dropped the books on the table and flipped to a picture of the farm the day Kari bought it and then dragged out the ones she had recently taken. "See?"

"Get me the negatives and the digital files I'll make a PowerPoint presentation. You can just click it when—"

"What is that?"

"Ok, Cheri will take care of it. Just get me the negatives

and names of the digital files. Once you see how it works, it'll be easier if you ever do it again."

"So do you think it's what Mrs. Lanzo wants?"

"It is." Chad smiled up at her. "I need to read this often."

"Why?"

"Close your eyes."

Willow protested, "What? That's—"

"Come on, close your eyes and pretend you're Cheri or even Mrs. Lanzo." As she tried to relax, Chad read a section. It took a moment for her to quit anticipating the next words and just listen. "'—live life as the gift of God that it is. This isn't the avoidance of the mundane aspects of life but the embracing of them. To live life deliberately and enjoy it as a gift makes simple tasks such as cleaning a sink or peeling potatoes an act of art and beauty. It makes the choice between a walk at sunset or another half hour in front of a TV show or movie you don't even like a non-question.'"

"I was afraid people might think that I was condemning the TV show or movie, but Mom said that they should understand the 'don't even like' to be what I mean."

"Well, and there'll be a Q&A afterward, right?"

"Q&A?"

Chad nodded. "Didn't you say they told you that there would be fifteen to twenty minutes of questions and answers?"

"Oh, yes. I see. They'll ask what I mean and I can clarify." She sighed. "Chad, I don't like it."

"What?"

"My words. They sound stuffy. They don't sound like me." She dropped her head in her hands, her elbows leaning on the table. "I don't think I'm any good at this."

"Tell me."

"What?"

Chad took her hand, gazed into her eyes, and said again, "Tell me. Tell *me*. Just explain your life to me as if we're having a conversation."

"Oh. Okay." She sighed. "I feel silly. My brain refuses to come up with anything."

Chad stood to fill his glass with water, lost in thought. "Okay then write your talk as if it was a letter—or better yet, one of your journals. If you were writing to explain what Mother tried to do here and how it worked in the practical and philosophical senses both, how would you write it?"

She reread several sections of the speech and then ripped them from the notebook, tossing them into the cook stove. "I know what to do, I think. You're right. I need to keep it conversational instead of formal."

Her fingers reached for her pen and she started again. Chad stood over her shoulder, reading for several lines, before he sat down beside her and watched as she formed words. After a few minutes, she hardly noticed his presence. The words flowed freely and relaxed as the familiar overtook her.

Willow slid the notebook across to Chad. "Is that part better now?" She stood over his shoulders, reading as he did, one hand on his shoulder in hopes of feeling his response before he spoke it.

Many people have told me about their desire to embrace a "simple life." I didn't realize, at first, that they meant my life—that they considered my life simple and "easy." My life, while simple compared to the busyness of so many that I've observed, is anything but easy. I work hard for most of every day and I have for my entire life. Even before my husband and I expanded our operation, I had full days of hard work. It is a beautiful, rich existence. It is all I know, but it is not easy despite its simplicity. We create beauty in work because to do otherwise is to exist in the mundane rather than embrace it and transform it. I cannot avoid peeling potatoes or scrubbing floors, but I can choose to see them as the brush strokes of a life lived in pursuit of beauty and deliberate living.

"That's it, lass. That's my Willow. That's the spirit of this place. Write the rest of your talk like this and either read it until you know exactly what you want to say or memorize it or even—" he hesitated before continuing. "No, don't."

"What?"

"Willow, I think this is the real problem. Write this out so you have an outline for yourself—so you'll have an idea how much information you can convey in the amount of time you're given. After that, print this out and hand out to the women there, but don't read it on the platform. Just talk to them as if you were giving them a tour of the farm and explaining your life. One on one—just you and each individual woman. You'll be great."

Marianne stood close, one hand reaching out for her half a dozen times a minute. "Now don't be nervous. They're excited to hear what you have to say."

"Shh... did you hear that woman? To lose every memory and have to start over with a family who knows her when she doesn't know herself—doesn't like herself. Wow." Willow strained to hear the next words, but rousing applause filled the auditorium. "Will she have a question and answer session too?"

"I assume so. Then we break for twenty minutes and it's your turn. Would you like a snack?"

"Probably. But would you go out and ask a question for me?"

Marianne nodded. "Sure. What question?"

"Ask her if she could go back and have all those memories back would she do it?"

The moment Marianne stepped from the room, Willow sagged in relief. She pulled out her phone and called Chad. "It's like the wedding all over again. She keeps trying to reassure me that my nerves are going to make it."

"Not nervous?"

"Not really. I'm just telling people what they asked me to tell them. Why should I be nervous?"

Chad laughed. "Remember how you felt when you first saw Rockland—the buildings towering over you?"

"Yeah..."

"That's how a lot of people feel when they see a sea of faces out there."

"I was picturing them as a garden, but okay." She glanced up and saw Cheri with a boy on each hip. "Oh, Cheri's here with the boys. I'm going to try to feed them before it's my turn."

She pocketed the phone, smiling at her husband's

bungled reassurance that all would be well with her lack of nerves. Even he didn't understand. What had been annoying became amusing as she fumbled with her shirt. Liam toddled to her knees and looked up at her, expectantly. "Hungry, lad?"

"I doubt it. They've been munching on everything in that bag," Cheri muttered. "I couldn't keep Mrs. Majors from feeding them absolutely everything."

"They'll survive once."

By the time each boy ate, she had less than five minutes to adjust her clothes, brush out her hair, and flip through her set of index cards. Those single word prompts had restructured her entire talk. She fingered the borders she'd drawn on each card, traced the outline of a maple leaf from one corner, and smiled at the word "Daisies" written in her best penmanship and with the "I" drawn as the flower.

Show the cards, lass. They'll understand you better from those simple cards than a thousand words can express. Maybe that's what they mean by, "A picture is worth a thousand words."

Chad's words echoed in her heart as she waited for the call to the podium. Marianne took the boys from Cheri as her sister-in-law came to join her. "Ready?"

Willow nodded. "Excited. I love what you and Chad did with the pictures. They'll help me not to talk too fast, too slow, too much—perfect."

"Be sure you don't forget to turn on the mic or people will only hear the music."

From the auditorium, Willow heard her name called. "—pleased to welcome, Willow Finley Tesdall of Walden Farm."

The applause startled her. Considering the applause she'd given and heard for the other speakers, it shouldn't have, but Willow hadn't really considered herself an "official" speaker. She stepped up to the podium, smiled, and fumbled for the mic. "I know it's here somewhere."

Cheri laughed and punched the button for her. Leaning close to the little mic pinned to Willow's blouse, she said, "Willow and technology—scary combination sometimes."

The room erupted in chuckles. Willow smiled and waved her cards. "I am under orders from my husband to tell you about these cards. So before Cheri works her magic with the laptop, I thought I'd tell you a little about them and why they are what they are." She frowned. "You know, I should have thought about making spares or taking pictures or something. I could have just passed them around the room."

"Willow!" Cheri's hiss behind her caught her attention.

"Yes?"

"Give them to me as you're done with them and I'll take them down."

"Oh, my sister-in-law has an idea. Let's get started then, shall we?"

Cheri started the presentation. Faint music whispered through the auditorium as the photos on the projection screen slowly faded from one to the next. Willow spoke of life on the farm, life with her mother, and faith at the root of every aspect of that life. She spoke of the journals her mother had left and how she now made chronicling her days a priority. "I never knew how much I would treasure Mother's words and wisdom. As a child, it even annoyed me when she'd sit down and write endless lists about when to cut the hay or how much soap we would need before spring and summer." She laughed. "You cannot imagine how much soap we go through on the farm! My mother-in-law says if she had to buy the soap we use, she'd be bankrupt."

Her stories continued through each of twelve cards. Work. Beauty. Joy. Peace. Life. Breath. Daisies. Card after card passed from her hands and into the hands of the audience. She heard the song coming to its final close and changed the direction of her speech.

"I promised to tell you about those cards and then I didn't. I think the most precious gift anyone has ever given me was a yellow colored pencil—the exact golden yellow of a manila envelope. Do you know the color?"

Heads nodded all over the room, but the expressions on those faces told her that she'd made the right decision. This was important.

"You see, part of that beauty is in the simple things like manila envelopes or index cue cards for a speech." She smiled. "Chad says he'll never forget the day I pulled out one of our decorated envelopes that held tax records. We always color them—make them beautiful. It's part of who we Finley women are. I expressed an interest in white envelopes when Chad mentioned them but dismissed it almost immediately and because of only one thing." She paused. "I didn't want the tops of the white envelopes to be different from the tops of the manila ones. It would bother me seeing them in a box all mixed up like that."

A smile crossed her face. "That is why the pencil my husband bought me is so precious to me. The day he brought it home is the day I saw that he not only loved me—he accepted and loved the life that we have. I never truly saw that until that day."

Chapter 165

Ida and Becca worked to fill the fifth wheel with Becca's things. Dishes, clothing, bedding, books, laptop, and few bags of groceries slowly turned a large trailer into a small home. Willow and the boys slowly walked across the property once Becca sent a text that she was all moved in and ready for company. By the time she arrived, Ida sat relaxed on the sofa with a glass of water in her hand. "This is so nice! I can't believe how much room is in this thing."

"So, are you going to move out here with me now, Gram?"

Willow laughed as Ida shook her head. "Not until I see how you do with a winter in this thing first. June is one thing. January is quite another."

"I thought Josh was coming."

Becca sighed. "He is...just not until later. Had to work after all. That Marie is getting more and more undependable, and they always call him when someone doesn't show."

"I'm hoping he'll wake up and—"

"Gram, please!" Becca looked miserable. "She's convinced that Josh will come rushing out here, begging me to marry him."

"As nice as that sounds, I'd miss my helper and I haven't even gotten to use her yet."

Becca shook her head. "I already told Josh that even if I hate it, I'm not quitting without three months' notice."

"Why that long?"

Ida interrupted before Becca could answer. "He needs to know there are consequences to waiting."

"Gram!"

"It's true! I don't know what is wrong with that man."

Hoping to diffuse what seemed to be a sore subject, Willow decided to speak her mind. "I think he is scared. He made a decision once—the wrong one—because someone told him something about himself that wasn't true. He has to live with that choice every day. I think it's hard to risk being that vulnerable again because it means he has to ask someone else to live with it with him."

"Well, he has time to think about it now. We've known each other for two years and if he needs more time, that's fine. I'll even wait. I'm just going to do something I love while I'm waiting in case my entire life becomes a matter of waiting."

Something about Becca's words didn't fit the Becca Willow knew. She remembered what Josh had told her and added one last encouragement before diving after the boys as they tried to climb the cabinets. "He once asked me to make sure you knew that he has no doubts about *you*. Whatever slows him down—it's not you."

Josh walked beside Chad around the square, up Market Street, down Elm, and back again. "I don't know what to do. I just don't know. She—that farm. I know it's your home, but do you have any idea how opposite we are in this? She loves it. I cringe at the dirt on my shoes or the smell of manure. Can you believe she stopped the car the other day when we drove by a house that had just spread manure over the lawn? Manure! She said, 'Man that smells good.'"

Chad laughed. "Yeah, I don't think Willow would say it smells good. She'd pull out the lavender and crush it, sprinkle powder through the house to try to combat it. But she wouldn't get rid of the cow."

"I can't even get a job in Fairbury. There's nothing here. I looked."

As Josh described his job at the fabric store, the

inspiration it gave him, and the frustration he felt when he couldn't act on that inspiration, Chad began thinking in a new direction. "You liked carding, didn't you?"

"Carding—oh the wool. Yeah. That spinning wheel was fun too. And the loom. See, I could do that all day."

"So why don't you?"

Frustrated, Josh threw up his hands. "It's called living. Maybe you've heard of it?" A pedestrian gave Josh a strange look, making the man lower his voice. "It requires money for things like rent, insurance, food, clothing, and gas to see your girlfriend sixty miles away."

"If she was your wife, you would only need enough to cover your insurance. The rest—food, shelter, money for clothing et cetera would be covered."

"So I do what?" Josh shrugged. "Make macramé plant holders and sing 'Kum Bah Yah?'"

"You create. You do whatever it is you've been wanting to do for the past however many years. You do it because you're in a position to be able to do it."

"So I marry Becca for her money."

Chad laughed. "You marry her because she's the right girl for you. You suck it up, get your testosterone in order, and show her exactly what she needs—that you're the man in her life. You give her that confidence in you." Josh started to interrupt, but Chad continued, talking over him for a few seconds until he grew quiet again and listened. "You do what men have done for decades—probably centuries. You let your wife help keep food on the table while you establish yourself in your field. You're not a doctor. She's not putting you through med school or college so you can be an engineer. Instead, she's milking goats so you can establish yourself as some kind of textile artist."

They turned another corner, Chad pointing to a car with a silent warning to slow down. He felt confident that Josh would see reason. In fact, if he could trust his gut, Becca would be engaged before midnight. Maybe there was something to matchmaking after all.

"Sounds like a dream come true."

Chad almost pumped his fist but managed to contain himself in time. "Sounds pretty perfect to me."

"Until she ends up pregnant and unable to mow hay or weed gardens or whatever this job is going to be. Then what?"

A sick feeling filled Chad's heart. Josh had a point. "Then you man up and do it for her until she can again. You find someone else to do it or you insist that she quit. You do what you have to do to protect your family—starting with your wife."

"She'd resent that."

"If you had proposed before that dinner with Willow, she never would have asked for the job, Josh. She asked for it because waiting around for another two years for you to get your courage up would break her heart." Chad stopped and gave Josh his best, "I'm an officer, listen to me" glare. "She'd go home with you today if you asked her. She loves you."

For an hour after Willow and her Gram left, Becca tried to wait for Josh. He should have been there hours earlier, but he didn't answer his cellphone and didn't respond to texts. The store had been closed for over two hours. Was he injured in some accident and unable to call? Had he decided that she abandoned him so the relationship was over? Why wasn't he there?

She tried reading a book. The words blurred together into nonsensical hieroglyphics. She tried watching a movie on her laptop, but when the scene replayed for the third time and she still didn't hear why the main character slapped the antagonist, she shut it with a little too much force. Becca tried everything, but she was too agitated to sleep before the sun went down and nothing else held her interest long enough to distract her.

Laughter filled the trailer—weak and a little hollow but the sound comforted anyway. She could leave the silly trailer. She could go into town, get an ice cream, go visit Adric and Jael, walk over and play double Chinese checkers with Willow, or just go for a walk along the stream. The latter won out.

Becca strolled away from the trailer and down the hill toward the stream. In the quiet of the evening, she could only hear the occasional car whiz past on the highway. Her eyes sought the little lane that led from the highway to where her trailer—and someday a house would be. Would she be the one to live in that house? Becca couldn't imagine not being the one, but that meant that Josh also was not "the one—" a thought that broke her heart every time she paused to think of it.

Somewhere, a car door slammed. Was it at Adric's house? Was she closer than she thought? It didn't seem likely, but she was much too far from Willow's house for it to be the Tesdalls. A voice called out—called her name. She smiled, turned, and ran. He came.

As she neared the trailer, she answered him. "Coming!"

Josh met her at the corner of the trailer. She started to throw her arms around him, but his hands never left his pockets—something she'd never seen him do. So this was it. He was there to break up with her. Though it didn't surprise her, Becca's throat still tightened as she struggled to find a way to assure him that she understood—despite the lie it was.

"I talked to Chad."

Becca didn't quite know what to make of the abrupt statement. "You did?"

"Yeah. I like fashion. You like farming."

"And we won't work." She sighed and nodded. "I understand."

"I don't."

Becca's head snapped up as she sought his eyes. "What?"

"I thought you cared about me."

"Josh, I love you. You know that."

"So why," he asked, his voice growing husky with pain, "do you say you understand that we won't work. Why won't we work?"

"You said—"

"I stated the obvious. People do that when they don't know how to say what they are afraid to say." He sighed. "Look. I want to say that I can help you with the farm stuff and we'll live happily ever after, but I know I can't. I can't promise, that is. I can promise to try."

"Josh—"

"I want to marry you. I want to make this work. If we

can't make it work here, then we'll make it work somewhere else. You can run tractors and butcher chickens. I'll design clothes or hand paint fabrics or something."

"Really?"

His lips traced her cheekbone to her ear as he whispered, "Really. Now will you marry me?"

"Definitely."

They sat on her couch, talking late into the night until Josh bolted upright. "Oh no!"

"What?"

"I asked you to marry me!"

Becca nodded slowly. "And that's a bad thing?"

"It kind of ruined the proposal I've been planning for almost two years." He sighed.

"What did?" Becca smiled.

Josh stared at her. "Asking—"

"No one asked me anything. You just came out here to admire my new house. If you have something to ask, can you do it some other time?" Becca winked now. "I really need to get to sleep early. I have a lot of work tomorrow."

"Sure. Call me." He made it halfway to his car before he called back, "Oh, and what are you doing Saturday night?"

Chapter 166

For days, whenever Becca stepped into the house, Willow disconnected a call and refused to answer questions about the conversations. She knew her new employee was suspicious, but it seemed ridiculous to pretend nothing was happening. Josh had practically announced something coming. When, where, how... that would be the surprise.

So, when Becca brought in a set of reprinted journals with questions flagged and Willow pointed to the table and stepped outside, Becca's exasperated expression amused her greatly. Once she was out of earshot of the windows, Willow murmured, "We're driving her crazy. You're a genius."

"Well, my idea wasn't going to work—not with this new life of hers."

"Yours."

"Right," Josh agreed with that same trace of nervousness he had every time they discussed it. "Ours."

"I think changing your romantic dinner the way you did is brilliant. It's perfect for both of you, and I think if you're going to take the time to do something special for a proposal, the least you could do is make it reflect each of your personalities and tastes."

For several seconds, Willow heard nothing. She called out for Josh twice, but no response. She stared at the phone, listening, looking, and almost disconnected when Josh's voice returned, laced heavily with emotion. "I needed to hear that. Thanks."

The emotional side of Josh often unnerved her. She had considered Chad to be quite sensitive for a man—probably thanks to Dad Tesdall's opinion—but once she knew Josh better, that idea had disappeared. Compared to Josh, Chad seemed nearly emotionless. Still, that kind of gentleness and sensitivity seemed to bring out the best in Becca. "And that's what a man should do."

"What?"

Willow nearly brushed it off as thinking aloud without telling him the source of her thoughts, but something seemed to compel her to explain. "I was just thinking about how you bring out the best in Becca. You make her stronger and yet you carry her burden for her at the same time. It's truly beautiful."

"If it's true, it's by accident and probably a lot of example. I've often thought that of you and Chad." She heard the hard swallow as Josh tried to rein in his emotions. "I hope it's true."

"It is. I wouldn't say it if it wasn't."

"So, we're good for tomorrow afternoon?"

The abrupt change of subject unsettled her thoughts. "Um—yes. Right. I'll have everything in the back of the truck. If you drive it out there and unload it for me, I'll set it up while you come back to change and dress."

"This is going to be great!"

Willow sighed, relieved, as she disconnected the call. Josh was back—the enthusiastic Josh that she loved. A thought filled her mind and refused to leave. Before she could act, Liam's squawk sounded from the upstairs window. "And the troops are up and ready for action. It would be cruel to strap them in those car seats," she muttered as she strolled to the back door.

Becca's feet were on the first steps as Willow reached the living room. "I'll get them. I have an errand for you."

The young woman stepped aside as Willow jogged up the steps. "What do you need?"

"C'mon. Let's talk." As she changed the boys, she told Becca her plan. "Look, we both know that Josh is planning something special, right?"

"Yeeesss…"

"Well, I think you need to have a new dress. Well," Willow winked at Lucas before she glanced at Becca, "I think the truth is I want to make one and don't need one and this is a good excuse."

"Sounds like you. What kind of dress?"

"You need to go to Josh's store and pick out something. Try to get his input, but I'd want some kind of printed or embroidered voile if I were you. Maybe chiffon, but voile breathes better."

"I think I know what chiffon is but voile..."

"He'll know."

Becca grinned. "Isn't it great? I've got a guy who is a great fashion consultant. I'll never be able to get frumpy and blah, because he won't let me."

"There you go. I doubt you would have anyway, but—"

As she took Lucas from Willow, Becca shook her head. "No, I would. I know me too well. I need that kind of encouragement. It's too easy to throw my hair in a ponytail, toss on jeans and a t-shirt, and go. I bet I'd become a 'sweats all day' kind of gal after a baby or two."

"Can you see Josh with a baby?" Willow giggled. "He's already nuts over these guys. He's going to be amazing."

"Sooo... buy fabric."

"Yep, fast. You need to get there and back as soon as possible or I'll never get it done. You might also have to add a bit of child care to your job description today and tomorrow."

"But..." Becca bit her lip and glanced around her.

"But what?"

"Well, wasn't the point of hiring me so that you didn't have these things to take you away from the boys?"

"The point," Willow corrected, "was not to have things that don't matter to me crowd out the things that do. I can afford an afternoon and morning devoted to a project I'm dying to do. That fits in the general scheme of 'living life to the fullest' and not being a slave to the 'next thing' that demands my time."

With both boys changed and ready for play, Becca and Willow took them downstairs, attached the gate that sometimes worked to keep the little climbers off the stairs, and stared at one another, grinning. Becca took a deep breath and exhaled slowly. "It's really happening, isn't it?"

"What is?"

"Me, getting married, and to Josh. Josh wants me!"

"He's nervous, you know."

Worry flooded Becca's eyes. "About what?"

"That he'll fail you. You did the right thing coming out here and living your life, but it's an adjustment for him. He really thinks he's going to have to learn to love large animals, shoveling manure, and tilling soil."

"But that's my job." Becca smiled. "He's going to learn to cook. He thinks he'll enjoy what he wants to call 'country gourmet.'"

"I don't know what that means, but it sounds good."

"Omelets made with expensive sausages and cheeses, meatloaves with whatever ingredients that make it incredible in some... incredible way." Becca blushed and shrugged. "I don't understand it all. We eat very plainly, but hey. What can I say? I don't know what I'm talking about, but he's amazing with stuff like this."

"That explains a lot."

"Of what?"

Willow shook her head and dove for the gate. Liam screeched his objections as she removed him from danger. Ignoring Becca's curiosity, she stared at her son, shaking her head. "No, Liam. Hush."

The tyke stared at her between wails, and let out an even more furious yell of protest. "Okay then. In you go. He who fusses can fume alone."

Becca shoved her hands in her jeans pockets and shuffled her feet. "Sheer fabric—blue."

"Blue. Now get out of here."

Chad's truck crept up the drive as he craned to stare at the odd sight before him. Two o'clock, no call from Willow so all must be well, but the house was ablaze with light. That thought prompted a snicker. Ablaze. A few oil lamps glowing near windows—ablaze. Sure.

Still, there were lamps lit—probably a candle or three

too—in nearly every room. Even the library seemed aglow with the amber light of the oil lamp. What could she be doing?

He stepped from the truck and shut the door softly. Portia rushed to his side, nudging him toward the house as if to say, "Something's wrong in there and if I can't get in to fix it, you must."

"It'll be all right, girl. I promise. If anything had gone wrong, she would have called—now." The memory of a time when that wouldn't have occurred to her filled him with gratitude for the change.

A strange sound—one he knew but couldn't place—filled the night air, interrupting the whisper of the trees in the breeze and the sound of a lone mockingbird in search of a mate. As he jogged up the steps, the sight of Willow at the treadle made him smile. Sewing. So engrossed was she in her project that she didn't notice him. She raced upstairs, quietly calling Becca. "Okay, I think I have the fit right this time."

Becca. It must be a dress for the big night. He shouldn't have been surprised. Willow had talked of nothing else, which he found highly amusing. A small smile crept over his lips as he heard gales of laughter fill the upstairs. A few giggles followed, and then laughter erupted all over again.

It occurred to him that she'd never had the slumber party experience. Girls giggling over boys, doing weird things to hair and whatever else Cheri and her friends had done throughout junior high and high school. He stepped inside and grinned at the sight of fabric scraps flung willy-nilly all over the room. Oh yeah, it was a Willow-fest of epic proportions. Blue and sheer—exactly as she'd mentioned. Becca would look lovely in it.

The kitchen showed evidence of ice cream, brownies, and Willow's canned cherries. His mouth watered. Chad peeked into the warmer at the top of the stove and sighed. His wife, without any doubt, loved him. In bowl and covered by a plate, a brownie sat waiting for him. That it was for him, he had no doubt. A glance into the icebox showed a bowl of ice cream waiting for him too.

Giggles wafted down the stairs as Willow and Becca returned to the living room. "Chad's home!"

Chad's heart swelled at those words. The joy, excitement,

and utter delight to hear he had returned—why had he ever resisted the idea of marriage? "In here, Lass. This better be my brownie and ice cream because I'm pretty sure no one wants it anymore."

Willow burst into the kitchen, Becca following with a smile on her face. "Yay! You're here. We're making a dress for Becca. It's going to be amazing."

"You're making it. Of course it will." He grinned at Becca. "Isn't she great when she gets like this?"

"I've only seen it a few times, but—"

"Now that you're here, you're going to see it more," Chad insisted. "This is the Willow I met. The one who hand paints fabric just so she can use up scraps from another project—that's Willow."

"She didn't!"

Willow nodded. "I had enough for one, but not two, so I made it work." She winked at Becca. "It's what we do."

Chad's laughter filled the kitchen. "How many times did I hear that?"

As a tickle fest ensued, Becca backed toward the door, grabbing a flashlight from the bench. "I'll be here in the morning. Don't stay up too late."

"I'm not going to bed until it's done." Willow pointed to the door as Becca hesitated. "You come back and help Chad while I sleep—if I get to sleep. I'm going to sew."

She turned and left the room, a small smile on her lips. Chad shrugged at Becca. "You heard the woman. Sleep. I'll get the goats, but I'll leave the watering to you unless you think you'll sleep past ten…"

"Ten? What a cushy job."

"When your boss keeps you up until all hours, I'd say ten is reasonable. It's past two-thirty." Chad opened the back door and pushed open the screen for her. "Let Portia follow you if she wants to."

Willow heard the shower shut off just as she finished sewing the lining and dress together. It would be perfect—perfect! She grabbed a sleeve and matched the ends. As she worked, her mind worked through the steps, trying to avoid missing a step in her sleep-deprived state. *Right sides—no wrong sides together. Sew. Trim. Flip. Right sides together. Sew. Press with the bone folder. Repeat.*

Chad stood at the base of the stairs, leaning against the bannister, his quarter inch hair plastered against his head. He didn't dry it in warmer weather. She glanced up at him, as she pinned the sleeve to the arm scythe. "Warm tonight?"

"Not much. Just thought I'd sleep well with my head cool. Long day."

"Did they get the new meters installed?"

A yawn preceded Chad's nod. "Yep. They remove the covers on Monday. We're pointing them out to everyone, but I bet our first month is a doozy."

"Well, if it pays for more officers, it's worth it." She held up the pinned sleeve and inspected it. "Almost there!"

"You're that close to done?"

"With the machine, yep." Willow grinned. "Then I just have to bind the armholes and hem all the edges."

"Will you be in bed before I wake up?"

"Probably not." She smiled. "I'll get the goats before I go to bed."

Chad pushed away from the bannister and came to stand behind her. Kneading her shoulders gently, he murmured, "Don't overdo it. You can always finish tomorrow afternoon."

"I have a restaurant to assemble. No time to do anything tomorrow. Oh," Willow tilted her head back and gazed into Chad's eyes. "Josh said thanks for the tent frame. He thinks you should sell them. I told him if he wanted to market them he was welcome to do it himself."

His chuckle rumbled as he kissed her forehead. "Got that right. We're not going to kill ourselves by trying to market every interesting idea we have."

As Chad climbed the stairs, Willow lost herself in the project before her. One sleeve, then another—the machine work complete. Needle, thread, two lamps to illuminate the corner, she sat to work.

Chapter 167

Chad rolled over at the sound of the boys' wails. His arm reached to pull Willow back, knowing she'd try to get them, but he grabbed air and a tiny amount of blanket. Lucas protested louder, calling, "Mamamamamamaaaaaa..." as if that would solve all that ailed him.

"Be glad you still believe it does, little man," he groaned as he dragged himself out of bed. Where was she anyway? Why hadn't she gone to bed? Surely it didn't take—he glanced at the clock—six hours to hem a dress and sleeves. Even at a leisurely pace that seemed excessive.

The boys grinned at him, the little white squares on their lower jaws expanding their cuteness factor by a factor of ten—maybe twenty. "*Buenos días, chicos...* or is that *los chicos*? I can't remember. Anyway, that's Spanish for 'good morning.' You might need to know that someday."

All through the morning routine of diaper changes, dressing, and washing hands and faces before breakfast—something that still seemed a waste of time to Chad—he talked. He told them about their mother's late night, how they needed to be quiet so she could sleep, and how much Becca would appreciate the dress. "It's going to be a beautiful dress. Girls like that stuff. You're going to have a sister, so you'll need to remember that. Girls like pretty things."

Liam cocked his head and stared at Chad as if absorbing every word. Just as Chad started to commend his son's wisdom, the boy belched as if he'd already inhaled his breakfast. "Well, son. That might be your opinion, but girls have the right to theirs too."

Halfway down the stairs, he saw Willow asleep—half reclining on the couch. Becca's dress hung from the library doorjamb, swaying in the breeze that blew in through the screen door. Her journal lay abandoned in her lap, and if his eyes didn't deceive him, she'd managed to scrawl across the page when she fell asleep—apparently mid-sentence. "Boys, I'm tempted to take you to the diner for breakfast. Tempted, but not stupid," he sighed as he imagined trying to feed them without creating a mess that spread across the restaurant.

In the kitchen, he felt the stove before setting the tykes down and rushing to wedge the stair gate into place. They seemed happy enough to play with the cloth blocks Willow had created, so he went to work. The breaker flipped on with a flick of the wrist. A morning like this called for his electric kettle. Willow wouldn't know and the boys would be safe while he made their oatmeal.

He dumped the oats in the bowl, sprinkled a bit of salt over them, and drummed his fingers on the counter, waiting for the water to boil. A glance over his shoulder showed Liam heading for the doorway and no sign of Lucas. Chad ran. He nearly vaulted over Liam in his desperation to reach Willow before their son woke her, but he arrived exactly one and a half seconds after Lucas jabbed his finger in Willow's sleeping eye. In the five minutes they'd been down stairs, she had readjusted herself to a horizontal position on the couch—a perfect height for their son's finger to explore.

"Aaaak!"

Lucas screeched. Behind Chad, Liam squawked. Whether Liam's objection had to do with the abuse of his mother or his inability to enjoy investigating cause and effect of fingers to eyes, Chad couldn't determine. Willow sat upright and rubbed her eye. "What—"

Now Lucas laughed. His little belly shook with mirth, prompting a similar giggle from Liam. Chad shrugged. "Apparently injured mothers are the next thing in stand-up comedy."

"Oh. I think I'll go to bed."

Liam reached for the journal that now lay on the floor.

Chad rescued it. "I think that's good. Did you stay up to milk Ditto?"

"Yes. I—" Willow frowned. "Um, I don't remember if I turned off the water on the stove."

"I'll go see."

Before Chad could grab either of his boys, Willow scooped them both up and started toward the stairs. "Okay, little fellows, it's nap time."

"Um, Willow?"

At the first step, Willow tried to wrestle with the gate as she murmured, "Hmm?"

"They just woke up. Their oatmeal is cooking as we speak. Go to bed. I've got this."

"Just woke up. What time is it?"

Chad chuckled. "Seven-thirty."

"Ugh," she groaned as she carried the lads back to their father and deposited them in his arms. "I haven't been asleep for more than half an hour. Good night—morning. Whatever."

She nearly tripped over the gate and paused, glaring at it. Her fingers fumbled before she sighed, grabbed the bannister and flattened one hand against the opposite wall. Hoisting herself over the gate, she took the rest, muttering as she went, "Two, four, six, eight..."

Chad listened for the door to shut—bathroom first. That made sense. Even with the new one downstairs, she rarely remembered it was there. "She'll remember when it comes time to teaching you guys to use it. That'll probably be a while. Let's see how that oatmeal looks..."

While Willow managed to feed them with an efficiency that would have impressed time and motion expert, Frank Gilbreth, himself, Chad took much longer and created a greater mess. That morning, his boys smeared oatmeal on every surface they could reach as he ineffectually spooned too-large portions into their eager mouths. As he did, he read the latest entry, trying to imagine what had prompted her to write on such a late night.

June—

I have managed another first today/tonight. I have

"pulled an all-nighter." *Cheri will be so proud. In the interest of full disclosure, since the written word is powerless to show expression without the author's inclusion, that line was written with a most definite roll to my eyes.*

However, the effort is more than worth it. Becca's dress turned out lovely. I need to tell Josh that my experiment with the lining worked. Having a lining just a hint heavier than the actual fabric ensured that the neckline rolled lovely—not a hint of lining showing anywhere. I wasn't certain it would work. In fact, I'm certain that anything heavier would have been just as bad as anything lighter. Why any of this matters, I don't know. However, the day may come when my Kari needs to know how to do these things, and we'll have the reference. I should put it down in Mother's sewing journals as well. Note: What does Chad think about adding to Mother's journals? Is it a bad idea to combine them like that—not the originals, of course. Just the reference ones. Hmm. We'll see.

Chad doesn't understand why this proposal thing is so important to me. I've seen him watching me as I work on things for it, and tonight, while I was sewing, I realized that he might think I am dissatisfied with his own proposal. Well, it wasn't much of a "proposal" by modern terms, I suppose, but it's ours. It suits us. I can't imagine anything more horrifying to me than imagining how I would have reacted if he had tried to be romantic with me back then. I don't know if we'd still be friends. That idea terrifies me.

So, before I fell asleep and didn't tell him, I wanted to write it down for posterity. I'm glad we did things the way we did. It fits us.

Chad's eyes closed in gratitude, and missed Lucas' next bite, dropping it onto the lad's shoulders.

Lily Allen's sedan sat parked before a meter about to expire. Chad glanced around him, hoping to see her, but saw no sign of her anywhere. He peeked into The Grind, tried to gaze through the window of The Market, and finally fished out a quarter from his pocket and plugged it into the meter.

Aiden Cox, arms wrapped around a skateboard and a helmet hanging from his wrist, watched the proceeding curiously.

"What's that for?"

"It's a parking meter."

The boy stepped forward, examining the machine with even more interest. "I thought it was called an extortionist?"

"I suppose people might feel that way, but these little babies are going to pay for another officer."

"Great. More cops to keep me choking." Though the boy sounded utterly dejected, his grin told Chad he had resigned himself to his fate as a cranial protected citizen. "So why did you put a quarter in it?"

"Because people aren't used to it, and if I didn't, I'd have to write Mrs. Allen a ticket. I don't want to do that, so I paid it this time."

"How long does a quarter give her?"

"Fifteen minutes." Chad smiled as Lily rushed around the corner, fishing in her purse for change. "Got it, Lily."

"Denise took longer today. She kept getting call after call. I thought I was going to end up with blond streaks by the time she got to rinsing my highlights." Lily passed Chad a quarter.

"Not necess—"

"It will be if you keep paying people's meters for them. You saved me thirty dollars. The least I can do is pay it back so you can save some other woman from irritating her husband. This will take some getting used to."

Chad pocketed the quarter, complimented Lily on her new hairstyle, and waved. Aiden stared at him. "Thirty dollars for what?"

"The ticket. If I hadn't put the quarter in there, it would have cost her thirty dollars in fines."

"Wow. That's a lot."

"That's why people should take notice of time." He inched toward the corner where an old burgundy Taurus had been sitting for far too long. "Drat. I missed Abe's car."

"Maybe you should check out the ones down there first. I've just got to go into the Diner for a minute..." Aiden attempted a wink that involved two eyes and a lot of nose scrunching.

Chad nodded. "You're probably right. Need to check that side. Haven't checked it at all." With a wave, Chad took off in the opposite direction, but when he reached the corner, he ducked behind the building and peeked around the corner.

Old Abe Fuhrmann shuffled out of the Diner, digging his fists into the saggy, baggy trousers he'd worn for the past three decades and plugged a few quarters into the machine. He grinned at Aiden as he shuffled back to the door of the diner, and handed the boy a coin or two.

Probably a quarter. Guys like that always think a quarter is the ultimate gift to a kid. That was nice. All along Center and Market Streets, and over to Elm, Chad strolled, checking meters, signaling citizens, and writing tickets when he couldn't place a vehicle. By the time his lunch break came, he'd written over four hundred dollars in tickets—most of which he assumed would be written off if the people complained. The city council had been most insistent that there be a long grace period for residents. Because of that, anyone willing to show up to contest their ticket would likely have it dismissed.

Judith strolled up to him, waving her book. "How many?"

"Fifteen..." He glanced at the book. "No, sixteen."

"Not bad...that's four per hour. I'll see if I can beat that."

"You can. I could have written a couple dozen more..." Chad realized where the conversation would go and tried to dissolve it.

"But you paid them yourself?"

He shrugged. "Mostly just found the owner and warned them—if I knew them."

"Softie."

"They'll get dismissed anyway," Chad protested. "I'm saving Judge Waller time."

An hour later, Chad resumed his beat, ticket book in hand and feeling a lot like a meter maid rather than one of "Fairbury's finest." Unbeknownst to him, as he wrote yet another ticket for an out of state plate sitting for well over an hour past the meter time, Aiden Cox observed from across the street. When Joe pulled up beside Chad and called him to the car for backup, Aiden stood, hooked his skateboard under his arm, and strolled toward the corner.

Chapter 168

Sunlight glowed around the edges of the curtains of Willow's room. She rolled over, pushing back one corner to see the time on the clock. Two o'clock. Exhausted, she pulled the light cover over her shoulder, rolled onto her other side, and closed her eyes. Seconds after she slipped into semi-consciousness, Liam's cry from outside sent a flood of milk through her ducts, demanding release.

"Ugh. If I had any doubt about being able to nurse Kari, these boys seem to ensure it won't be a problem." She stood, swaying from exhaustion and insufficient hydration. It took time, but she managed to stumble downstairs and plop herself in the porch swing with a mason jar of water on the window ledge.

Becca played with the boys in the yard, rolling balls in opposite directions. This drove Portia crazy as the dog tried to corral both boys at the same time. "Are either of them hungry? I'd rather avoid that machine if I can avoid it."

Lucas heard her voice and raced for the steps. He crawled up them faster than he ever had and practically flung himself across the porch and at her knees. "Mamama!"

"Hungry?"

Willow's son's eyes slid to her chest and back to her face as he grabbed her shirt. She shook her head at Becca and said, "He's all boy in one way or another."

"How's that?" Becca led Liam to the porch, much to Portia's apparent satisfaction. Once both boys sat near

Willow, the dog laid beside the swing, head on her paws, resting.

"He's either obsessed with food or with the source."

Becca's laughter filled the afternoon air. "Or both."

A glance across the yard brought a frown to Willow's face. "Where's Chad?"

"Oh! He got called into work. Brad got spit on by some guy with blood in his mouth, so they sent him—Brad that is—to the clinic to get tested or whatever they do."

Dread slowly washed over Willow. "Oh... so he probably won't be back by four..."

"Nope. He said he'd have to work the whole shift. Brad had just started and got called to a fight at the Aphrodite." Becca kicked her toe in a crack between porch floorboards. "Joe took over that case, so Chad got Joe's beat too."

"Poor Chad. They start ticketing today."

"Chad voted against that measure, didn't he?"

Willow nodded. "Yes. I'd like to say it was a philosophical objection to further taxation, but I'm pretty sure he said, 'I'm not voting for me to become a stupid parking inspector.' Pride, pure and simple."

"But if it gets them the officers they need..."

"I suppose." Willow grinned down at her milk-drunk son as he sat up and blinked. "Full?"

"Mmmm."

"Loquacious little tykes, aren't they?" she muttered as she reached for Liam. "When did they last eat?"

"Chad said he fed them a lighter lunch—just enough to tide them over. If you didn't get up by three, I was supposed to give them more." Becca pulled out her phone and glanced at it and smiled to herself before shoving it back in her pocket.

"Looks like I made it just in time. Can you go find me my phone?"

While Becca retrieved the requested phone, Willow's mind went into overdrive. She had an hour and a half to get reinforcements and kick Becca out of her yard. The moment Becca returned, Willow sent her inside. "First, you need to try on that dress."

Becca blushed. "I did. For the record, I think your

husband would like to see a very similar dress to that one on you."

"Oh?"

She shrugged and grinned. "I believe he said something to the effect of, 'She needs to make one for herself—in red.'"

"Red. Hmmm..." Willow shook her head. "I don't need any new dresses. If anything, I have too many. Did you know I have three different sizes of clothing in there? Half of them I doubt I'll ever wear again—maybe more."

"You like to sew, right?" Becca didn't wait for an answer. "So why don't you take those clothes, bundle them up, pass them onto someone who would love to have them, and make you things that fit. You win with something fun to do, and they win because they get a new wardrobe that they otherwise couldn't hope to have."

"I'll think about it."

Becca pointed to the strawberry beds. "I'm going to go do some more weeding. I tried with the boys, but they wanted to help. Let's just say that they consider pinkish berries to be weeds and leave it at that." She nodded at the boys. "Call me if you need me—to take a shower or whatever. I just really wanted that off my list today."

Just as Willow stood to take the boys upstairs for diaper changes, Becca returned. "Willow?"

"Hmm?"

"Make the dress. Even if you keep every single thing you own, make that dress. I think Chad needs to—" she stopped mid-sentence and turned. "Never mind. It's none of my business."

"I'd rather hear it, actually. What do you think Chad needs?"

The young woman froze, but didn't turn. Several seconds passed in which flies tried to annoy her boys and Willow grew impatient. Just as she started to repeat her question, Becca spoke. "I think he needs to know that you care about attracting *him*."

At four o'clock, Marianne pulled into the drive and

Willow carried out Becca's dress, covered in a muslin sleeve. She waved at her mother-in-law and carried the dress to her friend while keeping an eye on her wandering sons. Marianne picked up each in turn, swinging them in an arc. Calling had been the right decision.

Her eyes slid to the covered dress. Asking Josh to bring out some red chiffon and lining would also be an excellent decision. Yes it would. In fact, she had already imagined a slightly altered neckline for it—one Chad couldn't help loving. *Mother, you'd be amazed at what kinds of awkward things a woman will do for the right man. I'm going to put enough cleavage in that dress to make it utterly inappropriate.*

At Becca's side, she kicked the girl's shoe. "Weed eradication process complete. Now take this and get out of here. I expect you to spend the next three hours resting and getting ready."

Becca stood dusted herself off, and pulled off her gloves. "I was just cleaning up the weeds…"

"Which you can do tomorrow. Now go!"

"Bossy."

Willow nodded sagely. "That I am. It's my job. Yes it is. Now go!"

Three steps away, Becca turned and asked, "Is this going to be as amazing as I think it is?"

"What do you think it is?"

"I have no clue. I just have this feeling it's going to be incredible."

Relief washed over Willow. "It is. Now go."

"Go, go, go," Becca muttered as she passed Marianne. "She's just always trying to keep me on the go."

"You're supposed to be getting ready! What's wrong with this picture?"

Willow beamed. "Listen to my brilliant mother-in-law, Becca. She knows of which she speaks."

Before Marianne could respond, Willow's phone rang. "Hey, Josh."

"Is it safe?"

After waiting for Becca to step around the corner of the house, Willow relaxed. "Give it five minutes. I just convinced her to leave."

"Then I'm going to swing through town and grab a smoothie. Want one?"

"Yes. I'm starving."

Josh laughed. "I heard you were up all night. Bet you forgot to eat. Want me to stop at The Deli and get you a sandwich?"

Though tempted, Willow remembered the leftover roast in her icebox and shook her head. "No thank you. I think I'll make one here. See you soon."

Marianne shooed the dog away as she said, "You do know he can't see you shake your head, don't you?"

"Yes. It's a habit."

Liam tugged on Willow's skirt, practically jumping to get into her arms. She lifted him and nuzzled his neck. "Let's go help me make a sandwich, little man." She called for Lucas, but the boy chased something—what they couldn't tell—and refused to come.

"I'll get him."

"Don't let him get away with squawking at you. He thinks if he protests enough, we'll leave him alone."

"Takes after his father," Marianne muttered. "Chris started with the classic, 'no' and moved into negotiation. Cheri cried and begged. Chad just protested."

"Good. I'm blaming him."

Marianne laughed. "He's read your mother's journals, Willow. You'll never convince him that you are not equally to blame for any stubbornness of will."

"I can try."

Rolling her eyes, Marianne tweaked Liam's nose and said, "I rest my case."

Near a trio of tulip trees that sat out in the grasses of the far pasture, Josh and Willow worked to finish their preparations in time. While Josh unloaded the garden carts, Willow dug the first hole for the tent with the posthole digger. Each time she finished a hole, Josh came to hold the pieces in place while she hurried to set up the next one. Once assembled, the tent frame proved surprisingly sturdy.

"You guys really do have to find someone to build these. This is just amazing."

"It's pretty simple. Maybe Luke wants to teach Laird. That might be a nice side business for a boy."

"How old?" Josh sounded skeptical.

"I think... he's what, twelve, thirteen now?"

"My parents wouldn't have let me near power tools at that age."

Willow shrugged. "Who says it has to be power tools. Mother did everything she did with hand tools—or very nearly."

She helped Josh carry the dropped leaf table from her living room into the tent and left him to carry chairs and table settings while she went to work hanging the sheer curtains they'd made for it. "Whatever that machine you have is, these hems are amazing."

Josh paused and then shook his head. "Serger. Just did a rolled hem. It makes such a difference. I had all the panels hemmed in less than half an hour."

Willow's arms dropped and she stared at him. "You're kidding me! I spent six hours hemming—" She swallowed hard. "—a dress recently. I want to see how this machine works. Maybe I can learn something from it."

"You would—want to that is. I doubt you'll be able to replicate it. They use like four threads at once."

With the curtains hung, she stood back and eyed the effect. "I don't like it. It looks sloppy, and if a breeze comes up, they're going to fly up into your plates."

"I'll see what I can do in a minute." Josh sat in the chair and it rocked. "I keep moving this around until I find a solid place for it, but I don't know if I can."

"What about an old area rug? I have one that'll fit in here up in the attic. It's a bit worn, but—"

"Perfect. I'll pull everything back out and try to figure out how to make the curtains work better. Or do you want to do that and I'll go get the rug?"

The dread in his voice amused her, but Willow didn't have the heart to laugh. "I'll get it. By the time I explained which one I think would work, I could be halfway to the house."

When she returned, the rug filling their smallest garden cart, Josh had tied back parts of the panels to the posts and the others hung in straight, sheer lines on three sides. On the fourth side, he had looped the panel several times around the top bar of the tent and tied it to the bar in the middle. The panels rippled lightly in the wisp of an evening breeze that wafted across the pasture from time to time.

"That is perfect! How did you do it?"

"I pushed the posts down a bit further and it gave me just enough extra length to staple them to the bottom bars. It'll be a pain to get out without tearing them, but it'll work."

"How did you get the posts to go down more?" Before Josh could answer, Willow saw the digger abandoned at the side of the tent on the opposite side from where she'd left it. "You lifted that thing and dug more?"

"Well..."

"Don't tell me this is too rustic for you. You're becoming a natural already."

Josh shrugged. "Where's that rug. We're losing time here."

With the rug in place, very little grass remained inside the tent. The table sat in the middle and with a few adjustments, the chairs no longer wobbled beneath them. "There," Willow said with satisfaction. "Now what do you want where? I'll get it done and you go get dressed."

"I have almost two hours left. We've got time. Tablecloth first."

The incongruity of embroidered linen tablecloths, fine china, and crystal in the middle of a meadow touched Willow with its heart aching beauty. She pulled out a bucket of pink and pale yellow snapdragons and started to carry them to the vase Josh pulled from a well-padded box, but he reached into one of the coolers and withdrew a bouquet of pink and ivory roses.

"Think she'll like them—oh." He flushed.

"They're beautiful, Josh. Of course she'll like them. What do you think about me tying these to the posts with the jute?"

They worked in silence for a minute or two before Josh murmured, "Willow?"

"Hmm?"

"Thanks for not being offended."

"About what?" She carried the carriage lantern to the table and inserted the thick pillar candle he had purchased for it. Why her candles wouldn't work, she didn't know, but the faint apple scent did smell lovely next to the roses.

"The flowers. I know you cut those especially for her. I didn't think—"

"Oh, don't be ridiculous. This is about you having things how you want them for your fiancée."

"To be."

"She already said yes."

Josh shook his head. "Not officially. Officially, I asked nothing, she heard nothing, she answered nothing."

"You're both nuts." She stood back. "But it is beautiful."

Josh carried an old crate to the corner and tucked a boom box behind it. "Can you save enough of those to cover this or something? It'll look nice there in the corner."

Willow pulled several stalks of snapdragons from the tent corners and added them back to the bucket. She dug through everything she could find, but nothing seemed to work. "This bucket is too big; the bowls are too small... I need a pitcher. I'll be right back."

"Can you bring a few washcloths too? I just realized that something is likely to spill. It always happens."

At six-thirty, she and Josh stood inside the tent, glancing around them to ensure they had forgotten nothing. He had not left out a single detail. Candles, music, décor—everything looked out of a magazine. She pulled her camera bag from the cart and took dozens of shots—most of which she expected would be worthless. "If I can just get one or two really good ones..."

"I'm sure you will."

"Are you sure she won't mind me here taking the pictures?"

Josh shook his head. "I'm sure. You'll be subtle, and I intend to monopolize her attention." He winked. "And if I don't, maybe her ring will."

Dismay flooded her heart. She'd seen that ring. How Becca would be able to do any real work with something like that sticking up on her finger, Willow couldn't imagine. "She'll love every bit of effort you've put into all of this. What woman wouldn't feel cherished?"

He dug his hand into his pocket and pulled out a larger jeweler's box than she expected. "I got this to go with her ring. Do you think it's silly? Will she understand or—"

Willow opened it and smiled at the thick chain nestled in the bottom of the box. "That is a great idea!"

"I couldn't afford gold—not that thick—but I thought silver would work with the white gold—since it'll be worn inside her shirt most likely."

"You've almost thought of everything."

Josh's head whipped up as he stared at her. "Almost?"

"You've forgotten one important thing, but other than that..."

"What's that?"

Her eyes traveled up and down his filthy, sweat-stained body. "A shower."

Chapter 169

The camera and a note sat on the kitchen table as Chad came in that evening. His disappointment in not seeing Willow waiting for him took him by surprise, until he remembered how little sleep she had gotten. The note was brief.

Chaddie,
Look at the pictures before you come to bed. You won't regret it. I got two or three that even Wes wouldn't be ashamed to show! It was beautiful. And yes, she did say yes—again. Smart girl.
Thank you for letting me sleep this morning. I tried to stay awake tonight, but I couldn't.
I love you,
Willow

As he ate the reheated enchiladas from Rosita's, he smiled at the recollection of his mother's call. *"Chad! She forgot dinner—completely forgot. She just stared at me and said, 'I didn't make anything, plan anything—nothing. I have no idea what to fix.' It is probably the first and last time in the annals of Finley women forgetting to plan or follow one, and I thought you might enjoy it with me. Now what should I get to bring home?"*

Willow forgetting to make dinner. The only advantage was Rosita's shredded beef enchiladas. He couldn't imagine it.

Still, as he ate, he scrolled through picture after picture after the second one that he thought looked print worthy, he grabbed a notepad and paper from the windowsill and began writing down numbers. The angles told him she'd spent most of her time on the ground, crouching or kneeling. One showed that she had climbed a ladder to angle down at them. However, their eyes meeting the camera lens told him it would be the last.

How they had managed to create such an elegant "room" in the middle of a field, he still couldn't imagine, but the tent frame had worked well. In fact, it looked so nice that he suspected he should show it to Luke. Someone should take the design and run with it. "And I thought it would fall over..." he muttered as he took another bite and switched screens.

Six shots, almost identical, preceded the presentation of the ring. After several that looked like any snapshot, she had leaned forward precisely the right amount at just the right time and captured Josh's hopeful expression and Becca's excitement. "I know what she's going to say, Lord. She's going to say, 'I can't believe he looked even a bit uncertain. She already said yes!"

Monday's beat took on a new rhythm. Stroll the streets, slow down traffic, pass out a couple of speeding tickets, arrest a shoplifter, and watch Aiden Cox as he— Chad stared at the boy, confused. No helmet. No knee pads. No skateboard, scooter, or bike. However the kid did spend a lot of time checking out parking meters and running in and out of stores.

Each time Chad started toward the boy, something interrupted him. The emergency alarm at The Fox went off when two kids started fighting in the middle of the latest epic fantasy movie. Apparently Warden's forces were cooler than Fydrok's—unless you talked to the "Drokers" who preferred the Fydroks.

Still he stepped outside again in time to see Aiden dash around the corner and into the bank. He'd been there twice already. A meter near him showed expired. Chad wrote a ticket and slipped it under the windshield wiper and moved on to check the next.

A man stepped out of Bookends, protesting. "What do you think you're doing?"

"Writing a ticket for an expired meter."

"Since when does Fairbury have meters?"

Chad tried to keep his demeanor as pleasant and calm as possible, but inwardly he wanted to scream, *Even the Rockland news stations have talked about it. Where have you been?* Instead, he pointed to the meter, to the parking signs, and repeated the prepared statement Varney had given them. "There have been notices in the papers, on the news, and signs posted for weeks. If you object to the fine, I'm sure Judge Waller will be happy to listen to your grievances."

"That's ridiculous! I—"

In an attempt to diffuse an unhappy citizen, and to be able to follow Aiden Cox on his next mission, Chad leaned forward and interrupted. "Sir, it is not the official position of the department, but it is my personal opinion that you will find the judge very willing to dismiss first tickets. They don't want to antagonize citizens. They're just trying to pay for another officer."

The man's bluster fizzled. "I guess that makes sense— not that I like the meters— but forgiving the first ticket, I mean. This is what I get for taking a year to visit my cousin in New Zealand."

Aiden raced around a corner, capturing Chad's eye. "I think I've got a boy who needs something to do. Can't call it loitering, but he's up to something."

"That Aiden Cox? Man, he's grown. Still fighting the helmet?"

Chad laughed. "No... not today anyway. But he's been running all over the place. I can't figure out what he's up to. Seems odd, though."

"Well, at least he's out there doing something. Most kids his age seem attached to a screen of some kind." The man— one Chad couldn't name—shoved his hand in his pocket for a quarter and came up empty. "Man, I'll have to start carrying change now."

Before he strolled toward where Aiden disappeared from

sight, Chad fished out a few quarters from his pocket and popped them in the meter. "Just feed one for someone else sometime."

"And that's what I like about living here," the man called after him. "Small town atmosphere is highly underrated."

Two more hours passed before things settled enough for Chad to be able to watch Aiden. He had tried following the boy, but where a kid could run down the sidewalks, for an officer to do it would create a general protest. At last, he hid himself behind a large shrub at the corner and waited. Within seconds, the boy appeared and began scanning the meters. He paused at one, glanced at the car, and continued. However, the next one he stopped at sent him running. He dodged in and out of several stores until he went into the hair salon and didn't come right back out again.

Time ticked past at an obscenely slow rate. Chad couldn't see the meter, but it had been close to expiration when he had passed. Fran wouldn't like having to pay for a ticket. Torn between the desire to see what happened with Aiden and the feeling of obligation to help prevent Fran from getting a ticket, Chad inched his way around the shrub. Aiden flew out of the salon and plopped three quarters into the meter.

That seemed odd. Then again, Fran lived on Aiden's street. It was nice of the boy to warn her. Still, he seemed a bit obsessed with those meters. Just as Chad stepped out again to talk to the strangely good Samaritan, Aiden paused before a car that Chad vaguely recognized. It parked in the same spot of the parking lot at the church—every Sunday. He just couldn't identify it. However, apparently Aiden could.

The boy took off, dodging three pedestrians with an ease that seemed almost Olympian. If human hurdles ever became a "thing," Aiden would be a champion. This time, Aiden hurried into The Market without hesitation. How could he be so certain?

A tourist stopped him, asking directions to The Coventry. Chad missed Aiden's return, but saw the boy rush toward Bookends, pause at a car just outside, and then disappear inside the store. This time, Chad walked—the opposite route—but he walked and kept his eyes open as he did.

Aiden dashed from the store, plugged one quarter into the meter out front, and then raced for the other car, almost not waiting for a car that crept past the intersection. At the other meter, the boy inserted coins—how many, Chad couldn't tell—and then strolled down First Street. Chad continued around the square to Bookends and stepped inside.

"Hey, Todd."

"Chad! I've got a book for Willow, here. She asked for something on sustainable agriculture for Ryder, and it came in today."

"I'll stop in and get it tomorrow. What can you tell me about Aiden Cox?"

Todd shrugged. "He's a smart kid, kind of dare devilish but—"

Something in Todd's demeanor told Chad the man was hiding something. "Come on, spill it."

"Spill what? You know how the kid is."

"He was just in here. What was he doing?" Chad waited a moment and added, "I can ask all of your customers if you like—you know, interrupt them while they're relaxing and becoming attached to the book in their hands. You know how much people love to stay where an officer is asking questions..."

"You're mean when you want something."

Chad nodded. "I'll take that. Now what was he doing?"

"Just letting the patrons know that their meter was about to expire. Nice of him."

The words, though innocuous enough, did not ring true somehow. "Nice of him how?"

"Saving citizens the cost of a ticket? How is that not nice?"

"What are you not telling me?" Chad demanded. "I can see on your face that there's more to it."

"I'll tell you what; it was worth a quarter to save myself thirty bucks in fines." Wilma Vanderhausen beamed at Chad from the couch across the room.

"A quarter?" From the corner of his eye, Chad saw Todd making slicing motions across his neck. "Oh, for the meter."

"No, for Aiden. He has quite the business mind; that

little man does. He's probably making a fortune."

Slack-jawed, Chad turned to Todd, and caught the man choking himself, trying to stop Wilma from speaking. "What's going on, Todd?"

"He's just making a little money for his effort. People are happy to pay the kid for his services."

"Pay him what?"

At his elbow, Wilma beamed. "A quarter. I told you. He charges folks a quarter for every dollar he exchanges for change and for paying the meter for you. A lot of people seem not to have change on them. The poor boy said he'd had to go get more quarters three times already today."

"He's charging people a quarter to keep their meters fed?"

Todd nodded. "Yep. Like I said, smart kid. I bet he's made a minor fortune today."

"—can't believe that kid. I mean, that's extortion!"

"That's solid business sense if you ask me," Willow argued as she tore lettuce and tossed it into the bowl.

"Business sense! The kid is charging twenty-five— actually, technically one hundred percent if it's just a quarter hour!"

"And people are happy to pay it. Who cares what they want to do with their money?" Willow grabbed the tomato nearest her and began slicing. "Chad, is it illegal to charge people to provide a service to them? If he charges a quarter for picking up their mail every day they're gone on vacation, is that a crime?"

"Of course not, but this—"

"Is just another service. They're paying him for his time to procure change, watch the meters to see when they need to be replenished, let them know, feed the meter, and continue to keep watch. They could say no and walk out to pay it themselves. I'm sure some do. Those who would rather pay him the quarter—which is crazy cheap in my opinion—well, that's their business."

Frustrated, Chad shoved the chair away from the table

and carried his glass to the windowsill. "I'll go take care of the animals."

"If Becca hasn't beaten you to it. That girl—I swear, I'll be glad when the garden is in full swing or I'll never get to do anything again. She tried to beat rugs today!" Willow paused. "Wait, should you tell her to stop working and charging us for it?"

"Very funny." At the door, Chad paused. "You know what the sad part is?"

"What's that?"

Lucas threw himself at Chad's legs in protest as Chad pushed open the door. "C'mon, little guy. You can help me." To Willow, he added, "I bet if he didn't charge people, they'd give him the whole dollar and tell him to put in a quarter or two for the meter. He'd make more if he just let people tip him than by charging them."

Liam stood at the back door, calling for Daaaayyyyyeeee until it became readily apparent that his father would not return for him. Willow retrieved him before he managed to push through the screen and grabbed a chair at the same time. "Come help me."

Once she washed his hands, she pulled a handful of lettuce from the bowl and set it in front of him. "Can you put this in the bowl? One, two, three..." It took half a dozen pieces, but Liam caught on and tried to put away almost as much lettuce as he removed again. "You know, I think we should go into town tomorrow. We'll take the stroller, see the sights along the highway, and then maybe get some ice cream at the Confectionary too."

She glanced around the room before she added, "And we'll suggest trying the tip approach to Aiden. Maybe he'll make more."

With that secret told, she grabbed a washed carrot and the potato peeler. "Let's shred a bit of this in there too. I like carrots in my salad. I bet you will too. Carrots are very good for you. They have alpha and beta-carotene in them. You will probably love to gnaw on them when your teeth get a bit bigger."

Cucumber slices, yellow and green peppers, and homemade croutons came next. "What about Daddy's cheddar cheese? He likes that chopped up in there too."

Liam stared at her, hand frozen in mid-air as he listened to her question. After what seemed like several minutes, he nodded solemnly and said, "No!"

"How very contradictory, my son. I think we'll go with the nod, though. Maybe a bit of cheese will mellow him a bit. That might help me whoop him at chess. I've been in the mood for a game for days."

***

The trip to town changed everything in Willow's life. Nothing startling happened—perhaps that proved the point. Still, it became one of those days that defined a new chapter for her. The ability to leave the farm and take her sons to town to satisfy a whim soothed an aggravated and angry wound on her soul—one she hadn't realized she had been fighting. While she ignored the extra gardens, Becca hoed, weeded, and fertilized them. She would return to dry clothes flapping in the breeze and she would chase her boys through the sheets.

"Oh, look! See that?" No response from the stroller prompted her to peek through the top "window" of the canopy. Both boys snoozed. "You two are not allowing me the opportunity to instill any kind of information into those little brains. I'm supposed to talk to you all the time, and I'm perfectly willing to do so, but really, what's the point if you're sleeping through it. And, for the record, I thought that whole idea was absurd. Those magazines Mom brings are usually so ridiculous, but I found something in Mother's journal that said the same thing. How she talked to me because she heard something about how important it was for mental development. So, here I am talking to you, and for what? Nothing."

Considering herself excused from the responsibility of explaining the flora and fauna surrounding Fairbury on their trek to town, Willow lapsed into thoughtful silence. That silence lasted until just a mile outside town when her phone rang. The boys slept through the blast of some country song that Chad must have decided she needed to hear. William's name flashed on the screen.

"Hello, William! How is everything?"

"Good and bad, depending on your take."

Her heart sank. Lawsuit. They had been prepared for it, but William promised not to mention anything until he knew something definite. "And what are they—the good and bad news, that is."

"The bad news is that they did present the corporation's lawyers with a demand for damages."

"Is that common?" The question felt inadequate, but Willow didn't quite know how to respond. Knowing a lawsuit was imminent and hearing of it were two very different things.

"It's what we expected. The amount was excessive, which we also expected."

"Do I have to give up the farm?"

William laughed. "Not at all. The insurance lawyers drafted a counter settlement and submitted it for review."

"Insurance lawyers?"

"You do remember that you are covered against this kind of thing, right?" William must have taken her silence as denial, because he charged onward, assuring her that all would be well. "I think we'll settle out of court for about two hundred thousand dollars. That's the figure the woman from Mayflower Trust gave me."

"Oh, we can afford that!" The relief she felt nearly made her weak in the knees.

"Willow, you have insurance to cover this. Sure, there's a ten thousand dollar deductible, but that's all you have to pay. I was just calling to tell you that it's probably not going to court and—"

"Why do I only have—wait. Insurance to cover getting sued for my mother killing a man? Are you insane?"

"No, it's just a basic corporate liability account. Your mother wanted it in case you shot someone while—" he stopped abruptly. "Oh. Wow. Yeah, sorry."

"That's okay. She protected us. That's the main thing. She was wrong—so very wrong—but it was an accident."

At the turnoff to Fairbury, Willow disconnected the call and jogged across the highway. She stopped at the convenience store, wiped the boys' perspiring faces, brushed her hair, changed her shoes, and wrestled the stroller into the store to purchase a bottle of water.

The girl behind the counter waved. "Haven't seen you in a while. Wow! They're so big. Do they walk yet?"

"No." Willow winked at the girl's surprise. "They run, though. Run everywhere. Walking appears to be beneath them."

It took several passes up and down the street to find Aiden. The boy dashed out of the bank, his pockets jingling like a panhandler's cup. Willow called to him as he raced past her. "When you're done with the next one, come see me on that bench."

The boy froze. "Uh—Mrs. Tesdall..."

"Go ahead. You don't want to miss a customer. Just come see me over there. I have an idea for you."

At the square, she pulled out a fan and waved it gently to cool the boys, but both lads awoke once the gentle rocking of the stroller ceased. Liam met her eyes and grinned. "Eh!"

Taking that to mean, "Up," Willow unbuckled him and set him on his feet. "Whoa, son. Steady. Take it easy. One foot and then another. There you go." The toddler took half a dozen steps toward the street and glanced back at Willow as if for permission. "What's Lucas doing?"

That worked. The boy turned and rushed to the stroller, poking his brother's chest. A battle began, one that no longer seemed worth the hassle of keeping Liam out of the street. "Should have just walked him back," she muttered.

Willow produced balls from the bag on the back of the stroller and handed one to each boy. While Liam tried to bounce his on the grass, she unbuckled Lucas and watched the competition begin. The boys chased balls, each other, and the occasional butterfly. She felt a little like Portia, herding her sons away from the road and toward the center of the grassy area—repeatedly. As she kept them corralled, her eyes wandered the downtown area, watching Aiden.

He stayed busy; no one could argue that. In and out each store, checking cars, racing back. It took her several minutes to realize that half of his activity was a show, but whether for her benefit or to impress potential customers, she couldn't decide. As she caught his eye and beckoned. Slumped shoulders told her half or more of it had been a ruse. The kid had spunk. She respected that.

By the time he reached her side, Willow saw she was ready to bolt. "I heard about your little business enterprise."

"Officer Tesdall doesn't like it."

"I know. Men don't like losing to the competition."

Aiden cocked his head. "Competition?"

"Sure. Chad's job is to find people who didn't pay the meter and give them a ticket. Every meter you help someone pay is one he 'loses.' See?" Willow grinned. "It's healthy for his pride. You're doing good, but he said something that made me think."

"They're going to make me stop, aren't they? Man, I've been making good money too."

"No... but Chad said that you'd make more money if you did it free."

The boy laughed. "I almost believed you."

"No, he's right." Willow reached out and tugged Aiden's sleeve before diving to stop Lucas for running toward the road again. "If you just do it, some people won't give you a dime, sure. But most people just need another fifteen minutes, right?"

"Yeah..."

"If you go in and ask if they'd like you to run a quarter out to the meter for them, they won't have the quarter usually, will they?"

Slowly, Aiden nodded. "I see..."

"Right. So you pull out four quarters and offer to trade for a dollar. What's going to happen?"

A grin split Aiden's face. "You're right. They'll just give me the dollar!"

"Yep. And even if you walk past and see them there and plug in another quarter for them, you're not any farther behind than you were. But I bet—Lucas! No!" She dove to stop the boy—again. "I bet if you let them know they had another quarter hour, they'd offer to reimburse you—most of the time."

"So you're helping me beat Cha—Officer Tesdall."

"No..." Willow hesitated before she winked. "Between

you and me, it's just delayed. You'll go back to school in a few months, people will be used to you thinking for them, and then Chad'll get them. And, let's face it. Doing 'his' idea will help mollify him."

"Mollify?"

"It means to appease or soothe." She wrestled with her son as he fought her restraining arms. "He'll like that you liked his idea, and he'll respect you."

"You think so?" Aiden didn't give her a chance to answer. "I think that's funny."

"What's funny?"

"Your kid. He's fighting you protecting him—kind of like I do with the helmet." The boy kicked the ground with his toe. "I gotta go."

She waited until he took a couple of steps away before she asked, "Aiden?"

"Hmm?"

"Why *do* you fight the helmet?"

The boy didn't turn around. He hesitated before he mumbled, "Don't like it."

"Don't like it and..."

Willow saw him stiffen. He turned slightly, glancing over his shoulder. "Gives us—the cops and me—something to talk about."

With that, Aiden turned and jogged back to the crosswalk, turned around, and waved. She chased the boys, rolled in the grass, and tickled them until they gasped for air. The sun slowly arced toward the west, but still they played. Just before Willow decided they should start for home, Chad parked his cruiser and strode across the grass, swinging Lucas into the air as the boy met him halfway.

"Been watching you guys. Wanted to stop, but you know—"

Despite the very public place, Willow stood on tiptoe and kissed him, ignoring the fact that half the town could be watching. As she sank her heels back into the grass, she giggled at Liam's hands pushing Chad away. "I know that I love you. That's enough for me."

Chapter 170

From somewhere deep within her mind, Willow heard music—some song she couldn't place and didn't like. She rolled over, the sound growing more insistent. Her eyes opened, and she stared at the clock. Independence Eve. The music came again, this time recognizable.

"Phone..."

She dove for it, but not before it went to voicemail. Almost seven weeks too early for Chelsea—but it was. The message said simply, "Going to the hospital," before a cry of pain cut it off.

Willow hesitated. If she waited the hour until Chad got off work, it might mean Chelsea was alone for that time. Then again, waking Becca just for an hour difference... Despite her instinctive resistance, she punched Becca's number. "Chelsea—"

Becca didn't let her finish. "Coming. Give me five to get there."

Willow expected ten—even fifteen—minutes, but Becca arrived in six. Still dressed in her pajamas, her feet stuffed sockless into tennis shoes, she burst through the back door, with a blanket in one hand and her flashlight in the other. "Get out of here. Call when you know something."

She started listing off things for Becca to remember, but the girl waved her out the door. "Send me a text, call me and leave a message, anything. Just go." As Willow stepped outside the door, Becca called back. "Do you need your breast pump?"

As much as she hated the idea, the realization that she'd need to increase her milk supply immediately sent her to the pantry. "Thanks."

Prayers flowed from her as she drove along the highway to Brunswick. The boys had been three weeks early. How much more dangerous was seven and a half? Maybe little Kari would only need a few days in the hospital to make sure everything was working well. Maybe they would agree to Willow providing the milk, even if the baby couldn't nurse yet. Did babies have trouble nursing when they were early? She couldn't remember.

A horrible sense of déjà vu flooded her as she rushed through the emergency room doors and followed the proper corridors to the OB wing. Sharon Vernon stood outside the room, her purse dangling from her wrist and anxiety oozing from her. "Sharon?"

"I'm so glad you got the call. She's panicking, I don't know what to do for her, and—"

"Will they not let us in?"

Sharon jerked her head. "Go ahead. I'm not ready for it yet."

For several seconds, Willow stared at Chelsea's mother, stunned at the woman's words. "I imagine she isn't either. I know I wasn't." When the woman didn't answer, Willow asked, "Were you ready for Chelsea's birth?"

"Well, I was married and chose to get pregnant. I didn't just sleep with the first boy who showed me attention. So, in that sense, yes."

"It's probably best that you're not ready then. I'm sure she's not ready to be reminded of how horribly she has failed you—not tonight."

Before she said something she truly regretted, Willow stepped into the room and rattled the curtain before peeking around the corner. "Hey..."

Chelsea lay on the bed, her arms gripping the rails, pain flooding her features. Willow remembered those horrible hours of misery and nearly fled the room. Gathering every ounce of self-control she could find, she gave Chelsea a weak smile and said, "Pretty rough, huh?"

"Yeah."

The single gasped word told Willow all she needed to know. "Look, I don't know when they allow epidurals, but I went from truly believing I might die to relief almost immediately. Want me to ask them about it?"

"Won't do any good," a nurse said as he entered the room. "Poor girl has a long, long way to go and we're doing everything to stop the contractions so that it doesn't have to be now."

"What?"

"They said I'm not even close to labor," the girl whined. "If this isn't labor, I don't want the real thing."

Willow watched another contraction on the monitor, holding Chelsea's hand and frowning. "I can see the pain she's in. What do you mean this isn't labor?"

"Dehydration. It can cause contractions, but they won't accomplish anything. We've got an IV bag going and once the doctor gets here and says she can go, we'll release her all rehydrated and with orders to drink more."

"If I drink more, I can't sleep! I'm up every five minutes to pee. How am I supposed to get any sleep! Aaaaaaaahhhh!"

None of it made sense to Willow. The girl looked positively wracked with pain, and the spikes on the monitor clearly showed a strong contraction. "When is Dr. Kline expected to be here?"

"He's usually pretty fast, so I'd say fifteen or twenty minutes. He lives close."

Willow tried everything to help Chelsea, but nothing worked. Back rubs, leg rubs, arm—the arms nearly got her decked. "Sorry," the panting girl whispered.

"I remember some things just really drove me crazy—never any rhyme or reason."

"That feels like my entire life lately." Her eyes pleaded for answers as she whispered, "Where is Mom?"

"Just outside. Want me to get her?"

Chelsea shook her head. "I heard her when you got here. She's getting worse every week."

"Where's Ryder?"

The girl studied the light sheet that covered her. "I didn't call. I thought he'd feel pressured to come and then—"

"He'll be honest with me. Want me to ask?" Willow pulled out her phone.

"Let's see what the doctor says first. It would be crazy to call him if we're going to go right home." Another contraction built, and with it came a new, tearful round of pleas for help.

By the time Dr. Kline arrived, Willow had decided that her infertility had a side effect that could only be regarded as a blessing—no labor. The day would come—she knew it would—that she might hope to endure anything to carry and deliver another child. But with the boys at home asleep in their beds, the memory of the horrible hours of her labor with them, and now watching Chelsea, she felt perfectly content never to endure any of it again.

Willow stepped outside the room while the doctor examined Chelsea and found the hallway empty. At the end of the hall, a waiting area with one occupied chair drew her. "Sharon?"

"What do they know?"

"The doctor just got here, but the nurse thinks that she's just dehydrated and that they'll let her go home soon."

Sharon nodded. "I should have known she'd be one of those."

"One of those..." It took great restraint not to snap the words.

"Going into labor every other day for eight weeks."

"Well," Willow began, trying to find a way to keep the conversation civil. "Since she has just over seven weeks to go and this is her first possible false alarm, I'd say she's not."

"Why are you doing this?"

Willow glanced up at the woman, stunned. "Doing what?"

"Adopting the child. You have those boys. They're still very little. Why take another?"

"I can't imagine not taking her. I try to prepare myself for the idea that Chelsea may change her mind—"

"It won't happen. She wants that child less than we do."

"Or," Willow suggested softly, "she wants you to believe that in an attempt to get some kind of approval from you."

"Chelsea doesn't care about our approval. Getting pregnant is proof of that in itself."

"You think she did this just to show how she doesn't care what you think? You think this was deliberate?"

Sharon shrugged. "No, but if she cared what we thought, she wouldn't have been sleeping with that boy."

"Let's assume for a moment that you're correct—that she sl—was intimate with Ryder merely as a way of proving something to someone." Willow took a deep breath and prayed for wisdom. "I'd say that whoever she tried to prove something to matters very much to her. When you don't care, you don't act in a way to prove it... you just don't care."

The nurse appeared, calling for them. "Chelsea wants you there while Dr. Kline explains what's happening."

"Me?" Willow asked, "Or Sharon?"

"Both of you."

The women crowded around Chelsea's bed, waiting to hear what the doctor had to say. Dr. Kline entered seconds later and nodded approvingly. "Glad to see you both here. Okay," he squeezed Chelsea's hand before continuing. "What we have here is definitely a case of dehydration. There's no doubt about that. However, Maria here thinks Chelsea's cervix feels softer and a bit thinner than when she first arrived. So, we're going to wait an hour, check, and if Maria notices any difference at all, we'll give you a shot of Terbutaline and see if we can't stop the contractions that way."

Sharon spoke Willow's thoughts before she could formulate them. "Why not just give it to her now?"

"It's not something I like to give at all. All drugs have risks. However, keeping that baby in there for a couple more weeks at the very least is important. I just don't want to give it prematurely."

"Is there nothing you can do for her pain?" Willow flushed at the doctor's knowing look. "I just can't stand to see her hurting like this."

"If she can hold on for the next hour, we can make decisions then based upon a better knowledge of what is happening. If I start pulling out drugs now, it can affect how her body reacts and we might get a false reading. So, if she's willing—"

"I can take another hour," Chelsea gasped. "I think."

As the contraction built, Dr. Kline watched the monitor. "Getting pretty bad right about there, isn't it?"

"Ya think?"

He chuckled. "It must really be annoying for a man to watch a screen and tell you he thinks he knows what you're going through."

"Just slightly," the girl snapped.

As the contraction subsided, Dr. Kline felt around her pelvis, checking the position of the baby's head. "She's still down, but she isn't engaged. I just don't know what to think yet. I wish I could be sure now, but waiting would be best. Maria is usually right. If there was a change in the first hour, we hope to see just anything to hint as to what happened during the second."

An expression crossed Chelsea's face—one Willow had seen before. The girl wanted to see Ryder. She waggled her phone and stepped outside the door. It took several rings, but Ryder picked up, his voice groggy. "What's up? Something happen to the greenhouse?"

"Chelsea's at the hospital. I think she wants you here."

"Coming." The phone clicked—dead.

Dr. Kline stepped from the room as Willow returned. "How is she?"

"She's in pain, of course. I know it looks unbearable to you, but she's handling it pretty well." Willow's skepticism must have shown because the man laughed. "No, I'm serious. I can see the difference in your eyes. You looked out of your mind with pain. Hers is the, 'This hurts and I don't like it' variety. That can change in an instant, but I can guarantee that if it hurt as badly as you think it does, she wouldn't have agreed to wait an hour."

"That was a test?"

"Well, not intentionally." He patted Willow's arm. "I'll be close. If you have any questions at all, just have them page me." Dr. Kline took a few steps and turned back. "Is Chad coming?"

Her eyes widened. "I forgot—wow. Well, Becca will have told him by now. Ugh."

The tension in the room grew with each passing minute. Ryder stood miserably beside the bed, begging with his eyes for Willow to do something about Chelsea's pain. Sharon muttered unhelpful and irrelevant criticisms at the slightest provocation. Willow prayed. When Maria arrived to check Chelsea's progress, Ryder and Sharon disappeared. "Squeamish, eh?"

"Something like that," Chelsea muttered.

"Contractions getting any better, worse—about the same?"

The girl squeezed her eyes as the nurse's hand reached to determine her fate. "About the same."

Willow shook her head. "There have been a couple that were obviously worse than the others."

"Right, but I thought she meant in general. Ow!"

"Sorry." Latex snapped as the woman pulled the gloves from her hands and dumped them in the bin. "Let me call Dr. Kline down here and we'll see what he has to say."

"Can't you tell me—"

But the woman was gone. Willow grinned. "I think that means something is happening. When she thought it was nothing, she said so."

Chelsea's eyes widened and then tears filled them. "I don't want to do this today. I'm tired. I stayed up with Mia and watched movies last night."

Willow beckoned Sharon and Ryder back into the room. "The nurse went to get Dr. Kline."

"And that means..." Ryder looked positively ill at the idea of what it might mean.

"That we don't know," Willow answered.

"This is just ridiculous!"

Sharon's outburst began a semi-hushed argument that drove Chelsea to scream for them all to get out. Seconds later, she wailed for them to return. Frustrated, Willow whispered for her to hold on, and went to wait outside the door for Dr. Kline.

As he approached, she stopped him far enough away from the door to prevent anyone overhearing. "Sharon Vernon is not handling this well and it's adding stress to Chelsea.

Ryder is reacting to that and to seeing her in pain. If you could talk to them..."

"I'll take care of it."

The doctor stepped into the room and pulled the others out. With Willow there too, he left an ultimatum. "If you can't be quiet and supportive, keeping the room a conflict-free zone, you can leave now."

Silence hung as if freezing them in place until Chelsea's wavering voice called out, "Willow..."

After a glance at Dr. Kline for approval, she hurried to Chelsea's side. A minute or two later, the other two returned to the room with the doctor following. He examined the monitor strip once more and turned to them. "Okay, this is what's happening..."

Chapter 171

July 4th

 Chad worked from ten till six today. So, the boys and I did our best to celebrate without him—at least until he came home for dinner. After breakfast, I strapped them in the stroller and moved the animals around for Becca. She tried to stick to her usual schedule, but I insisted that she take the day off. So, Josh came and I think they're making wedding plans. I've had three phone calls about things that make me suspect that. And, I think it means I get to try to make a wedding dress. I can't wait to see what she wants to do! The fabrics, trims... I've never done anything like it! I hope it works.
 Speaking of fabrics and such, Josh brought me a fascinating bag of it for a surprise for Chad. I can't wait to get started on it, but I will have to find a good hiding place. We can't ruin his surprise. Of course, now that I write that, he will turn the house inside out to find it anytime he thinks I'm not watching. Let him. I have just decided how and where I will hide things and there is absolutely no way he'll ever, ever find it.
 I got sidetracked. The boys are sleeping, so I feel compelled to write this as I have the peace and quiet to manage it. They've been loud today—louder than I've ever heard. I wonder sometimes how the baby will ever sleep through their racket. I've tried to teach them to hush, but

they either cannot or will not understand. I suspect a bit of both. In fact, today was the first time I understood why people used to drug their children with "soothing drops." Ugh. As nasty as those things sound, the idea of settling them down with the squeeze of a dropper does offer a bit of a temptation.

And, sidetracked again. After the animal rotation, I took the boys out to Mother's tree and we ate cherries and watermelon. The boys love the melon, but they weren't fond of the cherries. Considering all the work it took to remove the pits, cut into pieces they could attempt to chew, and the stains they got on their clothes, I'm not sorry about that at all.

When they got tired, I lay down on the blanket with them and recited every poem I could remember. Mother would be ashamed of me, but instead of proper inflection, I finished "Paul Revere's Ride" with a decided sing-song rhythm. It put the lads right to sleep.

The Declaration of Independence impacted me more deeply than ever this year. I think having children who will have to live in the country we leave behind, and seeing the world as it is rather than through the eyes of a girl with the luxury of an idyllic existence, has made me more aware of how far this nation has come from what our forefathers pledged their "lives, their fortunes, and their sacred honor" to ensure.

Chad will say that I am too narrow-minded about these things. He will say that things like the Constitution and the Declaration of Independence began a process of America rather than establishing the definition of her. I cannot agree. Still, it makes for stimulating conversation—something I expect that will come again after he reads this. My question or him is this. These men risked their lives and their families to fight for less government intervention in their lives. Would he fight—risk his life and the lives of our children—to continue to have more restrictions placed on what we can and cannot do on and with our own property? He risks his life every day to protect others from those who do not obey the law. He is a brave man to do that. I would never imply otherwise. I just wonder if he would risk his life to fight for more laws—ones that tax him more, limit his ability to *protect his family, or restrict what crops we can grow or what animals we can raise here.*

Then again, does it matter? Probably not. I just can't help but wonder sometimes.

We played at the pond. The boys chased dragonflies and only Liam got too close. Nabbed that boy just before he fell in. Lucas seems to have a healthy fear of water. He was happy to splash downstream a bit as long as he held my hand. Liam, on the other hand, kept trying to get away from me. I think he saw fish. If so, I might have a fine fishing buddy in a few years.

I made hamburger buns yesterday. Chad came home tonight and found burgers, potato salad, "grill beans" as he calls them, and pie for dinner. He said it was the perfect "Fourth meal" he could have asked for. I guess it was worth throwing out two batches of botched buns.

But the house is quiet. The boys—all three of them—sleep but I can't. Something bothers me—something I can't identify. I feel as if I've done something terribly wrong, but I don't know what it is. As I read through this entry, it hit me, though. I said something uncharitable and unjust about Chad. Or rather, implied. I questioned his willingness to fight for what he believes in. I was wrong. Chad would—of course he would.

Chad's heart sank as he read the final words of the entry. Life had kept him busy—too busy to read it for over a week. Upstairs—directly above him, in fact—his wife slept with utter confidence of his willingness to stand for right and against anything he considered wrong.

With heavy feet he carried his dishes to the sink, extinguished the lamp, and followed his way instinctively through the house and up the stairs. In the bathroom he brushed his teeth, each movement slow and deliberate. He stopped by the boys' room, listening to their rhythmic breaths as they slept. Two little mounds, their backs pressed against each other, still occupied the same crib. Despite their attempts to introduce each to their own space, the boys didn't sleep until Willow capitulated and put them together again. She had already chosen a full-sized bed for them to share.

Why buy two beds if they're going to insist on one?

"Why indeed," he whispered.

A step into Kari's room—that thought froze Chad's thoughts. Kari's room would be little Kari's room. Was it a bad idea? Would it be harder on Willow than she thought? Should the boys have the bigger room? There were two of them. They might need or want the space. Then again, the room had always belonged to a "Kari." Well, it had since the Finleys moved in. It would be nice to continue that. His boys would understand because he would teach them to. Then the truth hit him. They would have shared the other room regardless of little Kari's presence. The room would have been kept as a guest room.

"I'm getting silly," he muttered as he closed the door behind him and stepped across the hall. The hint of a snore—that occasional whisper of a buzz on her exhale—welcomed him. Why did something so insignificant spell "home" to him in a way that nothing else could?

He crawled beneath the covers, his gut twisting again at the memory of her words. After several minutes of tossing and turning, he poked her. "Lass?"

"Hmm? The boys wake up?" She flung back the covers, but Chad reached for her, pulling her close and readjusting the sheet and summer coverlet.

"No." He took a deep breath. "I read your journal."

She rolled over and rose, leaning on her elbow. "What's wrong? You always read my journal. That's why I leave it out for you."

I wouldn't do it. That's what's wrong. If it would disappoint you, I wouldn't fight for what I believe. I would want to, but I couldn't. Even as the thoughts flooded his mind, Chad knew he couldn't speak them. *That would disappoint you too.*

"I just love you."

Willow kissed him and curled against him. "Love you too."

Becca stepped into the kitchen as Willow fed the boys

their lunch of scrambled eggs and apple sauce. "I was wondering..."

"Yeah?"

"Well, what if I delivered the milk to the customers today. I have to go get the order from the feed and seed. I could empty the fridge if I just toodled around town and dropped off milk first. That would give us room for more..."

"That works." Willow pointed to a journal on the windowsill. "The phone numbers are in there."

Without hesitation, Becca grabbed the book, flipped to section for milk customers, and frowned. "What are these strips?"

"Previous customers."

"Why didn't you just cross them out?"

Chad entered the kitchen, laughing. "Because my wife doesn't like how untidy that looks and says," his voice rose in a ridiculous falsetto. "'And this way if they come back, we have all their information.'"

"But it's blocked out!"

Willow shook her head. "Chad found me this wonderful glue stuff. You just wipe it across the strip of paper and press it to the page, but if you want it to come up again..."

"Repositionable glue."

"Yes. That!" Willow beamed and shoveled a bite of eggs into Lucas' mouth. "It makes me happy."

Becca stared at Chad. "She's brilliant—usually off the charts brilliant about a ton of stuff I have hardly heard about."

Chad's arms crossed over his chest and he leaned against the wall. "But..."

"But then she says stuff like this and goes all blonde on us!"

"Um, Becca?" Willow flicked a braid at her friend. "I am blonde."

Much to Willow's chagrin, Chad and Becca erupted in a fit of snickers. "Do we start a round of blonde jokes?"

Becca grinned. "Yes!" She winked and said, "A blonde brags about her knowledge of state capitals until a friend says, 'Okay, fine. What's the capital of Wisconsin?' The blonde says, 'That's easy. W.'"

Chad snorted, Becca snickered, but Willow stared blankly at them. "It's a fun play on words, but it's true."

"Maybe that wasn't overt enough," Chad admitted. To Becca he added, "But it's one of my favorites." He thought for a moment. "Okay, why did the blonde keep a hanger in her back seat?"

Willow shrugged. "Because someone told her she had a lot of hang ups?"

The other two snickered and even Liam grinned. Chad shook his head. "No, but that's a good one. She put it there in case she locked her keys in the car."

This time, Willow blinked. "You're kidding me, right? People think these are funny?"

After he exchanged a few blank expressions with Becca, Chad slowly nodded his head. "I get it. You don't get the 'blonde' aspect of the joke."

"I don't. What does her hair color have to do with it?"

"It's just a cultural joke. My favorite blonde jokes were told by blondes. There are redneck jokes, moron jokes, Jewish princess jokes, soccer mom jokes—"

"So, you could say 'Why did the police officer keep a hanger in his back seat?'"

Becca howled. "Yeah. That would be good. That would be really good."

With the blonde aspect removed, Willow seemed to appreciate the humor. Chad just shook his head and rolled his eyes at his sons. "Your mother overanalyzes everything. Remember that when you do something and she doesn't understand why. She wants to know why you shoved that piece of egg up your nose. She cannot comprehend that you just do it without a reason."

"Did he really—"

Lucas sneezed egg on her arm.

"Well, I guess he did." Willow rolled her eyes. "Why did the blonde boy shove eggs up his nose?"

Chad and Becca exchanged curious glances before Becca shrugged. "I don't know. Why did he?"

Willow wiped off the residue as she answered, "He's cracked."

Groaning, Chad tweaked her braid. "Not bad for spur of

the moment, but..."

To keep his wife happy, Chad spent a little time every day "searching" for her project. He looked in the pantry, in the craft room, in the attic, and in the barn. He found nothing in the greenhouse, the van, or under the seat of his truck. Under the couch cushions, behind books in the library, and even at Becca's trailer—nothing. Still, he pretended to give it a thorough search.

However, he knew she worked on something. As much as she mentioned Lacey of late, he suspected it was for the horse—a new blanket perhaps. That might explain what Josh had to do with anything. It didn't make sense.

Through it all, he still struggled with feeling like a fraud for not being the man she thought he was. He arrived home at three o'clock—almost an hour late—on Founder's Day, determined to confess and take the consequences. The thought made him chuckle. "Lord, sometimes I think Cheri is wearing off on me—all the drama. Ugh."

The house echoed with the silence that comes from empty rooms. No baby boys overslept their naps in their cribs. No squeals came from the sheets flapping on the line. That seemed odd. Willow rarely lost the chance to chase her boys through the sheets.

Empty gardens, greenhouse, and no sign of them leaving or entering the pastures. Chad turned to the barn and tried the summer kitchen. There he found Willow and the boys. Liam and Lucas were tied into chairs, munching on their biscuits, while Willow fried—something.

"Whatcha makin'?"

Willow leaned her head back, accepted his kiss, and returned to the pot before her. "Tortilla chips. Becca bought me a bunch of tortillas and I'm making chips."

"Any particular reason?"

Without answering him, she grabbed a chip, dipped it into a bowl, and passed it to him. "That's why. Isn't that amazing!"

Chad bit into the proffered chip. "*Pico de gallo?*"

"Yes! How did you know? That's just so good. Becca

asked if she could take home a few tomatoes, onions, cilantro—and said she made that to eat with tortilla chips. So I tried it. She said equal portions of everything. Oh, and she brought me this lime juice." Willow shook a little bottle. "It really adds something to it. Delicious."

The bowl of *pico de gallo* could have fed an army. She had filled one of her baking bowls with the stuff. "Um, Willow?"

"Yeah?"

"Isn't that a lot of *pico de gallo*?"

She shrugged. "I didn't know how much it would make, so I just filled the bowl. I thought we could share with her if—" Chad's laughter cut her off. She waited until he took another bite and asked, "What's so funny?"

"This is enough to take to a church potluck and come home with leftovers."

Her eyes widened. "Is it?" She shrugged. "Then I'll send some to the station after I make more tortilla chips. They can munch on it on their breaks."

"You're already the favorite wife of the station."

"I'm the only—well, other than Mrs. Varney—wife of the station."

Chad nodded. "Yes, but where she keeps a distinct separation between home and her husband's work, you just take them into your family and feed them. They love it." He bit into a new chip and moaned. "And with this—perfecto."

"I'm almost done with the chips. Are we still going to town? When you called, I forgot to ask."

After yet another chip, Chad nodded. "I thought I'd take a shower. Chief asked if I could wear my uniform—just in case."

"Sounds smart to me."

"And you could have called back."

"I'm not calling you at work unless it's an emergency. I'm just not."

Halfway across the yard, he turned around and returned for a bowl and a handful of chips. "This stuff is addictive," he muttered.

"And you thought I made too much."

The song of the cicadas filled the night air as Chad and Willow rocked in the swing. The boys slept upstairs, their little bellies full of fruit smoothies and shortbread cookies. Did they have memories of jugglers and daisies? Did they still hear the tight harmony of the local barbershop quartet singing "It's a Grand Old Flag?" Chad suspected they did.

Willow murmured something—something he didn't hear. "What?"

"I saw a quote on a card tonight. I liked it. It said something like, 'Life is beautiful. Take note.'"

"It sounds like something you would say."

Her head nestled into his shoulder and she curled up closer. "I feel as if I am living it again." She sighed. "Becca was complaining today."

"Is the work too much?"

"No, she says there's not enough of it. She wants me to 'stop coddling her and give her the real work.'"

It didn't sound like anything Willow would do, but Chad had to ask, "Are you?"

"Nope. Right now, we just collect eggs—lots of eggs—weed gardens, pick the vegetables for Jill, and relax a bit. The hard work comes a few weeks after the baby."

"Did you tell her that?"

Willow nodded. "I've been letting her ride Lacey. I hope that's okay. She's been all over the property. Oh, and she says there are fence problems at the north. She thinks the goats have been climbing on them to get to some of the leaves on the other side."

"Probably. I'll get to it next week." Something in Willow's silence made him hesitate. "What?"

"I told her she could try. Should I not—"

"Of course not. I can fix it if she can't do it. That's what we're paying her for." He nudged her. "What have you been doing?"

"Playing with the boys, cleaning house, working on your surprise—"

"I know what it is, you know."

She jerked upright. "You do not!"

"Sure do. Figured it out days ago."

Willow crossed her arms and leaned back again. "Then what is it?"

"And ruin your surprise? Not hardly." He squeezed her shoulder. "We'll have to have a date so I can show it off."

Her jaw hung for several seconds. "I can't believe—where did you find—how do you—what—"

"I'm good. You know it."

Despite his encouragement, Willow refused to answer. She changed the subject, closed her mouth, and even stood and tugged him inside. "It's time for bed. You're not going to tempt me to give anything away. I'll know when you see it if you were right or not."

"I am."

"You always think you are," Willow insisted, "But it's not always true. So, I'd be less confident if I were you."

Upstairs, she brushed her teeth, washed her face and hands, and changed into her sleeping shorts and top. As always, she wrapped her robe around it, refusing to walk around, even in front of him, without something covering her. "The boys are asleep, Willow. You can leave off the robe—especially in this heat."

"It's my summer robe. It's not hot." Even in the darkness he knew she blushed as she added, "It's just wrong to walk around half-dressed in mixed company. Even I know that."

"We're not mixed company, lass. I'm your husband, remember?"

"Yes, and—"

"I'm just pointing out that it's okay to walk from the bathroom to the bedroom in shorts and a skimpy top. There's nothing risqué about your pajamas. I saw less on half the people on the streets of Fairbury tonight."

"Should be arrested for indecent exposure," she muttered as she crawled between the covers.

"You don't like women walking around on display?"

"Nope. I don't want to look at 'em and I certainly don't want you to 'enjoy the sights.'"

Chad pulled her close and murmured, "That's obvious."

Uncharacteristically, she giggled. "Well, if you put it like that..."

The same guilt and dread that Chad had endured for four long days hit him hard. He hated it—all of it. Why wouldn't it leave him alone? She wanted to assume the best of him. Why not let her? Why couldn't he flirt with his wife without guilt hanging over him?

"Lass?"

"Hmm?"

The satisfied sleepiness to her voice told him he'd better unburden his heart before she drifted into slumber. "I've been avoiding something."

"Avoid it some more, will you? I don't want to hear how horrible I am about something until tomorrow, okay?"

He felt her sigh tickle his cheek and chuckled. "You're not horrible about anything, silly."

Sleepiness grew heavier in her tones. "So why are you avoiding something?"

"Because you're going to be disappointed in me. I hate that, but you are."

"Nonsense."

The quiet confidence with which she spoke told him it would be harder than he'd expected. "No, Willow. Really."

"Okay, tell me what horrible thing you've done so that we can sleep. The boys'll be awake before we're ready for them."

"Remember your journal entry—the one about how I'd fight for what I thought was right and against what I thought was wrong?"

She sighed again, nodding. "Mmm hmm..."

"I wouldn't."

Her answer came swiftly and with conviction. "Hogwash. You're the over analyzer this time. You would. Go to sleep."

"No. I wouldn't. I want to be able to say I would. For you, I want that to be true, but it isn't."

Again, she contradicted him. Again, he assured her of her overconfidence. He ached to admit the truth—explain himself—but hearing the disappointment in her voice... Chad dreaded it. However, now that he'd begun, he had to finish. Only one thing would be worse than hearing that disappointment—seeing it. He had to do something and fast.

"Chad, I don't know what happened to make you think—

"

"Willow," he interrupted before he lost the nerve to do it, "I wouldn't—not if it went against what you hold dear. I believe in a lot of things that you find distasteful—things like airport security and laws that sometimes intrude on property ownership. You believe that I would fight for these things or against people who tried to take them away. I wouldn't."

"But Chad, you—"

"No, I wouldn't. If I didn't know you, maybe—probably. But the idea of me fighting for or against something that opposed your convictions makes me sick. It probably means I'm a weak person or something, but I couldn't do it. I couldn't disappoint you that way."

The cicadas continued their late night lullaby, soothing Willow and unnerving Chad as he waited for her to say the words that proved she'd lost her respect for him. That they would come, he did not doubt. He just prayed that she would share some area that she still held some sliver of respect in. To lose it all—the thought nauseated him.

Long after he thought she'd drifted off to sleep, her quiet voice pierced his thoughts. "I know you believe that, Chad. I understand why you say it, and for some things, it might even be true. You don't hold many rigid convictions in the same way I do. I know that. But there are things you would fight for—things you believe with all your heart. You'd fight for Scripture—whatever the cost. You'd lose your job, you'd defend your family's right to own a Bible, and you would join with others in resisting a government that tried to take away our right to worship. This I know."

"But you would support that. It's not the same."

"No. Even if I didn't, you would do it. You would because *that* is what is most important to you. Other things you care about—prefer. But you don't have the same kind of conviction about them that you do about the Bible." She brushed his cheek with her fingers. "When it matters—even in our own little family—you fight for what you truly think is important."

Perhaps he had overanalyzed things. "Such as?" He held his breath, begging God to have her say something he could believe.

"Me driving a car. You didn't give me an option. I had to

learn. Period. It was important to you. You fought *me* over it. I could see from the moment you mentioned it that you wouldn't back down on it." He started to speak, but she continued. "The parolee idea. You killed it the second you decided it was dangerous. Even if I had fought you, you would have done anything to ensure it didn't happen—even if it meant I threw a first-class tantrum."

"So minor things…"

"Kari. Chad, you wanted Kari as much as I did, but you stood up for your right to have a say in our decision. It's not fighting physically to the death for a principle, but you stood up to me and put me in my place."

"Oh, lass! I didn't mean—"

"I'm not saying you made me into some doormat, Chad. Don't be ridiculous. But I stepped way out of bounds and you firmly and gently put me behind the proper line—beside you, not charging ahead and doing whatever I wanted because I thought it seemed like a good idea."

Willow's phone rang. She jumped, screeching out a high-pitched, "Eeek!" before snatching it up. "It's Chelsea!"

"Her timing is impeccable," Chad laughed as she punched the button.

"Is it time? I'm on my way! Do I need to call Ryder or—okay. Coming. Hang in there. Chad'll be praying."

As she dressed, Willow said, "I was still right about the idea of the baby—just wrong in how I went about it. You were right about both."

Chapter 172

Just after daybreak, Willow trudged up the stairs and crawled into bed next to Chad without bothering to undress. Seconds later, her shoes, one at a time, flew across the room and hit the floor. Chad moaned and rolled over. Startled, he sat up.

"You're back! Is she here? When can she come home? How big—"

Yawning, Willow stretched and curled up against him. "False alarm. She hasn't changed 'stations' or 'thickness' or any of that stuff. The minute they strapped her to that monitor the contractions slowed down and then fizzled to nothing."

"Dehydrated again?"

Willow shook her head. "Nope. Dr. Kline said Kari either can't make up her mind or she's a practical joker. I'm voting for the latter." She gave a half-hearted giggle that morphed into a yawn. "I forgot the bag too. She wouldn't have had her pretty little clothes or anything." Several seconds passed before she added, "I didn't even bring a camera..."

"How's Ryder holding up?"

No answer came. Instead, a soft snore told him she'd fallen asleep. Chad rolled over and gazed at his wife. The exhaustion she must have felt seemed gone—eradicated by the relaxation of sleep.

Several minutes passed before he gave up on the idea of returning to sleep. He slipped from the bed, unhooked the blackout shade from his side of the room and dropped it into place. Once he lowered hers as well, he crept from the room and peeked in on the boys. Chad quietly cleared his throat, but neither lad stirred. He had time to shower.

However, when he stepped back into their room to check on them before heading downstairs, he found Lucas alone in the crib. His feet took the stairs two and three at a time. The downstairs was empty, but the front screen moved at his touch. He raced around the house in his bare feet, wincing as twigs, stickers, and the occasional rock bruised his heels and toes.

Once certain his son hadn't escaped the house, Chad hurried back inside and climbed the stairs again. The craft room remained undisturbed as did Kari's room. However, the distinct sound of smacking lips called him into their bedroom. There, beside his mother, Liam lay nursing.

"Pretty soon you're going to have to defer to a little sister, bud."

"He will. I'm just trying to boost the supply," she murmured. I heard him stir and grabbed him while I thought about it."

Just then, Liam flopped onto his back, his arms thrown back and with utter contentment on his face. "You should look at this. I bet you can see it better than I can."

Willow beckoned for Chad. "Come take him. I'll look at my adorable son later. Right now, I want sleep."

"What about Lucas?"

"Is he awake?"

"Chad shook his head—useless gesture that it was. "No, I meant when he wakes up. Want me to bring him in to nurse then?"

"Yeah. Make me roll over first."

"Gotcha. I'm thinking about taking them to go get Danishes from the Confectionary. Want one if I do?"

"Sure. Cherry with the cream cheese. That stuff is amazing."

"Got it." Chad lifted his son and carried him from the room. "Night, lass."

"Mornin'."

As Chad carried Liam downstairs, he muttered, "Your

mother is always so precise. Did you hear that? When it comes time to pick a wife, make sure you get a good one—and that you can stand her quirks. She's got to put up with yours, so don't get too high and mighty about them, but still... Women!"

Liam stared at him and then nodded.

Every other night for a week, Willow grabbed hospital bag and camera bag and dashed out into the night—nearly always right around one o'clock in the morning. One night when Chad was working, Becca came to stay with the boys, sleeping on Kari's bed. Each morning around five or six o'clock, she dragged herself back upstairs to sleep for a few hours. At the boys' naptime, she slept. When they went to bed, if Chad wasn't home, she slept.

As her birthday drew near, she felt a little panicked at the idea of not finishing her dress in time. As if to make a difficult situation impossible, in her sleep-deprived state, she made silly errors that cost her much time and frustration. So, when the eve of her birthday arrived, Willow was near tears and the dress still incomplete.

So, despite her insistence that she not use Becca for babysitting outside of true emergencies, she called her new assistant into the house and begged her to keep the boys out of trouble. "Chad gets home in two hours. I can have this thing done by then if I don't have to rescue the books, the bathroom, and everything else from them."

"We'll go outside and play. I'll wear 'em out so they'll sleep good for you at naptime. That should give you a bit more time too."

"I have to sleep when they do. I'm on fumes, as Chad puts it, as it is. Oh, and while you're at it, pray that Chelsea neither has false or real labor tonight or tomorrow night. I want a nice birthday."

"What are you doing?"

"Chad's taking me out. He doesn't know it yet, but he is. Cheri and Chuck are coming to watch the boys and tell us their wedding plans when we get back." Willow rolled her eyes. "At least *some* people share their ideas."

"I don't know what I want, or I would."

Something in Becca's tone told Willow that the words weren't quite accurate. "Do you not know what you want, or do you not think it's possible?"

"That's probably more like it."

"What *would* you do if you could do anything?"

It took several minutes for Becca to answer. She had to change a diaper, soothe a bumped head, and rescue Willow's spinning wheel from curious fingers. Once she had the boys engrossed in their stacking toys, she turned to Willow and said, "I'd combine a simple church wedding with a reception that felt like my proposal."

"Then we do that. But to do it, you have to work fast or wait almost a year."

"Why is that?"

Willow shook out the dress and stared at the sleeve before deciding it was fine. "Because after September, it'll be too cool to do an outdoor reception." She picked up the needle and started on the other sleeve. "Or, you have a reception at that place in Rockland with the dome over the maze. That might give a similar feel..."

"It wouldn't have the rustic side of it and I can't afford it anyway."

"That would be an advantage to here," Willow mumbled around the pins she held in her mouth. "It's free. We even have the tables and chairs."

"I suppose two months is too short..."

This time, Willow didn't answer. She took her time, finished her pinning, and set the dress aside. "Look, if you want to do it, we can. It'll be a lot of work, but we can do it."

"I want things simple anyway, but you said August through October are our biggest months. We should probably wait until next spring or do something else for a reception. Maybe we could—" Becca froze and turned to stare at Willow. "That's it. That's what I want."

"What?"

"I want to turn the kitchens at the Mission into the nicest thing I can afford to do. I want the mission children to be my flower girls. It'll be a chance to do something really nice for them before we're both gone."

Despite the disappointment in losing the fun of decorating the pastures again, Willow saw the beauty of the idea. "I wonder..."

"What?"

"Well, if we can't take elegance outdoors as Josh did for your proposal; maybe we can take outdoors into the mission. We can have trees brought in—the ones we'll plant next spring, maybe. That would work."

Becca grinned. "You sew. We'll talk about this later. If we're not doing this in two months, then we have time. Maybe November or something." She took each boy's hand and urged them out the door.

Alone in the house, Willow went back to work. Stitch after stitch rolled the edge of her last sleeve until it hung perfectly. She used her bone folder to press the edge into a crisp line, saving the need for ironing. Excited, she rushed into the bathroom and changed out of her clothes. She slipped the dress over her head and zipped up the side. A glance at the mirror showed it to fit perfectly.

The cleavage it showed prompted a blush. Yes, Chad would like it. She could never wear it outside the house, but Chad would like it. His words hit her hard. *"We'll have to have a date so I can show it off."*

"Not on your life, bud," she muttered. A new idea occurred to her, one prompting a smile. "Then again..."

Willow carried Chad's dress shirt, slacks, and tie downstairs. "You dress here."

"Dress for what?" He crossed his arms over his chest and eyed her suspiciously.

"You promised me a date with your surprise. Today you get your surprise, so we're going on the date. Your sister and Chuck are almost here, so I suggest you get dressed."

"Okaaay..." He frowned.

"I want your promise to take me to dinner after you get your surprise."

"Sure."

She grinned—something in it making him quite nervous. "Then get dressed."

Within minutes, he paced the living room. Twice he called up to her. Still, she remained upstairs. After losing all patience and climbing the stairs, she hid behind locked door and ordered him back to the living room. Cheri and Chuck arrived and took the boys—where, he didn't know.

The minute Cheri's car disappeared down the drive, he heard their bedroom door open. This would be good. How or why, didn't know, but it would be good.

A red hem hit his line of vision first. Becca's dress. They had told her what he said. And she'd made it—just for him. Unaware he did so, Chad closed his eyes and thanked the Lord for her. As he opened them again, he saw her hair, still tousled after she had untied her braid. That he knew she did for him.

"Well..."

The uncertainty in her tone cut him. She—his eyes widened as he took in the full cut of the dress. Even the cut-off halter she wore whenever she thought no one was around showed less... topography. "Wow."

"I get that a lot." The uncertainty still hovered, but not as strongly. "I hear you have a thing for red dresses, so..."

"I love it, but if you think I'm taking you anywhere in that, you're crazy."

"I thought I did a good job," she teased.

"You did an excellent job. I'll sit here and enjoy leftovers and the view." He waggled his finger in the general direction of her chest, "But if you think I'm sharing that view with anyone, you've got another thing coming."

To his astonishment, Willow's face clouded. "Fine. See if I try to please you again. I'll change."

"Willow—"

His attempt to soothe her ruffled feathers failed. She stormed up the stairs and slammed the door. The idea that she even considered leaving the house so exposed astounded him. She wouldn't usually wear something so revealing in his presence alone, much less around others. Before he could decide what to do or how to explain, the door opened and to his further dismay, the red hem appeared again. Chad swallowed hard, ready to fight for this one, and laughed as she reached the bottom of the stairs. "Okay, you got me."

"When you mentioned date, I couldn't figure out how you guessed."

"Lass, I thought you were making a horse blanket." He brushed a tendril of hair from her cheek. "I didn't expect anything like this. I bought this one hook, line, and sinker."

"Stinker, is more like it." She smoothed the scarf around her neck. "Yesterday when I thought of making a fichu—"

"Bless you."

"Stop it!" Willow laughed. "I realized I could still surprise you, even if it meant more of a practical joke of a surprise."

"You surprised me, all right. When I imagined a server bending over your shoulder to place your plate, I imagined having to arrest myself for assault."

"I'm sure he would give you some if you asked him."

Chad frowned. "Some what?"

"Salt!"

Groaning, Chad led her to the truck and held the door. "You know, that was cruel of you."

"What was?"

"Coming down without that scarf-aahchoo thing."

"It's a fichu! They used to wear them all the time." She shook her head and said, "Okay so why was it cruel?"

Just as he shut the door, Chad murmured, "I'm going to be trying to imagine that dress without it all through dinner."

Willow caught it and stopped it from shutting. Her eyes rose to meet his. "That was kind of the idea."

The boys slept soundly by the time Chad and Willow returned home. Cheri and Chuck talked for a few minutes, but before they could leave, Willow's phone rang. She peeked at it and showed Chad. As she rushed upstairs to grab bags and change, Chad called out, "Um, Willow?"

"Yeah?"

"Happy Birthday."

Chapter 173

Chad met her at the door, a son wrapped around each leg as he walked stiff-legged through the house. Squeals of delight preceded his arrival, and shouts of protest came as he stopped to greet her. "Another false alarm?"

Willow nodded, yawning. "I don't know how she's functioning. But," she added with a weak smile, "Dr. Kline said next time we don't have to try to stop it. We can get her to walk around, squat, do whatever it is you do to urge babies to come. I've gotta read up on that."

He pointed to the stairs. "Sleep first."

"I—"

He shook his head. "Sleep first."

Liam toddled to her and lifted his arms up. She knelt to kiss him and held her arms out for Lucas. Chad tapped his toes until a slow smile spread across her sleepy features. "Husband card?"

"If necessary."

"I'll go peacefully." Willow squeezed each boy once more. "Wouldn't want you to have to play all your cards before our fifth anniversary."

Once she hit the landing, Chad stopped her again. "Hey, lass?"

"Yeah?"

"Would it be weird if we sent her flowers?"

"When the baby is born?"

He shook his head. "No, today. Kind of a 'hang in there'

sort of thing?"

She jogged back down the steps and hugged him. "And that's why I love you. Great idea. Can you do it? Call Wayne?"

"The minute he opens."

Before she reached the top, Willow called back down. "Can you call Sharon and tell her that we'll bring dinner tonight? I bet she's having a hard time managing work and coming home and trying to fix dinner and everything."

"Sure. I'll order pasta from Marcello's."

"Oh, and I don't know if I made Becca's work list for today, but the tomatoes and the zucchini are overrunning the garden. We've got to get them out of there immediately. Oh, and some inspector is coming—the notes are on the clipboard."

Chad stood each boy on one foot and walked them to the kitchen, their giggles and squeals filling the downstairs. "Bad idea. Mama's got to sleep. How about we go play outside. Just... as... soon... as..." He flipped through the paperwork on the clipboard muttering, "Where is it?" A carefully penned note attached to the egg quantities told him which inspector.

Lucas tugged on his pants as if to urge him onward, but Chad's finger slid over the back of the clipboard. "Look, buddy. See that? Your mama loves to make things pretty. Bet she drew that chicken herself."

The boy stomped on Chad's feet. "How do I know? Well," Chad explained, "it might have something to do with it looking a little too fat to be capable of walking."

Unimpressed Liam and Lucas raced from Chad's side to the counter, pointing to where Willow kept the cookies she made for them. Liam added to the request with his single-word mantra, "Some?"

Bleary-eyed, Willow crawled from beneath the sheets, hot and sticky. She felt cotton-headed and the stifling heat didn't help matters. A glance at the boys' room showed them sleeping, a fan blowing over the crib, sending cooler air down on them. Chad. A peek back into her room showed a fan there, the plug lying on the floor beside the outlet. "I must have gotten restless," she muttered as she grabbed fresh clothes from her drawers and a towel from the hall closet.

After a refreshing shower and clean clothes, Willow's energy rose. She hurried downstairs for food. Though her chicken sandwich looked good, the wilted lettuce in the box did little to whet her appetite. She tossed the greens in the compost bucket and grabbed a basket. The garden lettuces had all gone to seed, but she found options in the greenhouse. "Mother should have built a greenhouse years ago. Oh, she would have loved the variety we can get now."

"Did you say something?"

Ryder's voice in the corner made her jump. "What are you doing here? You're supposed to be home—sleeping!"

"I couldn't sleep, so I decided to come here and work for a bit—unwind. I'll sleep better later."

Willow cut the outer leaves of several lettuce plants. "Unless we get another call tonight." She glanced around her. "I can't believe how temperate it is in here."

"Keeping the air circulating helps, and the new shade cloth is amazing."

She glanced up at the cooler. "How long has it been running today?"

"About an hour."

Willow pointed to the lettuce. "How long can we keep them from bolting?"

"As long as I keep the cooler on from about two o'clock until five or so, we should be good."

"This is just so..." Her brain refused to think anymore. All she wanted was food.

"I believe the word you want is cool."

"Fine. Cool. Meanwhile, I'm starving. Want a salad?"

"No, but if you want them, there are peppers ready." Ryder pointed to the near garden. "Becca didn't know if you meant to put them on the list or not, so she didn't pick but..."

"I'll take a look. Thanks." Her eyes roamed over the greenhouse. "All seems well in here."

"It is."

"Then go home. Sleep. Watch a movie, but sleep."

Ryder went to rinse his hands. "You're right. Maybe I'll call Beth."

"Beth?"

"My girlfriend. Didn't you meet her? Yeah, back—"

"I met her," Willow said, her mind whirling, "I just didn't realize she was your girlfriend. I thought Chelsea—"

"No, that ended months ago. She's too much of a drama queen."

Stunned at his words, Willow nodded and stepped from the greenhouse, eager to get away and think. Why did he come, night after night, if he had another girlfriend? Did he think she wanted him there? Did she? Did she know about the girlfriend? Surely, Ryder would tell her—wouldn't he?

Questions bombarded her as she grabbed a ripe bell pepper and a tomato. Pickled beets sounded good too. However, as she stepped into the pantry, Willow found only two half-pint jars left. Disappointment washed over her. "I didn't pickle beets this year."

All enthusiasm she had for her meal dissolved in a puddle of frustration. What else had she forgotten? Willow tore lettuce, and mentally calculated the plans for salad greens to last them until late spring the next year. She chopped tomatoes and counted jars on the shelves and tried to remember how many plants they had left in the garden and greenhouse. As she sliced chicken and cheese, she realized she hadn't made cheese in weeks—or more.

She set down her knife and made a note for herself on her clipboard. Chad came in from a ride on Lacey as she finished and asked, "What are you doing?"

"We need cheese—I think."

"Oh. We out? I can go get some."

Willow shook her head, trying to think of what else she could have forgotten. "No. I just don't know how much we have. We're almost out of pickled beets. I forgot to pickle some this year."

"Well, we can buy some, or grow more in the greenhouse and make it later, right?"

"Yes, but that wasn't my point." She carried her salad bowl over to the table and set it in front of her place. "Forgot something."

"Fork?"

"Right." Willow retrieved the utensil and sat down,

poking at her salad uninterestedly. "What else did I forget?"

"Dressing?"

"No, I like to make that fresh—" As she took a bite, she sighed. "You meant on here. You're right. And I don't feel like making mayonnaise right now."

Chad stood and strolled out the back door. As illogical as she knew it was, Willow fought back tears. She stared at the bowl of unappetizing salad and wondered why it had ever seemed like a good idea. She speared a piece of chicken and forced herself to chew it. A tear splashed on the back of her hand.

"Oh, now you're just being silly."

"What?"

Willow glanced up and saw Chad standing on the other side of the screen door, a bottle of his favorite "ranch" dressing in hand. "I told myself I was being silly—crying over no mayonnaise and pickled beets. This is ridiculous."

He stepped inside and set the bottle in front of her. "Just try it. If you hate it, I'll go get you anything you want from town—anything."

Laughing, she took the bottle and unscrewed the top. "That's not much consolation. You'd do that anyway."

"After I picked myself up off the floor when you asked, maybe." Chad grinned. "Now what's up with you?"

"I don't know! I forgot to pickle beets. I love those things on salad! I—" She grabbed the clipboard and slowly wrote out the next item on her running "to do" list. "I need to do pepper relish too. We have an overabundance of those things. It'll be great in winter."

"So you forgot a couple of things. You're sleep deprived and transitioning from doing it all to having someone else do it."

"But I can't have her do it if I can't remember," Willow wailed. "I'm used to Mother telling *me*, not the other way around!"

He turned his chair around and sat backwards on it as he did every time he had something to think about or something serious to discuss. "Willow..."

"If I'm being unreasonable again, can you tell me tomorrow—or next week? I can't take it right now."

"You're not being unreasonable—not really. You know what you need and want done, and you know that you are capable of doing it."

Her head snapped up. "Exactly! That's what I was trying to tell you."

"I just think," Chad began with evident caution in his tone, "you're forgetting that there are other things that need to be done that you aren't capable of doing. It's not just about doing everything you've always done." He draped his arms over the back of the chair and rested his chin on them, gazing at her. "Lass, I think you forget that I tripled your work—at least. You added things like the clothing line. We added children—three of them in a year and a half."

Willow giggled. "Well, two anyway. Our third seems to have the good sense to want to stay as far away from here for as long as she can." Her joke seemed to wound Chad. He dropped his eyes and stared at the floor. "Chad..."

"This place—" his voice cracked. "It's not supposed to be a place people would want to avoid—even joking," he added as she started to protest. "That's the beauty of it for so many people. For them, this farm *is* coming home, and they've never lived here or anywhere else like it."

"I didn't mean that—" She frowned. "Wait, we've had this discussion. We've made changes. It's just going to take time. It's okay, right?" Before Chad could reply, another tear rolled down her cheek.

"So if you're okay with it, then why are you crying?"

"I don't know. I'm tired, I'm so hungry, I haven't seen my sons in days, we haven't gotten to go for a walk in..." Her eyes rose to meet Chad's. "How long? I can't even remember how long!"

"Too—"

Willow rushed on without allowing him to answer. "We'll just get adjusted with the baby and Ryder will be gone. Ryder..." Another tear followed. "He has a new girlfriend. Did you know that?"

"Beth? Yeah. She's nice—"

"Why didn't you tell me? All this time I thought he was there for Chelsea because they—"

"Lass," Chad began, trying to explain. "I didn't know you

didn't know." He paused, his forehead wrinkling. "Whatever. I just assumed Ryder—it's not like we talk about them."

"I just—" She swallowed hard. "I don't like it. I feel like something horrible has happened all over again."

Becca arrived at the door with a few envelopes. "The mail came. There's a packet from the social services office…"

Willow grinned at Chad, her disappointments forgotten. "The home study? It's finally complete?"

Chad opened the manila envelope and scanned the cover letter. His eyebrows drew together as he read, but concern lodged in Willow's heart as she saw him swallow hard. Her eyes sought Becca's but saw nothing there. "Chad?"

Without a word, he passed her the letter and began flipping through the papers. Willow read several sentences before her hand dropped. "You're kidding me. The social worker passed us off to another one so we have to have the inspection and home interview all over again? And what's with the electricity thing? Who cares! We have it. That's the point, right?"

"Read it all, lass. It says that the paperwork on our background checks and financials are complete. They just want to interview again because of a notation about the electricity."

"But what it says between the lines is that Maeve Zolora didn't want to make a decision as to whether it was appropriate to allow us to adopt because we don't always leave the electricity on in our house."

"That's not exactly accurate," Chad argued. "It's more like we rarely do."

"So, it always comes back down to the innate virtues of electricity. Fine." Willow stormed to the pantry to flip on the switch and frowned. Furious, she backtracked and paused long enough to say, "Maybe we should point out that I couldn't even turn it on for them. *It was on!*"

She stumbled twice as she rushed up the stairs and slammed the door shut. Her eyes widened and she waited, holding her breath as if it would help, for her sons to awaken. Not a peep followed. Relieved, she collapsed on their bed and wept.

Chapter 174

The new interview fell on a morning when Willow had been called to the hospital—again. Chad watched the nondescript sedan crawl up the long drive and berated himself for not grading it. The recent rainstorm had left it more rutted than usual—not the way to make a good first impression.

As the woman stepped from her vehicle, his heart sank. How had he never noticed that there was no walkway to the porch? The woman stumbled over the grass to the steps. By the time she reached the door, he held the screen open for her. "Ms. Claremont?"

"Yes."

When she didn't offer a first name or call him by name, Chad's throat went dry. "I'm Chad. Willow isn't here yet. Chelsea went to the hospital around eight o'clock."

"I see. Will she be here?"

Chad assured her that Willow had promised to try to be back before the interview was over—even if she had to return to the hospital when they finished. "Would you like some water? Lemonade? Iced tea?"

"Sweet tea?"

Chad shook his head. "No, but I can add sugar—"

Ms. Claremont gave him the slightest nod of approval. "No, iced tea is perfect. Thank you." He turned to go, but the woman spoke again. "May I come too? I've heard about your... unique situation."

"Um, sure." As he led her to the kitchen, Chad showed her the artwork and craftsmanship of the Finley women. From the painted "wallpaper" and the hand carved trim around doors and windows, to the hooked rugs—he gave the same tour that he had given so many other times. In the kitchen, he showed the wood cook stove and noted the tightening of the woman's lips as she listened to the explanation of the fence around it. "We also have an icebox in here—" Chad pointed to it and opened the door. "I'll never forget my surprise when I saw her filling buckets of water in the winter and setting them outside."

"And why did she do that?"

"For summer ice. We keep it in the cellar in an ice room of sorts. You'd be amazed at how well it lasts. We'll run out just before the first freeze if we haven't used more than usual."

"And why not just use a freezer—oh, no electricity."

Chad poured the woman a glass of tea and passed it to her. "That isn't exactly accurate. He popped his head in the pantry. "Looks like we have it on again today. It was pretty hot last night. I tend to forget to shut it off." Chad reached for the breaker box and flipped it.

"So you *do* have electricity. The report was so ambiguous. It implied that the barn had it but not the house. Which," the woman added, "obviously makes no sense."

"Well, there is some truth to it," Chad admitted. He gestured to the table. "Would you like to sit there or in the living room?"

"Here would be fine, thank you."

Chad saw a fine line of perspiration form on the woman's upper lip and stepped back into the pantry for a fan. He plugged it in and frowned when it didn't come on. "Oh, I turned off the breaker. Sorry. We get used to the heat."

Once settled, the woman opened a file folder and took out a pen. "Okay, why don't you tell me about the electrical situation again? I am thoroughly confused now."

"We have electricity to all parts of the farm. We choose not to use it in the house most of the time."

The woman scrawled notes as she listened. "When do you have it on then?"

Disarmed by the almost curt manner in which Ms. Claremont asked her questions, Chad had to ask her to repeat the question. "Oh, sorry. We've been a bit sleep deprived. Chelsea's body can't decide if it does or doesn't want to have this baby, so we're up and down every night almost." He thought for a moment, even further unnerved by her poised pen. "Electricity in the house—we usually use it if we want to watch a movie on the laptop or on hot nights to cool things down so people can sleep comfortably." He nodded at the fan that blew past the woman's shoulder. "And, of course, when we have a guest, we'll put a fan on to cool them down or flip on the breaker for them to use an electric razor or blow dryer."

"I see. And why is the electricity kept on in the barn?"

"The barn is where the freezer, washing machine, and things like that are. Next to the barn we have what the Finleys call a 'summer kitchen.' Willow does her canning and things out there. It's being upgraded to a commercial kitchen so that anything she makes can be sold if we ever decide to go that route."

"And what about plumbing?"

Chad laughed. "Well, we have the outhou—" His joke fizzled. "Sorry, bad joke. It's all modern. We're on a septic system, which..." a new thought occurred to him. "Maybe I should make a note to check records. I don't know when the last time they had it pumped was. It was probably something Kari handled." He reached for Willow's notes and scribbled a question at the bottom of a random list of ideas and questions.

"What is that?" Ms. Claremont's pen poised again.

"Just Willow's running list of things to do, to remember, to research. The Finley women are very... methodical. But they had clearly defined lines of work and planning that work was Kari's. Willow hasn't mastered the balance of it all yet."

"What happens when the work becomes too much?"

"Well, so far," Chad began, relaxing a little. "So far we've just hired someone to do it. If that becomes no longer feasible, then we cut back what we do here."

The woman glanced around her. "Can you tell me where your sons are? It says here you have twin boys who are... seventeen months old?"

"We have an employee who lives on the property. She has them at her place while we talk. I thought I'd be distracted from our conversation if I had to keep an eye on both boys by myself."

"May I meet them?"

Chad pulled out his phone. "Sure. I'll call and ask her to bring them and see where Willow is. Excuse me."

"May I walk around outside?"

A glance at her shoes made Chad wince, but he nodded. "It's a farm, Ms. Claremont. Please be careful."

"I will."

The moment she stepped outside, Chad punched Becca's number. "Hey, the social worker wants to see the boys." Becca asked if that was normal, but Chad didn't know. "Seems reasonable to want to see how we interact with the children we already have, so I suppose. They were just 'there' last time, so it wasn't an issue. Can you run them up now?"

That squared away, he called Willow. The phone went to voicemail and a couple of minutes passed before she called him back. "On my way home—had to find somewhere to pull over to answer."

"How far out are you?"

Willow's voice changed. "What's wrong?"

"Wrong?"

"I can hear it. Something is wrong. Has she indicated—"

"Lass, she's just..." It took him a moment to define the problem. "I don't know, cold—disapproving even. Every word she says, every expression, every question—it all makes me feel as if she's ready to order the boys removed from us or something."

"What! Can she do that?"

"No, no. I don't think she would; it's just so different from Maeve. Maeve was so friendly and interested in everything. It felt like a chat with an old friend. This feels like I'm at an interview for a job that we both know I'm grossly under qualified for."

"Chad..."

"Just come. I need you."

They sat stiffly on the sofa, a boy on each of their laps, and tried to be as relaxed and natural as possible. From the moment she had dragged herself up the front steps, Willow had felt exactly what Chad had described. The woman considered them unfit—possibly even to parent their own children.

Liam squirmed to get down, and Willow let him go, standing as he toddled toward the toy basket. Ms. Claremont commented on it. "Is there a reason you cannot sit, Mrs. Tesdall?"

"Not until I see what he plans to do and until I latch the gate." She wrestled the thing in place and watched as Lucas followed his brother to the toy basket. Exactly three seconds before the brouhaha began, Willow predicted it.

Lucas decided he wanted the little wooden train Liam held. Liam protested the attempted confiscation of his toy and jerked it away. Lucas leapt—as did Willow. She grabbed her son and seated herself on the couch, holding the wriggling, screaming toddler as he protested his thwarted train-jacking scheme. Chad shifted his concentration to Liam while Willow dealt with the tantrum.

Ms. Claremont watched in silence.

Once Willow felt Lucas shift from anger to frustration, she told him to hush. Unwilling to yield, the boy buried his face in her chest and wailed, albeit with much less vigor. In less than a minute, Lucas sat quietly on her lap and then tried to slip to the floor. "No, son. You stay with me for a bit." He protested. She didn't budge. Ms. Claremont seemed curious.

"Why keep him on your lap?"

Having already given up any hope of approval from the woman, Willow spoke candidly. "He just threw a tantrum for not being allowed to steal. I just want to be sure he's not going to repeat his attempt at grand theft train."

"Some would say," the woman suggested, "that he simply expressed his feelings. Do you not think that children should be allowed to express their feelings?"

"I don't know about that, but I do know it's cruel to allow

a child to form a habit of socially unacceptable behavior and then later expect him to break that bad habit simply because he's older. Why not teach him not to do it in the first place?"

Liam relaxed as Willow spoke; the last remnants of resistance dissolved and left him perfectly content to sit with her. She pointed to the basket of toys. "What about your ball? I'll roll it. Go find the ball."

The boy raced for the basket and dug out one of Willow's wool felt balls and brought it back to her, throwing it in her lap. "No, son." She handed it back to him. "Hand me the ball. Don't throw."

He cocked his head as his eyes traveled back and forth between his mother's face and the ball. He raised his arm to throw again, but she stopped him. "No... gentle. Like this."

With exaggerated movements, Willow took the ball and placed it gently in her son's hands. "See. Give me the ball..."

Excited, Liam handed her the ball, but with much more force than could ever be called 'gentle.' Still, Willow praised him. "That's better. Here..." She rolled the ball toward the dining room table, trying to aim for the center. Liam loved crawling around and between the table and chair legs.

"And yet, he still wasn't gentle and that is fine?"

The disapproving tone, the press of the woman's thin lips—everything screamed a big, red, rejection stamp to Willow, but she forced herself to remain calm. "Fine for trying. He was overeager, sure, but he tried to do what he was told. I consider that perfectly acceptable—particularly at his age."

"I see."

Those words made Willow want to scream. However, the woman closed her folder, stood, and gave them a weak and somewhat forced-looking smile. "Thank you for your time. You have darling sons." She glanced around the house before adding. "You have chosen a unique life. I don't quite know how to describe it, but it's very interesting."

They stood on the porch, the boys playing at their feet, and watched the sedan bounce along the lane to the highway. Chad draped an arm around Willow's shoulder. "Think I should go see what I can find out about requesting a new home study?"

"Probably. If Maeve left things so ambiguous, and this woman is so obviously unsatisfied with our situation, we'll have to appeal somehow, right?"

He nodded. "Yeah. I guess we shouldn't have assumed everything was okay when we didn't hear back."

She gripped the porch railing, trying not to scream out her frustrations. "We told them everything up front. We told them about Mother and what she did. We told them about how we live and everything. We went to all those classes and those office interviews. We did the medical stuff, got all the references, handed over the financial records…"

Chad laughed. "And I even wrote that 'life story' thing."

Willow snickered. "It was pretty funny…"

"Yours was more interesting."

"Well… it was different, anyway."

"I could have saved myself a lot of time," Chad mused as he turned and leaned against the rail, his arms crossing over his chest. "I should have just written, "I had the opposite life from Willow. If she did it, I didn't. If she didn't and it was legal, I did."

Willow dropped her head on Chad's shoulder and allowed herself to relax just a little. "Maybe my letter killed our chances. Maybe it's not the farm or the breaker box."

"How do you figure?"

"You know in that movie Cheri brought—the black and white one she used to torture Chuck with that night?"

Chad's chin dropped on her head. "Singing?"

"Right. Remember the guy who wanted to become a citizen and talked too much and the questioner said he should come back with shorter answers?"

The familiar feeling of the rumble of Chad's chuckle comforted her as she waited for him to speak. After a few seconds, he sighed. "The paperwork assured us that they just wanted a safe home—ours is—with room for the child—we do—and adequate resources to care for it—we have them—and to be well adjusted and loving people."

"Which we are—loving anyway. I make no promises about being well adjusted." A yawn escaped before she could swallow it. "I've got to get some food and try to sleep."

"You're not going back?"

"Nope. Dr. Kline says she's still not dilating, thinning, dropping, stationing... or any of the other '-ings' he wants to see before they encourage labor to keep going."

"Two more weeks." Chad's groan sounded suspiciously similar to Ryder's.

"Or four."

"What!"

"Well, if she's not ready, the dates could be off..." Willow laughed. "Just kidding. They're sure because they measured some bone in there and voila. It tells them everything."

Chad pointed to the door. "Okay, you go and eat then. You might be up all night again."

"At least they're not trying to stop it anymore," Willow murmured as she took each son by a hand and led them into the house. "That's progress." She yawned again, this time unable to suppress it.

His hand smoothed the back of her hair. "You know what?"

Willow paused, her eyes closing as she relaxed under his touch. "Hmm?" Good feelings flew as her sons tugged her toward the kitchen.

"Go upstairs, take a shower, and crawl in bed. I'll make one of your egg and sausage sandwiches. You can eat there and fall asleep."

She reached the kitchen door and hesitated. "But—" The boys rushed for their chairs. "—they don't want me anymore anyway."

"Food trumps mom any day. It's a guy thing." Chad pointed to the stairs. "Go on. You know you'll get a call an hour into that nap anyway." He snickered. "Can't wait to tell Mom you're gone again. For a woman who protested the idea in the first place, she's nearly going insane waiting."

"It's not even Chelsea's due date yet!"

"False labor messes with your mind—makes it seem like it has to be past time even when it's not yet there."

She shrugged and turned away. "You win—but only because I want that shower."

Chapter 175

When days passed without news regarding the home study, Chad grew impatient. Frustrated, he asked his father who offered an excellent suggestion. "Aggie had to have had something like that done when she took over guardianship of the children, right? Call and ask her."

Instead of calling, Chad stopped by on the way back from a transport to Brunswick. He found all but the youngest Stuart-Sullivan children around a table in the library, watching a rat chase through an elaborate maze. "What's going on?"

"Tavish trained Trapper to follow the long route to the cheese!" Kenzie beamed up at Chad. "Trapper is very smart."

"Greedy is more like it," Aggie muttered.

"Got a question for you, Aggie. Can we talk somewhere—the kitchen maybe?"

Aggie gave Vannie a look that clearly said, "Don't let that rodent escape into my house" and led Chad from the room. "Anything wrong?"

He crossed his forearms and leaned them on the island. "Home studies—what do you know about them?"

"I thought you did that a few months ago! I mean, that was back in what, April?"

"Yeah, well the first interviewer came out and left ambiguous statements about our electricity which prompted another interview. From what I can tell, Ms. Claremont is unimpressed with us and our home. We need to know what to do next. The baby could be here any day... or in the next month, anyway."

"Month? I thought she had two weeks!"

"And," Chad muttered, "who reminded us that a mother can go two weeks *past* her due date?"

Aggie giggled. "Well, you can, but I doubt they would after the misery that poor girl has been in. Why don't they just induce her?"

"Dr. Kline says she just isn't ready. He says it'll end in a C-section most likely." Chad ran his hand over his head in frustration. "We have to have this stuff done or they won't let us keep the baby!"

"I don't know, Chad. The court ordered a background check and fingerprints and stuff for me, but I didn't have to do everything, because I'm just the guardian. It wasn't nearly as involved as what you're doing." Her eyes widened. "But Ellene would know! Let me call her—wait, is she home?" Aggie glanced out the window. "I can't tell. Hold on."

Chad wandered into the library to watch the kids with their rat while Aggie chatted with her neighbor. Half a minute later, she appeared at his shoulder. "Murphy wants to know what the social worker's name is."

"Ms. Claremont."

Laughter came through the phone before Aggie could relay the name. She listened and then nodded, turning to walk away from the children's cheers as the rat neared the end of the maze—again. Chad followed, eager to hear why Ms. Claremont's name was so amusing. Still, it took several more minutes for Aggie to disconnect the call.

"Okay, first, Wendy Claremont is probably their best social worker. Murphy says you got a great advocate in her." Aggie ticked off her fingers as she counted. "Second, I guess the woman is kind of hard to read, but if there was a problem, you would have gotten a call the next day. Murphy says to call and request a copy of the report."

"Okay..." He sighed. "I just—I had no idea it could be a problem."

"It's probably not one. Just ask." She grabbed a glass and waved it at him. "Water? Tea? I might have some dregs of lemonade in there, but I doubt it."

"Water, thanks."

"Sandwich?" Aggie began pulling out lunchmeat as he hesitated. "Sandwich it is. Ham okay?"

"Sure. Thanks."

"So, why are they waiting so long to do this study? You've been going to all those classes and things, right?"

"This is just the final home inspection part. We keep calling it the 'home study' but the whole process has really been that."

"How has Willow handled that?" Aggie held up mayonnaise and mustard with a questioning look on her face.

"Both please."

"Watermelon?"

"Sure, but—"

Aggie interrupted him. "Okay so this is just the 'make sure the kid will have a bed and not be allowed to play with live wires' visit?"

"Second one. The first one just left notes about no electricity and questions about it and they sent a letter saying we had to have someone else come out to fill in the report."

"Sounds routine. You *have* electricity. There's no law that says you have to use it. You'll be fine."

Chad accepted a wedge of watermelon and moved to the sink before taking a bite. Juice ran down his chin and dropped into the basin. "Good watermelon."

"Luke knows how to pick 'em. I try to copy his technique and get mealy things that even my bottomless pits won't touch." She passed him the sandwich on a paper towel. "So everything else is in order? You just need this report on how safe your home is or isn't?"

"Yep."

"Want me to ask Mur—"

"Do you call Ellene that to her face?"

Aggie laughed. "Yep. She even calls herself that now and then when she wants to tease me. So, as I was saying before I was so rudely and suspiciously interrupted..." Aggie grinned. "Do you want me to ask her if she'd come give your place a once-over and tell you what she thinks could be an issue?"

Chad sighed. "I don't think she'd be allowed to do that,

and even if we could hire an independent social worker to do their own inspection, I doubt Ellene could be that person. Being your neighbor and friend—it's probably a conflict of interest thing." He took a swig of his water and swallowed a bit almost whole. "If she thinks it was probably okay, then we'll just trust—for now. If you talk to her again, can you ask her for a recommendation for a private agency if we need to hire a "rebuttal" inspection or whatever we do if we have to appeal?"

"Sure." Aggie winced at squeals coming from the library. "So help me if those kids let that rat get loose..."

After another quick swig of water, Chad grabbed his sandwich and gave her a quick hug. "Thanks. I've gotta get back. I just thought about you and the chief said I could have half an hour, so I took it while I had the chance."

As he stepped through the screen door, Chad heard screams of "Get him!" Seconds later, Aggie's voice wavered and began singing, "*When sore trials came upon you, did you think to pray...*"

A snicker escaped before he could stop himself. "Willow is gonna love that one."

Willow met Chad at the door. "I called the lawyer and he said that even if the home study is not finalized and approved, that we can sign a legal risk waiver and some kind of other documentation so we can still take the baby home. He thinks everything is fine, but he's contacting the social worker today to see if we need to do anything else."

"Shouldn't *we* be calling?"

"Dale said usually, yes, but since we're concerned about approval, it might be better to go through a third party—him. I asked Renee about it, and she agreed."

"Two lawyers—who can argue with that?" He sank into the rocking chair by the stove and closed his eyes. "I can't believe how relieved I am."

"I know what you mean!" She waved her hands over the table. "I've been playing with invitation ideas all afternoon.

It's like my creativity resurfaced once that weight lifted." Willow's eyes slid toward the clock. "But, those sons of ours will be up from their naps soon. I'd better clear it away."

Eyes closed, Chad nodded and said, "Let me see your favorite three."

"See? Sure you will. Right through those closed eyelids."

"Woman!"

Willow giggled and chose three of the dozen or so prototypes spread across the table. "Okay, what do you think?"

The first looked similar to the effect she'd used for their invitations, but with roses instead of daisies and lilacs. "I like it." The second, seemed too plain to him, but it did lend a certain elegance. "What's with the monogram and nothing else?"

"I thought maybe it might be something they'd want and then really liked how it turned out. I wish I could make it raised instead of flat, but I had a hard enough time trying to do that with the next one."

Chad stared at the third card, wondering at the holes in place of flower petals in several places. She had managed a decent attempt at an embossed surface, but the holes marred the effect and she hadn't managed to make the edges smooth. "I like the concept."

"Me too. I just can't get the right amount of pressure on top and hardness beneath it."

"What did you use?" He laid one of the other cards beneath it and nodded. "The alternate color behind that hole looks cool, though."

"Pencil eraser. I just dragged it where I wanted. I tried other things but everything I had was too sharp or narrow. I need something with a small ball on the end, I think."

"I bet Mom has something in all that scrapbooking junk she has."

As they talked, Willow began gathering her paper, watercolors, pencils, and scissors into a basket. "I'll call Mom tomorrow. She'd probably have fun helping me come up with ideas."

"And then she might not feel so weird asking you for help with Cheri's."

Willow turned, stunned. "Cheri's? Why would she want help? I thought they would order the kind of stuff they showed me in magazines."

"Maybe, but I got the impression that she was going to see if you could help them design something. I guess hand crafted is very 'in' right now."

"Who cares if it is or isn't? Do what you want. I don't get people."

Chad's laughter filled the kitchen. "That's okay, lass. They don't get you either. That's what makes it a very interesting world."

Her phone rang. Willow glanced at the name, dumped the basket on the table, and reached for her keys on the shelf as she answered it. "On my—oh. Well, that's good! Great. Okay. Have fun and try to relax."

"What was that about?"

"Chelsea went to Dr. Kline for a quick check before the weekend. He said she's thinning and that the baby's head is further down. He suggested she walk, so they're going to go to that summer faire thing in New Cheltenham."

"Sooo..." Chad shrugged. "Why'd she call you?"

"Just warning me to get a nap in case it starts the labor stuff again."

He stood, took the basket from her, and jerked his head toward the stairs. "She's right. Go sleep while you can. I'll put this away. If you hear the boys, ignore them. Sleep."

"I'm not tired. I'm actually quite energized."

Chad thought for a moment and nodded. "Okay, I'll go change and we'll take the boys fishing when they wake up. That way, you'll at least relax." Willow's squeal told him he'd made the right decision.

"I haven't been fishing in—when *was* the last time I went fishing?"

"Dunno. Let's get ourselves ready, eh?"

"I'll pack a snack. Want a sandwich?" She reached for bread without waiting for him to answer.

"Yeah... maybe a little *pico de gallo?* I've got chips in the truck. Grabbed them on the way home."

She grinned. "Sounds just about perfect. We'll have fish and fried okra for dinner. I'm pretty sure the plants closest to the house flowered a few days ago."

"Cornbread?"

"Definitely. I'll mix the dry ingredients before we go. Yay!" Her eyes rose to the floor above her and she winked before adding, "Yay!" twice as loudly as the last time.

One week before Chelsea's due date, Chad came downstairs in the wee hours of the morning. He put on his shoes, ate a bowl of the cold cereal Willow still refused to touch, and thumbed through her journal. The latest entry was one he hadn't read, and so as he ate the cereal that grew soggier with each bite, Chad read.

August—

The long nights of watching Chelsea not deliver a baby are harder on me than I expected. I think I have moved from relief that I will likely never have to endure something so painful again and an acute desire to take it from her. She's so young—so worn out with the normal discomforts of pregnancy. These sometimes nightly cycles of pain are wearing her out.

We took the boys fishing, and I haven't felt more relaxed and happy in such a long time. It felt like MY life again. Work always feels natural and good, but when I have time to take a walk in the woods, pick the flowers, fish a little, or just swing... those are the times that I feel as if my life is what it should be. I suppose because those are the times that feel most like Mother would approve. She was so firm in her conviction that each day needs a bit of "Sabbath" to it just as each week does. Not that we must observe some ritual to be "holy," but that God built the principle into our lives to bless and refresh us. I've always struggled with wanting to do more—try new things—and when I let that eagerness consume me, I lose sight of the things that truly do matter.

Nearly every day, Chad or I will say how blessed we are to have Becca. Hiring her has given me back the life I want to live. I work still, definitely. But this work I do is the work meant FOR me, not just work. Mom says that this is the problem with American society today. She says that we have become so addicted to doing more—being more—that we don't have the self-control to choose only things that fulfill us and our purpose here.

The thing is, isn't that what Chad and I did? We found good things to do—valuable things. We took what we already did and increased it. Somehow we turned the beauty of work in our lives into busyness in the name of business. Three or four times now we've rehashed the same idea—we're doing too much and need to cut back to what works for us. Each time it seems so overwhelming and as if we've failed or something, but when I talked to Dad about it, he said that Mother had to do the same thing when she first started here on the farm. She had to choose between existing without any electricity, all electricity, or a balance of it. She had to choose between chopping wood or holding me that first year. She kept just one plate, one bowl, and one glass for each of us. That was the perfect balance for her not to get lazy with her work. For us, we need more because there are more of us, we have visitors that Mother never had, and we have other things to occupy our time besides washing the dishes. So, if finding that balance took her time, why are we surprised when we keep having to do the same thing?

Speaking of Mom and Dad, they came for the weekend and Cheri came for a few hours too. Mom has this nifty little machine that does amazing emboss work. You just put paper in a little folder, crank the machine, and the pattern is perfect! She also had a stylus that works really well for me designing my own embossing. I don't know which one I'll use, but knowing I can do it really makes me want Becca to choose the new design I came up with. Cheri liked the monogrammed prototype. Chad is disgusted, but hey. I think it fits her.

The call came in from Ms. Claremont. Apparently, Ellene Tuttle knows what she's talking about, because Ms. Claremont was very direct—almost curt—but quite sincere about her approval of our home for Chelsea's baby. Apparently Maeve Zolora had a family emergency and the report she had on us just had the words noted that she wanted to be sure to address—not things she was concerned about. The assistant just typed up a letter to notify us and wrote it all wrong. I wonder if he or she has any idea what kind of panic she sent through us—especially after the meeting with Wendy Claremont. Wendy... no wonder she sticks to "Ms." I've never seen someone so utterly misnamed in my life. She should be an Alexandra or a Justine. Something formal and elegant but not excessively feminine.

Canning is in full force right now. Becca and I take turns doing batches. I want to keep up with what I can, but when the boys wake up, she takes over. I've been processing plums and pears until it seems like we'll have more than we can use, but even if we do, we can give some for Christmas gifts or to Becca and Iris. The boys like to watch. We give them bowls and pieces to play with. I don't know if they think they're helping or if they are just playing. I wish they would talk more, but Iris says boys talk later than girls and less. They like to make more noise, though. Why would that be?

Well, I should sleep. The call could come any time. I told Chelsea that if she ever calls midday, I'll know it's going to be the real thing since so far it's always been at night. I do not think she was amused.

Something upstairs interrupted Chad's reading. He stood, stepped into the dining room, and then grabbed his bowl to carry to the sink. Willow's phone. She'd be calling Becca now. "Lord, please let that baby come," he muttered as he washed his bowl and spoon and put them in the drainer.

Willow stepped into the room, her hair still tousled from sleep. "This one's it!"

"Wha—"

"Sharon called. This time, Chelsea's water broke! From

the sounds of it, she's already having a rough time."

"I'll come straight to the hospital after work."

She hugged him as she passed him on her way to the pantry. "I thought I'd milk myself before I go so that I'm not getting too full while I'm there."

"They should have them there too if you need one."

"True... maybe I should just take it and—" Willow shook her head. "Silly. We'll be busy trying to get her comfortable. I have to wait for Becca anyway."

"I'll go make our bed and make sure the sheets on hers are clean."

"They are," she assured him. "I changed them yesterday. The boys and I had great fun with them." Her eyes directed his to the clock. "Besides, you should go soon."

"Should or not, I don't want to now."

Willow handed him his covered coffee mug. "Get yourself one of those coffees from the Grind when they open." After a quick kiss—and one that took much too long—she pointed to the door. "Keep safe and keep Fairbury safe. I'll call."

Ten minutes later, as Chad pulled into the station, the reality of his life changing, yet again, hit him hard. He threw the truck into park and gripped the steering wheel. "Wow, Lord. Wow."

Chapter 176

Marianne arrived just as Dr. Kline insisted Willow leave to eat. "You'll need your strength.

Taking charge, Marianne gave Chelsea a quick hug and pushed Willow from the room. "I was going to see what you wanted and bring it back," she explained, "but this'll give you a minute to rest."

They passed the corridor to the cafeteria, prompting Willow to object. "Where are you taking me?"

"Somewhere quiet, where you can get a nice relaxing meal."

"But—"

They stepped into the elevator and Marianne allowed the doors to close. "No buts, girlie. You need to relax or you'll crash just when that poor girl needs you. Ryder is there. That's enough for now."

"Ryder's girlfriend is bringing him lunch. Won't that be awkward for Chelsea?"

Marianne shrugged. "I don't think he's the kind of boy who would allow his girlfriend to make the mother of his child uncomfortable during labor. If she's coming, Chelsea's probably fine with it." The elevator doors opened again, and the women stepped into the hall. "I like how he is staying with her until it's over. Too many boys would just disappear once they broke up and he signed away his paternal rights."

"He told me he would have paid child support, stayed involved in Kari's life—everything—if Chelsea had chosen to keep the baby."

"I believe it too." As they stepped from the building, Marianne pointed to her car. "I'm over there. You know, Dad and I think Ryder will become a Christian after all this. He's seeing 'pure religion' in action every day."

Willow opened the passenger door, leaning on it for a moment, and sighed. "I hope so. I can't help but wonder if maybe he'll regret it and then move away."

"Any boy willing to be a single dad is not going to move far from his child if the adoptive parents are willing for him to be close. Give him time."

As they pulled into a restaurant parking lot, Willow gripped the door handle as if it would somehow help her say what she wanted to say. "You know, I know one way to make him take a serious look at Christianity. I have no doubt it would work."

"Then why don't you?"

"It's manipulative at best." She felt Marianne's eyes on her and whispered, "All I have to do is say something like, 'Your parents consider Christianity to be a crutch for unintelligent minds, right?'"

"Oh." Marianne played with the keys in her hand. "I see. Just pointing out that his parents rejected something is a really good way to get him to explore it."

"And a really good way to reinforce bad feelings between them."

They had their choice of nearly any table in the restaurant. Marianne chose one in the corner—quiet and private. "Just relax. Do you know what you want?"

"I don't care," Willow assured her. She closed her eyes and tried to relax. "I wonder how the boys are?"

"They were fine an hour ago. I sent Becca out to do whatever she needed to do and then put them down for a late nap before I left."

"Oh!" Willow's head snapped up. "Thank you. That was—"

"Relax. It's what grandmas do."

"My boys have the best grandparents ever. I can't imagine how Mother ever managed without having someone to talk to—to learn from. I've always known she was an incredible woman, but when I think of all the help I need..."

"I don't think it's a matter of need as much as accessibility. You have it and are wise enough to use it, but if you *had* to do this on your own, you would. You could."

"Maybe," Willow agreed, "but don't you think if I had been twins she would have had to find help?"

"What if there was no help—anywhere. What if the world blew up and she was alone with those twins with no one to help? Would she do well because she had to or would she give up?" Marianne's hand crept across the table and squeezed Willow's. "I can't believe I'm the one reminding *you* of all people this, but your mother wasn't all alone. She had all the help she could ever need—in the Lord."

Those words spread across Willow's heart, coating it before slowly sinking into her soul. She sat unspeaking, lost in thoughts, even after the server brought water and took their orders. Once her mind and heart reconciled truth and emotion, Willow sat up, leaning against the table.

"I think..." Should she say it? Would Chad's lovely mother misunderstand—think less of her? "I think that I can only just now see the beauty of what Mother did. It took losing—" Her forehead furrowed. "Well, actually giving up is more accurate. I chose a different path. It took choosing another life to see how fully she had to rely on the Lord. I've always seen her as so fiercely independent, but she was more than that. She was also utterly dependent on the only One who could truly help her in need. That is something I don't have anymore."

This time Marianne kept silent, thinking. Their meals arrived, and still neither woman spoke. At last, just as Willow decided to reassure her mother-in-law that she did not regret the changes, Marianne said, "Willow? I think you have just as deep a dependence upon the Lord as your mother did. I just think it manifests differently. You have to choose to recognize that the Lord's provision and care for you is through His people rather than through yourself or supernaturally through Him. It's the same thing. It just manifests in a different way."

"I'm not sure I see what you mean."

"Well—"

Understanding dawned. "Oh! You mean that I rely on the Lord for help or emotional support and the Lord provides it through Chad. Mother relied on the Lord for help and emotional support and the Lord provided it through herself and later through me. It is more overt to come directly from Him or feel like it does, but that doesn't make it any less of a provision if He uses someone here to provide it."

"Right... and in a way, it's harder for you. You have to consciously choose to recognize the Source of your help."

Willow didn't taste her food. She ate methodically, robotically. Each bite cut without thought, chewed without notice, and washed down with a sip of water before repeating the process. The stress and interrupted sleep of the previous six weeks caught up to her in one overwhelming rush. Had Marianne not called her name in time, she might have collapsed into her plate of pasta salad.

"I think I'll be glad when I can take this baby home and get some sleep."

Marianne snickered. "Did you hear yourself? Sleep with a newborn?"

"They wake up often, but go back to sleep." Willow yawned. "I just want to begin my life."

The words hovered between them. Tears filled Willow's eyes. "I can't believe I just said that," she whispered. "Why did I say that?"

"It's the exhaustion talking."

"But, 'out of the abundance of the heart, the mouth speaks,'" she protested. "Have I really become that person? Have I given up everything Mother taught me? I—" Illogically, a new thought occurred to her. "Wait, where is Chad? Why hasn't he called? He should have been off work hours ago."

"He didn't call?" Marianne frowned. "He came by for something to eat and went right back—something to do with an accident on the lake. The Sheriff's department is out there too. I heard rumors of drug stuff in town, but I don't know how true that is. He didn't think he'd be off before six o'clock."

Willow pulled out her phone and sighed. "I forgot. I turned it off when Chelsea was sleeping. Any noise seemed to wake her, so I thought..." She inched her way out of the booth. "I'll be right back. I want to see if he can talk for a minute."

The afternoon drifted into evening, and Chelsea labored. The epidural kept her comfortable, but exhaustion took its toll. Sleep rarely happened, but when it did, Willow protected it with everything she could. She ushered the others out of the room, insisted the nurses stay away if they possibly could, and at one point, even asked Dr. Kline to come back later.

Chad arrived just after nine o'clock and suggested she eat again. The nurse checked Chelsea's progress and pronounced her at "eight," a number that did not impress the laboring mother or Willow. However, with the assurance that birth would be at least two or more hours away, she agreed to leave for an hour at most.

They ate at Denny's—a first for Willow. After eating a few bites, she frowned. "Well, there's a lot of food for very little money and doesn't taste horrible..."

Laughing, Chad waggled his burger. "That's why I recommended burgers. They do great with those. Roast... not so much."

She reached across the table and took his burger from him. After a bite she hesitated and shoved her plate across the table. "Trade?"

"I—" She smiled and raised her eyebrows in question. Sighing, Chad passed her his plate and picked up her fork. "Man, lass. You've made me into one of those pushovers."

"You always were one. You came back when you didn't want to, remember?"

"Either that," he teased, "or I'm just a sucker for a pretty face."

"I thought that was called being a man?"

Chad snatched the sprig of parsley from his plate and threw it at her. "You're so going to pay for that."

"Oh, yeah?"

"Do you want me to prove it now? I guarantee you'll be thoroughly embarrassed and I'll enjoy every second of it."

All Willow's bravado evaporated. "Okay, okay. I believe you." She toyed with the parsley before she added, "I call a five second head start."

"You're on. I'll even give you twenty-four hours to get sleep before I challenge you."

"It's gonna be pillows, isn't it?" Willow leaned forward. "What is it Cheri says at times like this? Bring it?"

"Yeah."

"Okay, then. Bring it."

Once she ate, Chad led Willow to the truck and reached behind the seat. "Brought the pump."

She stared at it, glancing around the parking lot. "Hey— that corner over there. Want to park there? I can't use this thing discreetly with this shirt."

For the next twenty minutes, they chatted as she let the machine do its job. Her eyes watched the truck clock, and she grew nervous as the time neared ten-thirty. "Shouldn't we get back?"

"You ready?"

"Yes." She hesitated. "Chad?"

"Hmm?"

"How important is it for you to hold the baby as soon as it's born?"

"Why?"

She swallowed hard and forced herself to suggest the one thing she did not want him to do. "I just was thinking... you've been up for almost twenty-four hours. That baby could come by midnight or it could be after two or three o'clock. If a few hours later won't make you feel like you missed out, maybe you should just drop me off and go get some sleep."

As if an answer, Chad yawned. "I don't know..."

"I'm not trying to get rid of you, but I do think it might be nice if one of us was semi-coherent. We know I'm not going to get any sleep, so..."

He pulled up to the emergency room doors and let the truck idle. "It just seems so wrong not to be there if I can. And I can."

"When do you work next? I can't remember."

"I work at two tomorrow afternoon and then I'm off for two days."

She reached for the door handle. "Go home, Chad. You need to sleep. The safety of our lovely town requires it."

As the tail lights of his truck disappeared down the street, Willow swallowed the lump in her throat and fought back tears. "He needed to go, Lord. I just needed—or at last wanted—him to stay."

All the hustle and bustle of the hospital during the day disappeared at night—except in the obstetrics wing. A woman screaming in a room two doors down from Chelsea sent nurses scrambling. Seconds later, another burst of people rushed to the other side of the wing. Willow stepped into Chelsea's room and found her and Ryder talking quietly. "How's it going?"

"Better here than in there. Why do people think it's so great to go 'natural?' Ugh. Mom says that when her mom had her, they just gassed her and she woke up with a baby. I think that sounds pretty much perfect."

"Have they checked you recently?"

The girl nodded. "Yeah. She said I was an eight-nine about thirty minutes ago." The girl sighed. "Of course, then she told me that I'll probably push for two hours."

"Really?"

"I think something's happening though. I can't feel much in my legs and the contractions are 'there' but that's about it. But I feel pressure 'down there.'"

Willow nodded. "Well, that's good, right? Maybe it means the baby is getting into place so you won't have to push so much."

"Maybe. It comes and goes in waves like contractions, so I thought maybe it was just everything pushing things into place."

"I could go ask a nurse..." Before she could turn, Chelsea shifted and the blanket slipped. Willow frowned. "Chelsea, are you feeling that pressure right now?"

"Yeah, why?"

She hesitated. "Mind if I look?"

At Chelsea's nod, Willow pulled back the blanket and blinked. "Strange, I thought I saw—"

"The pressure is gone now. Does that help?"

"Maybe... Don't tell me when it comes back. Let me tell

you when I think it does. Does it get stronger each time?"

"Yeah... why?"

"It's building now, isn't it!" Willow's eyes widened. "Ryder, go get a nurse!"

"Why—"

"Go!"

Chelsea's eyes widened in fear. "What!"

"I see hair—not yours. And oh... boy!"

"Girl. It's a girl, remember," the girl gasped.

The head slipped back inside as the contraction ended. "I think if you tried to push when the next pressure builds... just pretended you were going to go to the bathroom... I think that baby would come."

"Really? They said hours!"

All exhaustion left Chelsea's voice. Willow could almost see the adrenaline coursing through the girl's veins as it worked its magic. "It's building, isn't it?"

"Yeah... push?"

"Go for it."

"Without the nurse?"

"Do you want to wait?" The idea seemed preposterous to her, but what did she know?

"No!"

Grabbing the rails on the bed, Chelsea gave a push that Willow could see take effect. "Keep going... I think... oh drat."

"It went back in again?" The girl gasped, panting. "Water?"

Willow glanced around for Ryder and gave up. After a drink of water, cool rag to the girl's forehead, and a quick scrub of the hands, Willow glanced into the hall and rushed back to the bed as she saw Chelsea nearly pull herself upright and gave another mighty push.

"Pressure, eh... wow. I wish I knew if it was safe to pull on that head. I can almost grab it."

"Do it!"

She shook her head. "Can't. I have no idea if that's safe."

"Please!"

But the head slipped back inside once more. Willow

dashed for the door and glared at Ryder. "What are you doing! Get someone!" she hissed.

He shrugged and circled the wing again, but Willow couldn't wait to see. As she stepped back in the room, the nurse call button practically glowed at her. "Oh, brother." She punched the button and went to check Chelsea again. "Okay, do you feel pressure?"

"Not yet. Why?"

"The head didn't go back as far this time. Maybe?"

Determination set in Chelsea's face. "I'm pushing this time until that baby gets out of here. I'm done."

As if to prove her point, Chelsea held her breath, tucked her chin, grabbed the rails, and pushed, slowly exhaling as she did. This time, the baby's head completely emerged. "You did it!"

"I did? How can I not feel that?"

"Those epidurals can be amazing."

Chelsea looked down, trying to see what Willow was doing. "Where is the baby?"

"Just waiting for you to get another contraction."

"Why?"

"So you can push out the body?" Willow saw movement from the corner of her eye and called to Ryder. "Tell them to hurry! The baby is half born!"

"I'm trying, but I just can't walk into some woman's room and take away the nurse!"

"There's no one in the halls?" It seemed inconceivable.

"I've seen two and both said they'd be here in just a moment. They don't believe me when I say that the baby is coming now."

"Well," Willow snapped, "go tell them that they're almost too late. The head is born!"

Before she finished speaking, Chelsea pulled herself up and bore down again, shaking with the exertion. Despite the poor girl's weeks of labor and pain-filled hours and exhaustion, baby Kari slipped into Willow's hands with deceptive ease. Her tiny cry echoed faintly around the room, and Chelsea collapsed against the pillows, spent.

Ryder stepped in the room, eyes wide. "Did I hear—"

"Yep. Go tell those nurses that couldn't be bothered that

we did fine without them, but we'd like help knowing what to do about the placenta. I don't remember anything about placentas. My brain is blank. Oh, and will you text Chad? Oh! And what time is it?" Her eyes rose to the clock. "Wow, eleven eleven. That was fast. I got here around ten-thirty."

"Glad something was fast about this," Chelsea murmured.

Without a blanket to cover the baby, Willow reached for the sheet and pulled it over the infant, wrapping her gently. "Sorry, Chelsea. She looked cold."

"Why isn't she crying anymore?"

Willow shrugged. "She's just blinking as if trying to focus."

"But she's breathing, right?"

"Yep."

Chelsea rose up on her elbows. "Can I see?"

"Want to hold her?"

"Not yet. Just want to see that she's really here."

The appearance of the nurse cut off Willow's response. The woman stared at Willow holding the baby wrapped in a sheet that hung nearly to the floor. "Did you cut the cord?"

"No. I didn't have anything to do that with. I figured someone would come eventually."

The nurse, Loretta, shook her head as she surveyed the scene. "I don't believe it. She was going so slow and we had—whatever. Let me see. Did you suction her—him—out?"

"Her. With what?"

"Call Dr. Kline's service and tell them to get him here immediately. I'll take her..."

Willow went to wash her hands and glanced over at Chelsea, "Well, that'll make for a fun story someday."

"Maybe for you," the girl muttered. "I, for one, would love to forget this whole thing."

Chapter 177

Dawn broke over the countryside surrounding Fairbury, slowly filling their bedroom with the pinky glow of early morning light. Chad rolled over and felt the empty bed beside him. He inched his way across the bed and peered into the cradle. Empty as well. A smile crept over his face.

He found her downstairs, half-reclining on the couch, Kari asleep on her chest. *Oh, Lord. Look at that. Can you just look at that?*

She shifted, one eye opening as the baby stretched. "Hey..."

"Can I just say," Chad murmured, "waking up to see my girls like this—could life be any more perfect?"

Willow gave him a lazy grin. "Um, yes. Yes it could. She could have a fresh diaper."

"Disposable or washable?"

"She still had a bit of meconium last time. Better stick with the disposables." Willow shifted and the baby stretched again. "I love watching her stretch. I don't remember the boys doing that!"

"I don't either." Chad lifted his daughter and cradled her. The baby shifted, whimpering. "Shh... Kar-i-lee... Let's get you clean again while mommy," he gave Willow a pointed look, "goes back to bed."

"I was going to milk the goats first."

"I'll get the goats."

"And Kari?" She stood, stretching.

"If she doesn't fall back to sleep, I'll bring her up."

He changed his daughter, tried to soothe her back to sleep, and when Kari refused to settle, he carried her back up to Willow and grabbed his clothes. "I'll come get her when I'm done."

Life already had a new rhythm. Becca arrived to help with the goats, but Chad sent her to feed the chickens and gather eggs. Mornings of just he and Willow working together seemed over, and that thought discouraged him. Perhaps they should have "family" chickens and a single goat. Then again, they would have new things to do together, and life had proven that change would be constant.

He poured the milk into bottles, marking the date as he went. Milk pails glistened in the morning light after he scalded each one. Chad released the goats into the pasture for the day and stopped to pick up a kettle of boiling water before he strolled back to the house.

Oats in bowls, hot water covering them, plates on top. He stepped into the pantry for peaches and realized they'd already eaten the last jar. "Wonder if they're ripe..."

He reached for cherries and hesitated. She'd love fresh peaches—even more than he would. Without giving him a chance to talk himself into cherries, Chad hurried out the door and down the back steps. Becca saw him and waved. "Need something?"

He shook his head. "Gonna check to see if peaches are ripe."

"Oh—canning today?"

Chad shrugged. "I'll ask. Want a peach if they're ready?"

"Sure!" She nodded at the crate of eggs in her arms. "I could go after I put these away if you want."

"That's okay. I've got it."

Around the barns, past the alfalfa fields—they needed to cut those—and over to the orchard. Dew on the high grasses dampened his jeans, but Chad ignored them. He reached up and squeezed a peach. It seemed ripe, but he moved on, squeezing, touching, trying to gauge which would be best. A gentle tug—that's what Willow had suggested would indicate perfect ripeness—released a peach. He sniffed it, squeezing again. Not too firm, not mushy. Yellow skin with a blush. Chad rubbed his shirttail and took a bite. Perfect. With one success behind him, he found several more.

Willow's snapdragon patch tempted him. He hurried inside, set his peaches on the counter, and grabbed the kitchen shears. Within minutes, he had a nice vase of flowers on the kitchen table and their breakfast was ready. She'd appreciate that.

He jogged up the stairs and leaned against the doorjamb and watched as Willow rocked their daughter. "Hungry?"

"No, she ate already."

"I meant you," Chad murmured.

"What do we have?"

"Oatmeal and fresh peaches. I thought about making sausage, but…"

"Then we'd have to start the stove. Not on your day off." She nodded at the sleeping infant. "Take her? I'll go get dressed." As he reached for his daughter she smiled. "Is it terrible that I'm glad I have no recovery? I can carry her, go up and down stairs, lift the boys, work—I can work!"

He hesitated, his hand brushing her cheek. "It wasn't *that* bad, was it? I—"

"Chad," she interrupted, "I wasn't complaining. I wouldn't trade any of it with the boys for anything. I'm just enjoying the benefits of adoption too. "

"Just making sure. Kari and I are going to go say hi to Portia and see if Becca needs anything. Take a shower first. Give me a holler when you get downstairs."

With his daughter cradled in his arm, Chad descended the stairs, talking to her. "Your mama is the most amazing woman. Did you know that she can do anything! Anything! Well, anything that doesn't require work with a saw. She's pathetic with wood."

The lads played in the orchard, chasing Portia and then running from her as the dog urged them back to Willow's side. Kari slept in the playpen, a shade covering her from the sun's glare. Crate after crate of peaches filled the cart. Each time it filled, either she or Becca pushed it back to the summer kitchen and returned again.

"This is one bumper crop," Willow muttered. "I don't think we can finish picking them all today and still process everything before it goes mushy. We'd probably finish this cart full and then start peeling." She paused. "Can you go start the Dutch oven boiling in the summer kitchen?"

"What for—oh, to peel like tomatoes?" Becca hesitated for confirmation and then grinned. "I'm getting the hang of this."

Willow paused her picking as she watched her sons use a peach as a ball, each throwing it for the other to fetch. How long it would take for them to squabble over it—that was her question. Almost as she thought it, Liam tried to snatch it from Lucas. "Liam..."

He glanced at her and back at his brother. Lucas stared at her too—a distraction Liam used to his advantage. He grabbed the peach and ran, tumbling over his own feet. Lucas threw himself at his brother. Willow stared, torn between the urge to laugh and the desire to send them both to bed for such ridiculous behavior. "You two are unbelievable. Everything is a competition!"

Becca's voice startled her. "That's called being a child—and particularly a boy in my experience. It's like they're born with an innate *need* to prove themselves superior."

"At least we have one girl to give us a break."

"Unless she learns from them or has it too. There are competitive girls too, you know."

"I know. I was just hoping," Willow confessed. "I once told Chad that if children were such obnoxious creatures, that I didn't want any."

"Really? I always pictured you as a little girl dreaming of being a mommy."

"I thought about it sometimes. I always pictured myself with two sons and Mother. In a sense, I have that. Strange, isn't it?"

"Josh says we'll probably have five boys—all mountain men types who love hunting and football."

Willow laughed. "Or, you'll have five daughters—all mountain men types who love hunting and football. Just because that would be even more amusing. Can you see him trying to put pretty dresses on a tomboy?"

Becca grew quiet. Just as Willow started to ask if something was wrong, the young woman asked, "Do you think there's something wrong with marrying a man who would rather make his daughter doll clothes than teach his son how to fish?"

"Not at all. Why?"

"Just something someone said. I wondered if I was being blind."

"I don't know if you're blind," Willow said as she hurried to separate her boys before their screeches woke the baby, "but I do know that Josh loves you and put himself in a place where he might have to give up a lot to be your husband. I'd say that's a beautiful thing."

"Yeah... and people here don't know Josh. They only see what they think they know. So someone thinks he's not honest with himself. Who cares what they think?"

Willow separated the boys, giving each a cracker and a cup of water. They'd be soaked in seconds, but it would work. "I think what matters is what God thinks. Did God make a mistake when He made Josh? Are Josh's talents wrong? Should he ignore them and try to develop something else simply because someone thinks it means he's effeminate? That's ridiculous."

Becca stared at the cart. "I think we have enough. If we take any more, we'll never get it done, and he's coming tonight to talk about reception menus."

"Did you tell him you decided on a dress style?"

"Yep."

Willow raised her eyebrows. "And... what did he say?"

"He didn't say a thing." Becca blushed. "But based upon his reaction, I think he was excited."

"Where's Willow?"

Becca glanced up from the pile of blocks on the floor. "She came downstairs after her shower and said, 'It's beautiful outside, the baby is asleep, and the sun's going to set soon. I'm going for a walk in the pasture. Can you watch the boys?'" Becca smiled. "Who would say no to that—or them?" Her eyes slid to where the boys piled and toppled stacks of blocks with equal success.

"I think I'll go see if she's all right—if you don't mind staying a little longer."

"I'm good. There's a roast in the crockpot and she made a salad before she left."

Nodding his thanks, Chad strolled through the house, out the back door, and down the steps. Portia didn't come running as she usually did. The chickens still pecked at bugs in the evening grass; the goats stood in their overnight pens, milked and waiting for the morning. As he passed the gardens, he noticed how empty and dead much of them looked. Jill would miss the produce at the farmer's market. As much as the greenhouses produced, it wasn't nearly enough to provide what the gardens had.

The scent of cut alfalfa still hung in the air with that sweet scent that made the farm *feel* like one. He walked in a wide arc, following the flow of the animals until he reached the pasture they'd grazed in early spring. The grasses were higher there, reaching past his calves.

Chad shaded his eyes, staring nearly directly into the fading sun. A silhouette of Willow danced—literally danced—before his eyes. The music that inspired her must have been soft and slow if her movements were any indication. She swayed, her arms sweeping in slow arcs around and over her. She spun in circles, her hands outstretched to the sky, before sweeping down to the grass.

He'd never seen her like this—so moved by something that it overflowed in such a physically artistic way. She usually photographed, painted, sketched, or wrote. She turned flat pieces of fabric into art that moved and flowed, but never had he seen her dance with such utter abandon.

The beauty of it produced an ache in his throat that threatened to choke him. Would he ever know this woman that he called wife? Could he? Something about the carefree dance before him reminded him of a little girl—the one she had been once, he supposed. Would Kari be like her? Was it possible without the genetic code that had linked the Finley women? Would growing up on the farm with Willow as her mother be enough to give their daughter that joy for life and love for beauty?

"God, please make it so," he choked.

When his heart could take no more, when his lungs seemed incapable of cooperating any longer, Chad called to her. "Lass?"

Willow turned. She didn't hesitate. The moment she spied him near the edge of the pasture, she ran to him, laughing. "Chad!"

He caught her as she flung herself into his arms, swinging her in an arc and kissing her. "Having fun?"

"Mmm hmm…"

They walked back to the house, hand in hand, not speaking for some time. At last, Willow leaned against him and murmured, "I missed Mother today—more than I have since those first days. I came out here, talked with the Lord, cried—"

"Oh, Willow…"

"I'm not sorry. I haven't danced in the pastures since Mother died. We did that sometimes, you know. We'd go out in the grass at sunset and dance and spin… Today I did that by myself and you know what?"

Chad's voice cracked twice before he managed to choke out, "What?"

"It was good. Someday, I'll bring Kari out here and we'll dance together, but tonight it was just me and the Lord, and I'm good with that."

"It was beautiful."

She smiled up at him, kissing his cheek as she did. "Yes it was."

Chapter 178

The leaves had already begun to change. As she walked the highway to Fairbury, Willow noted the golden splotches in some of the trees and smiled. Autumn would arrive soon in all its glory. At the turnoff, she waited for cars to pass before jogging across the highway and making her way to the convenience store. In the restroom, she struggled to change her shoes. With her hat off, she brushed her hair, washed her hands and face, and stared at herself in the mirror. "Better," she whispered, adjusting the fabric wrapped around her.

In the store, she grabbed a bottle of water and pulled out her wallet. The attendant smiled. "Have a nice day, Willow."

"Thank you, you too."

Each step toward the center of town brought a different feeling—one she couldn't identify. She passed the street to the police station—the street that had led her to Chad only three years earlier. Her eyes scanned the little building, trying to remember the person she had been as she stepped into that unfamiliar room. Even now, she could feel the blast of cool air and hear Judith's jokes as she called to Chad.

Her hand curled around sleeping Kari's head. The long wrap that tied the baby snugly to Willow's chest made pushing the jogging stroller easier. A glance through the cover showed the lads leaning forward, curious about all they saw. Residents waved, calling her by name. Alexa Hartfield saw them and paused, kneeling to ask the boys about the trip to town. "Your daughter is so beautiful," the woman said as she continued on her way.

Willow nodded. "She is, isn't she?"

A couple of blocks ahead, Chad wrote a ticket and tucked it under a windshield wiper. "See there? Daddy's working. Someone forgot to pay the meter, so he has to give them a ticket. Aiden Cox is in school now, so Daddy says he's writing a lot more tickets these days."

Chad saw them and waved, hurrying down the street to meet them. Another expired meter—or possibly one near expiration—made him pause and he dumped a quarter in it. She suspected he did it simply to avoid having to stop to write another ticket. As he reached them, he kissed her, his hand sliding over Kari's head. "How're my girls?"

"Happy to see you!"

"Daddy!" The boys called to Chad in unison, each straining at the straps that kept them from climbing from the stroller whenever something interested them.

As Chad knelt to talk to his sons, a lump filled Willow's throat. A sense of awe washed over her seeing all that her life had become. Friends waved, some calling them by name. Her husband—husband!—lifted their sons—their sons!—from the stroller, holding one in each arm. How had life ever become so different? How had she ever resisted such a rich and beautiful existence?

"Lass?"

Chad's voice broke through her reverie. "Hmm?"

"Are you okay?"

She smiled up at him, her heart dancing at the love and concern she saw in his face. "I think I can truly say I've never been better." Her lips dropped to Kari's head. "I love you." She shook her head at the unexpected tears the filled her eyes. "I love my life."

To be continued ...

Past Forward. Don't miss a single episode of this serial novel. Check for them **FREE** on Kindle.

Coming Soon

Books by Chautona Havig

The Rockland Chronicles
Noble Pursuits
Discovering Hope
Argosy Junction
Thirty Days Hath…
Advent
31 Kisses
Not a Word

The Aggie Series (Part of the Rockland Chronicles)
Ready or Not
For Keeps
Here We Come

The Hartfield Mysteries (Part of the Rockland Chronicles)
Manuscript for Murder
Crime of Fashion

The Agency Files (Part of the Rockland Chronicles)
Justified Means
Mismatched

Past Forward- A Serial Novel (Part of the Rockland Chronicles)
Volume 1
Volume 2
Volume 3
Volume 4
Volume 5

Historical Fiction

Allerednic (A Regency Cinderella story)

The Annals of Wynnewood
Shadows and Secrets
Cloaked in Secrets
Beneath the Cloak

The Not-So-Fairy Tales
Princess Paisley
Everard

Made in the USA
San Bernardino, CA
01 April 2018